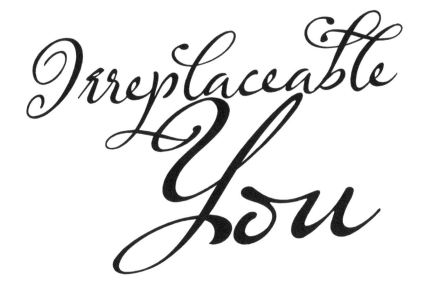

DURGA

PARTRIDGE

Library of Congress Control Number:		2020907619
ISBN:	Hardcover	978-1-5437-5803-0
	Softcover	978-1-5437-5802-3
	eBook	978-1-5437-5801-6

Print information available on the last page.

To order additional copies of this book, contact
Toll Free +65 3165 7531 (Singapore)
Toll Free +60 3 3099 4412 (Malaysia)
orders.singapore@partridgepublishing.com

www.partridgepublishing.com/singapore

This book is dedicated to my late mom, I pray you are watching over me.

Acknowledgement

I would like to say my thanks to a group of very special people in my life without their desire to motivate me this novel would not have had transpired as a hardcopy. My late mom, you never failed to encourage me striving forward and reach out for my goals; your endearing words imprinted inside my heart as a lifeline. Thank you, for guiding me to become a better individual to be as humble as you, the strength within me is part of your essence.

To my dearest papa, you have helped me so much in getting my first book published for the entire world to read. I am lucky to be your daughter. Your unconditional love is an inspiration in my life. Seeing you pray for my success, blessing me with goodness for my future.

The journey hadn't been easy with many setbacks; financially, pessimism, uncertainties, witnessing the detreating health of a loved one. At the beginning of Irreplaceable You, the ill written chapters were published on Wattpad but it was meant for my small numbers of readers. My gratitude to Carrillo, Carla, Cynthia, Cath, Lizah, Liana, Letti and Zohal; you ladies have a special place in my heart.

My heartfelt appreciation to Jen Robins, Vanessa Dean from the Partridge; your advices, encouragement, becoming my listening ear whenever the weight becomes unbearable for me without faltering the two of you chose to guide me forward. Thank you for being here through thick and thin.

And to the rest of the Partridge Team, your constant hard-work amazes me into making sure Irreplaceable You will be well loved by readers.

Chapter 1

Chiyoda, Tokyo

*T*he sleeping alcove was masked in the shadows of the crack of dawn. Drapery with a fuchsia floral pattern on a nacred background barricaded the world beyond the shut window. A quaint study desk beside the single window stood diametrically opposite the foot of the bed frame. Cream-tone blank walls complemented the entire set-up. Then an ear-splitting buzz from the radio alarm shattered the noiseless atmosphere.

Suhana "Hana" Akiyama drowsily yawned and sank her dark head beneath her coverlet as a bolster toppled over the edge. Her mind felt sluggish as she nestled her button nose against a feathery soft pillow.

"Tekken," she softly hummed. "Mmm …."

Soon an insistent knock sounded on the closed door. She listened to the footfalls of her workaholic mother, a sure sign that another crucial day had begun. Hana burrowed her nose and inhaled a lungful of mouth-watering fragrance. Then she dragged her sleepy body, clad in cotton pyjamas covered with a multitude of tiny dogs, from under the tumbled duvet. The air conditioner blasted cold air as it hummed in the background.

Hana wobbled on her feet as she stepped into the dimly lit corridor. Another tear-inducing yawn twisted her jaw as she contorted her body and hands upward until she heard a satisfying "pop". She passed a bronze sculpture of Lord Ganesha on a table next to a wide bowl filled with floating flower petals. Her mother, Neena, had a keen eye for interior design and had decorated the household to duplicate their own version of a museum.

Before Neena had officially moved to Japan, she had worked in a gallery for the historical and cultural department. Her work trips to Japan increased her ever-growing interest in the country and led to her life-altering resolution in their current lives. Six months later, Neena was forging a career as a curator at a local university library just as she gave birth to a baby girl.

In a span of three winks, Hana swung the toilet door open, taking in its citrusy smell as she opened her eyes wide. She halted in the midst of applying toothpaste to a brush and stared at her reflection in the circular mirror. She turned her head from side to side, studying a pimple on her olive-coloured skin.

"I hate you," she whispered at the blemish.

Hana was deeply critical of her own appearance; she suffered from low self-esteem and disliked her image. She habitually compared other girls to herself, and the comparison had slowly poisoned her point of view on beauty.

After a reviving lukewarm shower, she put on a fluffy bathrobe and hurried to her bedroom to start on her makeover. Thick raven-coloured hair curled to her waist as she fought to detangle the wet mess, gritting her teeth from the pain on her scalp. She plopped her bottom onto a quaint chair to face the dressing table mirror as she quickly secured her mane in two pigtails. Her attire consisted of a collared white button-down shirt and a black tie that matched both her coat and pleated skirt, although on summer days they ditched the outerwear. She rolled knee-high ebony socks onto her slender ankles. To cover up the reddish spot, she improvised with concealer and gave an approving nod to the final result.

She hunted for her messenger bag as the curved HD television switched to a random news channel, kept at a low volume; the minimalist apartment had a picturesque ambience. She heard clinking tableware and headed to the kitchen.

"Good morning," Neena said with a radiant smile. "Breakfast is ready; hurry up."

"Morning," Hana replied as she salivated over the heap of pancakes. "What's for lunch?"

"Ham sandwich with salad dressing and your favourite chips," Neena drawled with a brow raised, "and strawberry yoghurt drink."

"I love you, Mom." Hana giggled when she saw her mom's face.

Mother and daughter sat down at the dining table. They ate in silence, each lost in thought. They were polar opposites; Neena was an extroverted person who oozed confidence, whereas Hana was a failure who avoided contact because of her nervousness. However, she harboured the same exhilaration for the history of Japan as her mother and had carved out her career path as a librarian.

Mind wandering, Hana set aside her cutlery and thought about school. She figured the day would not be terrible since she had somebody who protected her from troublesome attention. When Jin's profile flitted across her brain, she smiled, and a warm feeling spread inside her. She was a target of bullying; a small group of boys had chosen to surround Hana at the playground when Jin came to stand up against them—their first meeting. Since then, the pair had become inseparable, and Hana was grateful to both Jin and his mother for accepting her.

"What's the matter, Suhana?" A voice broke into her thoughts.

"Nothing." Hana got up to clear away her dishes. "I have to leave right now."

"Take care," Neena said before her voice took on a serious tone. "Don't stay out too late."

"'Kay," Suhana groused, rolling her eyes. Before she finished her sentence, the older woman was busy on the phone.

Hana gingerly pecked her mother's dewy cheek and shuffled towards the front door, where she hunched to slip into her school shoes before letting herself out. A middle-aged man nodded in her direction as he breezed along to the elevator in the lobby. Hana was nervous, as she always was on school days, but she silently gave herself a mini pep talk as she waited for the next elevator to pick her up.

Upon reaching the lobby, Hana gripped her bag tightly and raced out of the building. Her pigtails jostled against her voluptuous breasts, and a calm settled over her at the familiar sight of a boy casually perched on his bicycle. He had earphones plugged in as his hands slowly mimicked a pair of drumsticks over an invisible drumming set.

He glanced over at Hana as she halted beside him. "Stop running," Jin Takami drawled with a disgusted snort.

"Morning to you too," she huffed, short of breath, as she adjusted the front of her uniform. "Why mustn't I run? Everybody does."

"It's disgusting to see you running," Jin complained as he mimed cupping a pair of breasts in front of him.

"That is so rude!" Hana gasped aloud, but she was accustomed to his crude jokes. "Are you afraid that you might fall for my body?"

"Hell no." Jin rolled his sleeves up. "Your body doesn't fascinate my teenage curiosity."

In a fit of pettiness, Hana mercilessly grabbed a tuft of Jin's hair and yanked it as she climbed onto the bicycle's rear fender. Jin yelped in agony, and the vehicle shook. Hana emitted a chortle of pure glee at the look of pain plastered on Jin's handsome face.

"That hurt a lot, idiot!" he moaned as he rubbed the smarting area.

"Serves you right." She leaned over Jin's shoulder and poked his cheek.

The pair of piercings on his left ear twinkled at her. He was popular among their classmates, and even students from other classes were aware of his presence. Jin preferred to be laid-back, and his aura resonated with anyone who sat with him. Hana was not close to any of his friends and vice versa.

"You always make us late," Jin complained as he pedalled forward. He made sure she was able to stand upright without toppling over to the side.

"Be quiet." Hana playfully knocked a closed fist atop his messy hairdo. She spied blonde streaks incorporated with his natural raven-coloured mane.

His broad shoulders were warm under Hana's fingertips. She shut both eyes to enjoy the cool breeze caressing her face as she felt his muscles move. In comfortable silence, both friends travelled to their school. They chattered amicably as they turned, went over bumps, and paused at traffic lights. The dangling chains attached to Jin's black pants made a familiar sound, the tyres squeaked under the weight of their bodies, and she caught his masculine scent. Both of their bags were settled properly in the front basket alongside his hastily rolled-up sweater.

"Oi!" Jin called loudly to be heard over the noises from the streets. "I have Chupa Chups in my breast pocket; take one."

"Thank you," Hana replied happily. "My parents will be away this weekend for a company function; can you overnight at my place?"

"Anytime," Jin murmured, slowing the bicycle as Hana gingerly prodded his pocket. "I'll bring along the PlayStation."

"You are the greatest friend anybody can have," Hana said as she squeezed his broad shoulders.

"I wish some other girl besides you invited me over," he groused playfully. "Hopefully this changes sometime in the future when you get yourself a boyfriend."

"Say that one more time," Hana warned as she hopped on the pedestal a few times. "You don't have a girlfriend, sore loser, and when I get myself a boyfriend, you'll be so far behind."

"Stop jumping, or you pay for the bike!" Jin shouted at her. "I just got the chains fixed the other day."

"Fine," she huffed in annoyance. "You're riding too slow."

"Your fault," Jin shot back as he peered over a shoulder. "I finally beat the highest score."

"Not fair!" Hana whined and puckered her lower lip. "You promised to wait for me!"

"I couldn't sleep well last night," he said, shrugging nonchalantly.

"Without me?" Hana sneered with a gentle tug on his ear.

"You don't even know how to play that game very well," Jin chortled, earning a light punch on his back. "Just come over after school later; we'll do battle and see who wins."

"Good." Hana had a mock-savage expression. "I'll prove to you that I'm getting better."

Hana tugged over a piece of an earphone to insert in her ear and began humming along with RadWimp, one of their favourite rock bands. As they approached the school, they saw students along the pathway either in clumps or aimlessly walking individually. Jin rode the bicycle in between a row of stands, where Hana got down to allow him to lock it in place. He retrieved their bags as well as his vest, and they headed toward the entrance.

"So have you completed the English assignment?" His blank expression altered as she watched.

"Fuck." He halted in mid-motion to gawk at her. "I forgot all about it!"

"What were you up to yesterday?" Hana shook her head in disappointment, still walking.

"I was hanging out with the guys at the arcade before we went out job hunting," Jin replied hopelessly, hurrying to catch up. "Hana …."

"You can copy during the break period." She had a good inkling as to what he would say next. "I'll give you my notebook later in the classroom."

"You are an angel," Jin exhaled in a sigh of relief and gently squeezed her upper arm in a show of gratitude. "I'll buy you a drink at your favourite café before we head back to my place."

"Right," Hana sniffed haughtily as she peeked sideways at his smiling face. "See, I'm the only girl who can handle your tardiness."

"I take back my words," Jin replied in a dry tone. "Perhaps I'll ask the favour from Mahiro."

"Oi!" Hana yelped, giving him a scowl. "I was only kidding, you know?"

"Me too." Jin chuckled while he wrapped his stomach with an arm. "Well, are you ready to face school? Hana, at least learn from me and try to make more friends."

"It's not as easy you say," Hana muttered when Jin was accosted by his group of male friends. "Unlike you, I'm not confident of myself."

Chapter 2

The corridor bustled with students and teachers alike, the cacophony of voices drowning out Hana's footstep as she climbed the staircase to the second level; Jin casually ambled far behind alongside his friends. In silence, she lugged her bag to keep from bumping into others until she caught sight of their classroom and sped her feet towards her destination. Jovial faces met her gaze at the surrounding room; faintly envious, she paused to admire the teenagers still mingling with each other. She was still rooted in the entryway when a group of boys arrived to stream around her on both sides. A playful fist knocked atop her head, breaking into her reverie.

Hana jerked a little at the sudden contact to glance. Jin passed by to halt beside his desk at the back of the classroom, two seats away from the window. A pretty classmate saw him and offered a gleaming smile, and soon a group had gathered around him, chatting up a storm. Hana shuffled to her own spot situated at the front in the same row as Jin's and plopped down unceremoniously. To pass the time, she pulled a comic out of her bag that was neatly hung at the corner hook of the desk and flipped through the pages of drawn characters. Her ears perked every time the group broke out into laughter, she yearned to be a part of the rest.

Finally, Hana became engrossed with reading until the school bell signalled the start of their day. She dazedly glanced up just as their homeroom teacher breezed in with files and assorted papers in his hands. All the students stood, accompanied by screeching of chairs and tables, to bow to the male mentor. Hana hurriedly slipped a frilly bookmark into the comic and stuck it back in her bag.

The middle-aged teacher, Ino Hayamoto, rearranged his desk in silence as a few students murmured somewhere behind. A clipboard visible in his hand, Mr Hayamato lounged sideways with a hand in his front pocket to call out their names for attendance; then lessons resumed as usual. Their first period consisted of mathematics, a subject Hana secretly enjoyed; she thrived solving problem sums. She fought the urge to peer towards Jin, knowing he abhorred numeric subjects.

Mr Hayamato spoke in a loud voice while jotting on the whiteboard. The man was short and surveyed them with a sharp gaze from behind tortoise-shell glasses anchored on a regal nose. Hana groaned inwardly when his eyes stopped at her. He nodded for her to come forward whilst stepping aside for her to take the marker pen from him. She fidgeted as she took it.

"Silence," he warned the class. "Miss Akiyama will solve the problem."

Hana ducked her chin low as she stumbled towards the whiteboard, and a few chortled at her odd behaviour. With a sweaty hand, she gripped the pen before staring at the problem sum and scrawled the answer, only to erase it quickly before rewriting in bigger letters. A crumpled piece of paper hit the board, startling her, and rolled to a stop against her feet. A murmur of laughter behind Hana only spurred her on to finish her task. She was once again startled by their mentor's bark for the offender to step forth.

"Pick up that paper before you step outside my classroom," Mr Hayamato said, glowering at the culprit.

"But, Mr Hayamoto," the boy whined, drawing more chuckles.

The teacher remained unfazed by the lad's antics. Realising there was no room for escape, the boy stood amid a barrage of mockery to nonchalantly walk forward and retrieve the fallen ball of paper. Hana never moved from her position, all the while staring a hole into the whiteboard. Then she glimpsed him as he bent low to snatch the rubbish. She fumbled nervously to cap the marker before putting it down with an audible rap. She returned to her seat and flushed when she found Jin gazing at her raptly. He gave her an encouraging thumbs up.

"Miss Akiyama has written a correct answer," he beamed. "Well done."

Their homeroom teacher instructed the rest to copy down the answers. Hana doodled on the corner of her notebook to compose her runaway emotions. She bit her lower lip to control a sudden rush of tears and tuned out her surroundings to daydream. Soon, to her relief, the session ended.

The midday break period came, with students cheering, much to the teacher's consternation, and changing seats to be closer to their friends for lunch. Hana worked the kinks out of her stiff neck, rolling it whilst massaging with her fingers. She stowed the rest of her books underneath the table and got out both the comic and her lunchbox to set them atop the clear surface.

Meanwhile someone brought a chair next to hers and straddled it from behind to rest both arms on the back. Jin peered into her open lunchbox. "What's for lunch today?"

"Go get your own lunch," she retorted slyly. "Stop hogging mine."

"Well then, I'm just helping you cut down your serving size." As he delivered this deft comeback, he snatched a leaf from the salad dressing and started chewing it loudly.

"I don't eat that much, you liar." She scowled agreeably at her best friend's teasing.

They had been sharing lunch together ever since she had learned that his ill mother's exhaustion after double shifts kept her from waking up on time to help cook lunch for her son. Hana had asked her own mother to make extra for two people. Both Jin and his single mother were taken aback by their thoughtful suggestion, which further strengthened their bond.

Now they ate in comfortable silence until his continuous typing on his cell phone caught her attention. "Hey, who are you texting?" She tilted her head. "Somebody mysterious?"

"Nobody," he murmured offhand. "Be quiet and eat your lunch."

"You have a secret girlfriend, I just know it." She nudged his foot with her own. "Just tell me already."

"Quiet, I said." Jin finally looked up with a raised brow. "Stop being so nosy in somebody else's business."

"Whatever." She rolled her eyes and twisted her lips in a pout.

"Not cute," he said, choking out the words. "You have a long way to go to make a boy feel enthralled with your expressions."

Before she could complain, he leaned forward to steal the comic from her hand. She snarled in reply when he evaded efforts to snatch her beloved treasure. Jin casually browsed through the pages, at times pausing to gaze with rapturous attention, which elicited a deep blush from her when he finally glanced up to waggle his brows salaciously at her.

"There are a lot of smut drawings," he said, helpfully pointing out the obvious. "Hana, you bad girl."

"Shut up, and give it back. That belongs to me," she hissed with a red face at the same time wiggling her fingers. "Jin, I said stop—"

"Ryuunosuke, touch me there." He read the words aloud in a breathy voice, earning a smack of her hand on the side of his head. "Ouch, that hurt!"

"Serves you right." Hana bit the words out. "Why are you so annoying sometimes?"

"Hana, you don't bring porn into school." Jin raised his voice when several heads swivelled towards them. "I just learned about my friend's love for porn. This is too hilarious."

Hana figured it was useless to ignore him. "For your information, it's not *porn* but a romance genre comic with sweet coupling between the characters."

She was still speaking when Jin stood up, straightened his chair, and sat back down but this time with both legs on her lap. He slouch backwards and curled both arms against his lean chest.

"Jin, what are you doing?" Hana blinked. "Oi, people are watching us."

"I'm trying to catch a wink," he mumbled with eyes shut. "Just do your stuff."

"Really." Hana shook her head in defeat before picking the comic to read whilst adjusting her sitting position.

"They look like any other couple."

Hana gasped at the whispered words drifting from a small entourage from another class who visited their friend in her classroom. She peeked over a shoulder to confront several disgusted faces, in her confusion unaware that her free hand had drifted over to clutch Jin's calf.

A deep voice broke into her reverie. "Ignore them. Concentrate on your reading."

In truth, Hana couldn't summon annoyance. Others were frequently surprised when either of them mentioned the term friends. Many were dumbfounded since a girl and a boy being friends was a taboo. She dismissed the crazy notion that they might fall for each other and patted on his calf for his focus.

He peered at Hana with one eye open. "What?" he said, stifling a yawn.

"Jin, do you think I'll ever have a boyfriend?" she asked in a whisper.

He slid his legs away and scooted closer to hear. As Hana repeated the question, he rested an arm on the table with his head perched on it to gaze deeply at her. "Where did this question come from?" he murmured low. "Do you fancy anyone? Maybe I can help you."

"Um—" The rest of the sentence was cut off by the bell. Still, Hana sensed relief. "Forget it; there isn't anyone who comes to mind."

Jin stretched languidly to his full height, and they both heard a loud popping sound from him. She spied the edge of his boxers and glanced away without much thought, only to hear a chortle followed by a ruffle of his hand over her head. The ghostly weight of his hand lingered even after he had left for his seat.

Hana stole a glance behind her at Jin's retreating back. He was busy tuning in to a girl chatting him up and barked a laugh. Then he sat down, revealing a row of buttons undone to his collarbone and a plain white T-shirt worn underneath: he sported a dainty silver chain, a gift from his mother at his last birthday. The formal shirt hung over slouchy black pants that were rolled at the ankle above a pair of school slippers. She returned her gaze to the front, feeling like a lucky girl to have a handsome boy for a best friend.

Soon the entire group surged outside the classroom to start their next lesson—science, another geeky subject appealing to her. The female teacher greeted them inside the spacious lab room; the boys were hyped once her cheerful smile caught their eyes. Hana admitted that she too was a bit enthralled with her science teacher; she was a graceful, well-spoken, and pretty adult. Everyone was able to grasp the difficult subject because of her flawless teaching, but today, she directed everyone to form groups of four.

Remain calm, Hana thought in a mantra tone. But her calm evaporated when other girls drifted over to team up with her. She was reserved and had trouble socialising. Sweat beaded on her forehead, but she pretended not to notice as they spoke amongst themselves during one session; two of her teammates were grappling with the answers. Without a second thought, Hana came to their rescue, which caught them by surprise. She slowly and coolly explained the confusing concept.

"Hana, you are really good at this," Ikumi acknowledged with an awestruck look. "Can you help me with this one?"

A glow of happiness spread within Hana at her regard, and she dutifully helped out with a grin, taking the proffered pencil to write the answers.

"Jin informed us that you are really good at keeping notes," Maichiro spoke in a fake kind tone. "Can you help us, please?"

"Sure, just hand over your notebooks," Hana smiled although internally she vehemently denied their request. Teamwork soon became a one-person task. Several notebooks crowded Hana's area, but she maintained a positive attitude without focusing too much on their actual motives.

"Suhana, you are so generous," Aika lamented, arranging her papers as the end of school drew closer.

Hana rested her forehead against the cold metal, undeterred by the commotion at the surrounding lockers. She squeezed her eyes shut, depression heavy on her shoulders; she strongly wished she had rejected those girls' demands. For now, the notebooks bulged inside her bag. Then she felt a presence by her side, but instead of lifting her head to see who it was, Hana remained motionless.

She figured her best friend had found her moping when a wide palm mussed her hair in a circular motion, making her feel like a bobblehead doll. The idiot was oblivious to the bleak atmosphere and toyed with her until Hana had had enough.

"Stop it, Jin!" she snapped. "I'm in no mood for your hyper mode."

"Somebody is really pissed off," Jin chortled, seeming oblivious to her raging emotion. "What's the matter? You can't find yourself a boyfriend here?"

Hana paid no attention to his banter, apparently about their earlier conversation. With her toes she forced off the school slippers and replaced them with regular shoes. She slammed the locker door shut with a gratifying bang, hoisted the bag to her shoulder, again reminded of the extra work, and stepped away when from behind Jin attempted to trip her by placing his foot at the back of her shoe. He cackled on cue as she tripped and fell with one foot out of its shoe.

A few others saw her unladylike tumble and joined Jin's laughter. Ferocity darkened Hana's thoughts and she pivoted to slap Jin on the chest with her bag. She bared her teeth, unaware of the tears collecting in her eyelashes while he casually rubbed his chest.

"Jin, you are definitely a true idiot at moments like this," Hana scolded him while jabbing a rigid finger at his face. "I need to be left alone right now."

"Can you tell me the reason—?"

"Forget it," she snapped, putting on her shoe.

Jin stuffed both hands into his front pockets. "What about our promise to battle in the game?"

"I'm not free." She marched off, and he fell in step beside her. "Just leave me alone."

"Stop with your petty behaviour." He finally took an annoyed tone while hooking a finger inside her collar, forcing her to halt and almost choking her in the process. "You can confide in me when we kick each other's ass during the game."

"But—" The fight drained out of her when he rest a comforting hand on her head.

That single touch also made her face her runaway emotions whilst she bit her cheek, struggling not to cry. Guilt assailed her for lashing out at Jin when he was only concerned for her well-being. True to his words, he remained by her side as a best friend should to lend moral support. Hana realised that she was forever indebted to him.

Chapter 3

The sound of cutlery echoed across the ensconced kitchen as Jin, clad in a plain white tee over his school trousers, busied himself by piling snacks on the plates. He had purchased them at a convenience store as they walked to his house. Unwashed plates decorated the basin, and scraps from yesterday's meals remained on the counter. He sighed; it was his duty to clean the house whilst his mother slept away after working two shifts. Sweat rolled down his forehead, and on cue, he pressed an arm over the sticky skin and sauntered towards the refrigerator where he pulled out two soda cans.

He carefully arranged the full plates on the tray before bringing it out of the kitchen, taking measured steps through the colourful beads hanging over the entranceway. He passed along the corridor to ascend the staircase to the second floor, going by family portraits before pausing outside the slightly ajar door to peek inside the shadowy room when someone hacked a phlegm-infused cough. The breadwinner of the house, his mother overworked to put food on the table, yet she never pestered Jin to either hunt for a part-time job or curb his spending habits. Guilt fell heavily on his drooped shoulders. In fact he had been searching for a job that paid well in hopes of lessening the burden.

Quietly, he continued towards his bedroom, even more downcast when his mother coughed again just as he walked in to spy Hana sprawled with several open books in front of her. She was chewing on the tip of her pencil; sunlight filtering in from the open window cast a glow over her. She was unaware of Jin, who absently watched her legs swinging back and forth to reveal her upper thighs and a glimpse of her panties. He blushed in the face of such innocence.

"Hana," he called as he walked in, not sure what to say next.

They were so accustomed to each other's presence that at times Jin almost forgot Hana was a girl growing up just as he was, even though her attitude often resembled that of a toddler. Yet Jin had no romantic feelings towards her and vice versa, for which he was grateful. He considered Hana to be one of his closest friends; he could easily relate to her and share with her his innermost thoughts.

He placed the tray between them and peered down at the page before her with a befuddled expression. The handwriting was somewhat familiar, as well as the book itself. She finally peered up at him, half dazed, and he sprawled beside her on the wooden flooring. "Are these their notebooks?" he asked.

"Yeah," she muttered. "I have to complete them as soon as possible because they never bothered to write much about the subject."

"I'll help you." Jin grabbed for a pencil and a notebook. He examined Hana's neat, feminine handwriting, preparing to copy it.

"Jin, they will find out." Hana panicked a little. "Wait, you're serious?"

"I'm always serious," he murmured. "Look, is this all right?"

"It's not nearly the same." She gasped. "Jin, you're making it even worse!"

"It really doesn't matter if they know, right?" He glanced up at her. "As long as the notes are correct for them to look through?"

"I guess so," she said doubtfully. "Thank you for helping me out."

"This is me repaying you for helping whenever I forgot to write down my homework." He smiled. "Now, we're even, right?"

"Jin," she said, with tears welling up, "you know I'm weak when it comes to my emotions."

"You're too soft," he retorted in annoyance. "If you never wanted them to hand over their books, you should have just said no."

"But I'm doing my best to make friends." She sniffled. "Even if I hate being the mule for their work, as long as they see me as a friend, that's fine."

"I'm sorry." He heaved a sigh. "Sooner or later, they will learn how kind you are, Hana, and before you know it, they'll be your friends."

She sat up and hugged her knees. "I had that same thought before, but nobody besides you cared enough to talk to me."

"Don't lose hope," Jin answered whilst writing briskly. "You need to ooze with confidence to garner their attention."

"How do I do that?" she asked, inclining her head. "I want to be as good as you, Jin."

"Just—be confident."

The bedroom smelt of hair gel, socks, potato chips, and the breeze coming through the window. A thick mattress that had seen better days was thrown on the floor with haphazard pillows and a blanket. A small TV sat on the opposite cupboard, whilst knotted wires connected to his PlayStation were tangled across the floor. The cupboard held trophies he had won from middle school softball as well as during high school as a freshman. Home clothes mixed with school clothes were flung over the mattress, and Hana decided to help him by rearranging the place whilst he wrote in the notebooks. He saw her tottering every direction when he took a break to ease his wrists, frustrated by the bunch of girls who were too lazy to jot a single word.

"Is it all right if I use the laundry room?" Hana spoke at one point. "I'll help with the—"

"Oi." Jin jerked his head upright, looking flustered. "Hana, you don't have to."

"I've been your friend for so long." She shook her head. "Stop acting like I'm a guest."

"Well, you are," Jin mumbled with a pout. "My mother would kill me if she saw you doing the housework."

"I'll drop everything when I hear her waking up." Hana beamed. "You just help me with those notes. Do you need mine?"

"Huh," he scoffed. "I can be smart when I want to."

"Oh-ho, look who's talking." She poked fun at him, but he only smiled back.

By the time Jin finished the notes, a notification beep drew his attention. He fished the device from his front pocket and saw a message from an older girl. He was exhilarated at the idea of hooking up casually with this gorgeous flirt who had taken a liking to him. Hana hurried back into his room after completing her task, looking frazzled as usual. Jin sent a quick reply before putting aside the cell phone; he did keep some of his personal activities a secret from her habitual prying.

"I'm done here," he said and rolled himself upright. "Change of plan: I have to be elsewhere."

"Eh?" She blinked at him. "I thought we were about to play video games."

"Some other time." He shrugged. "Is the laundry done?"

"Yeah," she said whilst packing up her belongings. "Is it from the softball team?"

"Yup," he lied without missing a beat. "I need to change from this."

"Give me a second." She crab-walked across the floor to pick up some of the clutter before standing up with her bag. "I'll wait for you downstairs."

Jin took the time to tidy up his appearance, choosing a shirt and a jeans whilst spraying in every direction. Once satisfied with his look, he whistled merrily on his way out of the bedroom, in a hurry to meet up with his experienced partner. He did tamp down his excitement in front of Hana, who thankfully never caught on to his sudden brightness of mood as they left the traditional-looking house.

"Thanks for today," she said, once they were riding along the pathway. "I appreciate your help, Jin."

"No worries." Jin pedalled in a steady pace. "We are best friends, after all."

"Yes." Hana giggled. "I love you, Jin."

"Love you too," he replied.

He felt her leaning closer to embrace his neck as she perched her chin atop his head. The sensation of her bosom against his neck almost took him off the road. Although he regarded her as one of the boys sometimes, a moment like this was a strong reminder for him. Warmth crept across his cheeks, but he kept himself in check because he could never see Hana as someone to be intimate with. Still, he was a boy going through a riotous puberty, and even an accidental brush from a girl's frame turned him into a human rock.

"Hana, stand properly, or else we'll topple over," he gently chided her. "Also, I will be busy this week with practices for the upcoming tournament."

"Okay." She gripped his shoulders firmly. "I'll be spending more time in my club activity then."

"Reading club, right?" He touched on the subject earnestly. "What do you even do there?"

"Read," she replied with a snort. "What else do you expect from that club?"

"I don't know," he retorted. "I thought there must be something happening every week."

"The students including myself are a bunch of quiet and introverted beings," Hana lamented. "Even when we discuss, it's only about the books that catch our interest."

"How … boring." Jin cringed at the mental picture. "I'd probably die of boredom."

Finally, they reached the front of her apartment, and she hopped down to retrieve her bag from the basket. She bade him goodbye with a smile before trudging towards the entrance.

When she disappeared into the building, he rode the rest of the way to the meeting area at Takeshita District in a blur of wind. Soon he spotted the slender female smoking at a corner.

Gin Chiyo was the girl who took Jin's virginity the first time. They had been partners for about six months, and he had finesse in bed, much to her amazement. That sealed their bonds with no strings attached, even though Chiyo had a boyfriend also attending the same school as them.

"Hey, Jin," she said with a wave.

"Chiyo," he replied. "What's the matter?"

"I fought with him again." She took a final drag and dropped her cigarette on the ground to grind it with her shoe.

"Wanna go?" he inquired with raised brow.

"Eager, aren't you?" she said, toying with him.

"I'm not the one to text for a meet-up." Jin never missed a beat.

"Let's go to my house," she said as she sat on the seat behind him. "Be careful. I'm in a bad mood."

"All the better for me," Jin grinned lopsidedly.

"You're finally awake?" Chiyo smiled down at Jin, half-dozing and lethargic. "Are you okay?"

"Yeah," he groused. She sat beside him hugging a pillow. "It's late."

"Time for Jin to head on home." She stepped away from the bed and carefully picked up his clothes.

"I have to use the bathroom." Jin got up, unabashed by his nakedness. "Is it all right if I take a shower here?"

"Of course." She kindly showed him into the bathroom. "I'll join you in a few minutes."

By the time Jin returned home, it was close to midnight. Exhausted, he collapsed face down on the soft mattress. The house was void of human noises except when his stomach growled from hunger. He was too bushed to move yet, and too hungry to push the thought aside.

He was able to build a sandwich from the leftovers inside the refrigerator and was taking a bite when his cell phone alerted him to a message. Under the dim light in the dining room, Jin read the simple text from Hana. Sometimes he was able to shed his worries about his and his mother's circumstances, as well as the loneliness he was accustomed to ever since the only adult in the family had decided to work two jobs. Still, sometimes it was difficult to see her aging face.

He texted back pronto: *Good night, Hana, and sweet dreams - Jin*

Chapter 4

Shinjuku Gyoen National Garden

The warm breeze toyed with strands of Hana's hair while she sat on a wide wooden bench under a shade; leaves floated downward to gather on the ground whereas strangers passed along. The sunny park was full of activity, with beautiful landscape adorning its entire length. It was a tranquil destination for Hana when she needed to think and yearned for peace. A book in one hand, she ate a croquette, lost in her own world, often smiling when the characters within the book caught her interest. She didn't know that somebody was nervously watching over her.

Actually, Hana had skipped today's club activity to visit the park by herself, not bothered that one of the members would be peeved at her absence. It was rare for either one of them to miss class, and today was such a day. Without Jin, Hana had a sudden urge to drop by and enjoy the scenery.

"Suhana!" A boy called her name out of the blue.

Hana jumped at the interruption, blinking as she returned to her surroundings. A figure appeared before her, blocking her view of the garden, and she furtively glanced at the newcomer only to gawk at his presence. Her classmate was huffing and puffing nervously, not meeting her gaze. Then she saw something clutched firmly in his hand, and she narrowed both eyes behind her reading glasses.

"Ino, what is it?" she asked, concerned. "Did Jin ask you to come here?"

"No, no." Ino gulped before shuffling one foot on the ground and then raising his eyes to hers. "Can I talk to you, Suhana?"

At the mention of "talk," Hana's heart skipped, and again she peeked at the highly suspicious material in his grasp. Setting her book aside, she straightened to face Ino, who was rather chubby and a few inches taller than herself—a quiet, likable character who minded his own business. Hana reminded herself to breathe evenly and tamp down her excitement that this might be her first ever confession of interest from a boy. Jin's countenance materialised before her inner eye with a stunned expression if she informed him that one of their classmates had confessed to her.

"Suhana, is it possible that you can hand over this letter to Suzumi?" he said, extending the letter with both hands.

"Oh." Hana cleared her throat, feeling a warm flush creep across her cheeks. "Sure, I'll give it to her tomorrow."

"Thank you." He bowed in a show of gratitude.

At that moment, a group of college students walked past them. Misunderstanding the scenario of a shy boy confessing to an awkward girl, they burst into a riot of encouraging applause, and a few of the guys wolf-whistled at them.

Hana could only shy away from the embarrassing display, whereas Ino quickly turned around to wave both hands in front of him as his face reddened, and he stammered at them, "Please, you're getting the wrong impre—"

"Ino, leave it; they won't care," Hana snapped without thinking.

"I'm sorry for causing Suhana so much trouble." He gazed miserably down at his shoes. "I wish I were brave enough to face Suzumi and give the letter to her personally." He sighed in defeat.

"That's all right." She mustered up a smile and shrugged. "I also wish Ino all the best."

"Yeah," Ino said through a nervous chuckle. "Also, this is the first we ever talked with one another."

"True." Hana turned to insert the letter at the front zipper of her bag. "I'm used to not being approached by anyone inside the classroom unless they have something to gain out of it."

"I'm sorry," Ino whispered, clearly flustered. "I don't mean to bother you."

"Please, I should apologise for sounding so rude to Ino." She shook her head. "I only said the truth without putting you under the spotlight."

"But you have Jin with you," Ino said with a faint smile. "He is really popular with everyone."

"Jin is the only person who doesn't mind being seen with me." The thought of him brought a smile to her face.

"Are you two … dating?" Ino raised both eyebrows. "Of course, I don't wish to pry—"

"We are not *dating!*" she said, forming an *X* with her two hands.

"Oh." Ino blinked once, confusion written on his face. "Jin is really a nice guy."

"He is," Hana agreed.

"As a show of gratefulness for helping, allow me to treat you, Suhana," Ino volunteered, awkwardly loosening his bag straps.

"It's all right." Hana took a step back. "I really don't need Ino to treat me."

"Really, it will be my pleasure." He offered her a carefree smile. "You are not a bad person to talk with."

"Thank you." Hana grinned wide, realising she had found another friend in Ino. "I'm happy that you think so."

"Do you want to have a drink?" Ino glanced at her. "We can sit together and get to know one another better."

"Sure!" Hana was beyond thrilled, for once not bothered to be receiving a confession.

They quickly bonded over a shared love for comics and games and chattering about their favourite authors. At the back of her mind, Hana wondered if Suzumi would actually accept Ino's feelings for her because the girl was rather flighty and had an "I'm too good for anyone" nature, but the two girls had never spoken much during their occasional encounters in class.

The day went by in a blur. Later, Hana was at home getting ready when her mother surprised her by saying that she'd been invited to dinner by some workplace colleagues. "Will you be okay alone, Hana?" Neena pecked her on the forehead. "I'm sure you will; Suhana is my big girl."

"Yeah," Hana said with a nod, though shaking inwardly. "What time will Mom return home?"

"I am not sure. If I'm late, don't wait up for me," Neena replied tersely on her way to the threshold.

"Have fun." Hana waved before shutting and locking the front door. *Now what?* she thought to herself. She ambled toward the wide window frame to gaze out at the night, hugging herself defensively. She recalled the afternoon, and a corner of her mouth tilted higher. At least she had someone besides Jin to be friends with, even though Jin would always be the first in line. Yet now she would be able to greet somebody else within the classroom and move away.

Jin hadn't messaged her today, but she was feeling antsy, so she dived onto the mattress to pull the cell phone off the charger and dropped a text to her best friend. He replied moments later:

Yo, sorry, just got out of shower - Jin
No worries - Hana
How was today? - Jin
I made a new friend - Hana

Suddenly she was receiving a video call from Jin and couldn't help chortling at his reaction. When she slid the icon, she saw a shirtless boy arranging the phone on a kitchen counter. She noted Jin's serious expression while he adjusted the device, steadying it with both hands.

Finally, he peered into the screen and gave her a grin. "Care to tell me about this new friend of yours?" he asked, pulling out a cutting board to make dinner for himself.

"It's Yoshino Ino from our classroom." She told him about her afternoon as he got busy on the other end.

"Whoa." Jin paused in the middle of cutting meat to look at her. "Suzumi will reject him."

"Jin, stop being so negative," Hana chided him. "Maybe Ino will win her over with his niceness."

"You think Suzumi wants a goody two shoes?" Jin retorted with a snort. "Ino is a good lad with a kind heart, but he is looking up the wrong side of the tree."

"What do you mean?" Hana lay flat on her back. "Did Suzumi do something?"

"No." Jin sighed. "She's somebody who's a thrill seeker."

"Jin are you not telling me something?" Hana furrowed her neat brows. "I actually asked him what he sees in Suzumi, and the poor thing said she has a nice ambience around her."

"I don't see that going anywhere, but Hana got herself a friend." Jin walked off the frame momentarily to return with a rice cooker.

Hana shifted onto her side. "He says Jin is also a good person. I was almost thrilled at the idea that I might be confessed to today."

"Don't lose hope." Jin leaned closer to the phone. "You'll definitely meet someone soon."

"Really?" She rolled her eyes. "I'm just tired of waiting."

"Hey." Jin grinned wickedly, rubbing both hands together. "Read what he wrote in that letter."

"No." Hana narrowed her gaze at him. "Stop intruding into other people's business."

"Don't lie!" he shouted, pointing a finger at her. "Hana read it, but you don't wish to share with me."

She giggled. "I did not."

"You are too good," Jin lamented. "Anyway, we are going to a softball tournament at another school."

"Really?" Han raised herself on an elbow, careful not to drop her cell phone. "When?"

"Next week," Jin announced as he began to cook a simple dish. "Wanna tag along to show moral support?"

"Of course! I'll start by making some handwritten cheers on coloured papers." Her brain was already working on it.

"Just don't add up anything embarrassing, or else I'll fling it across the ocean," Jin warned her with a severe look.

"Stop acting so cool." She poked her tongue at him.

"How's your mom?" he asked with a chuckle.

"She's out for a dinner." She flinched to recall that she was alone. She abhorred staying in a quiet atmosphere, especially by herself in a dark house. She thought of her stepfather; hopefully he would return from his business trip. Even then, he headed out often for meetings.

Jin's voice brought her wayward attention back to the screen and saw him gazing back softly. "Why didn't you tell me sooner? You know I'd bunk down in your room."

"No worries. It's not as if my mother is going out for any business trips." She put on a brave front. "If she sees you in my room, there'll be a lot of commotion."

"Tell her not to worry too much because I'm helping by taking care of her young daughter's vir—"

"Jin! You idiot!" Hana yelped in embarrassment. "Stop acting so cool."

"You've already said that twice," he said with a wink. "Keep the lights on in your room."

"My mom will scold me for wasting the electricity," she moaned. "Jin, can you accompany me until I fall asleep?"

The boy was setting up dinner for one at the table and moved the phone there before answering her. Hana for her part was yawning, and her eyelids drooped several times. Yet she got out of the bed to shut off every single light and dashed inside the bedroom to shut the door.

"I'll be here," Jin said after swallowing a bite. "Go to sleep."

"Good night," she replied, already drowsing off.

"Sweet dreams," he said in a gentle tone.

She soon fell into a deep slumber. Jin waited patiently on the video call until she dozed off.

Chapter 5

"Morning, Hana; morning, Jin." A new voice approached the two of them in front of the shoe locker amidst a cacophonous hall.

"Morning, Ino," they both said, turning to greet Ino, who paused nervously beside them.

"See you guys in class." Ino sketched a quick bow and scooted away—nearly colliding with his secret crush.

Jin shook his head sympathetically when he saw Ino fumble with his bag; Suzumi never bothered to glance in his direction. He had a good inkling as to how the situation would end, with Ino's confession rejected, but Jin still hoped for some miracle for his classmate.

"Why do you have that expression?" Hana broke into his reverie.

"Suzumi didn't even blink when they crossed paths," Jin explained in a bored voice. "But now it's your turn; she's here."

"Wait a minute!" Hana hissed at him, visibly panicking. "I'm not ready to meet her."

"Are you the person confessing to Suzumi?" Jin leaned closer, arching one perfectly plucked brow.

"Not funny," she muttered, but she set sights on her target. "Just my luck the entire school will watch this moment and assume that I am the confessor."

"Hey, as long as Hana is popular enough to actually land a boyf—"

"You are cutting too close right now," she growled, only to huff a discontented sigh. "Why did I decide to help him out?"

"Because my little Hana is a good girl with a big heart." Jin smiled warmly down at her grimace. "Hurry up, you'll lose her soon."

"Here goes nothing," she whispered.

Once again, Jin leaned casually against the locker to watch Hana sidle over to Suzumi, who was chit-chatting amongst a cluster of other girls from different grades near the stairwell. When she noticed Hana's lingering presence, the rest of them looked her way as well. Hana froze up, bit one corner of her lip, and crossed both arms.

The two of them exchanged several words before Hana dug for the letter and handed it over. Suzumi's eyes flickered in Jin's direction. She grinned shyly, but he had a feeling it was a practised look and did not reciprocate, not wanting to complicate the circumstances. They often came across each other during lesson periods, and he was aware of her interest in him.

He patiently awaited Hana's return to his side before leading in a round of applause while she slammed her forehead against the locker comically. Jin grasped her by the arm and marched her forward as she whined for him to let go. He came to a sudden pause at the stairwell and pivoted languidly to stand behind a curious Hana. Her smile was radiant as his big hands rested on her shoulders.

Jin leaned closer to whisper in her ear. "Hurry up, we'll be late for class."

"Jin, everyone is watching us," Hana said, suppressing a laugh.

"Don't care," he said in a loud voice. "I have the authority since Hana is my friend."

"Idiot." Hana finally let loose her mirth. "Push me!"

"The two of you stop playing on the staircase," a stern teacher cautioned them from the landing above. "One of you might slip and cause a human avalanche."

"Sorry," the pair apologised in unison.

They managed to enter the classroom unharmed. Just then Ino glanced up from an open textbook to stare at them. Hana gave him a thumbs up as they approached his desk to announce that the confession letter had been delivered. The burly lad laughed nervously and gave a jerky nod whilst Jin continued towards his own desk and plopped down there.

"Hey, are they dating?" Tenka prodded on his arm.

"No, they are good friends now," Jin said to his friend, a bit annoyed. "Why don't you mind your own business?"

"Oi, don't have to get your hackles up. I was only curious, that's all."

Before the lesson began, Suzumi returned to the classroom with a sour look; Jin assumed that she must have had read the note. She ignored Ino, passing between desks to her seat. She sat down with a little huff, and Jin shrugged the moment he made eye contact with Hana who sat at the very front. Her wary eyes shifted to the hapless Ino, whose head was hanging, and Jin knew she felt sorry for him.

"Ino," Hana called out during recess period, "do you want to sit with us?"

"Um …." Ino paused near the sliding doorway holding on to his own lunchbox to glance at her oddly until Jin nodded for him to move closer. "Sure, why not?"

Jin grabbed a chair to drag over and straddle the seat to share lunch with Hana, who placed a bento box in the middle of the table. He scooted closer to peer into the box and salivated. Just then fresh memories of the past assailed his mind; the dish was a staple food for both Jin and his mother. She would cook fried rice with an omelette draped atop, carefully writing his name in ketchup sauce amidst little crooked hearts; his own heart clenched at the memory.

During their dinnertime, his mother would retell stories about Jin's father, whom he had never met because he had passed away due to cancer before Jin was born. But Jin had come to adore him, wishing deep within that his father could have lived on for the two of them to bond. He had worked as a banker, earning a decent income, and she was a housewife, but as luck had worked out, everything went downhill the moment he became ill.

She had a choice to remarry; her relatives flew from Osaka, hoping to see her adapt to a relationship, yet she declined firmly. Jin understood his mother's decision but wished at the same time that she had taken the offer. If she had, the two of them would be able to spend time together rather than finding themselves in this current rut with her health deteriorating.

"Jin, are you okay?" Hana's concerned voice broke into his reverie.

"Huh?" He blinked at his surroundings. "I'm sorry, I just feel tired."

Ino inserted his well-meaning opinion. "Maybe you need to rest. The weather was too hot for us to do all those laps at the field."

"I almost died," Hana said, laying one hand dramatically on her forehead. "That teacher is crazy!"

Jin stood up. "I'll be going to grab some drinks. Wanna order?"

Hana raised one hand. "A strawberry yoghurt, please. And hurry up, don't be late."

"What about you, Ino? My treat."

"Iced tea, thank you," Ino said with a smile. "Should I follow you, Jin?"

"No worries," Jin said with a wave and left the stuffy room. He had to make a beeline to escape from his inner thoughts because a tinge of depression had taken hold of his heart. He had no normal family life, unlike Hana. She was blessed with two parents, since her mother had remarried, making a wise decision. Once outdoors he stuffed two hands inside his front pockets and strolled casually towards the drink machine located at the corner of the school building. He nodded at several students in greeting, and his mood slowly lifted. He felt a tad better, returning to his usual self and softly whistling a merry tune.

Once at his destination, Jin paused to stare at a lone female in front of the machine he was headed for. She had shoulder-length raven hair with side-swept bangs partially concealing her features.

She had a tall, slender frame and gave off an alluring, feminine charm at first glance. Yet he had seen her occasionally stopping by the softball practice. At some point, he had begun to notice that her eyes tracked his every movement on the field, but he pretended to be oblivious, even as other players joked about the girl's attentions.

He partially took cover behind a pillar to watch her. She was having trouble with the machine, now and again slamming a hand against the device on cue. At last an ominous rattle and thud startled her. A drink had fallen into the dispenser. She bent low to retrieve it and turned to face his direction. At the same time Jin ducked out of sight, and the ringing of the school bell startled him. Since he had been fixated on the girl, he was able to discreetly observe her, and what he saw had pleased him. Then he turned for one more look and realised she was staring wide-eyed back at him.

To save himself, Jin coughed behind a fist avoiding eye contact while surreptitiously peeking at the stunning features of his admirer. A faint blush stole across her pretty complexion, and he adjusted his school uniform awkwardly before hurrying away—in fact almost stumbling in his haste. The moment he was out of her sight, he cringed whilst halting mid-motion to scrub his flustered face with both hands roughly and emit an embarrassed groan before continuing to the classroom alongside a sea of teenagers. He could hardly form a thought amidst the squeak of their slippers on the floor along with the general noise.

"Where's my drink?" a peeved Hana accosted him the moment he breezed inside.

"What are you doing, guarding the doorway?" he mumbled while pouting.

"Oi, I waited for you to bring us a drink." She crossed her arms. "Did you forget?"

"Shit." He smacked his forehead. "It slipped my mind."

"What were you doing?"

"I was busy gawking at—" Jin quickly shut his mouth. "I'll buy you one after school."

"I won't be able to go home with you because the reading club has some meeting," she said in a high voice.

"I'm sorry," he said, although his voice hinted that he was not.

"Hopeless," she muttered whilst stomping off to her desk, and he turned to reach his own.

Sometimes, Hana's behaviour irked Jin, but he let the matter drop because this was his fault, too busy spying on a stranger. The memory elicited another groan from deep within. He covered his head beneath both arms atop his desk to calm his distressed emotions.

If Hana won't be hanging out with me later on, then I might as well go out to look for a job, a mental voice whispered.

Chapter 6

*T*he sound of harried slippers slapping against the cold tile floor echoed in the quiet of the school corridor. In a flurry of arms and legs Hana ran for the bathroom and shoved open the swinging door. She located the nearest empty cubicle and slammed it shut, locking herself in. After undoing skirt and shorts, she plopped down on the toilet seat with a sigh of satisfaction. Out of nowhere, more voices began to fill the break room, and soon it rang with feminine laughter. Hana leaned sideways to peer through the crack and saw Suzumi alongside several of her friends.

They were from the band club, perhaps getting ready for the softball competition while Hana sat patiently toying mindlessly with the roll of tissues listening to the sounds of flushing and nonsensical chit-chat. She was waiting for everyone to disperse until a new topic of discussion perked her ears. Even though she felt uneasy at eavesdropping on their conversation, she silently beckoned them to continue.

"I thought the letter came from Takami Jin," Suzumi lamented in a high-pitched voice. "What a waste of energy."

"You were that happy?" one of them commented.

"Of course, remember that girl walking towards us with the letter? She's good friends with him, and my brain instantly put two and two together," Suzumi complained.

"I'm jealous of her friendship with Jin," another remarked.

Hana carefully and quietly arranged her clothes and tiptoed closer to the door where she could press her face closer to the crack and watch the four or five girls huddling at the sink counter. She was supposed to return to the book club for the current meeting but found she could not stop listening. Soon the girls were babbling about the weather, and besides never feeling welcome in such idle talk, she better understood Jin, who couldn't be bothered with girlish chatter.

"—Have you thought about what to do with him?"

"Of course, I will not accept his confession," Suzumi spoke in a breezy tone while adjusting her bobbed hair. "Ino is not my type of guy."

"You are so cold-hearted, Suzumi."

"I'm not," she snorted. "I just want a boyfriend desperately."

"You girls need to learn from me," another one piped in. The speaker was tall and shapely with beautiful straight hair set in a high ponytail. She carried an untouchable aura. The girl pivoted away from her reflection in the mirror to lean one hip against the counter. She loosely folded her arms with a look that was both mischievous and haughty.

"Amiya, why do you look so smug? It's disgusting," said a girl beside Suzumi, rolling her eyes.

"All of you are so crazy about wanting little *boys* to be your boyfriend," said the tall girl, "but I prefer a man." She gloated over the rest, and even Hana stunned by the confession.

"Eh? What do you mean?"

"I have men lining up to be my partner." She turned to study her reflection. "Their numbers are saved in my cell phone."

"You're crazy!" Suzumi squeaked, but her awe-struck look clashed with her protest. "Go on, tell us you're joking."

"You think?" she retorted, showing them her phone screen. "Is this proof enough?"

"What?" exclaimed the gaggle of girls in disbelief.

She's experienced! Hana thought.

"When did you lose your …?" Suzumi asked without finishing the sentence. "You had all of us fooled with your good-girl appearance."

"It's none of your business." The tall girl bit her lip, watching the others with a good-natured smirk.

"Just talking about it excites me already," one of the others sighed whimsically. "It's been a long time for me."

"Find yourself friends with benefits," the tall one advised, giving them crazy ideas. "You don't have to be in a relationship to have intercourse."

"You mean like tap and go?" another piped in. "But I'm still a virgin."

"If you're still wet behind the ears, it may pose a problem."

"Really?" The virgin's voice dropped several decibels. "That's fine, I'll wait for the right one."

"Good luck with that."

"Can you trust those men?" Suzumi brought up the main point.

"Well, it's tricky, but I follow my gut sense. Mostly they are gentlemen." The tall girl smiled. "My suggestion: be with someone you can trust not to take advantage of you."

"Hm," the girls hummed thoughtfully.

"If it is your first time, please, get yourself a guy who will be generous in the act, being extra careful and gentle with you."

"Where can we find a boy like that?"

"Ino."

All of them burst out laughing. As they left the bathroom, their screeching voices kept echoing as Hana finally emerged from the cubicle. She frowned in thought as words replayed inside her head. At the book club she sat staring with glazed eyes at the pages because their discussion for some reason caused a domino effect deep within her.

I want to experience intimate acts too, a childish inner voice declared.

Everyone else seemed to be enjoying their youthful splendour, gathering wonderful teenage memories while Hana sat woefully by. After the club was over, she was able to walk out of the school facility to gaze at the surroundings. When she got to the pedestrian crossing, she stood waiting for the light to turn green. Then she felt her phone vibrate in her pocket. It was a short message from her mother saying that she had a colleague's birthday bash after work and wouldn't be home till late. Hana felt another crack in her armour; her mother had excellent communication skills, while Hana was a disappointment in every way.

I hate myself, Hana vehemently spat mentally.

The apartment was brightly lit, and soft background music distracted the lone girl setting up for a long soak in a tub. She flung a bath bomb into the gushing water, releasing a sudden kaleidoscope of bubbles in vibrant colours. Hana, in her birthday suit, hunched at the edge to poke a finger inside the bubble froth enthralled by the vision as well as the bubblegum scent filling the bathroom. In a careful motion, she stepped one leg into the tub before her whole body was engulfed by the soapy texture and warm water, gently surging from the slight disturbance. With her hair bundled high in a haphazard bun, Hana leaned backward with eyes fluttering closed to focus on the music.

I should be out with friends too, whispered that same dark voice.

Hana squeaked at the sound of a thud before she realised it came from the neighbours upstairs. She stood up to rinse with lukewarm water before donning a fluffy robe, securing it warmly around her. She basked in the tranquillity of silence, although the fear of darkness kept her from actually wishing she lived by herself. After rummaging inside the refrigerator for a late night dinner, she finally managed to prepare for the night. After switching off every light in the apartment, she cuddled onto her soft mattress and rolled onto one side.

"I'm stupid to allow those girls to sway my mindset," she reminded herself. "I have to focus and be the girl everyone will admire."

With that thought in mind, Hana drifted off into a dreamless state. Someone calling her name from outside her door woke her to a tenebrous morning. She checked the glow of the clock, guessing she was up earlier than usual. Before she got ready for school, she dropped a quick text for Jin to meet her along the way before she set out on autopilot.

"Hana! Wait, don't forget your umbrella." Neena rushed out of the apartment to catch her waiting at the elevator. "Be careful. I love you."

"Love you too," Hana mumbled while kissing her mother on the cheek.

Soon she was ambling across the side path watching most of the stores preparing to open when something caught her eyes. A note was posted on a closed door saying they required either a full-time or part-time cashier, including students. Hana made a face but shrugged and jotted down both the email address and a hotline number, thinking she might call them during lunch break. As she swung her umbrella wide, someone whistled, and without looking, she knew the person could be none other than Jin. As if on cue, the bicycle screeched to a halt beside her.

"Somebody is up early" was his greeting.

"It's not a surprise," she said in a low voice. "Where's your umbrella?"

"There's no need for me," he commented while moving to the other side of the vehicle. "But those dark clouds are ominous."

They advanced in amicable silence. The morning passed at a snail's pace; perhaps the weather was the cause, or maybe only Hana felt the time drag. For the hundredth time, she sighed, even knowing that outdoor physical education was cancelled. At one point the clouds open up to a murmuring downpour. Finally the hands on the clock pointed at the right numbers, and the bell disrupted the quiet classroom.

"Ino, do you want to eat with us?" Hana called out.

"Um, I will be having my lunch at the canteen today." He pointed a thumb towards the doorway. "The two of you should sometimes visit the cafeteria."

"Hana's mother cooks up a delicious breakfast." Jin dragged a chair closer as usual. "Ino, you have to try it."

"I'll ask my mother to—"

"It's all right! Hana, you don't have to trouble your mother, but thank you for the kind offer." Ino smiled as he left the classroom hastily.

"Suzumi did not accept him," she whispered.

"I figured that earlier," he muttered. "Poor guy, but that's only the beginning, so he mustn't lose hope."

The rain stopped, but inside the building was a cramped chaos of students and teachers. Hana neatly repacked her empty lunch box; Jin had vanished the moment he stuffed the last rice ball deep into his mouth. Hana raised a brow, briefly puzzled about his odd behaviour.

Then she took matters in hand to call the bakery about the cashier's job. On the other end a lady greeted her in a cheery tone. Nervous, Hana stammered a little but inquired about the vacancy. By the end of their talk she had a strong inkling that she might soon be called for an interview. She bit the inner corner of her lip. Maybe she was taking a step forward to open up and change for the better. *Talk about a goody two shoes!* she thought with a quiet chuckle.

Students poured out of the gate in a sea of bodies as a prefect stood by with a teacher to check on them. In the middle Jin and Hana strode side by side meaning to visit the town area. They were hunting for a ramen stall. She mounted the bicycle behind Jin, and they rode off at a gentle pace. She had one hand clinging to the cold metal and the other around his warm waist. Her fingers tightened on the cloth of his shirt. She was enjoying the cool breeze and the puddles splashed through here and there.

"You okay back there?" Jin said. "You seem out of focus today."

"Really? You noticed me?" She peered at his face. "Very observant of you."

"Of course."

Jin chose a stall beneath the train track. A charming vintage vibe came from the humble shop along with a strong fragrance. They decided to perch at the counter, and each ordered a bowl of ramen noodles. Side dishes were prepping inside the kitchen while a cold drink was offered. They filled their growing bellies with delicious food. The old box television had a comedy show on set to a low volume. Soon office workers in formal attire were lining up for places to sit.

"I went out job hunting yesterday," Jin told her while sipping on the broth. "I have decided to help my mother financially."

"Any luck?" Hana asked, beaming at him. "Don't lose hope!"

"I won't, but a few stores told me that they give a call on the weekend for an interview." He shrugged. "Not too sure about that."

She laid a hand over his. "Have faith. Where did you go?"

"Takeshita District." He glanced at her. "You've got chilli paste on your chin."

"Where?" she said. "Here?"

"Lower … on the right." Hana patted aimlessly without success. "Allow me."

All of a sudden, the two best friends were up close with his hand gentle on her warmth face. Hana conjured a forbidden mental image that seared her brain, and for the first time in her life, she felt sensitive to Jin's touch; his brow was furrowed in concentration; his eyes the colour of dark chocolate with black flecks; his streaks of blonde hair and his piercings twinkling at her. Her eyes drifted lower to focus on his neck. His masculine build contrasted with her femininity. His Adam's apple bobbed, and that image persisted when his eyes met her wide ones.

"Done," he said.

"S-sorry!" she sputtered, standing upright only to topple against someone behind her.

"Hey, watch out!" the man yelled.

"Hana! Are you all right?" Jin shot out of his seat to grasp her arm firmly.

"No, yes!" She faltered on her feet. "I'm sorry!"

"It's okay." Jin spoke in a concerned voice. "Let's go home."

He hoisted their backpacks. The moment they exited from the crowded stall, they peeked up at the dark clouds just as a sudden heavy rain soaked everyone in sight. Once again, Hana was struggling to overcome her awakening senses when Jin took hold of her hand in his big one to race for the nearest shelter, their feet splashing on wet concrete as they dodged people also ducking for cover. Still holding hands, Jin and Hana paused underneath an awning, but it was not enough to keep them dry as a strong wind drenched them. Too late, Hana realised she had forgotten the umbrella in school. She caught sight of Jin shoving both hands through his wet hair. Water rolled down his face whilst the warmth of his palm still burned in Hana's own.

"You okay?" he asked softly. "Damn, you look like a drowned rat."

"Hm." Hana narrowed her eyes at him wondering if this "awakening" was a signal of her time of the month. *Stupid*, she scolded at herself.

"I'm sorry for getting both of us wet," he apologised out of the blue.

"Please, I was the one to forget my umbrella, or else we wouldn't be shivering here," she said through chattering teeth.

Suddenly her eyesight was obscured, and she felt something soggy over her head. She caught Jin's familiar scent and realised he had draped his school jacket over her to shield her from the cold rain—another chivalrous action from him but nothing new to Hana, although she seemed to be nitpicking his every motion. She clutched the lapels and stifled a sneeze. Then, peeking from below the jacket, she saw him bend low to roll up the hemline on his pants. "Jin, what are you up to?"

"I'm retrieving my bicycle, but just wait for me." He straightened with a slight bounce. "I'll ride back to school for the umbrella."

"No, I'll come too—"

"Request is denied." He leaned closer to tug the jacket over her face. "You will wait for me, right?"

The simple sentence brought tears to her eyes. Unable to speak, she only nodded jerkily. Jin raced into the downpour without hesitation. As she thought about him, the conversation in between the girls came barrelling into her mind. The tall girl's voice rang clearly in her ear:

"Be with someone you can trust not to take advantage of you."

"If it is your first time, please, get yourself a guy who will be generous in the act, being extra careful and gentle with you."

"Jin is that boy," Hana said with confidence.

He was out of sight, but Hana hunched low to hide beneath the jacket because in the back of her mind a voice kept on whispering about the image from earlier: the two of them kissing. The feeling was utterly natural.

She was not in love.

Chapter 7

"Bye, please come again," Hana said with a bow from behind the cash register.

"Well done," her older companion said with an appreciative nod. "For a beginner you are learning quickly."

"Thank you, Mrs Noshita," Hana said, returning her bow. "But I'm still nervous when dealing with the cash register."

"Everyone goes through that at first." Mrs Noshita waved a hand casually, returning to the back room. "I'm amazed that for a foreigner you grasped our language with so much ease and pronounce really well."

Hana cocked one hip. "I'm a local."

"Eh?" The woman peeked out from the back room with a stunned expression. "You're a local?"

"Well, yes." Hana shrugged gingerly while clearing her throat. "My mother became a permanent resident before giving birth to me; she loves the Japanese culture and decided to live here."

"Amazing! I am happy to know that your mother thinks our culture is interesting," Mrs Noshita said with a wrinkly smile.

Hana turned to stare at the front of the bakery. It had been pure luck during that early morning walk to school that she now had a part-time job. When she announced the news to her mother, Neena both congratulated her as well as urging her to be a sensible human being. When Hana received the email confirming her hiring, the two of them went out for dinner—a rare occasion, but Hana enjoyed their bonding moments together. They dined in an expensive restaurant before heading out window-shopping. A week later, she was slowly but surely getting along with the few workers, although her nervousness at conversing with strangers often made her tongue-tied at certain moments.

Hana was also discovering new sides of herself. She realised she was a natural in customer service, which surprised her because of her hesitancy around strangers. Still, she was proud to know this; it was a small link to her mother that now and then filled her with warmth.

One of the bakers popped out from behind with a tray of steaming loaves. "Hana, can you help restock the breads, please?"

"Yes!" Hana said a little too enthusiastically.

A part-time baker, he lived in a hostel close to his university and had been part of the team for almost a year now. When Hana first saw him close up, she felt uneasy about her appearance: slightly plump, with tanned skin and hair that badly needed a trim, she basically felt unpresentable. Yoshi was handsome, with a very open personality. He seemed to adapt quickly, like a chameleon, and he was kind towards Hana—a rare experience, since the boys in her school were picky about girls.

Carefully balancing the tray on one hand, Hana stacked the bread neatly. There weren't many customers compared to the weekend; it was just as her luck that she had begun her work when traffic was heavy. By the end of her shift, Hana had a strong inkling she smelt from perspiration, and her body ached from standing too long and rushing back and forth. At one point, Hana regretted her decision to work so as to pass her time and earn little sums of cash until her mother's compliment changed her mind. Neena had surprised her by fetching her from work, and they once again went out for dinner instead of cooking at home. Hana reminded herself that it was only a matter of time until she would work like a pro just like her colleagues.

The tinkling bell alerted Hana to three young men entering. They attended the same school; thankfully they were first years, while both Jin and Hana were second years. The boys lingered to choose a mountain of assorted desserts and bread before sauntering towards the cash register; still, Hana's hands trembled a little, as she didn't want to muck up her task. After ringing up the purchase and returning their change, she let out a sigh of relief and beamed merrily.

"Bye, Hana." Mrs Noshita paused at the back room entrance to wave at her. "My shift has ended. See you tomorrow."

"Have a safe journey home, Mrs Noshita."

When the coast was clear, Hana fished out her cell phone to check for messages when she caught Jin's name. It reminded her of the disturbed scenario at the ramen stall, and heat crept up her neck to flood her countenance, She rubbed a hand over her suddenly fatigued expression. She truly was not in love with Jin, yet, she could not deny the *lust* she had experienced. Just that tiny jolt had shifted her view forever. Still, she knew she should not take that step forward because Jin would not accept such a crazy request from her.

"Yo."

Hana glanced up only to come face to face with the devil. She shrieked in startled fear when the rest of the crew came bursting out from behind to check up on her. Another heatwave suffused her face, and she stammered an apology, guessing it was really rude to scream in a customer's face. After a terse explanation they were mollified, but Yoshi chuckled, grateful that none were irked by her reaction.

"I messaged you that I was standing outside the store." Jin leaned an elbow on the counter. "That is so rude of you."

"Shut up," Hana hissed, still working to calm her mind and slow her heartbeat. "Are you here to buy something?"

"Nope, just curious to see you working." He chuckled. "This is a new step in our life."

"Please keep your philosophy about life for later." Hana spoke with her teeth clenched. "Stop bothering me now."

"You mustn't talk like that to your customers," Jin said, scowling. "Now that you pissed me off, I'll buy a loaf from some other bakery."

"Sorry, sorry!" Hana clutched his sleeve as he turned away. "I don't mean to be so uptight."

"Forget it." Jin shrugged her off and marched towards the door.

She guessed it would take enormous patience to calm her friend, especially if he was in a dark mood. Jin had little to no restraint when it came to his emotions; even his own mother had given up cajoling her moody son. Hana bounded from behind the counter to chase after Jin. Meeting him at the entrance, she yanked Jin's arm, almost toppling him sideways. She grabbed a tuft of his waxed hair to comically wobble his head like a puppet on a string.

"Calm down," she chortled when she saw his pouting face. "You are so easily triggered."

"Let go," he told her in a deep voice. "I'm heading home."

"No you don't. My shift will end soon, so wait up for me. My treat, okay?" She fluttered her lashes at him until he finally snorted.

"Okay." Jin nodded and left to wait for her outside.

She shook her head. *What a little kid.*

"Is he your boyfriend?" a feminine voice inquired from behind.

"Eh?" Startled, Hana turned and saw Miko, a girl her age who attended a different school. The two had started work at the bakery only a week apart, even though Miko never spoke much to Hana unless it was about work. She was a beautiful girl who religiously took care of her appearance. She had a shoulder-length curly mane and wore coloured contact lenses and manicured nails. Her simple makeup merely accented her standout looks, as did her fashionable attire.

"He's my best friend," Hana explained awkwardly. "Sorry about just now."

"You frightened us," she said, but Hana caught her gently scolding tone. "Don't ever scream like that because you might cause an accident."

"Sorry," Hana whispered, a bit irked by her attitude.

Yoshi interrupted them with a smile. "Hana, you can head home now. Thank you for your hard work."

"Thank you." Hana bowed, feeling her throat clench on rising tears. "I will take my leave now."

"Bye," Yoshi said with a wave.

After changing from work uniform to her usual shirt, Hana hurried out of the store with a solemn expression. She had a feeling that she and Miko would not be in good terms, and her heart squeezed a little at the sour thought.

Just then someone placed a soothing hand atop her head to rub gently. "Are you all right?" Jin hunched low on his knees to glance at her downcast face. "Are you still angry about just now?"

When Hana shook her head without replying, he nudged her shoulder with his own, urging her to gaze up at him. She started forward whilst exhaling slowly to cut off the overwhelming urge to weep pitiful tears. The day had been going fairly well, yet there are always people who doesn't have the courtesy to give someone a space to breathe.

They paused to purchase a set of dangos and mochi ice cream. Hana was sure that her weight had recently gone up but not bothered about it today.

"Jin, why do people hate me?" She whispered the words once the two of them were settled on a bench at the park.

"What?" He blinked in surprise. "Is it because of me? I'm really sorry for bothering you at the workplace."

"No, it's not you—just some people who don't seem to like me at first glance." She put her dessert aside to gaze blankly at the calming scenery.

"Do I know this person?" Jin asked, showing some concern. "If it's someone from our class, I'll talk—"

"That girl from my work," Hana blurted, cutting off his sentence. "She has this aloof aura whenever I'm around."

"What about the rest of them?" he asked with brows raised. "Are they also treating Hana the same way?"

"Well, no." She shook her head once while stretching her legs. "They seem rather nice for a change."

"Focus on them and ignore her." He slouched back on the bench. "If she has a bone to pick, then don't care about her nasty attitude. Put your attention on the good stuff."

"But we're working in the same place," she said with a ragged sigh. "I'm doing my best to make friends with everyone."

"I can see." He smiled at her. "I'm proud of you, Hana."

"It's all thanks to you, Jin." Hana finally took a big bite out of the mochi ice cream, enjoying the burst of flavour.

"Give yourself some credit too." He leaned his head back on the bench to stare at the sky.

"Jin, you may continue about that life philosophy," she said, bumping her knee against his own. "I'm willing to listen to you."

"Really?" he drawled went on without shifting his gaze. "We're now approaching adulthood. Placing tiny steps forward, you and I, the two of us will take the last leap as third-year high school students."

"Hm." She tuned in with a concentrated expression. "It's scary, don't you think so?"

"Along that line, we may be separated, heading on different paths, but I don't want Hana to think I'll abandon you." His gaze swung back to her. "New relationships will come, and we'll be working hard to build a positive future and lifelong careers."

Hana had an out-of-body sensation at the mention that they might actually follow different paths while creating new bond in life. Without Jin, she was sure, she would drown and never be able to float on the surface. The boy was her lifeline, yet she couldn't selfishly keep Jin by her side forever. He was an adolescent male who yearned to explore the world, making new everlasting friends and perhaps settling down with a better partner.

She felt ashamed of herself. Jin was already thinking ahead about their future, whereas she had one-sided thinking. She gulped audibly, the taste of the ice cream dissipating in her mouth. "Yeah, Jin will always be my best friend even if we stop seeing each other someday along the way." She lifted her water bottle for a drink.

"Idiot, I'm not talking about ending our friendship. Hana is somebody I'll always trust." He chuckled softly. "Maybe it's best if the two of us are some in sort of relationship."

She suddenly choked on her water at his bizarre mention of them being in a relationship. Jin patted firmly on her back to calm her hacking cough. Finally she glanced at his blossom-tinted features as he struggled to control his amusement at her expense. She was lost for words.

"What the hell happened to you?" Jin chuckled. "I thought you were dying!"

"Oh, so the idea of me dying has you laughing merrily?" she moaned.

He waved off her lame retort. "No, no. You're mistaken."

Before she could give him an earful, he silently leaned his head onto her shoulder. The soft strands gently tickled Hana's neck. Even as her body tensed, she peeked at his dyed mane; his eyes were closed, and both arms were folded against his chest. She let her rigid frame relax and let a smile lighten her features.

"Hana, are you really afraid to be in a relationship?" he inquired out of nowhere. "I thought you wanted a boyfriend."

"I do," she said in a low voice. "But it won't be easy for me."

"Why do you say so?"

"Because I'm me," she replied in a monotone. "Let's drop the subject, shall we?"

The warm breeze carried the floral scent of the wide park; squirrels hopped from branch to branch in the oak over their heads. A distant dog was barking in a frenzy, and a few joggers enjoyed the mild weather. Scattered ivory clouds dotted the cobalt sky, while huge oaks lined both sides of the jogging path where the teenagers sat enjoying each other's company.

Out of the blue, Hana carefully reached a hand to caress the top of Jin's head without disturbing him, feeling suddenly protective. He was the most precious person in her dull life. Then she laid her head against Jin's own, and they were still for a long time.

"Hey, Jin," she said into the serene quiet. "Do you mind me saying something?"

"What is it?" he murmured in a sleepy tone.

"Even if you or I get into a relationship, let's not break this bond that we share."

"You have my promise. I won't be able to go further without your annoying presence," he joked.

"I'll introduce Jin to my future boyfriend, and the four of us will have double dates," she said whimsically. "We'll attend each other's weddings, and our children will grow up together and become best friends."

"That sounds nice," he affirmed with a chuckle. "I can clearly picture that."

So, please, Hana silently pleaded, *help me erase this crazy notion about the two of us in bed together.*

Chapter 8

In the middle of the night, Jin stirred awake from a deep slumber to rub his eyes in a daze. Then feeling his body went tense, and he listened for any sounds in the house. He peered into the shadowy corners of his bedroom, noting the time at half past twelve, and sighed aloud to have left such a peaceful rest. Chilly air floated in from the open window, and then his ears perked up at the sound of a hacking cough. He sat upright to shove the blankets away.

He shuffled out of the room covering a yawn and frowned at the light filtering from his mother's bedroom. He peeked past the barely open at his mother, who sat at the far side of the mattress. She poured a pill from one of the medicine bottles on her bedside table and swallowed it before downing a cup of water.

"I hate this cough," Sayomi complained in a fatigued tone.

The light flickered off by the bedside when she lay down after another assault of wet coughing shook her slight frame. Jin never budged from his spot, distressed that he was not able to aid his mother. Cold anger curled his upper lip, and he fought down the urge to slam a fist against the wall. That wouldn't cure his mother's health, and he backtracked from the position to re-enter his bedroom to sprawl face-down on his bed. He used a pillow to shut out noises, yet sleep evaded him. He blindly rustled for the cell phone on the floor beside the mattress and typed a quick message to Hana; after several minutes of silence, a vibration signalled her reply. He flopped on his back to study the text.

I'm still awake, you okay, Jin? - Hana
My mother's health is deteriorating I'm worried sick now - Jin
Want to meet? - Hana
What? Your mother will kill you - Jin

He shot upright when Hana actually gave him an exact location for a meetup. Panic settled within his gut. He typed furiously in scrambled letters, but no reply came. At lightning speed Jin hopped on his feet and threw on a pair of jeans hanging behind the door. He dug through a mountain of shirts in search of a long-sleeved T-shirt as well as a jacket to keep from freezing.

Once again, he checked the phone screen and saw a new message: she was out and about, much to his shock and excitement at their reckless behaviour. Hana's imprudent attitude to his problem touched a place in his heart. Noiselessly he let himself out the door, made a beeline for the bicycle, and zoomed off like a wild bat from a cave.

He caught a glimpse of Hana at the Shinjuku Gyoen National Garden, arriving just as he had by a transport of her own. A sudden laugh of disbelief burst from him as he gawked at either her stupidity or her bravery, alongside a twinge of guilt for getting Hana in trouble if Mrs Akiyama should find her daughter's bedroom vacant.

The adorable girl was cloaked in a thick jacket; her breath steamed in the chill whilst she stood on her pedals to bestow Jin a wide smile as they screeched to a halt face to face. Their gazes connected, and without a word she climbed off her bike and ran to Jin's and then flung herself against him for an embrace.

The two of them stood clinging to one another, and tears leaked from underneath his squeezed eyelids as she tightened her grip around him, lending her quiet strength. Her soft fingers twined through his hair in a mesmerising gesture. Amidst the utter absence of people and the chill breeze, with the eerie glow of street lamps on the pathway, the pair made not a sound.

Jin pulled her closer, seeking for comfort from someone who read him like an open book. The cold fingers of fear crept up his spine at the thought that he might lose his mother to sickness, and fresh tears rolled down his pale cheeks. He hiccupped, embarrassed to be crying in a girl's arms, but the night shielded them from prying eyes.

"She won't leave you so soon," Hana whispered close to his ear. "Be strong for your mother."

"You think so?" he mumbled against the curve of her neck.

"Yes." She caressed his back. "Perhaps both of you should sit down for a long talk."

"She doesn't have the time." He gritted his teeth to keep the rage away. "Work is always calling her to return."

"I'm sorry," she said, never loosening her arms around him. "Is there anything I can do to help?"

"You being here gives me the strength to face this," Jin whispered. "Thank you."

"We are friends after all," she replied without missing a beat. "I'll always be here for you, Jin."

When Jin had calmed his runaway emotions, he gingerly pulled away from Hana, instantly missing the enveloping warmth of her embrace when he saw her nervous expression. They acted like a regular couple, but it had never occurred to Jin that feelings might encroach between them; in fact, he figured that the two of them would never dare to step over the line of intimacy in the future.

In hopes of dissipating the heavy atmosphere, Jin chuckled, glancing away while rubbing the back of his head as well as wiping away wet stains on his cheeks. "Hey, do you want to play the swings?" he mentioned out of the blue. "Since the two of us are out, we might as well take advantage and enjoy the night scenery."

"I'd rather ride on our bikes around the neighbourhood," Hana suggested while resuming her seat. "Hurry up! We're going on a tour!"

With urgency in his movements, Jin mounted his bike to take the lead as they set out, feeling the last bit of depression slipping away. He let go a thrilling shout, and Hana answered with her own.

They sped along in the middle of the road to take in their deserted surroundings. A freezing blast chilled their rapt faces whilst above their heads a full moon hung over the serene indigo sky, and a spangle of stars twinkled prettily. They were biking through an otherworldly ambience.

Out of nowhere, Hana passed his bicycle, and her hazel eyes met his with a salacious wink before she put on speed as if to outrace him. Wickedly grinning, Jin followed close behind. A buoyant scream often came from Hana when he now and again closed the distance between them, even daring to kick the side of her bicycle as they weaved back and forth.

At one point, they ventured inside a convenience store to purchase snacks and sat on the kerb in front of the brightly lit space to nibble them and rest. An amicable silence prevailed between them as they soaked in the night-time sights and sounds. With wide eyes they gazed at the streets, where an occasional car would zip by, leaving a red blur of tail lights.

Finally Jin glanced at his phone screen to check the time and turned his head to gaze at her. "Let's go home."

"Okay," she whispered, crumpling discard paper in one hand.

"I'll fetch you to the apartment." He extended one hand for her to grip it firmly and pulled her upright.

"You feeling much better, Jin?" She stood on tiptoe to observe him.

"Much, much better," he said with a warm smile.

The next day, as school was ending, Hana stopped inside the classroom door. "I'll see you tomorrow." She waved as she pouted at his amused face. "I'm staying to clean the room."

"Good," he replied. "You'll learn new skills for tidying up my bedroom when you visit."

"Why, you …," she squeaked comically. Jin tugged at her braids before drawing back from her flailing hands. "Wait, wait!"

He danced away from her only to return to her side when she began digging inside her bag. She retrieved several books and shoved the stack against his chest. Confused, he fumbled for them to keep them from falling. Surveying the titles, he saw the school logo stamped on each cover and groaned loud enough for her to hear.

"Just return the books for me, please. Today is the date they're due." She bowed low. "Thank you."

"Fine," he groused, gently knocking one of the books on her head. "See ya."

At the library, Jin entered to see a few students either seated with open books on the desk or browsing amongst the sections in the quiet atmosphere. A brow raised sceptically, he ventured further inside and cleared his throat to catch the attention of a teacher behind a wide desk; a computer stood on the table before her, and behind her more books were stacked in boxes. A student paused to lift one of the cartons and carry it off; perhaps a school librarian, he thought.

"Where can I return these books?" he whispered.

"You can hand them over to me." She stretched both hands towards him to receive them. "Thank you."

"Thank you, too." He bowed tersely before rushing for the entrance. Just then he heard a sneeze off to one side. He saw a girl engrossed in a book that she held to the side as she sneezed again. She furtively glanced around as if apprehensive about disturbing others. All of a sudden, their gazes met from afar; he remained immobile at the entrance, one hand on the metal bar to swing it outwards.

The teacher sidled up behind him. "Excuse me, please do not crowd at the doorway." Jin was startled by her sudden appearance.

"Sorry," he muttered abashedly but saw only an empty place when he looked back at the girl. *Where did she go?*

Curiosity drew him across the room to stalk the space, hunched over to peer through the stacks. He ignored a few heads turning to watch, puzzled at his actions. His head jerked to peek around a corner, yet nobody hid from his sharp gaze. He continued to tiptoe further until he accidentally bumped the shelves. He grabbed for the toppling books and heard a quiet yelp. He pulled out a book to stare at a pair of onyx-coloured eyes blinking back at him. His heart quickened at the sight, and when he casually walked around the corner, he came face to face with her.

She was even prettier up close, and Jin gasped at the sight. She blushed under his open scrutiny and was about to flee when Jin let go of the books nestled in both arms. As they tumbled to the tiled floor, he extended tapered fingers to encircle a dainty wrist and interrupt her escape. Without letting go of her, he shuffled the few steps to block her path. With nowhere else to turn, she leaned against the shelf.

"I'm sorry," she apologised out of the blue. "I know my behaviour was very rude—"

"What is your name?" he asked in a soft voice, cutting off her words.

"Shouko Mitsunari."

"Excuse me, are these your books?" the librarian came into view, looking displeased. "If you are not reading, please maintain the tidiness of the library."

"I'm sorry." Jin bent low to aid the grumbling worker, only to hear a noise behind him. His admirer had found a perfect opportunity to escape.

Finally Jin left the stuffy atmosphere to inhale the familiar outdoor air of the school. He leaned against the side of the building and closed his eyes. With a faint smile he imagined bits of conversation he might share with his supposed admirer, but he was baffled as to how he should approach her with this new revelation.

Shouko, what a nice name, an inner voice whispered.

A week away from the softball tournament, Jin figured he had enough time to explore. Then someone whistled for his attention, and another emotion overtook him. Chiyo waved a hand to indicate that they should walk home together. The only reason she was interested in him was because of their casual fling. He pushed away from the wall to saunter towards her.

"Yo," he said by way of greeting.

"Wanna come over to my place?" she said, tucking a lock behind her ear. "That is, if you aren't busy with extra classes."

He shrugged. "I'm free today."

"Great," she said with a happy smile. "I'll meet at our usual place so we won't be seen by anyone here."

The two of them separated to walk from different locations, although today his head was filled with visions of Shouko—her innocent eyes never wavering from his own, the softness of her small wrist clasped in his hand, and the top of her head just below his chin. Indeed, Jin was experiencing a whole new territory.

Chapter 9

The bakery staff finally sighed in relief when their last customer for the afternoon left. Workers began to clear the mess from earlier. Usually the peak hours were chaotic as they matched pace with their customers. Mrs Noshita handed a bucket and mop to Hana on her way out after her morning shift.

As Hana aided her colleagues, a bounce to her steps drew an inquisitive look from Miko, perched behind the counter. She leaned over to rest both elbows on the cold surface and watch. She propped her chin on closed fists with a Cheshire cat grin. "Why are you looking so happy, Suhana?" she asked with a hint of curiosity.

"She is happy to be heading home soon, right?" Yoshi chuckled while cleaning up the trays.

"No, my stepfather is returning home tonight after a business trip," she answered happily. "I miss him so much."

"Do you have a crush on him?" Miko raised a thin brow drawn with a pencil liner. "I've heard about stories where the—"

"No!" Hana slammed the mop inside the bucket, splashing soapy water. "That's crazy! Who thinks about their stepfather that way?"

"It's a forbidden relationship." Miko waggled her brows, earning a groan from Yoshi. "So that isn't why you are feeling giddy with happiness?"

"Of course not, that is disgusting." Hana made a comical face. "We happen to be really close."

"I see-ee." She dragged out the syllable before straightening.

"Miko, where do you get such ideas?" Yoshi lamented.

"It's nothing new from the grapevine," she said with a shrug. "But our Suhana is so funny, and we girls are excited when the time comes to meet our boyfriend. But she's excited to see her stepfather."

"Do you have a boyfriend, Suhana?" Yoshi said, smiling. "You're so pretty, I'm sure many must be queuing up in front of your doorstep."

"Are you spoiling for a fight?" Hana muttered beneath her breath.

Miko rolled her eyes. "Yoshi, you can tell that Suhana has never had her first kiss. That poor thing stiffens up whenever you stand too close to her."

"Leave me alone, Miko." Hana doggedly kept mopping the floor. "I wasn't bothering you."

"She'll quit unless you stop," Yoshi warned her as well. "We don't bully our colleagues."

"I'm not bullying her," Miko said with a snort.

Hana resorted to one of her usual excuses. "I want to concentrate on my studies instead of wasting my time on a baseless relationship."

"What an intellectual retort," Miko grumbled while walking out from behind the counter to swing an arm over Hana's shoulder.

Hana paused at her task with a wary glance at Miko, who continued to smile at her. This close, she could see Miko's contact lenses, her striking blonde weave, and a smooth makeup job. A tongue piercing peeked out whenever she opened her mouth to speak. The two girls were polar opposites in many ways, but Miko was loosening up little by little around Hana. They were able to be in the same room together without awkwardness or a heavy atmosphere, although Hana was not thrilled that Miko often passed such casual offhand remarks.

"Don't mind our Miko," Yoshi chortled. "She's the type to ignore sensitive emotions."

Miko jabbed a thumb in his direction. "You can always date, Yoshi."

"I am still not over the break-up, sorry," he said, raising both hands.

"I'm beginning to think something is up with you, not the girls you've dated," Miko said.

"Stop assuming it's me," he snarled. "Those women are too much."

"Because you only date the materialistic ones." She moved away a little, releasing Hana from her clutches. "But you can start dating homely girls like Suhana."

"What?" Hana felt heat rise in her cheeks.

"I see Suhana as a little sister," Yoshi answered in an apologetic voice.

"See what I mean, Suhana?" Miko turned back to Hana, who fidgeted. "Guys don't see you much as a girlfriend but more like a sibling. Do you know what's wrong?"

"No," Hana said, pouting.

"Because you are too rigid." Miko crossed her arms. "Have you had your first kiss?"

"Oi, that's too far," Yoshi chided her. "Stop meddling into somebody else's life."

"I'm only helping her loosen up." Miko waved a hand in the air. "It's my habit to step in and point at the problem."

"I've had my first kiss," Hana lied while shrugging nonchalantly.

"Is it the father-daughter kind, or does it involve a romantic feeling?" Miko chuckled at Hana's uncomfortable expression.

"Remind me not to date you." Yoshi pointed a finger before returning inside the kitchen. "Miko, you're too wild."

Hana said, "I don't have a boyfriend—"

"In this day and age, who waits for a boyfriend?" Miko said, sauntering towards the counter.

"Who doesn't, unless you're talking about a one-night stand?" Hana pushed the bucket aside and leaned the mop against a wall.

"You know about one-night stands? I thought you were too prudish," Miko said without glancing at Hana's deadpan countenance.

"I am not a prude. I have books that describe characters making love." She wondered why she was going on with the conversation.

"It's a shame we're the same age." Miko finally looked at her. "You resemble an old hag, so just live your life."

"I plan to." Hana collected her bag. "I'm leaving."

After she had punched her attendance card, Hana breezed out of the store feeling sour. Miko's annoying face floated before her eyes. She wished she'd had better comebacks, but nothing could shut that girl up. Hana unchained her bike for the ride home, allowing fresh air to cleanse her mind and soul. After a minute or so, she could smile again and paused at a florist store to admire beautiful blooms ranged in the window. The strong fragrance enveloped her senses before she cycled away, listening to her earphones.

Soon she came across a group of girls along the opposite side of the street. At first she ignored them, but common courtesy tugged at her heartstring as she recalled her own past. She made a U-turn and rode back to confront them. They were all wearing similar high school attire different than Hana's.

"Um, excuse me," she said in a halting voice. "What's going on?"

"Nothing." One of them broke from the group to explain. "We're just talking, so you may leave, please."

But the girl was in tears, with several bruises visible on her arm; books were strewn on the ground next to a garbage can. Her collar was crumpled as if someone had pulled at it roughly, and Hana saw herself in that victim. She grew angry to realise that many were still going through bullying. She turned to glare at the rest of them.

"Stop messing around," she said in a loud voice.

"Who are you?" a tall girl standing at the front line said in a street slang. "Get the fuck out, stranger."

"Do you know her?" someone else chimed in nearby.

"I don't have to be acquainted with someone who might require my help." Hana's tone dripped with disgust.

"I've never seen a Japanese so tanned," another joked, laughing pathetically.

"I've heard that Japanese people are very kind, but you must not be one of them." The words were literally spilling from Hana's mouth.

"You asked for it!"

Suddenly several of them charged Hana and the weeping girl. They were beaten up, but their cries alerted the neighbourhood so that a few adults came rushing to their aid. The group of bullies fled from sight, leaving the two of them to sit dazedly on the ground. Pain exploded from Hana's ribcage, and tears leaked onto her bruised cheeks. She gingerly tapped a finger on her lips, coming away with blood.

"Come to my house," a young housewife said to Hana. "I'll treat your wound."

Trembling, Hana shook her head. "I'll be l-leaving for home," she said, choking back tears as she retrieved her bicycle. "Thank you."

"Thank you for rescuing me," the other girl said, bowing low. "I'm sorry they hurt you as well."

"Young lady, you must report to your school …," said the housewife, but Hana was quickly out of earshot. She gave in to her runaway emotions, crying aloud while walking beside her bicycle. She came to a stop staring at Jin's entrance gate and the small yard behind it. Panic-stricken, she stood for several minutes while crying her heart out.

The front door opened to reveal Jin's mother dressed up for work. Sayomi gawked at Hana until she saw that the girl shedding fat tears was her son's friend. She rushed to Hana's side. "Hana! What's the matter?" Sayomi gasped at her dishevelled appearance. "Jin! Come outside now!"

"What?" he called from his window. Then: "Hana?"

The head disappeared as Sayomi walked Hana into the yard. The door slammed open, and Jin bounded to her, wearing a black singlet and knee-length cut-off jeans. He cradled Hana's face between warm hands and leant closer to look her over, anger swirling in his narrowed eyes.

"Who did this to you?" he said quietly.

"I'll call your mother now." Sayomi was already re-entering the house.

"Please, no," Hana said, clutching the woman's sleeve. "I don't want them to worry over me."

"The how did this happen to you?" Sayomi asked, concerned. "Are you being bullied, Hana?"

"I tried to rescue someone being bullied, but they hurt me too," she said and wailed again.

"You could have walked away!" Jin spoke in a stern tone. "Are they boys?"

"Girls!" she hiccupped a few times.

"Ma, you can go to work," Jin said above her head. "I'll bring her home after taking care of the bruises."

"Okay," she replied with a nod. "Hana, you shouldn't have confronted them."

"But it could be me someday," she replied in a wavering voice. "I wanted to stand up for someone."

"It's all right," Jin cajoled her while drawing her in for an embrace. "I'm proud of you."

"Take care," Sayomi rubbed a motherly hand over Hana's arm. "If you need anything, Jin is here."

Hana clung to Jin as the two of them went inside the house. They went to the back with its full view of the flower garden. Sayomi had been an avid gardener before moving on to double shifts, resulting in Jin having to take care of her plantings. With clumsy hands and a book as his guide, he managed to tend them, even finding it therapeutic. Now he sat her down on the tatami mat to gaze out at the backdrop while he went for first aid supplies. A sense of nostalgia hit her when memories of bygone summer holidays spent in the Takami household: memories of cracking open a juicy watermelon and of dipping bare legs into a tub of icy water, a small fan cooling their backs, wind chimes tinkling gently as they ate.

When did we grow up so fast? she wondered.

"You okay?" Jin was back with a medical box. "You became so silent."

"I'm just reliving the past," she murmured.

"Look here."

Hana twisted to face him, and he pulled out an antibacterial ointment. He put it on a bit of cotton wool before gingerly dabbing it on her swelling upper lip. She gasped, and he paused for a second before going on to clean up her wound. They sat cross-legged, hearing the cries of cats nearby and the more distant bark of a lone dog. She kept her gaze on Jin's features as he concentrated on her split lip. She was still battling her devious thoughts; the forbidden images grew more vivid each day, and it felt more natural to conjure them.

To her, Jin was a person she could always rely on to make her feel comfortable when she was around him. Although she had gone through a series of tiny crushes, nothing had lasted; boys had drifted off to be with others; only her friend had remained by her side throughout their life. But how long would they be able to enjoy each other's company before one of them stumbled on someone else?

With no warning, Hana felt her body drifting forward, acting of its own accord. Jin reacted by grasping onto her body, apparently thinking she was falling, but then her fingers cupped his jawline, and she tilted her head and locked lips with him. Her other hand was on the floor, holding her up, and with her eyes squeezed shut she had no inkling of the shock etched on his face. She fluttered her eyes open to connect her gaze with his just as the reality of what had transpired finally slammed into her awareness. They gasped at the same time, and she reeled backwards to slap a hand over her gawking mouth. Without a word, she stumbled onto her feet and raced out of the house, her legs almost collapsing as she got on the bike to cycle off.

What have I done? she screamed inwardly.

She couldn't erase the image of Jin's expression as he sat rigid, staring at her in horror. Even when she ran away, he never bothered to follow or continue with the kiss, which was a proper explanation of how he felt about her. She pushed herself to the limit, skidding at one point and falling down, scraping her elbow. Even that did not help her cope with her bold action.

Evening was approaching when she was greeted at the front door by her mother, whose smile quickly vanished at the grisly sight of her daughter. "Hana!" she screamed. "Who did this to you?"

"What happened?" said another voice in the kitchen. "Is my daughter home yet?"

"She is hurt!" Neena cried while gathering a dazed Hana into her arms. "Tell me, who did this to you?"

"It was a scuffle," she mumbled against the woman's tight grip. "Mom, you're hurting me more."

In an instant, Neena released her death grip to wipe tears from her eyes while Abe Akiyama came to stand beside her. He assessed her face grimly; he had a stout, slightly chubby figure and a thinning hairline, but he enjoyed a good laugh and was a good listener. Abe wore glasses perched on the bump of his nose, which had suffered a soccer injury during his high school years.

"Hana, were you in a fight?" he inquired in a gentle voice. "We can report to the school."

"I came across someone getting bullied, so I intervened. Only this bunch of high school girls beat me up too." She shrugged. "I'm okay now. Jin took care of me."

"He was there with you?" Her mother pushed a lock of Hana's hair behind one ear.

"No, I happened to find myself there afterwards," she answered, although the questions began to bug her. "Mrs Takami was willing to call you, but I told her not to."

"Why?" Neena raised her voice. "Hana, I have the right to know that you're injured."

"Darling," Abe said, calming his wife, "Hana is not feeling well. She must have been scared to phone you."

"I want to be in my room," Hana mumbled. "I'm sorry, Father, but I've ruined your welcome home dinner."

"Of course not," he chided softly. "Come, we'll bring you to your room where you shall rest."

"Thank you." Her voice shook under another onslaught of tears.

"You are a brave young girl," he said, beaming with pride. "Although it pains me to see you in pain like this."

"Here," Neena returned with a glass of water while Hana sat on the edge of the bed. "I'll bring dinner for you."

"I'm not hungry," she whispered.

"Eat for my sake." Abe sat down beside her. "I have a gift waiting for you."

"Thank you, Father," she said and cosied into his arms.

"The best for my favourite daughter," he said with a chuckle.

In the middle of the night, Hana lay awake under her blankets, staring blindly at the ceiling. The kiss she had shared with Jin was settled in her mind for now. She had calmed somewhat, but she could still feel his lips pressed against hers when she touched a finger to her mouth. It truly felt normal: she had given her first kiss to her best friend, and a small smile lit up her face. Then it quickly faded; he had sent no messages, nor had he called. Perhaps he was in shock.

I don't blame him, she said to herself.

Chapter 10

Stars scattered across the indigo midnight sky twinkled one by one, greeting the people beneath. Jin sat on the edge of the window, watching the road below. As street lamps blinked on, a few cars slowly filed through the lane; the headlight of a lone cyclist crawled along beside them. Even though the scenery possessed a calm ambience, yet Jin's heart was full of tumult aroused after what had transpired in the afternoon between Hana and him. He absently bounced a tennis ball on the floor while slouching on the wide ledge.

The house creaked eerily. As a toddler Jin would jolt awake to cry for his mother, stumbling clumsily to reach at the other end of the scary hallway, where familiar arms wound around his small frame. Sayomi would carry him back to his bedroom and lie together with him, singing a lullaby while Jin tucked his head close against her breasts. The distant memories returned one by one, bringing a faint smile to his lips.

Earlier, when a dishevelled Hana had appeared, he was startled by her appearance. Jin felt his heart lodge in the back of his throat while he ran to her side as she wailed beside his mother. He was overwhelmed by the urge to protect the heartbroken girl and had no clue of who had hurt her. When Hana explained, he was both relieved as well as enraged by the group of bullies. For the first time, Hana had taken the initiative to help someone else; for her trouble she took a beating in turn, yet he was proud of her, even while sad about the bruises on her pale features.

The ball rolled away from his grasp, and he watched in silence before turning in for the night. Jin sprawled face down, his head sideways atop both folded arms. He shoved away images of the kisses and fiddled with his phone to switch on the radio in hopes of falling asleep. Hours later, Jin was still staring at the four wall when his eyes finally drifted shut. Soon he was dreaming incoherently.

"Look this way," he said in a gentle tone.

Hana turned sideways to face his concerned expression, and his eyes traced over her marred features. Anger overwhelmed him once again with the wish he had been there to teach those girls a few lessons. He began to minister to Hana's wound carefully, making sure he did not add too much pressure, only distantly aware of her emotional gaze trained on him. Now and then, he leaned closer to clean up dried blood after dabbing more antiseptic onto new cotton wool. All of a sudden, she moved forward, startling him as her soft fingers cupped his jawline. His mind went blank just as her honey coloured eyes drew closer and their mouths fused together.

Birds chirped merrily over the high-pitched laughter of children, and someone rang a bike bell, but within the room the two of them remained still as a statue. Jin's wide eyes were fixed on Hana's forehead when her eyes flickered open to stare into his own, She pulled back hastily, and his shock slowly settled. He never budged from the spot. Just as she was about to leave, Jin did the unthinkable: he shifted forwards and resumed the kiss, tilting his head for better access, one hand resting on her cheek and the other holding her shapely waist.

"Jin—," she squeaked against his mouth.

"Suhana …."

Jin woke up in a cold sweat. He sat up and scrubbed his face with both hands, calming himself from the weird dream. The sweet lilt of somebody singing from below finally calmed his nerves. It must be his mother ensconced in the kitchen; a wonderful fragrance enveloped the house.

Jin decided to take a shower in hopes of catching his mother before she headed out for work. With a towel around his waist, he went to the upper landing where he leaned out to check whether the voice was still audible. He rushed back to his bedroom to get ready and soon ran down the stairs, still adjusting his wax-tinted strands. He surprised his mother just as she was opening the front door.

"Jin! You're up early." She smiled. "Good morning, dear."

"Morning," he greeted while embracing her. "Off to work?"

"As usual," she replied with a hint of a sigh. "But I decided to make lunch for you to take to school."

"I miss your cooking," he said with a straight face.

"I'm sorry for not spending more time with you. If only …."

"If only?" He pushed her to finish the sentence. "You're exhausting yourself working double shifts."

"Not many of us have the luxury to choose." She place a hand on his cheek. "But I promise that sooner or later, we'll get back to normal."

"I'll help you—" But Sayomi shook her head, cutting off the rest of his sentence.

"Concentrate on your studies, Jin, I'm doing this for you." Her tone brooked no argument. "As a parent, my duty is help you grow up after attending a successful university."

"But I can work too, just like every other teenager," he insisted. "Hana is working too."

"As long as it does not affect your grades," the woman stepped back. "I don't need your help being the breadwinner."

"Your health is getting worse." Jin spoke calmly and knew he'd hit the target when her eyes flashed. He felt a tightening behind his chest.

"Nonsense," she said, laughing it off. "I have to leave. Have a good day, son."

The door closed, and he went back to the kitchen to retrieve the warm lunch box neatly tied in a kerchief. He carefully tucked the box inside his bag. Then he paused to drop a short text to Hana saying he wouldn't be able to pick her up. The awkwardness would be unbearable; in fact, Hana might need some space too. She might be embarrassed by her action.

Jin's eyes bored a hole in the back of Hana's head as everyone jotted notes. Instead he lounged at his desk with his chin propped on a fist. His face was blank as he ignored their mentor's lecture about the history of Japan and the announcement that a mock test might come up this week. When the bell rang to indicate lunch, Jin dragged his chair back noisily with everyone else.

Lunch box in hand, he was manoeuvring between the desks when Hana called to him from her seat. He turned to see her blink at him before her eyes shifted to his lunch. A smile lit her sharp features, and she looked up at him. The two had not spoken earlier, since he was already in his seat when Hana walked in by herself, although she had waved at him from the front of the class and he reciprocated.

"Where are you going, Jin?" she inquired.

"I'm gonna have lunch by the garden," he said, shrugging one shoulder. "See you."

He left quickly in case Hana had it in mind to follow. He realised that he was the one who needed some distance at the moment, until he knew he could face her without dredging up the images from yesterday. In fact, he now had to deal with the vivid dream as well. He cautiously glanced over his shoulder and heaved a sigh of relief that she was not following him.

He entered the garden and saw a vacant place to relax underneath a tall tree. He sat down on the green grass to undo the kerchief before digging into the simple fried rice, enjoying the familiar cooking. Moments later he had gobbled it up while drinking a juice box, surveying the ground and tuning out the noises from the rest of the students.

Jin walked slowly back to the classroom as students were gathering. He hesitated at Hana's empty chair. He shrugged, not giving it much thought, and went on to plop into his seat with a weary sigh, turning several heads around him. Even as the bell rang, her desk was not occupied. Beginning to worry about her, he leaned forward to link fingers while conjuring ideas as to where she could have ventured off to. Abruptly Ino was standing in front of him looking concerned. Jin glanced up in alarm.

Ino leaned down to whisper, "Jin, you might need to fetch Hana. She has been crying on the rooftop."

"'Kay, thank you." Jin rose and left in a hurry. *I shouldn't have avoided her.*

At the top of the stairs he pushed open the heavy door and stepped onto the broad roof searching for his friend. He caught sight of Hana sitting against the fence, arms around her knees, crying. He heard pitiful sounds from the girl as she wailed. He silently walked over, both hands in his front pockets. He frowned slightly as he came to a stop beside the curled figure, who was still unaware of his presence.

He squatted beside her. "What's the matter?" he finally said out loud.

"You hate me," she whimpered. "It's my fault!" She finally peered at him, and he knew his irritation was visible because of the sudden kiss shared between them.

He turned his head to view her tear-streaked face. "Hana, don't pull that stunt on me again."

"You hate it?" Her voice trembled from suppressed emotions. "You don't see me as a girl, right?"

"I hate it," he replied bluntly. "Hana, I only see you as my friend—"

"Why can't you look at me with a different perspective for once?" Her voice had risen.

"I don't think that will ever happen." He leaned his head back. "Why are you doing this?"

"Everyone thinks I'm ugly to be with them," she shouted, looking away from him. "If I was someone else, my life wouldn't be such crap!"

"You're arguing about nothing, Hana," he said briskly. "This has nothing to do with how you look."

"I don't even take after my mother's extroverted lifestyle." She glared daggers at him. "Even you abhor my approach."

"Hana! Are you even listening to me?" Jin grabbed her shoulders roughly. "You are my best friend. For me it's the same as kissing a guy friend!"

"Shut up!" Hana yelled at his face and suddenly shoved at his chest, toppling him over. "You are such an idiot!"

Jin remained where he was for several moments, coming to terms with her blow-up, before righting himself. Amidst the turbulent feelings he slowly realised that Hana in some way had confessed to him. As if on cue he sensed her arms encircling his waist from behind, but he was too angry with her to bother turning to look. Her soft body weighed against his back, and her head rested on his shoulder blades. He listened to her sniffles while dainty fingers crumpled the front of his shirt.

"I'm sorry, Jin," she apologised in a quiet voice.

"Are you in love with me?" he inquired, still not looking at her.

"No."

"Then what was your motive?" His voice was strained.

"I wanted to know what kissing a boy feels like," she answered truthfully. "The only boy that I trust is you, Jin."

"You chose me?" he finally turned in her arms.

"I gave you my first kiss." She moved away to peer up at his stunned face.

"Oh."

"Jin, there's more, but I won't tell you." Her eyes gleamed in determination.

"What is it?" He crossed his arms. "You know I hate getting left in the dark."

"You won't like it," she cautioned him.

"Try me."

She released him and stood up, folded hands at her heart. Her next words tilted his world upside down. "I want to spend the night with you."

Chapter 11

"What did you just ask of me?" Jin shot to his feet, towering over Hana, who timidly stepped back. He grabbed her by the arms, his fingers digging deep, eliciting a gasp. He leaned closer so she could see the storm of emotions on his face: disgust, befuddlement, and plain annoyance.

The words had actually spilt from her mouth without warning. In fact, she'd been trying to figure out the right time to broach the subject. But she had her answer clear as day.

"Do you hear yourself, Hana?" Jin hissed.

"I know what I'm asking of you," she replied in a high-pitched voice.

"Why are you doing to this to us?" he yelled, startling her.

"I'm not doing anything, just asking Jin a simple bid to help me—"

"Help you with that?" He chuckled dryly. "You must be out of your mind."

"Listen to me—"

"I won't!" He shoved her aside. "I'm returning to the classroom."

"But—" Hana's sentence was once again cut off by his single glare. "It's only one time; after that we can pretend nothing occurred."

"Hana, you think it's so easy?" He stalked back to point a rigid finger. "You don't respect the boundary of our friendship?"

"I do!" Hana was grasping at straws because doubt had begun to creep into her mind.

"So?" he whispered. "You should be ashamed of yourself for even bringing this up with me."

"Is it so wrong that I trust Jin because you are the only boy who won't hurt me?" Hana's lips trembled while fresh tears trickled onto her cheeks.

"We will hurt *each other*, Hana, trust me on this." Jin shook his head slowly. "Also, the one thing you asked of me is not something you handle casually between friends."

She gazed up at him. "So where does the term *friend with benefits* comes from?"

"I don't want to be with Hana in that way," he stated. "You have to wait for the right guy, someone who will respect you—"

"You are the one!" Hana wiped at her angry tears. "Nobody will like me enough to be my special someone."

"This is too much for me to take in," Jin whispered in a strained tone. "I'll just head back to the classroom by myself."

Hana collapsed on the warm surface as the door slammed close. Her mouth was open wide, yet not a sound escaped. Instead, tears dripped onto her skirt. She was shocked by her own actions, but it was too late. Jin had walked off without a backward glance, and she knew that her insolent behaviour had caused him to walk away. Hana wept behind her hands, bending under the weight of regret. Her choices in life left her feeling childish compared to her peers.

Out of nowhere, rough hands pulled her upright to drag her body against a rock-hard masculine frame. Hana was caught off guard until she caught a glimpse of the familiar earrings twinkling at her. Jin's fragrance enveloped her senses, and she squeezed her eyes shut to wrap both arms around his shoulders. He was on his knees, rocking her as if she was a child In fact, rhetorically speaking, she had a lot of growing up to do before she could imagine being in a relationship.

"I'm sorry," Jin whispered in a cajoling tone. "But, Hana—"

She cut him off. "I know. I'm ashamed of my own blatant attitude. When Jin walked away, it was eye-opening for me, and I understand that this can never happen between us."

"I know you're growing up, Hana," Jin said against her neck. "But you are looking at the wrong person, and I don't blame you. We've been friends for so long that I'm the only person who's always by your side. So naturally you think of me first."

"I won't act so stupid again," Hana said and sniffled aloud. "I don't wish to break our friendship, not with my behaviour."

"Let's get back to the classroom." He drew away to peer at her tear-swollen eyes.

"You go ahead of me," She wiped her face with her sleeves. "My face is a wreck, and everyone will wonder what's up."

"Then the two of us can relax here." Jin scooted on his butt to lean against the fence. "In the meantime, Hana will ponder the mistake of even thinking that the both of us—"

"Stop!" Hana shouted feeling heat climbing up her neck. "Thank you for setting me straight, Jin."

"What did you say?" He opened an eye to glare at her. "Girls pant after me."

"Really?" Hana gingerly waddled on her knees to sit sideways. "Jin, you're not a virgin, right?"

"No," he said, clearing his throat nervously. "But, I want Hana to wait a little longer because it will be a different experience with somebody you love."

"What about yourself, Jin?" She tilted her head.

"I'm waiting," he said in a faraway voice.

At that moment, Hana straightened up. She saw a flurry of emotions on his face. He was in love. Her best friend was in love with somebody else. She turned to lean back, drawing her knees against her chest, trying to cope with her own mixed emotions. She was unsure of how she should be reacting to his newfound romance. When she peered at him again, she caught him snoring softly. She sat for a while just watching his serene expression.

Hana gazed out the window without noticing the bright sky from within the sanctuary of the school library. Her head rested on her folded arms atop the wide table. Books were stacked haphazardly in front of her, but they were set for display. She had to study for an upcoming mock test, but her mind had been restless all week after the traumatic incident. Thankfully, the two of them had returned to their usual comfort zone as best friends, never mentioning the stolen kiss or her request for a one-night stand.

A bird flew near to nestle on the opposite of the closed window, its wings fluttering once in a while. Hana was mesmerised by the creature's beauty; the colours of its feathers made it more beautiful than herself.

Suddenly, the bird flew off into the bright sky. When the table shifted a little she was aware she had company. She looked up to see a girl apologising softly with a guilty expression. Hana shook her head and greeted her with a smile. For now, Hana focused on the book laid open on the table, yet the words bounced against an invisible brick wall in her brain, and she sighed aloud. Tomorrow she had work; the latest schedule allowed her to work on weekdays as well, to her relief, because staying up at home alone often brought on irrational anxiety.

She flipped the textbook closed to arrange the rest of her notes when someone cleared her throat daintily, catching Hana's attention. The girl across from her waved a hand shyly, and Hana nodded once, wracking her brain to see if the two of them had met before. She flush of excitement that someone might wish to make friends with her. She leaned her arms on the desk to move in closer, and her companion did the same.

"You are Hana Akiyama, correct?" the girl asked in a soft voice.

"Yes." Hana was taken aback by the her feminine allure. "How do you know me?"

"I know you from afar." She pushed a lock of hair behind a pink-tinted ear. "My name is Shouko Mitsunari. Pleased to meet you."

"Hello, Shouko," Hana said, beaming. "I'm amazed that someone took notice of me."

"It is easy for anyone to recall you," Shouko said but quickly shook her head. "I never meant to sound so rude."

"I don't mind," she said with a wave. "Sometimes, it's great to feel a little different from the rest."

"That's true!" Shouko's loud voice prompted a librarian to hush the two girls. "Sorry, again. I forgot that we are in the library."

"Do you want to walk out?" Hana shrugged. "Then we can speak in our normal tone."

"Sure, that's a good idea." Shouko quickly gathered her belongings while Hana replaced the books on a nearby trolley.

They exited onto the school ground while chattering amicably about their classes, teachers, and prospects as third-year students next year. Hana was amazed that she had made another friend without even bothering to try; perhaps her luck was running well. A bloom of happiness unfurled in her heart.

"May I ask you something, Hana?" Shouko spoke in a nervous voice.

"What is it?" Hana chewed on a strawberry donut, wiping at the excess sugary powder on her chin.

"Are you and Jin dating?"

Hana choked on her bite of dessert, and Shouko rapped helpfully on her back. Once she had regained her oxygen, Hana dabbed at her mouth, wondering at this girl's motive to start the conversation at the library. Shouko stepped back with a worried look when a fleeting memory of Jin's forlorn expression startled Hana.

"Are you that girl who Jin likes?" Hana's words tumbled out before she could stop them.

"What?" A faint blush painted Shouko's cheek. "Jin ... likes me?"

"He never told me her name," Hana answered, her voice a little hollow. "How do you know him?"

"I watch him play softball. We've spoken a couple of times, but my shyness always intervenes," Shouko murmured.

"Oh." Hana blinked once.

"Is it all right if Hana tells him my name?" Shouko took her free hand. "I like him very much, but if you are dating—"

"We aren't dating." Hana shrugged. "The two of us are best friends."

Although I kissed him, Hana's inner voice whispered.

"Thank you, Hana," Shouko said, bowing low.

"You're welcome." Hana's attempted smile felt more like a cringe. "You are lucky to have his affection."

"Oh, thank you, but we are not certain—"

"I know Jin very well," Hana spoke above her. "He likes you, but I'll inform him that his affection is reciprocated."

"If you don't mind, I want to be that person confessing to him." Shouko glanced at her feet.

"Sure," Hana said, nodding. "Let's eat our donut."

The two of them walked side by side, and Hana forced herself to match the other girl's enthusiasm as she points at various objects in the windows of different shops. It was a test of her resolution to take the path she and Jin had talked about. Hana was keen to know if her friendship with Jin remained the same, because somewhere deep in her heart she was certain of a change. She had not been the same after she and Jin had raced out of that ramen stall.

During the weekend, Hana stared blindly at the front of the store. She had yet to pass the news to Jin, and he was dropping by later to pick her up. Someone slammed a hand on the smooth surface, startling Hana. She let out a squeak when she jerked her wide eyes at Miko who pursed her mouth in wonderment.

"What is it?" Hana gasped at her.

"You seem out of it today." Miko leaned her hip against the counter. "What's the matter?"

"Nothing," Hana said, shaking her head.

"Keeping it locked up in your heart is poisonous for the mind," the other girl observed casually.

A customer breezed in, interrupting their little chat. Hana didn't acknowledge Miko's hovering presence. She pasted on a smile to greet the person, who smiled back while choosing a variety of baked goodies. Mrs Noshita waved farewell to them, as her morning shift had ended while Hana began an hour ago. After liasing with the patron, Hana counted the money within the cashier's box. At the backdrop she overheard Miko laughing at something while Yoshi's voice drifted out once in a while.

Out of nowhere, she wanted to confirm Miko's stupidity. On cue the girl walked in with a soft smile when Hana stepped in front of her.

"I want to have a word with you," Hana said gingerly. "I think you are a person who's blunt enough to help me figure something out."

"Did you just compliment me or insult me?" Miko drawled.

"Please, it's something important—"

"Yo." Someone spoke coming through the tinkling door.

Hana whipped her head around at the sound and saw Jin strolling in with a handheld lunch box. At once she recalled searching for it with her mother this morning when she had to leave for work. As usual she smiled at Jin, although inwardly, she was nitpicking at her behaviour towards him. As time passed, she had grown aware of a mixture of unwelcoming feelings for him.

"I met your mother on the way, and she told me to bring this lunch pack for you." He set the object on the counter.

"Have we been introduced?" Miko butted in.

"Miko, this is my friend, Jin."

"Please take good care of her," Jin said with a bow. "Nice to meet you, Miko."

"She is in good hands." Miko smiled warmly. "Are you here to pick up Hana? She just began her shift."

"I'll drop by late." Jin returned his gaze to Hana. "I have an interview soon."

"Really? All the best, Jin!"

"Thanks, I'm nervous as hell." He wiped sweaty palms on the seat of his pants.

"You'll be just fine. Win them over with your charm." Hana giggled. "They'll hire you in no time."

"I'll be going now." He glanced around at the store. "So, uh … you said there's something you want to tell me?"

"After work." She watched his expression crumple adorably. "It's a mystery, so go work on your interview answers."

"Is it important?" he pressed.

"I don't know; could be important for you." She ignored his probing look. "Jin, I'm working."

"Fine, I'll see you later." He shrugged. "Be a good girl; just don't spontaneously kiss your customers."

"Jin!" Hana pivoted, showing her back as Jin chortled on his retreat to the entrance. Hana put one hand to her flustered face.

"You seem so close." Miko had been watching their banter from one side. "How long have you known one another?"

"Since our childhood," Hana said in a quiet tone. "I look up to him."

"Yoshi!" Miko called out towards the kitchen. "Can you come out for minute?"

"What's the matter?" He poked his head out.

"Do you think you can man the counter while Hana and I take a break?" she said, walking into the back room.

"Two at once?" Yoshi looked at Hana while she gulped nervously. "We don't have enough hands at the kitchen."

"Sure you can." Miko had a pack of cigarette in one hand.

"I'm sorry, Yoshi." Hana felt a tad unsure. "Maybe we can talk here, Miko."

Yoshi adjusted the white cloth tied on his head. "If it's personal, then go ahead, but don't be late."

"Thank you!" Miko bowed, earning a laugh from him.

Once outside, Miko lit a cigarette. "What do you wish to talk about?" she asked after taking a long drag.

"I don't have gal pals," Hana began, picking her words carefully. "Jin is the only person close to me. I think my nervousness and lack of confidence get in the way of me growing up."

"Seeing how you are living in Japan, I cannot blame your self-esteem," Miko pointed out.

"Yeah." Hana squatted. They were at the corner of the store tucked in an alleyway. "I've been bullied before; it often happens now, but Jin helps me recover. In fact, his presence is my strength."

"And?" Miko gazed at her face intently. "That face you're making …."

"What face?" Hana blinked, returning to the moment.

"You look really pretty." Miko grinned a little. "Usually, you have a solemn expression, rather unemotional, but your features softened just now."

"Really?" She gingerly touched her face. "I didn't know I have a gloomy face."

"You do, rather unattractive." Miko flung her cigarette butt on the ground. "But tell me, what's going on in between Jin and yourself?"

"I don't where to begin." Hana felt a twinge of unease. "I want to think that I'm overreacting."

"I'll be the judge. Just begin wherever you feel is right." Miko hunched down beside her.

"I kissed him," Hana said without a hint of emotion. "Recently I became fixated on letting go of my virginity, being held by a guy. It all began when I overheard my classmates gossiping inside the school bathroom, and I eavesdropped on their conversation."

"Isn't it normal for teenagers to feel curious?" Miko looked at her. "Why are you beating yourself up?"

"Because Jin was against the kiss." She gazed at her companion with visible pain in her eyes. "I'm against it too."

"You … fell in love with him?" Miko sounded astonished. "Just by one kiss?"

"Is this love?" Hana asked. "I've never been in love."

"Judging by your face, you could be." Miko paused. "You seem more carefree when he is around."

"Because he oozes a comforting aura," Hana countered. "Jin has a laid-back nature, instantly making you feel calm."

"How did you feel after the kiss?" Miko peered closer. "Disgusted? Bland? Happy?"

"It felt right to me," Hana spoke with honesty ringing in her voice.

"You're in love," Miko declared. "What are you gonna do about it?"

"So it is certain I'm in love?" Hana's voice wavered from fear.

"You have to give yourself some time to confirm it. A simple case of lust can muddle your brains, confusing it with love," she said matter-of-factly.

"Okay." Hana nodded slowly. "Thank you, Miko."

"Have you confessed to him about your feelings?" Miko asked.

"I don't plan to, because he fell for someone else, and she reciprocates his feelings." Hana shrugged casually. "Honestly, I'm happy for him."

"At least confess to him," Miko persisted. "Allow him to hear your voice."

"I can't, Miko. When I asked to have one night with him—"

"What?" Miko squealed.

"Jin walked off, and he was disgusted."

Miko laughed, grating on Hana's nerves, but the other girl had the right to mock at her fearful behaviour. It took some time for Miko to compose herself, wiping away tears and patting Hana on the shoulder like a proud parent. This earned a pout from Hana, but she chuckled despite herself. They squatted together in silence; somehow they had established a bond without favour from each party—a true friendship, unlike the rest she had come across.

"I support you," Miko said all of a sudden. "Fight for him."

"Miko, I want him to stay by my side. Eventually this feeling will fade away." Hana got to her feet. "I don't want to lose Jin because he is irreplaceable to me."

"If I were you—"

"But you aren't," Hana interrupted and then waited for Miko to stand up. "We are two different characters."

"All the best then." Miko sighed aloud. "I hope what you feel is not love."

"Me too, Miko," Hana agreed fervently. "I want to look back later and chide myself along the lines of 'You're crazy, Hana.'"

"I feel depressed right now," Miko complained. "But this only motivates me to chase my crush."

"Really?" Hana beamed as they walked together. "Who is it?"

"Yoshi," Miko said calmly, but her voice softened a little. "That man has developed an aversion to relationship after his last break-up."

"You two would make a good couple," Hana said after envisioning the duo. "Yoshi keeps you grounded."

"Hah!" Miko snorted as the two of them enter the store. "I think so too."

Chapter 12

*J*in rubbed his hands for warmth while dressing in a sweater waiting for Hana's shift to end. He was happy that he now had a job as well; he was more than willing to begin any time of the week so as to help lessen the burden for his mother. The woman had been plagued with exhaustion; it was written on her aged face. She bravely put on a smile for him, although Jin was not fooled. His urgent drive to land a part-time job was finally satisfied.

He was eager to share this happy news with his best friend, imagining Hana's ecstatic expression before pulling him in for a tight hug. He sat on the metal rail, with both feet anchored to balance his frame, and peeked inside the store. Hana and a few of her colleagues were cleaning the place to close for the night. She seemed more carefree than usual, even laughing aloud at something her companions said, and that made Jin feel even better. Hana was finally opening herself up instead of hiding behind an imaginary wall. Finally, the two of them were walking along the same path to adulthood, ready to face the world side by side as change surrounded them.

Jin was finger-combing his messy hair just as noises poured from the bakery's open door, and he saw Hana standing beside another girl, the same one who had complained before. At this moment, the two of them painted an entirely different picture, standing close with their heads literally touching, each wearing a serious expression.

"Time for us to go home," a tall male announced after locking up the door. "Hana, your boyfriend is here."

"He—"

"She isn't—"

"Yoshi, he is my friend. Meet Jin."

The two of them talked over each other, rushing to correct Yoshi's mistake. He slowly flushed, realising his error, and apologised to them. After waving farewell, everyone separated while Jin and Hana slowly walked away, letting themselves calm down. Jin cleared his throat, prompting a sideways look from her. He chuckled at her wary face; the poor girl was worried sick that he'd been offended.

"I have good news to tell you," he began. "I got the job."

"Jin!" She squealed like a small child. "I'm so happy for you!"

"You are the first person I've told," Jin said with a chuckle. "I want to surprise my mother."

"She'll be so proud of you, Jin." She gazed up at his face. "I am too."

"Thank you, Hana. I'm the only male in the house, so I have to take on the responsibility."

Once again, silence fell between them—piquing Jin's awareness of her mood shift. The two of them easily picked up on one another's emotions, which lent a deep meaning to their friendship. He recalled that she had invited him because she had something to say to him. He playfully bumped shoulders with her, watching her startled eyes as she bestowed a smile on him.

"Hey, is there something bothering you?" he asked softly. "Also, you have something to tell me, right?"

"I ...." Her voice trailed off, and he saw her face alter in an instant as if she had changed her decision. Then she swivelled to walk backwards with an impish grin. "I forgot what it is."

"Oi, don't lie to me," he said, sighing aloud. "Hana, you know it bothers me when I am clueless."

"I'm telling the truth." She was as stubborn as ever. "I'll tell you when I remember."

"I can tell that you are lying," he accused while grabbing for her arm, but she evaded him.

"Why are you so desperate to know?" she bantered. "What if I don't wish to tell you?"

"Minx," he muttered under his breath before shifting his weight to chase her. "You're a high school student right now, so act like one!"

"Are you saying that I'm childish?" she retorted, only to emit a surprised gasp when he was able to capture her.

"You've been childish since forever." He spoke the truth, albeit in a caring tone, as they resumed their gait side by side. "It will be a hoot to see Hana mature someday."

He paused when she halted in mid-step. He glanced over a shoulder to stare into her eyes, where he saw a mixture of unknown emotions. A strong breeze with a hint of rain blew against them. Hana's lustrous long hair fluttered around her face; only then did he realise she had let her hair down during their walk. Naturally, he rarely noticed such details about her. He felt guilty for making fun of her and was about to make an apology when she suddenly stepped towards him, closing the short distance.

He inhaled sharply just as her cold hand rested on his chest. His heartbeat was bounding because of her action, and his eyes widened in shock. Hana gazed at him intently, and he saw tears leaking onto her cheeks and her lips trembling with strong emotion. He took a measured step back when she grabbed a fistful of his shirt, pressing into his chest. He was glaring at her, but even then she never budged from the spot.

"Don't," he cautioned her in a quiet voice.

"Jin, you taught me to stand on my own feet," she began in a wavery voice. "I always look up to you, Jin, because you are my support pillar, somebody who lifts me up when I'm about to break apart. Your presence calms me down like nobody else can; you cheer me up with your crazy jokes and annoying prank. You become a human brick wall against anyone who dares to hurt me because of what an easy target I am to negativity."

"Why are you doing this to us, Hana?" Jin said, raising his voice. "I don't want to break our friendship!"

"Listen to me!" she screamed before going on in a pleading tone. She was giving way to a flood of emotions. "People only talk to me when they have a favour to ask. Nobody sees me as a person with feelings, but that is my fault because I *allow* them to use me. All this time you have been telling me to be more confident and learn to be the one who takes that step forward instead of idly waiting for something to happen.

"And so I did, but it was the wrong way, I thought being mature meant I had to chalk up experiences so people would see me changing, especially myself. Instead, it backfired on me. Seeing you leave me behind woke me up.

"Jin, I want to be confident. I want to grow up in front of your eyes, to be that girl you can rely on instead of the opposite. Before anyone else confesses, I want to be that first person."

"No—" he whispered in terror, but she cut him off again while shaking the front of his shirt, her cries resonating in his ears.

"I love you, Jin," she screamed tearfully. "I love you very much!"

"Hana!" he shouted back, begging her, yet the calamity had occurred, and neither of them could turn back time. "You're hurting both of us!"

"I want to prove to Jin that I can change too!" she said, weeping brokenly as she finally let go of his shirt beneath his wide jacket.

"Why now?" he yelled in rage. "Is it because of that stupid kiss?"

"No." Her voice shook from violent emotions. "I suddenly developed feelings for you …."

"This cannot be happening." He snorted a laugh, glancing around haplessly. "I cannot reciprocate your feelings because I fell in love with someone else."

"I don't want to lose you," she hiccupped while reining in her sobs. "Jin, you are precious to me—"

"Hana, you have lost the right to call me your friend." Jin felt his lower lip tremble as he slowly backed away.

"Jin ...." Her eyes cutting him to pieces inside. "Trust me, I will prove my worth to you."

Without looking back, he raced off, arms pumping, and left her standing alone. He finally came to a stop when his lungs burned from the exertion and his legs wobbled. Hands on knees, he leaned over, exhaling in short puffs, gulping loudly. He hated Hana for creating a riff between them, for her blind stupidity and confusing her feelings of "love" for a fleeting lust. He hunched low on his elbows to hang both hands between his spread legs. Then he stood to take a calming breath, only to inhale the stench of diesel from vehicles polluting the area.

"Hana, you idiot," he lamented in a strained voice. "Why ...?"

Seconds turned to minutes, and soon he set out for home in a daze. He felt as if he had just undergone a traumatic event. He wondered what had changed between them for Hana to behave in such a drastic manner. The gate squeaked as he dragged himself in. He opened the entrance doorway and stared into the empty home, listening to white noise. Everything was normal, yet everything had changed.

He had a strong inkling that Hana was somewhere crying her heart out, but he could do no better than force himself to return to her side and spout lies of comfort. He collapsed against the wall and slid downwards. Closing his eyes, he could easily picture Hana in tears, her voice crystal clear as if she was standing beside him—but anger contorted his features once again as he succumbed to disbelief that the bond they once shared was now frayed.

The next morning, Jin walked to school with a blank expression. His hair fluttered in the wind while his eyes were strained from lack of sleep. His hands were jammed in his front pockets. His phone was muted, but he had no messages with the blinking name *Hana*. He was glad she was sharp enough to pretend everything remained normal; if not, Jin might snap and utter words that would wound her heart beyond relief.

Waiting for the pedestrian light to turn green, he spotted a familiar figure strolling along the opposite side of the road—the same girl who owned his heart. A flare of excitement drowned his misery, and in his haste to cross the road to keep her in sight, he first made sure the street was clear of vehicles

"Morning!" he greeted her from behind. Her tall frame jumped in fright. "Sorry, I didn't mean to startle you."

"Huh?" she blinked in confusion before recognising him. "Oh, morning!"

He jogged to her side, and the two of them resumed their casual walk towards the school. They were quiet for several minutes while Jin searched for a topic, but then the girl timidly started off. Her adorable act squeezed his heart, and he had the urge to plant a kiss on her plump lips. Still, he kept a good distance out of respect, while they zigzagged amidst the rushing crowd as if re-enacting a dance step on autopilot.

She turned her head to face him. "Um, I don't know how to put the words together …," she stammered, pushing a lock of hair behind one pink-tinted ear. "But has Suhana mentioned anything to you?"

"Mentioned what?" Hana's name sent a jolt through his frame like a shock. "Is there something that requires my attention?"

"Nothing important; forget it." She brushed off his question by waving a hand and laughing.

"Not you, too." He sighed in frustration. "Can you at least tell me what it's about?"

"I told Suhana to relay my message to you," she said, peering at him through lowered lashes.

"What message?" He stopped, and someone walking closely behind bumped into him.

"Oh, so she hasn't …?" the girl said as if to herself.

"Are you two friends now?" he said, quirking an eyebrow at her.

"I don't know, but I came up to Suhana in the school library," she explained. "The message isn't too important."

"It is to me," he replied huskily. "Look, this isn't the proper location while I'm still in the dark about your name."

"Shouko Mitsunari," she supplied with a laugh. "You could easily ask someone."

"But I wish to hear it from you," Jin said, watching a blush creep up her neck. "Shouko, you have a nice name."

"Thank you, Jin." She hid her face behind a book, but he caught a smile, which brightened his morning. "As for the rest, I will tell you when the time is right."

"Okay, Shouko." He enjoyed the taste of bliss at speaking her name. "Do you always walk to school?"

"Sometimes," she replied.

Silence fell over the pair once again, yet a comfort also enveloped them. As if in tune, their bodies inched closer with each step until he felt her arm brush against his own. He licked his bottom lip, reverting to his childlike self, as if watching his favourite dessert come to the table and feeling the rush of innocent optimism. They reached school before the opening bell rang. In the hallway crowded with students they waited on each other to change into school slippers.

Then Jin heard a familiar voice calling his name from behind. Emotions surged in his heart at the sound her voice, but when he turned around, he wiped away any trace of expression to show a deadpan countenance. Hana smiled at him radiantly as she walked up but faltered at the sight of Shouko standing beside him. He figured she had kept the information to herself last night, but he brush past her to stay with Shouko, who looked down as she walked ahead of him. People began to take note of the new girl walking along.

"I'll fetch Shouko to your classroom," he announced.

"Okay." She nodded once but gingerly looked back. "Do you think she's all right?"

"Yeah," he replied in a terse voice.

Soon they paused at Shouko's classroom, realising they were actually closer than he imagined. He looked up to check the sign above before returning his gaze to Shouko, noting that a cluster of girls looked on. Perhaps they were Shouko's friends, because they looked interested as they talked amongst themselves.

Shouko drew his attention back to herself. "Thank you," she said with a soft smile. "I'll see you soon, Jin."

"Yeah," he said, nodding with a lazy smile while leaning his shoulder against the door frame. "I look forward to hearing what you wish to say, Shouko."

"You will soon," she said, biting her lower lip. "Bye."

Jin retraced his steps towards his own classroom. There he paused to spy upon Hana in her chair. She was wearing her reading glasses and absorbed in a book. But he saw her white-knuckled grip on the book, displaying her inner turmoil, but he continued on the way to his seat. At one point his hand reached out as usual to tussle the top of her head affectionately, but he quickly retrieved it. He didn't see her peer over her shoulder to give his back a forlorn look before turning again to pretend that she was busy with her comic instead of hurting inside.

No more, his inner voice whispered.

Chapter 13

"Suhana!" Neena squealed from the front of the kitchen sink. "The chapatti is burning!"

"Shit," Hana muttered at the same time. She reached to clumsily flip the bread only to burn the tips of her fingers.

"Oh my God, what were you doing?" Neena chided as she watched her daughter hissing in pain.

"It's this stupid chapatti!" Hana yelped in frustration.

"Come here." Neena set down her vegetable knife on the wet counter. "Suhana, come over here and let me see."

The girl marched towards her mother, adopting a peeved expression. The throbbing of her fingers was unbearable. After a thoroughly assuring herself that her daughter was safe from any severe burn, Neena walked off to fetch the first-aid box. She pointed with her chin towards the dining table, and the pair sat down there while Neena began to dab an ointment. Meanwhile Hana mewled. She was a wuss when it came to pain.

"This is my fourth time making sure you are not dozing off at the stove," Neena scolded. "What's the matter with you?"

"Nothing," Hana replied in a dull voice. "I'm too tired."

"You could have told me earlier." The woman sat back with a frown. "Is something bothering you, Hana?"

"Of course not," she said a little too harshly. "I'll be in my bedroom," and she stood up to leave.

"Suhana, wait, Suhana!" Neena stood, bristling at the girl's tone.

Hana was wearing a traditional Indian ankle-length kurti in a cream shade. Her unbound wavy long hair fell over her shoulders. She was in no mood to converse with anyone else, particularly her mother. Hana figured that Neena might catch up to her easily, since her emotion was easy to read from her vivid expression. The cooling room greeted the girl as she quietly shut the door to lean against the plank momentarily. Both eyes shut, she inhaled the aromas wafting into her bedroom from downstairs. She grabbed the soft toy perched on her study table and made a move towards the mattress, where she plopped down against the headboard.

She glanced at her cell phone; no missed calls or messages from Jin, since clearly he was avoiding her like a plague. She felt many emotions all at once, especially pain, misery, and anger. It might be easy for him, yet she suffered watching Jin from a distance or knowing he was closer but still too far for her to reach out to him. The challenge she had boldly set for herself was rapidly deteriorating day by day. Her existence had grown bleak, a sign that Jin was a light to her gloomy life. She swiped away a tear while blinking a couple of times; then she scooted downwards to roll to her side and stare at the wall.

"Suhana, lunch is ready," her mother announced in a muffled tone just as she clicked open the door. "Baby?"

The soothing voice almost caused Hana to break down like a child. Instead of replying, she pretended to snooze, listening to the soft footsteps coming closer. The mattress dipped under Neena's weight, and her hand gently stroked her forehead. Hana felt enveloped by Neena's motherly love as well as a faint scent of flour, green tea, and her unique fragrance. The two of them remained in the same position while Hana sniffled quietly.

Finally, Neena gathered her heartbroken teenager in her arms while propping herself against the bed frame. Hana allowed her mother to move her like a rag doll in any direction, and soon she was resting on her mother's thigh, watching the outside world beyond the single window frame. Amidst the quiet of the apartment, with lunch waiting in the kitchen, Hana had composed her runaway feelings.

"What is wrong with my girl?" Neena tried once again. "It's been a while since the two of us have sat down and talked like this."

"Nothing," Hana whispered. "I'm fine."

"I'm sorry that I am not a perfect mother to you," Neena said with an exhausted sigh. "All I think about is my work, but, Suhana, being a workaholic mother, I have learnt to pick up changes in people, especially you. If I can provide just the slightest comfort, please, give me the chance."

"Mom, what were you like during high school?" Hana inquired after pondering Neena's words for a moment.

"Me?" Neena tilted her head up as if to look into the past. "Hmm … I was a boring kid in school."

"I'm serious, Mom." She tsk-tsked but didn't budge from her spot.

"Of course, I am serious here too." Neena's voice rose in disbelief. "Did you concoct some sort of scenario about me being a diva in high school?"

"No." Hana released a long sigh. "Never mind—"

"My parents thought becoming a Permanent Resident of Canada was a splendid idea." Ignoring her daughter's weak protest, Neena related her own story in melancholic tones. "I was only a toddler; to be an Indian residing in a foreign country was a challenge. Everything was a contrast to our daily routines. Although they'd got a new lease on life, in my home, your grandparents were strict about upholding our culture. In fact, rules had been set up specifying all the protocols I must follow. As I grew up, it was easy for me to follow them and please my parents—right up to the time I entered high school. Then my view drastically shifted. Making friends was never easy for me, with all the insecurities, different cultural backgrounds, our differences in minor details. I kept living up to my parents' expectations, while the girls around me were simply enjoying their teenage life. But little by little, few of my female classmates saw my determination."

"What about Dada and Dadi?" Hana was deeply fascinated by her mother's life story. "They were that strict?"

"Yes, my freedom was stripped away. In fact, I had none to begin with." Her voice was soft with reminiscence. "I soon learnt that girls, even under proper upbringing, can be independent. Our faith still rests in our mind and soul, but we ladies can achieve a certain distinction in life. My father wasn't too keen about the idea that I was beginning to change. He had marriage in mind, whereas I wanted more than just settling down with a stranger and taking care of his family. We butted heads; at one point, he said he regretted living in a foreign country because it had brainwashed me, but I am grateful to the two of them for changing my life. During college, I met your biological father. He was really kind, supportive, loyal, and honest. In my heart it was a stroke of luck to meet someone who was capable of understanding me. Everything went downhill when he learned that I was pregnant with you, and his awful words hit me as a slap in the face."

"What did he say to you, Mom?" At last Hana peeked up at her mother's shuttered expression.

"Many things, but what stood out the most was 'I cannot bring shame to my family.' That was the last straw." Neena grinned. "At the same time, I was no longer alone because you were here with me."

"I am sorry," Hana cuddles against her. "I didn't mean to hurt you."

"You didn't, baby." Neena laughs at this sudden show of affection. "My other friends were either married or becoming a role model for other girls as well."

"You have amazing friends," Hana whispered in awe. "But you don't meet them anymore."

"We live in different parts of the world, love," she said, cupping Hana's cheek, "although a few of us share emails once in a while."

"I wish to be just like you," Hana blurted. "I am not strong like you."

"Suhana, you are only sixteen years old, with a long way to go before adulthood settles in." Neena adjusted herself on the bed. "I don't want to see you grow up too quickly."

"But I want to," Hana insisted. "I am childish, hopeless, a coward, hoping somebody else will take care of me."

"You are not—"

"Yes!" she yelled in defeat. "Yes, I am, Mom!"

Neena stared in bewilderment. "What makes you think so?"

"He—" She bit the tip of her tongue. "I came to realise how badly I've been behaving. To tell the truth, my social life is a bore because of my anxiety, nervousness, and being a stupid kid."

"Stop labelling yourself stupid, Suhana." Her mother climbed to her feet. "It's normal for you to feel that way, but if you wish to step out of your comfort zone, then all the better."

"I want to be strong," she said adamantly.

"Suhana," Neena said, beginning to randomly tidy up the bedroom. "You have to learn in life that taking small and measured steps is the key."

"What do you mean?"

"It is good to be a strong girl, but rushing along blindly will make matters worse." She turned to pierce Hana with intense eyes. "Walk forwards, but be prepared to learn more about yourself. It will take some time to shrug off your old habits, but you can if you set your mind to it."

Out of nowhere, a notification beep alarmed Hana, who bolted from her spot to snatch her phone and frantically unlock the PIN code. A wave of giddiness overwhelmed her because of that one person—except the number belonged to an unknown line. Crumpled by crushing disappointment, she tapped on the icon to view the message, wondering if it might be merely junk.

This is Miko, I found your number just curious to know about that friend of yours since our shifts are no longer together we can chat here - (unknown number)

Miko! I don't know how to explain but do you want to meet up? - Hana

Minutes dragged by, and Hana became a little skittish, thinking that Miko might not wish to see her. She was asking via a text while Neena looked on when a reply came that altered Hana's mood. Beaming, she jumped off the bed.

Her mother paused amidst folding dry laundry to gaze at her, one brow raised. "Where are you going?"

"I am going to meet a friend of mine." Hana's movement became slower. "Um, may I go, please?"

"Who is this friend of yours?"

"My colleague. Her name is Miko; she's a great person." She stumbled over the words.

"I only gave you permission to go alone to school and your workplace." Neena's voice brooked no argument.

"Mom," Hana said, rolling her eyes. "Please, this is urgent."

"I said no unless I will be dropping you off." Her mother turned away. "By the way, where is Jin?"

"He's busy," Hana lied. "Mom, I have to go meet her."

"Fine, I'll drive you to the location and sit in a nearby café." Neena pointed a finger at her. "Call me when you are done."

"But you once craved for freedom too," she complained, stamping in frustration. "I won't get lost so easily."

"Don't argue with me," Neena said, stepping out of the room. "I am a daughter, so I can understand where they were coming from."

"Not fair," Hana whispered, only to fall silent when her mother peeked inside the room to look at her.

"What did you say?"

"Nothing." Hana slapped a hand against her thigh nonchalantly, figuring the two of them would not budge from this subject.

"What about your lunch?" Neena cocked a hip. "It's on the table cold right now."

"I'll have that as my dinner." Hana put on a T-shirt and knee-length jeans. "I'm ready."

The vehicle lurched to a stop beside the sidewalk opposite the restaurant. Hana quickly unbuckled. Before letting herself out, she bent low to peek at her mother settled in on the driver's seat with a laptop bag situated behind.

"Call me," Neena instructed. "Don't venture off too far."

"Yes." Hana dragged out the word, stepping behind to watch the car moving forwards. Then she pivoted like a drunk ballerina towards the entrance doorway.

The atmosphere was raucous; patrons occupied every seat. Hana rose on tiptoe to look for Miko when someone waved a hand, catching her attention. She made a beeline and soon found Miko in her school attire; loose curls over her slender shoulders, manicured fingers reached for the fries, a light makeup job on her heart-shaped countenance. A vest covered her white formal shirt, checkered skirt and a pair of slouchy ivory socks. She was a fashionista even in her school uniform. She offered a smirking grin while Hana slid onto the sofa. After a word of greeting, Miko pointed at the counter as if beckoning her to order lunch.

Finally, the duo were settled down to consume fast food while boisterous voices surrounded them.

"How did you come here?" Miko chewed on her cheeseburger.

"My mom dropped me off," she said, hungrily wolfing down a chicken burger. "What about you?"

"I came with my friends, but they left." She shrugged casually. "Your mom drives? That's amazing."

"Yeah," Hana agreed while leaning back to pat her belly. "Wow, I was so hungry."

"I can tell." Miko cleared her throat. "Anyway, how are things between you two?"

"Not too great. In fact, I took the bait and confessed my feelings after you saw us that night." She lowered her head and launched into her story.

"You wanted to keep it a secret?" Miko planted her elbows on the table. "Did something happen between you?"

As Hana explained the situation, her throat seemed to squeeze shut, and her heart pounded. She waved her hands haplessly once as her words gave way to a rush of overwhelming emotions. Miko looked on with an empathic expression. Once again, she inwardly saw Jin's face, and she missed his casual handsomeness, the sound of his voice when he relentlessly annoyed her, and his masculine scent that enveloped her senses.

"Shouko—that girl likes Jin, huh?" Miko whispered. "I don't think we can do anything about it."

"I know." Hana's voice was husky. "I'm up against a wall, knowing Jin is lost to me."

"What will you do?"

"Just be there for him, maybe," she said with a shrug. "I have learn to stand on my own two feet."

Miko tilted her head. "Prove to him that you are capable of changing to be someone he can respect."

"I want him to love me," Hana whispered in a strangled voice.

Miko got up from her seat to move over beside Hana and wrap both arms around her as she began weeping. They sat immobile for a while. Then she said, emotion in her tone, "You know what's worse than being a teenager?"

"What?" Hana inquired.

"Being a hormonal teenager in love." Miko laughed while she blinked away tears. "I am soft at heart when it comes to this matter, but, Hana, you will overcome this."

"Everything was wrong from the beginning." Hana's tears slowed as she gained control of her feelings. "Approaching Jin boldly, falling in love with him—it was only a matter of time."

"I trust in you, Hana. You can always correct your mistakes."

The words rang true in Hana's heart. She could find a way to earn Jin's forgiveness, but she could never lie to him about her feelings. She really was in love with her best friend. Perhaps tomorrow was only the start of her new journey. Knowing he would not be by her side made her even more aware as well as determined. One reason Hana demanded that Jin should watch her make progress was because she yearned to catch a glimpse of recognition in his eyes.

"You're right, Miko," she said, smiling through her tears. "I'm just a kid finally learning how to handle her life."

"If it's meant to happen, then it will, Hana, or else be prepared to move forwards without him by your side." Miko took her hand firmly. "You are weak in heart and mind. Times will come when you will collapse, but don't let that stop you from showing him that *he* changed you."

"I'm glad to find a friend in you, Miko." Hana giggled with a new sensation of well-being.

"Me too," Miko answered. "I never thought we would be sitting here together."

"Hm." Hana nodded once. "I agree."

Chapter 14

$\mathcal{J}$in let out an elongated sigh. He was sitting at his desk, alone in the classroom. He had finished his cleaning duties, and now the afternoon light streamed into the room. He glanced nonchalantly at the window before clearing up his desk. Shouldering his bag, he casually started out while fishing out his cell phone. Just outside the classroom he met with Hana, hunched beside the door. Startled, he almost dropped his device.

On cue, he gasped aloud, feeling the strain of guilt. Then he swallowed nervously when he glimpsed hurt flashing in her expressive eyes.

They stared at one another without moving before he shifted his gaze to another direction to push past her. Just then, he felt his sleeve tugged backwards, and he paused with eyes squeezed shut. He didn't dare glance behind, knowing his rigid stance would dissolve and he would forgive her. Still, his stubbornness stuck, blocking his other emotions. When he shrugged of her grasp, he was able to take only a few steps before she clutched another handful of his shirt, forcing him to halt.

"I have to leave," Jin said in a monotone.

"Jin, we need to talk," she said in a soft voice. "Please."

"There is nothing we can speak of now," he said a little louder. "Now let me go."

"No." Her voice wavered. "You are avoiding me."

Jin finally turned around to stare at the girl. Her eyes were wide, brimming with a mixture of feelings; he kept his face blank. Truth be told, he experienced pain internally for hurting his best friend, just as anyone would. He had behaved cruelly, but he had a good reason. He realised that Hana had a sensitive character, and she was easily swayed by negative feelings.

"What do you want now?" he sighed, exasperated. "Haven't you caused enough trouble for the two of us?"

"Trouble?" Hana blinked once before her eyes darkened in anger. "My confession is 'trouble' to you?"

He looked all around the corridor for fear someone might overhear their conversation. Then he grabbed her arm to drag her inside their classroom, and slammed the door shut. Hana tripped a little from this sudden manhandling, but he was overwhelmed by a tumult of thoughts, making his actions seem more jumbled and forceful, and he shoved her forwards. Jin was never good at expressing his feelings and became a little volatile in action.

"You have talked enough," he said, jabbing a finger at her. "Now listen to me."

"It hurts!" she shrieked aloud as tears dripped below.

All at once, Jin felt his rage draining away. He listened to her cries while scrubbing both hands over his face, trying to sort his emotions. As if of themselves, his legs began to move forwards. His eyes blurred with suppressed tears, and a strong feeling displaced the rest: he was pining for her. If he'd learned only one thing from their current dispute, it was that he now perceived how much her presence meant to him.

"Hana, I want you to listen to me," he said in a soft voice, wiping at her wet cheeks.

She glanced up at him, her brows furrowed but letting him dry her cheeks. It had been a long time since Jin had touched her, but for now, it felt different from the past, when they were able to cling to each other without much thought. He was trembling inside. He snatched his hand away as if burned. Again he blamed Hana for giving him misconceptions.

He took some time to pull together the words that had to be said. A forlorn sensation tugged on his heartstrings, but Jin doubted whether this was best for the two of them. For several minutes he battled with his inner self about his next course of action, but he caved in to nervously wrap his arms around her.

Hana gasped in surprise. Jin winced, guessing that his spur-of-the-moment display might have given her a false sense of hope. When he tensed up to recoil backwards, she grasped the front of his shirt and buried her face on Jin's chest. He inhaled and exhaled aloud through his nostrils; the sun dipped behind straying clouds, blocking the glow of golden rays on the couple.

"Tell me," she whispered ever so quietly.

"Hana, I do not want the two of us to go on with bad blood in between us." In response, she tightened her fingers against the soft material. "Your careless behaviour hurt the two of us, and I'm torn up inside, to watch you suffering because of my harsh attitude towards you. But, Hana, if what you meant is the truth, then we cannot return to our former relationship. I hope one day you come to realise that this infatuation for me is just baseless."

"What if my feelings remain the same?" Hana peered close, and Jin saw his reflection in her eyes.

"We'll still be friends, although frankly speaking," he said in a rush just as her eyes snapped wide, "I don't wish to hurt anyone."

"You won't ignore me?" she asked with a warm smile.

"Hana, this is the first step to saying goodbye." He began to pull away one step at a time.

"Jin ...." She shook her head slowly.

"It's for the best, Hana." He remained firm in his decision. "You have been my one and only closest friend."

"Jin, wait." Hana's voice reeked of desperation. "We can still be friends because you don't have to worry about me—"

"Are you crazy?" he said, flustered. "Do you want me to drown in my own guilt?"

"It's not that you love me back." She hiccupped several times. "I'll be fine."

"Your choice of words reminds me that you have a long way to grow up." His voice rose a little higher. "I am being nice to you, Hana; don't frustrate me again."

"Is my love for Jin a disease?" she persisted. "Why is it so wrong for me to fall in love with someone who has been a part of my life?"

"Stop it," Jin said harshly, unaware of a figure standing just outside the closed door eavesdropping on them. "You know what? I am wrong to even think we can still remain friends."

"Are you afraid that your feelings may one day match mine?" Hana swayed on her feet to lean heavily on a desk.

"You don't have to worry about my feelings." Jin couldn't control his tongue. "My view about us will never change."

Hana wept openly before crumpling on the floor while Jin gulped aloud. Cold sweat covered him as he watched her unravelling. Fresh guilt overcame his sense of judgement, and he cursed aloud. They were both stubborn to a fault; often the duo would bicker, sulking, stuck in disagreement. Yet always, one of them made sure to calm down and approach the other to apologise. His heart caught in between, the caterwauling of his friends grating in his ears, he could still see a younger version of herself sobbing after she was bullied because of her difference in appearance. But why was his heart splintering in two?

"I hate you," Jin said vehemently, even though his action said the opposite when he marched towards her.

With brute force, he pulled her upright to embrace her short stature. They fit perfectly when her arms wound around him. Jin was not a person to hurt someone else intentionally, yet Hana's behaviour brought out the worst in him.

He released himself from her tight grasp, and their gazes met. "Do you mean that?" she asked in a tearful voice. "You hate me?"

"Who knows?" Jin shrugged. Suddenly the door rattled open, and in came the one person who caused him to catch his breath.

Shouko stared at them, her eyes flashing with betrayal. When they halted on Hana, Jin reflexively stepped between them, shielding his friend, too late to note that his act stung the newcomer. Shouko wheeled around to rush out of sight. Jin called out her name after hurling Hana a look that clearly read blame before racing out of the classroom, leaving her to deal with the situation alone.

He literally ran down the stairs to chase after Shouko, who never bothered to wait even as he called her name several times, but at length he caught up to her. He fell into step behind her, leaving a space between them. In silence, the two of them walked along in file. He saw Chiyo watching them, and she was stunned by the duo, but Jin never glanced back.

Out of nowhere, Shouko halted in mid-step, and Jin collided with her from behind. He apologised at once, moving around to look at her dark head hanging low. He smiled softly at the same time, gentle urging her to look up by curling his fingers beneath her chin, and she complied.

"Is it wrong of me to be jealous?" she asked in a tense voice.

"No," he whispered. "That only means you care for me."

"Why do you choose me, Jin?" Shouko inhaled and exhaled a ragged breath. "Hana is your friend—"

"And I only see her as my friend," he said, cutting her off. "But I fell in love with you."

"What?" She blinked at his slip of the tongue.

"Crap," he muttered, rubbing the back of his neck. "I never meant to blurt it out like this."

"Too late," she said in a hurried tone.

"It wasn't until I got a good look at you back at the vending machine when my feelings changed." He shrugged uncomfortably.

"What about her?" she demanded.

"It's one-sided," Jin replied haltingly. "I love Hana, but it's platonic. Even now, I don't wish to hurt her."

"Maybe she's threatened by me," Shouko murmured in a thoughtful voice. "I feel sorry for the girl, but at the same time, I'm surprised that she could do this to me."

"Please don't hate her." Jin grasped her fingers, linking them with his own. "She has gone through a lot."

"What about you?" She looked up to peer deeply into his gaze.

"Me?" he raised a questioning brow.

"Jin, you hug her so easily." Shouko looked away. "Anyone can mistake the two of you as lovers."

"But I see nothing wrong in that. I'm talking about the past." He tightened his grip when she made a move to let go.

"Would you hug your male best friend?" she shouted at him. "The two of you are so toxic."

"Toxic?" he yelped in surprise. "There is nothing toxic about the two of us."

"Answer me!" she yelled at him. "If Hana were a boy, would the two of you be so close?"

"Of course!" he replied in a shocked voice. "I don't judge people."

"So you would often embrace, coddle, and spoil him?" she sneered. "Jin, I have watched the two of you from afar."

Jin's heartbeat began to race at the clarity of her words. Suddenly his mind was muddled in confusion and panic. "Quiet," he scoffed at her.

"Which is why I asked Hana once if she and you were dating," Shouko went on, ignoring his discomfort. "The two of you behave so differently than how friends should act towards one another."

"You're wrong," he said vehemently. "My reason for how I behave towards Hana is not what you think. She has been the only person who understands me. Our friendship is strong because of the times we've spent with one another. We can finish sentences for each other, more often than not, catch a change of vibe without needing to explain. Look, it's difficult for me to put this into words, but Hana is special to me."

"Then what's wrong in loving her?" She pushed his hands away. "Don't you think it's better to be in a relationship with someone who can understand you better?"

"She is my friend," Jin emphasised, his voice cracking as if that single word was a reminder to him. "Losing this friendship hurts me, but I can't envision Hana and me in a different light."

She shook her head at him. "Jin, why do I sense that you're fighting with yourself? Do you know that some friendships can actually blossom into romance if that other person comes to a conclusion?"

"But our friendship is not one of them," Jin said, rejecting the idea. "Shouko, if you had a guy friend, would you prefer to test the water or remain friends so as not to hurt one another?"

"I don't know." She shrugged and then sighed aloud. "Jin, I think we should consider carefully before taking the next step."

Without hesitation, Jin stepped forwards and watched Shouko's stunned features as he leaned down to plant a kiss on her gawking mouth. He remained in the same position; the thought that this girl might leave him shocked Jin. He knew that what he felt for her was real. He was serious when it came to Shouko, for once falling head over heels for somebody else with no casual mindset. He blamed Hana for confusing his thoughts, for giving him a moment of doubt for even thinking in that manner, although that inner voice taunted him mercilessly, calling him a coward.

"Shouko, go steady with me," he whispered against her lips. "I really want to be by your side."

"Why?" she sulked pettily. "What if you hurt me?"

"I won't," he said, smiling. "If I wanted to love Hana, we wouldn't be standing so close here."

"Are you sure about this?" Shouko stared into his gaze. "You won't regret it?"

He shook his head firmly. "No."

"Then will you kiss me again?" she asked in a shy voice.

They fused their lips in harmony, and they shifted in unison until the two of them were embracing each other. A spark of joy surged in him. Then, envisioning Hana's lonely expression, her tears falling continuously, and his last words to her, Jin deepened the kiss to erase the memory.

The next day, the school was abuzz about the new relationship. Girls watched Shouko in quiet envy, but many came forward to offer congratulations to the blushing pair. Still, it was quite different in the classroom. Hana's face spoke of blatant devastation; her eyes, puffy from tears, and her silent retreat gave the other side of the story. Most of the girls in the room either looked on with guilt or murmured as to what might have caused Jin to behave ignorantly. Meanwhile, Jin was getting an earful from his male comrades.

Of course, their dissolving friendship was another subject for the gossiping peers shocked by their pretended indifference towards each other. Their camaraderie was out of joint, while Jin spent more time with the others. He was becoming just like the rest of them, a faceless counterpart.

Chapter 15

$\mathcal{J}$in let out a heavy sigh and rubbed the back of his neck. Done waiting tables for now, he collapsed on a chair inside a cramped room that had a row of lockers against one wall, a rectangular shaped table with foldable chairs in the middle, and a strong chlorine scent. Today was his third day of manoeuvring orders; he'd done well for a first-timer, only accidentally offering the wrong menu a couple of times. Thankfully, those customers were understanding of his situation.

"Jin, you are doing well," said a cook, appearing with a steamy dish of seafood pasta in his hands. "Don't mind me joining in?"

"Of course not." He quickly stood to offer a formal greeting before plopping down once again. Both his feet were throbbing. "Thank you for the encouragement."

"How are you feeling so far?" The middle-aged man sat down, shaking off his own exhaustion. "I hope you won't quit this job."

"No, that's not an option for me." He felt a little nervous in front of this man.

"Hard-working kid, eh?" the cook said with a chuckle. "Does your school allow their students to work?"

"Um, y-yes, as long as our grades are not affected." Jin folded his hands gingerly. "I hope I'm not causing too much trouble with my clumsiness."

"It's all right, you're only on your … fourth day?" He paused, holding his next forkful ready.

"No, my third day." Jin smiled uneasily.

"Oh." The cook blinked in surprise. "I'm sorry for losing track. My brain is getting sluggish with all the orders coming in."

"No worries." Jin peeked down at his smart casual attire. "My shift will be over soon."

"You can make this work. Our manager is really kind, and so are the rest of us. We're one big family," he continued between big bites. "The only time we become busy and often snap is when our hands are full, so please, don't take it to heart."

"I understand." Jin smiled when the door clicked open to reveal another colleague heading inside for her afternoon shift. "Hello."

"Oh, Jin," she waved at him. "Good to see you here."

Aoi had cropped hair atop a short, slender figure with an athletic built. She was clearly a person who regularly lifted in the gym. She was a high school senior and had worked for the past four years and was light on her feet. Someday Jin wished to be pro just like her, but he had a long way to go; perhaps if he'd been in the same restaurant for half his life, he'd be proficient.

That thought reminded him of his mother's health. Her phlegmy cough was getting worse, and he was getting more frustrated. In fact, he had planned to urge his mom, urgently if necessary, to take a week off from her fucking workplace.

"Jin?" someone called out loudly. "Your break ended five minutes ago."

He shot upright, banging his knee beneath the table. Ignoring the answering laughter, he hissed aloud from the agony, rubbing his knee, and then hobbled off. His companions in the locker room offered him encouragement when he apologised to them for his tardiness. After they warned him not to let it happen again, he set off around the restaurant with a notepad and a pen hidden in the apron tied around his lean waist. He wore an onyx coloured formal dress shirt with long sleeves, slacks in a similar tone, and dress shoes. His hair was tied in a short ponytail while a headband anchored his hair in front. Jin looked dapper in his uniform, surprising even himself.

By evening, Jin bade farewell to the rest of his colleagues after changing out of his work clothes and slinging his bag across his chest. Exhausted, he trudged along while people passed by hurriedly. He put on earbuds to cut off the hectic reality and settle into his own thoughts.

Suddenly someone collided with him head-on. He looked up and saw a laughing couple, who bowed in apology. He nodded once, keeping his irritation at bay. Then he slowed down and turned to stare at the giddy pair. Their merry expressions reminded him of Hana and himself. He smiled faintly at his memory the past, but his smile faded as he continued walking. He was excited about his budding relationship with Shouko, but a corner of his heart yearned for Hana's friendship. In fact, Hana now greeted him at every opportunity, but he was reserved in response.

He did see little changes in Hana. She was more perceptive of the people around her, surprising a few. Of course, Jin was assured that Ino would remain by her side, timid though he was. Jin would never dare to approach him with the topic, and perhaps it was for the best. Whenever Hana was close, Jin's resolve to avoid her crumbled, but he had to remind himself that she had erected a fanciful hope about them being together. An unwelcome image of them kissing made him blush beet red, and he covered his face. *Hana, you are an idiot.*

The next morning, Jin woke up early, hoping to run into his mother, but the house was empty and silent. He angrily punched the wall, unbothered by the stinging pain, and then stomped off to get ready for school. He was confused as to why she was so fixated on her job when their daily budget was spent carefully, and he never dared ask for extra allowance. Warm water splashing on his face awakened his senses, though he sighed aloud that every path he decided to take was covered in pain.

After assembling a pitiful lunch for himself—he had been practising ever since the fight broke out with Hana, deciding to be more resilient—and heading for his bike, he was startled by his ringing phone. A feeling of joy spread through him at the name on the screen.

He tapped on the icon to hear the other person's adorable voice. "Good morning," Shouko greeted him nervously.

"I'm on my way," he told her, holding on with just one hand as he pedalled. "Don't go anywhere."

"Um, I won't," she said with a giggle before ending the call.

The girl was obviously very shy. Jin was patient around her, letting her adjust to him and to the relationship as well as what might follow in the future. At that thought, he almost wrecked the bike against a pole, spewing colourful curses. He had been pleased to realise that their houses were not far apart and that they could go to and from school together. He was looking forward to their first dates, already planning for the summer holiday in case she had no other commitments.

"Jin!" she called, having seen him from a distance.

"Get on," he said, beaming at her.

Once she was settled on the seat, they set off to school. The indigo sky was turning pink, and sunlight had not yet come. The gentle touch of her hand against his back felt like fire. Of course, he could not hold back his wide smile because he officially had a girlfriend. The bicycle rocked to a stop at the road junction, and they were waiting for the red signal to turn green when he spied Hana straight ahead across the street. She was strolling slowly, unaware that he was even there, so close that if she turned her head. they would see each other.

Just the red changed to green Jin pedalled forward, his heart thumping louder in his buzzing ears. Hana's back came closer and closer while Jin broke out in cold sweat. His initial plan was to drive past her, yet his actions seemed to follow without his will. Their eyes connected just as he rang the bell for safety reasons so she would move out of the way. He caught a glimpse of her exhausted gaze.

"Morning, Hana," he called out, surprising himself.

She halted to stare at them as he pedalled away. Shouko's fingers tightened on the back of his shirt when he quickly peered over his shoulder. Hana stood rooted on the spot, a hurt expression on her otherwise blank features. He turned back to focus forwards, gripping the handles firmly while speeding up. A heaviness settled behind his chest, and he bit the corner of his lip. He was at a loss. Of course he did not regret his decision, but the two of them had faced one another in an unfortunate way. Clearly, Hana was adamant about what had caused him to behave so harshly towards her.

"Jin, are you listening to me?" Shouko's clear voice startled him, and he pressed on the brake a little so he could peer behind. There he saw a troubled face glancing downward. Guilt ate away inside him, because now he had to think about his girlfriend's feelings too. He paused the bike to set one foot on the ground. He hung his head but then sensed movement before she turned his face towards her. He looked at her beautiful face up close, lit with a smile, and she affectionately brushed his fringe back. "Jin, I love you," she confessed in an earnest voice. "This is not the right place or perfect time for me to be so bold, but I realise I have no choice. My apologies if I seem out of line—"

"Wait," Jin interrupted. "Let's walk to school."

"Okay," she agreed, and the pair walked on in silence.

It was a crisp morning with blaring noises from vehicles in the street, shops opening for the day, and pedestrians streaming through it all. It was an overload for the senses, but Jin was accustomed to the pace of this big city. He recalled the last time he and his mother had ventured to the countryside many years ago. The memory startled him, and somehow he kept from smiling in disbelief. The two of them were on a visit to her late relative's house. Jin could only summon bits and pieces, but mostly he felt a tinge of nostalgic euphoria from childhood recollections. For a split second he yearned to return to that period when his mother doted on him. Then another image assailed him: when they returned home the next day, a younger Hana came straight to Jin with much to say about his absence.

"What do you want to tell me, Shouko?" he sighed quietly. Everything was different compared to the bygone years.

"Nothing," she whispered.

"What?" He blinked, finally focusing on the present. "Shouko, what's the matter?"

"It's all right, I forgot what I was about to say." She shrugged but had a moody expression. "We have to hurry, or else we'll be late for school."

"Yeah." Jin nodded once. "I'm sorry, Shouko, if somehow my behaviour has hurt you."

"It's my fault," she whined adorably. "Jin, I'm actually envious of the friendship that the two of you have for each other."

"Huh?" He turned to gawk at her.

"I would admire both Hana and you from afar for the respect and love that you have for her." She squeezed his fingers nervously. "It's easy to read your mind, Jin. You are not happy with the circumstances."

"But"—he groaned, rubbing his face roughly—"I'm stuck. My head tells me to give her the cold shoulder, but my heart wants to be by her side."

Jin never saw the glimmer of realisation lighting Shouko's countenance at his casual honesty. They made it to school on time to find a teacher standing beside the entrance. As students acknowledged his stern presence, Jin, followed by Shouko, strolled towards the parking space for bicycles. To make the ambience lighter again, Jin cheekily wrapped an arm over Shouko's shoulder to drag her against his chest. A blush rose on her face while he leaned to peck a kiss on her gasping mouth.

"Jin", she said, giggling merrily, "someone might see us."

"Let them see." He nuzzled the girl's neck. "I love you."

"Me too." She ruffled the top of his head. "But I think you have to patch things up with your best friend."

"I'm scared," he whispered.

"What did you say?" she said, tilting her head.

"Nothing important; let's go." He moved back and took her hand, twining their fingers together.

Shouko, I'm scared of uncovering an emotion that still remains close behind that mental door swirling in my heart, Jin's inner sentimental voice declared.

Chapter 16

Droplets of sweat trickled down Hana's olive-toned countenance. The sun was beating down upon the rest of the team as their PE instructor announced a five-minute break after a series of runs around the perimeter of the school. She sat struggling with each rasping breath to calm her racing heartbeat. She stood at a wall overlooking the little garden, while her mind was elsewhere.

This morning Jin had surprised her with a hasty greeting, but his attitude changed once they were inside the school. She was befuddled by his behaviour even though she expected it from him. For once, she was open to being hurt by someone else. Suddenly she found it hard to breathe, and she clasped both hands onto the edge to loom over the wide basin.

The sight of Shouko nestled behind Jin on the same seat Hana once occupied had lacerated her heart. It took her a long time to calm her ragged emotions. She didn't know she was being watched from afar by Chiyo, the senior student Jin had once been with in a physical relationship. Chiyo gauged the situation and took off in another direction, allowing Hana the space to mourn her pain.

She pressed a fist against her chest and squeezed her eyes shut. It was hard to prove to Jin that she was a whole new person, and just now the effort seemed idiotic to her. She let go a sardonic laugh, but when she overheard girlish voices approaching, she regained her composure. Her classmates lingered around her in small groups.

Although she knew she was putting herself and her fragile heart out on limb, she had recently decided to converse with classmates, beginning with the girls. While it had been easy with Ino, her self-consciousness made it hard with the girls. The only thing they had in common was that Hana was their note-taker. Even though in the past she had once complained to Jin about that, now it might prove a slow and measured first step to gain their notice.

Still, nothing seemed to change. The groups ignored Hana's presence, keeping to themselves and chattering merrily above her head, sounding like water splashing on a metal basin. Just then, Suzumi caught her eye. As the girl approached, Hana reminding herself that she had more hurdles to jump across.

Suzumi paused in front of her. "I'm curious: what happened between Jin and you?"

"Huh?" Hana glanced around at the rest of them.

The girls around had fallen quiet, pretending to ignore the sudden change of subject. Hana returned her wary gaze to the one standing in front of her. She had figured the classroom would catch up sooner or later with the weird vibe going on, yet nobody had dared to ask except Suzumi, and Hana wasn't comfortable with her to begin with. They were in a different level; even though the rest were able to accept her little by little, she felt Suzumi was unmovable.

"Nothing," she finally blurted out. "Why do you ask?"

Suzumi rolled her eyes. "Don't act stupid."

"I'm not," Hana said. She gulped, feeling uneasy. "Jin is my best friend."

"You've been replaced, right?" Suzumi snorted. "The second year are aware of the relationship between Jin and that other girl from class 2-B."

"I was never his girlfriend to be replaced by someone else." Hana forced out the words that seemed lodged in her throat. *Don't panic now,* she told herself.

"Suzumi, don't be so rude," Aika piped up, laughing.

"Jin doesn't bother talking to you any longer," Hanabi said as she leaned casually against the edge.

"I don't care." Suzumi shrugged while flicking drops of water off her hands. "They do look better by comparison; it's rather odd to see him with a girl who looks so out of place."

"Suzumi", Aika warned her friend nervously, "let's go, shall we?"

"Yeah." Suzumi never gave a backward glance at Hana, who bit the inside of her cheek.

The moment the other girls left the area, Hana hunched on the ground, and a soft keening cry came from her lips. She could not run off to Jin as before; instead, this was a personal battle against a bunch of bullies.

Suddenly she heard running footsteps, and she had not time to straighten herself before a classmate caught her weeping alone. "Suhana? What happened?" Aika walked over, though she looked hesitant. "Um, is it because of what Suzumi told you?"

"I'm fine," Hana said, shaking her head. "Please, don't tell anyone about this."

"I won't." She glanced around, looking unsure. "Will you be okay by yourself?"

"Yes," Hana replied in a strained voice.

Aika had rushed over to retrieve her towel, and now she jogged off, first giving Hana a sympathetic look. After some time, Hana strolled towards the group of students gathering near the teacher. He stood to one side with a clipboard in one hand. After he gave her an earful for vanishing, she was let off with a warning. A few of the boys sniggered; it was a rare sight to see a good pupil getting scolded by the authorities.

During recess break, Hana headed for the rooftop. She sat at the same spot where she and Jin had quarrelled, and there she munched on her meal, consisting of a simple Indian dish. Below, many voices lulled her senses. She put off the thought of Jin walking off with Shouko, who had dropped by to pick him up for lunch. When both girls accidentally made eye contact, Shouko had quickly looked away.

Hana leaned her head against the fence to study the cloudy sky, wondering where everything had gone wrong. Out of nowhere a smiling Ino startled her as he approached and sat adjacent to her with his own lunch. Without a word he began to eat. It struck Hana that he might be here to lend moral support, even though it took courage for him to even be here.

In silence, Ino looked up at her sniffling. Clearly there was no hiding that indeed some trouble had come between the two friends. Hana mentally berated herself for constantly bursting into tears, yet there was more grief locked up within her.

"Thank you," Hana whispered ever so softly.

"Anytime," he replied in a hushed voice.

Finally, the two of them ambled towards the classroom when the school bell rang. Hana sneezed from crying too much in one day, her nose stuffy and eyes puffy. Upon entering they found their homeroom teacher waiting for the rest of them to take seats.

"Oh look, another Ino is here too," someone joked, and soft laughter filled the room.

"Get out of my classroom," the teacher snapped while flipping through pages.

Hana plopped down on her chair telling herself firmly not to look at Jin's face at the back. Once everyone was settled, the teacher glances at each of their faces, adding tension to the atmosphere.

"All of you are aware of the rules and regulations about taking up jobs, correct?" he began while looking directly at everyone. "We have learned that our students are working without the school's consent."

Without a thought, Hana glanced over her shoulder towards Jin, and his gaze met with her own. Both of them jumped as their names were called out by the teacher, who told them both to meet him after school in the teacher's office. Many were expressing their shock, mainly about Hana. She shrank further in her chair; apparently Jin's friends had known of him taking up a job.

Hana's senses were working hard as Jin stood beside her in the teacher's office. She heard the low buzz of the fax machine and the mentors' voices as they chatted amongst themselves; she saw one or two class representatives walking in with stacks of paper; smelled the strong scent of coffee intermingling with the pervasive aroma of books. When the two of them had walked towards the office, neither broke the heavy quietness; she kept her pace slow to view his back.

"The two of you broke the school code." Mr Hayamato sighed while taking off his glasses. "Care to tell me about your labour?"

"I work in a bakery," she announced in a high-pitched tone.

"What about yourself, Jin?"

"I recently began working at a family restaurant," he said in a low voice harbouring nervousness.

"Why didn't either of you approach me in the first place?" Mr Hayamato leaned back on his creaking chair.

"I'm sorry." Hana looked at the teacher haplessly. "But I wanted to save up my allowance money by myself."

"I'm sorry, but you know the school rules." Mr Hayamato shook his head. "Students are strictly forbidden—"

"Please, Mr Hayamato!" Jin yelled, frightening the others, and hastily bowed low. "I need this job really urgently!"

"Jin …," Hana whispered in pain.

"Tell me the reason, Jin," Mr Hayamato said, heaving a sigh. "Even then, I have no choice in this matter."

"My mother is working two shifts, and the work is taking a severe toll on her health." He stood still, dogged, ramrod straight. "I am the only male in the household. If I don't support her, then who will?"

"Where are your relatives?" Mr Hayamato's tone said he alone would lead this talk.

"They live in the countryside. My mother's only living relative is my aunt." Jin continued in a pleading tone. "Please, let me work to help her."

"If you are facing financial difficulties, the school has options for students, so why didn't you come to us?" He looked sympathetic. "Jin, if your studies are affected, then how will you help your mother in the future?"

"I work on the weekend," he argued, tightening his fists. "She hasn't taken leave for a long time."

"He's right, Mr Hayamato," Hana put in. "Both Jin and his mother are going through difficulties."

She moved her hand to clasp Jin's, and he gave her a surprised look. Even though she held on to him firmly, he never curled his fingers. Hana, ignoring the signs, gazed steadily at their mentor, who eyed them in an unnerving silence.

"I can quit my job," Hana said, "but please, take Jin's plight under consideration." She stood steadily at her friend's side. "Mrs Takami is carrying a heavy burden, so my friend has taken the alternative route to help her in every way."

"I am very sorry, but there is no way I can allow one of my students to continue to work when everyone else here may not do so." Mr Hayamato shook his head. "However, I will have a talk with the headmaster to look into Jin's financial situation."

"I want to work by myself," Jin said with a frown. "I don't wish to ask for help."

"Young man, I want you to tone down your ego," the teacher barked. "Jin, it is time for you to learn that stubbornness will only put you in more trouble. We can discuss your scholarship as well, so wait for my reply. Until then, the two of you had better quit."

"Okay," Hana whispered in a gloomy voice.

"Suhana," the teacher called just as the pair reached the door. "Which store are you working at?"

"Why?" Hana inquired after giving the name.

"I never pegged you to work in a bakery," he said with a chuckle.

"Oh, we have sales going on. Please show your support," she said with a quick bow.

"I might drop by later," he remarked. "Run along now."

Once the two of them had exited the office, they ambled alongside one another. In fact, Hana did not wish to leave his side as he adopted a sombre expression. She peeked at the corridor and saw a noticeboard fluttering with papers. When she glanced back at Jin, he caught her eye. Once again, Hana figured her act would be out of line when she grasped his sleeve to keep his attention. She offered a small, nervous smile, but he shifted away from her, dropping her hand. She felt pain slice her heart. She was collecting years of scars wondering if they would heal properly in the future. She was matching his pace when he paused to look at her. Her eyes widened at the torn look in his eyes.

"Why, Hana?" he whispered.

"Because you are still my friend," she said in a simple fact. "Should there be a reason for me?"

"I cannot do this," he told her in a hurting voice. "Are you making me feel guilty?"

"No." Hana peered deep into his eyes. "You are taking this the wrong way."

"Jin, are you done?" A voice came out of nowhere. "What's the matter?"

Shouko was waiting by the staircase, her eyes studying them both. Emotion flashed in her eyes when she walked over to curl her arm over Jin's and turned to glance at Hana, who was taken aback by the hostility. Then Shouko seemed to mask her true emotion before putting on a concerned expression for her boyfriend, who looked flustered as if afraid of being overheard.

Hana took the hint. "I'll leave for now. Bye."

She fled the suffocating atmosphere, a heaviness like a boulder in her heart. Even the outdoor air could not clear her mind. The heartbroken girl could not have guessed what life-changing events might be looming just ahead.

Chapter 17

"Jin, what will you do now?"

"Hm?" He blinked and focused on Shouko. "I don't know."

They sat opposite one another in a quaint café within the Shinjuku District while indulging desserts. They had come here from the school after the meeting, at his girlfriend's insistence. Jin's brain was having a meltdown once the teacher had announced he must quit a job that he had only began last week, a decision he disagreed with. Even though the teacher had offered to aid his household through the school's financial system, he figured that might not stop his mother from continuing the double shift.

"Jin." Shouko's soft voice and gentle touch on his hand pulled him back from reveries.

"I'm sorry." He sighed in defeat. "I am searching for a way to work without the school noticing."

"But that will only get you into trouble, Jin." She paused to bite into a crisp wafer. "Your teacher has warned you about working while schooling."

He rubbed his face. "Shouko, I don't have a choice."

"You can wait for summer holiday, because I plan to work too," she said in an encouraging tone.

"I cannot wait till then," Jin explained while slowly pushing aside his unfinished treat.

"If that's the case, why not work for my father?" Shouko's face brightened.

"Where?" He peered up at her from beneath long lashes.

"My father is a carpenter; he designs furniture based on orders."

"I'll think about it, but thank you for the offer." He smiled, hoping to make her feel better.

"Jin, you are desperate to work, so why not just accept the offer?" She was adamant.

"I'm not good around carpentry, but it's a different matter when taking orders." He linked their fingers together.

"It's all right; I'm sorry," she said, waving her free hand nonchalantly.

He frowned a little. "Are you mad, Shouko?"

"Of course not." She glanced away looking flustered. "I wish to help you in any way."

"Thank you," Jin's voice conveyed his pride and determination.

"Well, you don't have to thank me because I'm not helping Jin lessen your burden," she whispered.

"Shouko, your presence is comforting for me," he reassured her.

"But it's not enough for me." She finally gazed at him with a tight countenance. "I want to be there for you."

He squeezed her hand. "You are, Shouko, right now."

"If … it was Suhana then she might know what to say to Jin, correct?" Her voice tightened with suppressed emotion.

"What does Hana have to do with our topic?" Jin asked calmly.

"I heard everything between you two, Jin," she whispered, slipping her hand out of his firm grip. "She knows more about you than I do."

"You're my girlfriend, Shouko. We have lots of time to learn about one another," he replied measuredly.

"So why do I feel that I'm not close to you?" Her piercing gaze connected to his own.

He sighed. "Shouko, you're imagining things."

"Jin, may I know what transpired inside the teacher's office?" she asked, toying with the dessert spoon.

"I told you everything."

"What about Hana's case?" Shouko bit her lower lip. "Is she working too?"

"She began working before me at a bakery." Jin shrugged. "She willingly told the teacher that she will hand over the resignation letter. Hana comes from a well-to-do household. Her mother works in a museum, and her stepfather is a businessman. everything is going fine for her."

Jin's eyes widened in shock at the condescension he heard in his own voice. He sat upright, guilt filtering internally, it was true that Hana's status was better than his own. Like everyone else, Jin reacted to the girl's foreign background, which made Shouko realise that he might have harboured unwanted feelings towards her.

"Suhana's family are rich?" Shouko inquired in an awestruck voice. "You mean to say that her mother married a Japanese man?"

"It didn't come out right; let me rephrase. Hana may come from a comfortable situation, but she wants to be independent and not rely on her parents' income." Jin smiled a little. "She's childish, stubborn, and naive, but her heart is in the right place."

"So why is she studying at our school when she could benefit more from a private school?" she asked, tilting her head.

"I have to admit that Hana has good grades, but she's had social anxiety and is introverted," he mused while recalling her reasons. "Our school is open to foreign students, whereas Hana was born in Japan making her a local. But mostly, she joined in because of me."

"Really?" Shouko chewed on a slice of kiwi thoughtfully.

A sudden sense of loss hit Jin as he reminisced over the past. She had stood up to Mr Hayamato without budging; she could have walked away easily after what had occurred between them. The warm grip of her hand, even though Jin didn't return it, was a silent reminder that she was by his side.

"Jin, what's the matter?" Shouko pulled him back from the agonising sensation.

"I'm just wondering about my current situation," he lied so as not to hurt her. "Let's get out of here."

"Sure." She nodded once. Then, as they packed up to leave, Jin received a call from an unknown number.

"Hello?" he answered with a concerned expression and then went rigid at the reply.

"Jin Takami, I am calling from the hospital about your mother—"

"What happened to her?" he roared, startling everyone in the café. *"Why is my mother in the hospital?"*

"Jin!" Shouko clutched onto his arm. "Calm down."

"Please calm down, Mr Takami. We have sent you the hospital location, so please come over as soon as possible."

"S-she is dying, right?" Jin wailed aloud, torn by a thousand mixed emotions.

"I'll call someone to fetch you—"

"No, I'm coming over now," he said through his tightened throat, sniffling aloud and blinded by raging tears.

"Be careful on your way." The phone call ended giving way to a beeping tone.

Shouko dragged him out of the café, supporting his weight even though she had trouble manoeuvring the two of them on the path. Passersby gave them a wide berth, looking at the teenagers curiously. Then someone actually stopped to inquire because the boy was sobbing uncontrollably, mumbling incoherent words. The kindhearted Samaritan flagged a cab to follow them to the hospital.

Through all this, Shouko never let go of him. "Jin, don't harbour negative thoughts," she murmured while patting his head, which was leaning on her shoulder.

"How can I not, Shouko?" he hissed in agony. "She was getting worse, but as a son, I have failed in taking care of her!"

"You have not," she reassured him. "Your mother loves you very much."

"Love cannot maintain someone's health," he said between wracking sobs. "I don't wish to lose her, Shouko. She's the only person that I have in this world."

"You have me," she declared. "Your mother will be fine; the three of us will sit together around the dining table."

"I love you," he said brokenly. "I love you, Shouko."

"I love you too, Jin." She kissed his forehead.

"We'll be there soon," the stranger spoke up from the front passenger seat. "Don't worry about the cab fare. I'll pay for the ride, young man, and I will pray for your mother."

At the hospital, the pair shot out of the cab. Shouko bowed in thanks before chasing the speeding Jin, who skidded on the floor and almost collided with several people. He was not bothered by the nurse's shout not to run until he reached the reception counter. Out of breath and reeking of perspiration, Jin cursed in frustration.

Shouko stepped up to question the admin behind the desk. "We are here to see Mrs Takami. This boy is her son," she said in a clear voice while rubbing his back soothingly.

"Wait here." The young woman got up and went to speak with a man sitting in the visitor's section. After a moment, the two of them came over. "He is the manager of the workplace who came along with your mother—"

Before she could finish, Jin attacked the man by throwing a punch. His furious voice all but shook the walls of the hospital. The man stumbled backwards, stunned by the sudden blow. He touched his smarting jaw with a look of disbelief. Then he responded with an angry insult to Jin, and the two grappled in a scuffle. A couple of nurses rushed over to separate them just as a security guard arrived. Raised vocals distracted many others, disturbing patients and their visitors.

"Jin, stop it!" Shouko screamed in fright. *"Please!"*

"You bastard!" Jin roared, spittle flying. "It's because of you my mother is in that room!"

"You'd better learn some respect! If not for me, your mother might have died some time ago!"

A head nurse came over. "If you two do not end this bickering, neither of you will be allowed to visit the patient."

"Tell that idiot! He hit me in the face first!" the man said, before a couple of men pulled him away.

"Get out!" Jin shrieked.

The main aimed a rigid finger at him. "I'll send her the relief letter, but after we've handled her bills, Mrs Takami will no longer work for us."

"Fuck off!" the boy was dragged away from a weeping Shouko as well as a few others. "I'll sue your fucking company!"

"Go ahead!"

"Enough!" the security guard finally intervened to push the bristling man towards the exit doorway. Staring at Jin, he said, "You, stop this disturbance."

"Jin!" Shouko wailed, and her trembling frame at last focused his attention. "I'm scared!"

"I'm sorry," he apologised in a hoarse voice.

A nurse hunched closer to hand over tissue towards Shouko who gladly took it to blow her nose. "Miss, please take him to the cafeteria. Once the two of you are calmed down, you may return here."

An hour or so had passed by when a numb Jin alongside a mentally exhausted Shouko strolled towards the front counter. The same nurse brought them to the level where his mother had been admitted. Jin's heartbeat began to accelerate as they came closer, and he was hyperventilating; the clinical odour of medicines immersed him as if he were floating in mid-air. He found himself in a dreamlike state; all sounds melted into a buzz, and everything else became sluggish.

The curtain was pulled aside to reveal his mother lying motionless on the bed attached to several tubes. Her pale face was etched with exhaustion, and an oxygen mask was strapped to her face. At the sight he broke down once again. He wobbled on his feet to stand over the bedside and gingerly wrap cold fingers against her own.

"Don't leave me, please," he begged, unaware of a chair placed behind him. Firm hands on his broad shoulders urged him to sit down.

That evening, when visiting hours ended for the day, a nurse walked in and saw the two teenagers sitting side by side near the bed frame. She acknowledged them with a smile to announce that it was time for them to return home. When Jin cleared his throat and explained the situation, he was allowed to stay overnight. The nurse left, and he shifted on the chair with a sigh.

"Come," he said to Shouko, "I'll walk you to the taxi stand." He had a major headache, a sore throat, and a pain in the chest.

"I can go by myself, but what about your clothes, Jin?" She gently swept his hair to the side. "Is there anything else I can do for you?"

"No, you've done so much for me." He leaned over to give her a lingering kiss before pulling away. "I'll handle the rest on my own."

"I don't want to leave you alone," she said softly. "Please call me anytime, even if it's in the middle of night."

"I will. I'm sorry for dragging you—"

Shouko silenced his apologies with a deep kiss, cupping his face with both hands. The only sound was the regular beep of the machines by the bed. Just as she started to stand, Jin nuzzled his face against her chest to inhale her feminine scent. Then he reluctantly pulled away as she rose. Before she left, she stood close to the bed to pray; her soothing voice calmed him somewhat.

"Remember what I told you," she reminded him while holding the bag strap tightly. "Don't get into trouble while I'm gone."

"I won't," he promised. "Just drop me a text when you reach home."

"All right. I love you, Jin."

"I love you too." He waved at her with a forced smile and then let out a sigh, looking back at his mother. *Just don't leave my side, Mother, please*, he thought and went on in silent prayers.

The next day, Jin called the school to explain his problem, asking the teacher not to announce his news to everyone else. He preferred to keep this hidden so as not to be disturbed by unnecessary calls from his classmates. He had his hands full going through paperwork, especially when he received the final medical bills, but he never faltered. The only person calling him now and then was Shouko. But in the back of his mind, he wondered whether or not he should inform one other person. His mother had been in hospital two days when the weekend arrived. Until then, he was unsure, but then his heart caved in, and he pulled out the cell phone to send a text.

Hey, just to let you know my mother is in hospital - Jin

He sent the message along with the address. No answer came, and he figured she must be at work or caught up in some other task. For some odd reason Jin felt his heart expand in relief when the phone did not vibrate with an incoming message. If he were to look more closely, though, Jin would feel a little better to have his best friend closer at such a crucial time.

Chapter 18

Hana got busy during the peak hours at the bakery. Even though she'd been ordered by their homeroom teacher to quit work and had given a week's notice, her heart swelled in gratitude when her colleagues voiced their displeasure at the latest news. They were glad to have her working alongside them. When the manager suggested that she could return to work during the school holidays next summer, Hana instantly agreed. In high spirits she worked efficiently, yet at the back of her mind she was preoccupied about Jin. Ever since the meeting with their mentor she'd had no contact with him.

She was afraid to text him, confidently guessing that he wouldn't bother replying; visiting his house was out of the question. She was growing worried for him; even though he whined about school and homework, Jin would never dare skip school, and his absence certainly bothered her.

Suddenly her mood sank as she was counting the money within the cash register, and she glanced upwards to heave a deep sigh. Her unease ballooned as she realised he must be in some sort of situation, and rather than contacting Hana, he avoided her. In the past, he would make a phone call or text her if something was amiss. She resolved to drop him a short message during break time, hoping he would at least be courteous enough to reply.

"Hey," Miko said, breezing in from her lunch break. "It's your turn now."

"Okay," Hana muttered.

"You don't look so good. Stop being a coward and just ask him."

"I'm planning to," she agreed with a nod. "He hasn't been to school, but strangely, the teacher never reacted."

"Something is going on." Miko stepped close beside her. "You mentioned his financial situation; what if he quits school?"

"What?" Hana gasped aloud. "I'm sure his mother would be furious."

"But you don't know the details right now," Miko said with a shrug.

"I'll give him a call," Hana whispered. She bent low to retrieve a bag from under the counter and fished out her phone. She was not aware of the message blinking until she slid the icon. There was the name *Jin*, clearly written for her to notice. At first she gasped and smiled, but her happiness drained away after she read the short, formal text.

She pressed a fist against her shuddering chest. "Jin .... Oh no, he needs me!"

"What's wrong, Hana?" Miko asked. "Is everything okay?"

"His mother is in the hospital!" Hana jerked her head upright. "I have to go!"

"But you're working—" Miko blinked in surprise when Hana grabbed her bag and bolted from behind the counter. "Wait, where are you going?"

"The hospital," Hana spoke numbly. "He wants me there."

"What's going on?" Mrs Noshita came out of the back, looking from one to the other. "Suhana, you are leaving?"

"Something urgent came up. I have to go," she implored. "Please."

"Does the manager know about this?" the older lady asked, looking concerned.

"No," Hana tightened her grasp on the strap.

"Hana," Miko said, clutching her upper arm, "call Jin to let him know you'll head over in the evening after your shift ends."

But her phone calls went unanswered, as the three of them stood together in a small circle. Hana's fingers grew more clammy from anxiety every time the operator prompted her to leave a voice message. She cursed out of nowhere, her gaze connecting with the duo.

When Yoshi came out asking for Mrs Noshita, he paused in mid-sentence to observe the heavy atmosphere. "What's wrong?" he said, looking puzzled. "Miko, Hana, did you two fight?"

"I'm sorry," Hana whispered in a strained voice. "But I have to go right now."

"If you walk out, the manager will not be pleased, Hana," Mrs Noshita warned her.

"I've put in my resignation letter," Hana explained in a determined voice. "Right now, he needs me the most."

Miko had exasperation written on her face. "Hana, he has a girlfriend right now, she will take care of him."

"Guys, can we set aside your personal matters and focus?" Yoshi look at each of them. "We have stock count today."

Without a word, Hana slipped away from them. The only sound in her ears was her erratic heartbeat. The moment she stepped out of the bakery, she sped into a run and was soon out of breath. Yet she never slowed in her quest to reach her destination. As she went, she sent countless messages telling Jin she would arrive soon, figuring she wouldn't receive any replies.

In a panic, she restlessly surveyed the J-Line map and decided to travel by taxi. She glanced around before sprinting for the side path and waved madly until one came to a halt. Hana literally flung herself into the back seat, and the vehicle jolted forward, Hana fidgeted, struggling to ignore Miko's words. She shut her eyes, feeling like an idiot to behave this way.

He needs me, she fervently repeated to herself.

It was late afternoon, and she guessed that visiting hours were still open. The building came into view, and the same antsy feeling returned. After handing her cash over to the taxi driver, she bolted out in a hurry. It took some time for Hana to locate the front desk. Approaching the lady behind it, she stammered unintelligibly before taking a deep breath. She said, "May I know the ward number for

Mrs Takami?" Her lips trembled in fear of what she might find behind the curtain.

"Miss, this is the bed number at level three. Turn to your right," the nurse said with a nod.

"Thank you," Hana muttered before fleeing off.

Her footsteps squeaked over the tile floor as she searched for the elevator and checking the location. Finally, she was standing outside the room, which Mrs Takami shared with other patients, trying to calm herself down. Quietly, she stepped inside the ward, ignoring the other patients and their visitors, and came to a halt behind the curtain. With shaking fingers she reached for the material to lift it enough enter, and a sob escaped from her mouth. Jin's mother was hooked to several IV lines, and Jin was asleep on a chair beside the bed, close enough for him to lean both arms on the woman's blanket-covered leg.

Hana walked over to regard the older woman and was stunned speechless. Her beauty was no longer visible; instead, wrinkles of exhaustion predominated. Petrified, she gently caressed the woman's forehead as if fearing she might harm her from mere contact, aware of a tear rolling down her own cheek. A tug on her uniform caught her attention, and she was surprised to see that Jin had grasped her shirt with one hand.

"It's alright," Hana whispered quietly. "I'm here, Jin."

His broad shoulders shuddered as he broke into sobs, and Hana thrust her fingers into his messy hair. He sat upright with a tearful expression, and she pulled him against her stomach, tightening her grip on his shoulders. He was crying into her stomach and wound both arms around her waist to pull her closer. She felt his warm breath as he wept, caressing his soft hair and murmuring to make him feel better.

"She hasn't woken up yet," he explained in a choked voice. "I've lost her, Hana."

"You have not." She lifted his face by cupping with both hands. "She will wake up soon."

He stared up at her with wet eyes as she leaned to kiss him on the forehead. Then, looking back at the woman, feeling uneasy, she sent up prayers for both Jin and his mother.

"Have you eaten lunch, Jin?" she asked.

"I have," he said haltingly. "Um, Shouko drops by after school."

Just then, jealousy coupled with anger moved her to act without thinking. She pushed him away and fled through the curtain, crying behind her hand. Common sense had forsaken her; they were nothing more than friends, even though she saw him as more than that, whereas Shouko and Jin were in a committed relationship. Once upon a time, Hana would have been the first in line to receive either good or bad news from him, but everything had changed.

"Hana, wait!" Jin called from behind her.

"I'm going!" Just as she reached the closing elevator door, she forced herself in.

Jin inserted a hand to stop the door from closing. Then he walked in without a word and dragged Hana into an embrace. The elevator shut them both out from the real world, enveloping them in quietness. She struggled at first within his strong hold but soon caved in to slide her hands upward and wind them around him. They soaked in each other's vibe, and Hana leaned her head against Jin's chest to flutter her eyelids closed.

"Why didn't you call me?" Hana asked in a hurt voice. "Do you hate me that much?"

"Shut up and let me hug you," Jin whispered closer to her ear.

She glanced upward to read Jin's flustered features. Confused by the strange atmosphere, she wondered if he was feeling vulnerable but kept silent and embraced him. Just then, the elevator door slid open, and a startled couple stepped inside. The two teenagers jumped away from each other, and strained awkwardness prevailed as the four people descended to the ground level. As soon as the couple had walked away, both Jin and Hana began to laugh until they were wheezing.

"Their faces …," Jin choked out the words while holding his belly.

"I know!" Hana was cackling aloud only to be hushed by a nearby nurse. "Are you feeling better?"

"Slightly." He nodded once. "Thank you, I needed that."

"You're welcome." She smiled warmly at him. "Jin, don't lose hope about your mother's condition."

"I am at a loss," he said with a sigh before leaning against the wall to slide downward. "She isn't responding."

"What did the doctor tell you?" Hana crouched beside him.

"He said it is both a positive and negative sign," he said, sounding winded. "Her blood pressure is fine. Perhaps she's just fatigued to be sleeping this long."

"Keep that thought in mind," she encouraged him, digging her fingers into his hair.

"I'm sorry, Hana," he apologised. "I should have contacted you as well."

"I'm hurt, you know," Hana told him frankly. "But I don't wish to drag it any further; your mother is our concern right now."

"Yeah." He nodded once. "I'll treat you to lunch as my way of repenting."

"You don't have to," she said, shaking her head.

"Come on." He extended one hand to her. "Up we go."

The two of them walked side by side towards the canteen in amicable silence. Once they were seated, he jogged off to order lunch for her. She bit the corner of her lip, rejoicing in the hug they had shared, and curled her hands around herself to keep Jin's warmth closer—although something else crept out of nowhere: guilt. Her smile vanished when she pictured Shouko's face. Even though it was a simple embrace, Hana was felt as if they had wronged Shouko. Yet she put on a determined expression; Jin was her best friend, and she would be there for him.

"You okay?"

She jumped when Jin's voice interrupted her deep thoughts. She peered at him as he slid a tray in front of her and then plopped onto the chair opposite to look at her intensely. Suddenly she felt nervous as she dug into a bowl of ramen noodles, with steam drifting upward.

Now and then she surreptitiously peeked at Jin's face, only to catch him observing her, causing warmth to creep onto her face. Then he laid his chopsticks aside to connect their gazes together.

"What is it?" Hana muttered.

He jerked his chin towards her. "You are wearing your work uniform."

"I ran out of the store." She pushed a lock of hair behind an ear. "When I saw your message, something snapped in me."

"What?" He blinked several times. "You ran?"

"I was working," she said with a shrug. "I might be fired for my careless behaviour, but that's not the point."

"Hana." Jin's voice rose, only to be cut off by her.

"I have given my resignation letter, so I'm not at a loss." She smiled while curling her fingers over his own.

"Hana, you have to stop being irrational." He rubbed a hand over his eyes. "You're drowning me in further."

"Drowning you?" She tilted her head. "What do you mean?"

"Idiot, do you want me to kiss your feet?" he hissed while glaring at her. "I've been hurting you all this time."

"Jin, are you sure you want to discuss this right now?" She let her face convey her forlorn feeling at his words.

"No," he replied after a moment. "I'm sorry."

"Never mind that. Where have you been sleeping?"

"Here," he answered while slipping his hand gently from under hers. "I only take showers at home before rushing back."

"I hate the idea that you are by yourself," she said, leaning back.

"This is my family matter, so I have to be here," Jin said softly. "I don't wish to burden anyone—"

"I won't listen to you," she said, pointing a finger at his shocked face.

"What?"

"You, Mister, will be coming over to my place," Hana ordered.

"What?" He sputtered several times. "Hana, what do you mean?"

"You heard me right, Jin!" she snapped at him. "You're only a teenager but pretending to be an adult—"

"Hana!" he shouted at her.

"Stop it! You have no right to keep all of this burden to yourself, you stupid boy!" She loomed over the table. "Do you think this will make everything better? No! Jin, it is all right to share this burden with someone you love."

"Don't make me lose my temper, Hana." He was looking downwards. "Stop this right now."

"Look at me. I said look at me!" She stomped over to his side to turn his head with her hands. "You will collapse if you don't stop this. Jin, what will happen to your mother if she learns that her actions caused her only son to be hurt?"

"No," he said, his lips trembling from his strong emotions. "I don't know what to do, Hana."

"You have me," Hana whispered to him. "Jin, my parents will welcome you to stay in our house until your mother heals."

"But what if Shouko—" He cut the sentence short. "I did not mean to—"

"We don't have to inform her." She sat back down to look at him directly.

"She'll be angry at me," he finally added.

"Jin, I won't force you." She put on a smile, but it never reached her eyes.

"I …." He scrubbed his face with two hands, grunting wordlessly, before nodding once. "I'm tired, Hana; all of this is taking a huge toll on me."

"My stepfather will drive you here in the morning." She placed a finger on his lips to silence his complaint.

He smiled in a carefree manner. "I am glad to have you as my friend, Hana. Thank you."

"You're welcome." She tilted her head and winked at him. "Come on, we can sit at the ward after I make a short call back home."

Chapter 19

The entrance door to Hana's apartment swung open to admit her and Jin after a hectic day at the hospital. They both had weary features, and the sun had long ago dipped below the horizon. She went further into the living room barefoot, whilst Jin remained stoic in a corner, showing a blank expression. She switched on the lights, resulting in a bright ambience.

The atmosphere had been rather tense during the phone call earlier with her parents. Hana had completely forgotten about their travelling to a hot spring with a few colleagues. Yet they agreed wholeheartedly to allow Jin to reside for a night or two. She had handed the device over to him and watched his nervous face as he talked briefly with them before returning her phone.

Hana came over to look at him. "Why are you standing here? Are you feeling all right, Jin?"

"Yeah," he said. "I'm just not sure how to act right now."

"What do you mean?" She tilted her head, a little confused.

"Usually, your mother is quite overprotective when I'm here," he said with a shrug.

"She doesn't hate you, Jin." Hana shook her head. "Sit down, I'll bring a glass of cold water for you."

"But thank you for having me here," he said with a little bow.

Her heart squeezed slightly. "You're welcome."

Hana brought a chilled mug from the kitchen and watched him take a drink as she sat on another sofa. After his protest, Jin finally relented after Hana persuaded him. She had talked herself down from the obvious reasons behind her action, advising herself that he was in dire need of somebody closer to him. She glanced down at her fingers clenched onto her knees as silence went on between them. In the past, Jin had often dropped by to play or during festivals such as Diwali, some of which had taught him about their cultural differences. Both his mother and Jin would leave the apartment with smiles on their faces. Then puberty had struck, and Hana's mother lectured her about being alert as an adolescent female, but that never deterred her from visiting Jin's house on a daily basis. There was no reason for them not to be in the same space.

"Hana?"

She jolted slightly when Jin's voice snatched her back to the present. She blinked several times and focused on his face. He was leaning forward with a concern look, and she realised he must have been calling her, but she never replied.

She got up smile down at him. "I'll bring my stepfather's shirt for you to wear," she said. "You can take a shower after me."

"Sure," he mumbled while not glancing upward from his cell phone.

Hana left the living room after switching the television on for Jin. Inside her bedroom she grabbed her sleeping dress. Distracted, she regarded the material bunched in one hand. It was a plain long-sleeved kurta in a cerulean shade. She thought, *It never did much for sex appeal*, only to gape in shock at her wayward thoughts.

Just then, she overheard a baritone voice outside her room. She tiptoed to peek past the slightly open door. Jin was speaking on the phone. She slipped out of the room towards the bathroom when she paused at the mention of Shouko's name. She turned halfway around to view the back of Jin's frame as he chattered on the phone. He was not aware of her presence and continued speaking quietly as if fearing someone might overhear the conversation.

"I'm fine, I promise," he said softly over the phone. "Yeah, I had my dinner earlier; what about you?"

All the while, Hana remained in the same position, feeling bitterness creep into her heart. She recalled Miko's words before she left the bakery without thinking about the circumstances, further hurting herself. Even then, her selfishness wouldn't allow Hana to hang back.

Jin began to walk in a circle while Hana hid from view, spying a small smile on his lips. Unlike before, Jin was more at ease while on the phone, but his next words shattered her emotions into a thousand shards, piercing her heart even more deeply.

"It's all right. I understand why your parents won't let a boy live under the same roof." He sighed, rubbing the back of his neck. "No, I'm overnighting at my neighbour's home. Yeah, the old man has known our family for a long time. Thank you, Shouko. I love you too."

Heartbroken, Hana locked the bathroom door, a sob climbing up her throat while her lips trembled with emotion. She leaned backwards against the entrance to breathe evenly. When she was able to move forward, she stripped off the rest of her clothes to stare at her reflection. She saw another resembling herself, with eyes swollen from crying, her tanned face exuding exhaustion. In fact, Hana was both mentally and physically drained. She choked on a sob, and when another slipped out, she was crouching with one hand clutching the basin while wailing behind her palm so as not to let out the sound.

She had brought all of this upon herself; the agony of hearing him being sweet and gentle yet cold and distant to Hana cut her even deeper. They'd had a good chemistry before, but everything was disrupted after her sudden confession; even though she had other plans, she had fallen in love with him. It took a long time for Hana to climb into the shower and the hot droplets pelting her. She spent the time collecting her lost composure and breathing slowly and carefully.

At last, solemn and subdued, she got out of the bathroom. She went to where Jin was collapsed on the sofa, randomly switching channels. He glanced up, surprising her with a smile, although it didn't seem complete. With a prolonged sigh, he got to his feet, passing her on the way but coming to a halt when Hana spoke up.

Without turning to look at him and lowering her head to study the tiles, she whispered, "Do you hate being here, Jin?"

"No," he said after a moment of reflection. "Hana, stop worrying over me."

Why did you cling to me at the hospital? her inner voice said mockingly.

The click of the bathroom door separated the pair when Hana moved on to the kitchen to cook a simple dish for the night, since the meal at the hospital wasn't up to her taste standards. Languidly, she resumed cutting, Soothed by the staccato beat of the chopping blade. By the time she was stir-frying eggs with vegetables and rice was set to a timer, someone came to peek curiously over her shoulder. He took in an elaborate sniff, earning a laugh from her.

"Go away," she said and pushed at him, only to be startled by his bare body. "Where's your shirt?"

"You never lent me one," he replied in a casual tone.

"I'll bring you one—"

"No, thanks, because it will make feel weird wearing your stepfather's shirt," he chortled while taking over to stir the condiment.

"You'll feel cold later in the night," she said listlessly, trying once again, but Jin was adamant: he would walk around without a shirt on.

"I'm used to it." He gave her a heart-warming grin, and she could not argue further. "Hana, I want to thank you for being here for me."

"I'm not going anywhere," she whispered.

"You're a strong person," he said after a while. "I don't think I'd have the ability to face someone I had confessed to."

From the corner of her eyes, she caught Jin halting in the middle of stirring to draw in a deep breath before glancing apologetically her way. He was having trouble with the current situation, but Hana was grateful that they were able to stand side by side while interacting just as before. She playfully flicked water towards his face, eliciting a shout of surprise. Soon the pair, in a comradely mood, ventured out with heaping plates to settle down on the couch while the television played in the background. Suddenly Jin let loose a moan of appreciation, flustering Hana even while she giggled.

"When did you learn to cook?" he said, chewing on a big bite.

"Not too long ago," she replied, one eye on a game show. "I realise cooking helps me to focus."

"I must be the cause for making you lose focus," he said beneath his breath.

"Why do you say that?" She turned to look at him.

"Because I hurt you, right?" he whispered. "I'm sorry that I could not fall in love with you."

You never gave us a chance, Jin, her inner voice said forlornly.

"You don't have to apologise," she said with a straight face while shifting her gaze elsewhere.

Silence fell between them, neither of them able to focus on the screen. At last Hana rose to clear away the plates; he did the same and then helped by washing the dishes. Then the ambience suddenly became tense; she figured it was time for her to retreat within her bedroom. She saw Jin focusing on text messages; he must have put his device to silent mode.

"You can sleep on my bed while I head over to my—"

"No," he cut her off in a stern voice. "I'll take the couch, thank you."

"But—"

She squeaked in shock when Jin used both fists to rub her temples roughly. Her heart skipped a beat to see a smile lighting his handsome face, and she was surprised by a strong urge to give him a kiss. She pushed aside the idea, figuring it might scare him enough that he would abandon her just as before. The memory brought a bitter taste to her mouth.

Or even worse, he won't think twice leaving you for her. The inner voice dripped with jealousy.

"I'll be all right, Hana," he said with a smile. "You've given me so much to be grateful for."

"Okay, I'll bring out the pillows as well as a blanket." She took several steps back, aware that something could definitely transpire if choices were given.

After arranging the pillows on the couch while Jin went off to the bathroom, she doused the lights while keeping the kitchen switched on in case the boy got thirsty. She paused at a little temple with a small statue of Goddess Durga Ganpati adorned by flowers and folded her hands in prayer. She asked for strength, for bravery to face the upcoming obstacles, and for Mrs Takami's fast recovery so that Jin could suffer less. Then she moved on to her bedroom. Acting a little petty, she had lent her friend pillows of her own when she suddenly thought about drool spots or odour. She made a quick detour to retrieve them, only to bump into Jin.

"Oi, where are you running off to?" he asked, keeping a firm grip on her arms.

"N-nowhere," she replied in a thready tone. "Have a good night. If you need anything, just knock on my door."

"Right." He nodded once and let go of her. "Um, I wish I could hug you, but that's one boundary I don't wish to cross anymore."

"Because Shouko would not be pleased; I get it." Hana stared up at his embarrassed face with her hurt one.

Without another word, she strode back into her room to close it in front of his face. She leaned sideways against the door, emitting a sigh before moving off to the mattress and climbing on top to roll on her side. Just then, a giddy happiness took over her system at the thought that Jin was beyond the shut doorway. It was amazing how a change in feelings allowed her to see things so differently. One hand slid over a pillow belonging to her mother while she stared into darkness. She curled her fingers into a fist, wishing he would walk in and confess about his feelings. Yet it was only a dream woven by a girl lost in her own fantasy realm.

Finally, Hana drifted into a dreamless state. The glowing red numerals showed it was half past one when a weird noise roused her from her deep slumber. She blinked to scan the room with a trickle of fear before acknowledging that she was not alone in the house with a sigh of relief. The she tuned in again to the sound and hastily jumped out of the bed to rush out, tripping on her way towards Jin, who was making a fuss in his sleep. When her hands came in contact with his skin, she discovered perspiration all over as he choked on a cry.

In panic she tried to wake him up. "Jin!" she called aloud. "Wake up; it's only a dream!"

"Ma …." Jin's breath hitched, and he was thrashing. "D-don't!"

"Wake up!" She shook his bare shoulders roughly while sitting on the edge of the couch. "Jin, stop it!"

Hana gripped his face firmly until his eyes snapped open. His pupils were dilated, tears leaked out to mix with sweat, and he was breathing in short gasps. He jerked wide eyes towards her face looming over him. Deeply concerned, she hushed him softly. At last he was breathing normally, although they kept on gazing at each other as if seeking comfort. She caressed Jin's forehead, ignoring the stickiness; she leaned slightly forward, her breasts resting on his forearm, and grasped his hand, which clutched onto her like a lifeline.

"It's all right," she whispered in a soothing tone. "It's all right, your mother will be fine."

"I'm scared, Hana," he said in a quiet voice. "What if she has passed away?"

She shook her head. "Don't think so negatively."

"But I can't stop myself." His face crumpled under strong emotions. "You know how much I adore my mother."

"I know." She gave an encouraging smile, even though inwardly she too was worried about his mother.

Taking a huge leap, Hana touched their foreheads together, letting her own emotions loose, hating the fact that she had the right to make him feel better, to comfort the boy she loved so much that getting hurt repeatedly was becoming normal for her. Her eyes widened when she sensed strong arms wrapping around her shoulders, pulling her head closer to his neck where she nuzzled deeply, realising that her tears were flowing as well.

A shudder ran through her when Jin burrowed his face against her hair. "Lend me your strength," he said in a low voice.

"Jin, you always have me by your side, come rain or shine," she said, sobbing quietly.

"You are strong," he acknowledged.

"I'm not." She shook her head—awkwardly, in this strange position.

"I was wrong about you." His breath warmed her ear.

Hana felt the first thump of her heartbeat as she curled her fingers behind his neck as they remained in close contact. Her feet were still on the floor while her upper body lay on his. Just then, he pushed at her face so they gazed at each other. She saw her reflection in his dark brown eyes. Then she climbed to rest fully on top of him, pulling the blanket over them both.

I love you, she promised silently.

Out of nowhere, bravery seized hold of her, and she brought his hand closer to kiss each finger. Then a gasp was torn from her because she was staring up at Jin, now looming above her. They sealed their mouths together in a kiss that sprang from unknown feelings. With no words spoken between them, Jin lifted her in his arms; with her long hair draped over an arm, he manoeuvred towards the open bedroom while she clung to him, breathing in his masculine scent, still in a euphoric state. Something else was about to transpire behind the now closed door. On her back, she stared at the familiar wall until he covered her soft frame with his own.

Chapter 20

*J*in rested both hands on either side of Hana's head to push himself upward while gazing down at Hana, their bodies touching, eyes locked together. Even though quietness blanketed them exception for their breathing in shallow puffs from exhilaration, he experienced comfort. For tonight, he was letting his inner emotions to rule instead of keeping them bottled up. Hence the explosion, although he was too proud and fearful to admit what the feelings actually meant for his best friend.

Then her soft hands caressed his face before tugging him downward to fuse her mouth with his. He moved his lips over hers while tilting sideways for a better access.

The room became warm even though an air conditioner whirred in the background. Sweat began to pop out all over him. It was a different experience with Hana, and he trailed butterfly kisses over her breast, sniffing her delicate scent.

A tear leaked from Hana's eye to roll down her flushed cheek. In an instant her smile gave way to a serious countenance. Ever since that confession she had been weeping by herself. He tugged her forward so that their bodies aligned, and he pressed his puckered lips onto her forehead with their palms connected; a newfound feeling enfolded him from the depths of his heart. Then a realisation struck him, how they were compatible both in body and in their personalities. Tonight it was all about Jin and Hana learning behind the tenderness.

By morning, the unlikely pair were snoozing, wrapped in each other's arms. Jin fluttered his eyelids open to stare at the other end of the bedroom where a wedge of sunlight beamed through the partially open curtain. He was resting his head on Hana's soft breast when he moved to perch on one elbow to regard the scenario: amidst little hickeys all along her neck he spied beard flush. She slept on like a babe when he sat upright to scrub his hands over his face, sighing aloud.

Last night was both memorable as well as hazy. He had let the fragility of his circumstances lead to a mistake that could not be undone. Just then, Hana murmured in her sleep; as if on cue, a message alarm beeped. He reached over her to peek at the phone and felt blood draining from his face. Shouko's name struck him motionless. He began to hyperventilate and widened his eyes in horror, replaying last night like a silent movie. He inched backwards to lean on the cold wall because of the new emotion that had surfaced—the lovemaking frightened him to the core.

What have I done? he shouted mentally.

"Love you," she whispered, giggling as she drowsed.

This cannot be happening, Jin said to himself, in rising panic. *I cheated on my girlfriend.*

"Jin?" Hana woke up, increasing his panic. "Good morning." She sat up to give him a big hug, her smile vibrant.

But Jin had already shut down. He noticed dried blood droplets staining the cover, and he let his anger carry him away. He clutched Hana's arms firmly, drawing a soft yelp from her. He held them apart so they could see each other, and when Hana realised that he was not pleased, a more distant look came over her.

"You", he seethed, "took advantage of me."

"What?" Her eyes searched his face. "Jin, what are you saying?"

"You took this opportunity to sleep with me!" he roared, frightening her.

"No!" Hana began to tremble in his grasp, tears welling up. "It's not like that!"

"You've wanted to fuck me ever since that idea came over you!" He was breathing loudly.

"Jin!" she sobbed, abruptly looking hurt.

He hopped out of the bed as if burned. In jerky motions he collected his scattered clothes. Just then his cell phone rang, and the his anxious heartbeat slowed when he saw the hospital number. He glared at Hana before walking out of the bedroom to answer the call. A huge weight lifted off him when the doctor attending his mother gave him the positive news that she was awake with no further complications.

Suddenly he felt a presence by his side. "Jin?"

"I'm going home," he said without looking at her. "Leave me alone."

"But—"

"I said it once; don't make me repeat it!" he yelled in her ashen face.

"Why are you so angry at me?" she wailed in a high-pitched tone.

"Because you seized this chance to fuck me. Hana, you have used me when I'm feeling lonely!" he replied while marching towards her.

She back-pedalled until she bumped against the wall. "You were willing to be with me!" she screamed at him.

"Shut up!" he shouted turning a blind eye to the truth.

"You could have stopped anytime—"

"I said be quiet, Hana!" he yelled even louder. "You have officially lost a friend in me."

"No," she pleaded tearfully. "Jin, please …."

He quickly put on the rest of his clothes, ignoring her cries because he felt the same way. Panic and confusion surged inside him as he headed for the front door. Then she flung herself onto his back, arms wrapped around him. Jin pushed her arms away without turning around and let himself out the entrance. Hana's sorrowful cries following him to the elevator.

When the elevator door opened in the lobby, Jin exited at a run, slipping on the tiled floor before straightening to continue fleeing from the hellish place. He had cheated behind Shouko's back; the poor girl didn't deserve his unfaithfulness. At the same time, he was too much of a coward to explain why it had happened, and hoped to keep it a secret from her.

He ran all the way to the hospital. When he stepped inside, he collapsed on his knees, filling his labouring lungs with oxygen, when someone offered a paper cup, concerned over his dishevelled appearance.

When he stood up at last, he realised he had been barefoot the whole time. He cursed his stupidity, but there was no way he would dare return for his shoes. Instead, he would purchase a new pair. When he reached the ward, he overheard her familiar voice from behind the curtain. He shoved it aside and saw his mother sitting comfortably. A smile lit her pretty face.

In silence he walked over and embraced her. Then, still nuzzled against her, he murmured, "I miss you, Mom."

"I'm sorry, my dearest, son," she apologised in a soothing tone.

"Don't ever scare me like this again," he said tightening his arms around her.

"I promise, Jin."

Chapter 21

Two Months Later

The evening sky was a vivid mandarin tone intermingled with a roseate hue forming a beautiful backdrop. Yet Hana stared blankly out her window, tears dripping from her chin and blurring her vision. In the last two months, her health was deteriorating, but she could not lessen her suffering and heartache. Jin had torn her heart and taken it with him when he had stormed out of the apartment like a tornado as she grappled with the sudden loss of her close friend. The hurtful event replayed endlessly in tiny fragments, piercing her over and over again.

In the classroom, Jin pretended not to notice her existence, and one by one, everyone came to see the tense situation between them. Still, nobody said anything; after all, she was not an important figure. The rest of them were busy with their own lives. Meanwhile, she had to bear the agony of watching Jin and Shouko together, merging their paths and leaving Hana to pick up the debris left behind in the recesses of her aching heart.

When a noise from outside her bedroom announced her mother's arrival, Hana glanced at the shut door. She'd been tuning into her parents' footsteps recently, as they had been acting strangely whenever they thought she was not looking at them. But she was too consumed by her personal dilemma to focus elsewhere. She crossed to the bed frame and collapsed on the cool coverlet, placing her back towards the doorway.

Neena had returned to her workaholic ways. Although this was the old "normal", Hana yearned for some warmth from her but never asked for it. The woman often holed up inside her bedroom to murmur over the phone, her low voice audible through the ajar door. Finally Hana dozed off in a fitful slumber, waking up to cold sweat and Jin's voice ringing in her ears.

She looked at the alarm, watching the numbers change. Like every other day, she went through her routine before heading out to school. Summer was approaching, but even the idea of smiling hurt her. It was a torture to sit in the same class as Jin. She moved around in a daze, the rumble of her belly reminding her that she'd forgotten to eat dinner last night. But she was falling into the habit of ignoring meals and wallowing in misery; she wiped away a trickling tear, looking downward.

Standing in one corner, Hana surreptitiously watched Jin running in every direction within the gym hall, engrossed in the activity. He was soaked in perspiration, his face flushed a vivid peach hue from the exertion, yet he looked determined as he swung a badminton racket. She had been sitting out the most vigorous activities more often than not.

Just then Jin burst into fits of laughter. Hana sat down on the floor, hugging her legs closer. Jin had adapted the role of ignoring Hana effortlessly, which always gave her a twinge because she could not push him aside on cue. She felt the first stab inside her gut, a hint that she might be suffering from a stomach ache, but she bit her lip against a wave of mind-numbing agony and leaned her head against her knees, inhaling and exhaling carefully. Still, nothing much changed. Just then, something hit the top of her head, and she looked up to view Jin's sombre features nearby as he picked up the shuttlecock before resuming his game.

Time for my medication, she thought with a sigh.

Someone mentioned her name. "Suhana, do you want to play with us? We need one more player."

"I'll pass, sorry." Hana shook her head and stood up to ask permission from the instructor to return back to the classroom. "I am having gastric issues right now."

"You seem to have fallen ill quite frequently," her classmate frowned slightly. "Maybe you should stay at home to recuperate."

"It's all right, and a test is approaching. It's no time to dilly-dally." She shrugged, attempting a smile. "But thank you for your concern."

This will not do, she thought, groaning aloud.

When the pain became unbearable, with one arm around her belly she paused to speak with the gym teacher. Then she left the stuffy lot to amble towards the classroom. After retrieving the medicine from her backpack pocket, she downed the pill with a swallow of water. She spent most of the school hours sleeping off the drug, which was supposed to ease her gastric problem. Although her mother had firmly insisted she stop "dieting", Hana threw caution to the wind.

Little by little, she had grown conscious of her body issues. She was losing weight rapidly but dismissed the symptoms, but when her monthly menstruation stopped altogether, she couldn't help feeling nervous.

Hana attended the last subject, but fatigue overcame her, and before she knew what had happened, someone was rousing her from sleep. Her head was on the desk, and her arms were hanging on either side when her eyes snapped open; she barely stopped herself from drooling. She sat upright with such force that she jarred the desk, making Mr Hayamato jump.

Hana blinked and stared at him in surprise. "Huh? Class has ended?"

"Yeah, everyone had gone home," the teacher said with a shrug. He watched her clearing up her desk. "I've been meaning to ask … what happened between Jin and you?"

"Our friendship is now in the past," Hana mumbled. Saying the words out loud put more strain on her.

"I tried to ask him a couple of times, but he simply shrugs me off." Mr Hayamato tapped his feet repeatedly on the floor. "Jin acts so different now."

"He is different," she whispered. "Mr Hayamato, can we talk?"

"I'm bad at giving advice," he said, stiffening when she sighed aloud. "But I can listen to you."

"Never mind, let's go home," she said with a half-hearted smile. "Exams are finally here."

"Summer too, which means the sports festival." He groaned.

"True. I hate sports."

"Me too," he chuckled as they walked out in silence. "I'll see you tomorrow; good luck."

"Thank you, Mr Hayamato. You too."

Walking under the cloudless azure, Hana was lost in thought, feeling sweat trickling low on her spine. The heat was growing unbearable since summer was around the corner. She felt a yearning to drench her palate with an ice cream. After purchasing a cone, she found their usual spot on the park bench empty, and she sat down.

Licking the sweetness of the melting cream, she whimsically wondered how many times she and Jin had sat here. With a bittersweet smile, she whispered, "Too many times to count. I'll begin counting the times I've sat alone before I can move on."

I don't think moving on is an option for me, an inner voice said to her.

By late evening, Hana returned home. She had no sooner stepped inside when she accidentally overheard the adults talking in the living room. Her mouth snapped shut at what she heard as she quietly secure the heavy entrance door without a sound. She tiptoed to peek around the corner at her mother and her stepfather, their features a mixture of emotions.

"This might be our last time as a family."

"What about Hana?"

"What about me?" Hana announced her arrival, surprising them.

The two of them jumped to their feet as if caught red-handed. As before, Neena was too absorbed by the alterations in her life to notice what was transforming her daughter. Neena and Abe exchanged nervous looks but pasted on brave smiles. Still, Hana spied the glimmer of tears in her mother's gaze, intensifying her suspicion.

"Are you two divorcing?" Her voice was a little higher than she'd intended.

"Of course not!" Neena shook her head. "We were discussing our trip for the summer holiday."

"What makes you think we'll be able to go for a vacation?" Hana never budged from the spot, glaring at them. "I'm not sure about my grades …."

"With you, Hana, I can be assured the scores will be high," her mother acknowledged with a wide smile. "Have you eaten?"

"Yeah," she lied boldly before shuffling off for the bedroom. "I'm tired. I'll have dinner after my short nap."

"By the way, Hana, I saw Jin along the pathway," her stepfather said out of the blue, putting an invisible strain on her. "Does he have a girlfriend right now?"

"I don't know," she continued without looking behind. "Why don't you ask Jin if he has one or not?"

"Hana," Neena snapped at her, "why are you talking so rudely?"

"Oh, the upcoming sport event? I'm not participating." She paused at the doorway to glance at them. "Please don't come."

From the other side of the locked door, Hana heard them talking about her moody behaviour, but her stepfather concluded that all teenagers have their moment to rebel. While she lazed on the mattress, still in her school uniform, her eyelids drooped shut. The only good coming out of being alone was that she could sleep and conjure makeshift dreams with happy endings. Once again, she skipped dinner using the same excuse repeatedly of being exhausted. At least it was partially true; she was mentally and physically tuckered out.

Of course, school was hectic. Between studying and nursing her ill health, Hana was getting even more worried about her delayed menstruation. Meanwhile, their class president had decided that those not participating in the sports would be responsible to create banners and a cheer squad for their classmates. Amongst the divided group Hana was required to decorate the cardboards, once again pitted beside the usual girls. Although Suzumi paid her no attention, the rest of them were slowly getting along better with Hana, who took the extra step of helping them.

"Suhana, I'm buying lunch. What would you like to eat?" Hanabi said, standing to stretch her back.

"You don't have to get me anything," she said, concentrating on her sketch on coloured paper.

"I've been meaning to ask, Suhana, you aren't eating much ever since we began to work together," another piped in with a furrowed expression. "Are you still embarrassed around us?"

"No, I just don't eat much anymore," Hana replied with a shrug.

"Hey, both Jin and you really broke apart as friends?" Suzumi paused from shading an alphabet.

"Yeah, we needed some space between us." She nodded dismissively, hoping to close the subject, but the other girl became persistent.

"Well, you aren't fooling me." She tilted her head while leaning backwards on both hands. "It's embarrassing, but many of us can read you like an open book, Suhana. We've caught you staring at him."

"Suzumi, I think we must respect Suhana's privacy," Aika butted in. "Why are you always attacking her?"

"As if you girls haven't gossiped about her!" Suzumi retorted, her face turning beet red. "I'm just being vocal, unlike the rest of you."

"But we stopped attacking her," another responded. "Stop dragging us into your petty fight."

"Can we stop, please?" Hana whispered in an attempt to break up the bickering. "I really don't care about all that."

"Suzumi, we all know that you've been jealous of Jin and Suhana's friendship," Maiko spat out.

"Shut up!" Suzumi yelled aloud. "Why are you defending Suhana suddenly?"

"Because we are so used to seeing them together, it feels different right now," another explained while looking at Hana who was trembling inwardly. "Suhana, you should eat and stop hurting yourself."

"Please—" She choked on the plea.

"Suhana, we apologise for behaving rudely to you," Hanabi said in a low voice.

Out of the blue, Hana released one quiet sob as she sat like a depressed rag doll. Unsure, the rest of the girls watched her unfurl when Suzumi began to pack her belongings in a jerky manner. The sound of her slippers hitting on the concrete tiles just then, she was obviously perturbed,

Suzumi returned to glare down at Hana who was swiping away the tears. "Have some dignity. You're mooning after a guy who is in a relationship with someone else!" Her voice rang outside in the empty corridor. "Jin must have felt your possessiveness over him to push Suhana far from him."

"Suzumi!" someone gasped at her audacity.

"Enough!" Hana screeched, standing upright to glare back. "You have no right to judge me or my relationship with Jin because Suzumi is an outsider. As far as I'm concerned, he never cared about how you felt for him."

Suddenly she felt the blood draining from her brain. She began to weave on her feet while black spots appeared in her vision. The group of girls rushed over to grab her, but she pushed them away. She was hyperventilating a little, shaking, hardly hearing their words asking her to remain behind to complete half of the work. She ran out on unsteady legs with tears blurring her vision. No matter the places, she was still unwanted, and the truth hurt her more than she could admit.

She came to a halt beyond the school gate, leaning over with two hands on her knees, crying her heart out.

"Everyone hates me so much," she whimpered quietly. "All of them …."

Chapter 22

The summer sun glared mercilessly while students gathered from many schools. Sports Day was held on the weekend, a two-day event, when parents came in to support their children. Some adults joined in to hand over bottled drinks as well as meals throughout the afternoon. Teachers blowing shrill whistles and cheers erupting from spectators filled the air; the school ground was covered in tents with colourful banners proudly displaying the name of each school.

Between lugging boards and standing to wait, Hana wiped her perspiring forehead with her short sleeves as they marched back and forth looking determined.

"Suhana, please wait here while I take Hiro to the nurse's office," she said, beaming at her.

"Sure." Hana nodded smiling a little. "Be careful."

"Oi, I don't need to be coddled from a girl like you …," said Hiro.

The bickering pair walked away into the sea of students. Then Hana caught sight of Jin's mother arriving to settle on a patch of grass underneath the shade of a tree. In the meantime, her son was flexing and bending to warm up for a relay race on the other side, surrounded by his friends. Suddenly Hana felt the urge to empty her stomach. Dumping the boards on the ground, she made a beeline for the back of the gym class and crouched to vomit heavily.

She took her time to return, catching sight of the rest of her classmates giving her peeved looks as she slowly approached. They were clutching the decorative boards she had dropped. When Hana caught Jin's gaze, he only turned away.

Suzumi began to berate her in a loud tone, turning many heads. "We put so much hard work into this, so don't throw it on the ground!"

"I wasn't feeling well. I'm sorry," Hana told them. "I promise not to act without thinking the next time."

"Suhana, maybe you should sit down somewhere," Aika remarked.

"Suhana!" a familiar voice called out to her. "Over here!"

Dreading what was next, Hana glanced towards the woman calling her, who was waving a hand, beckoning Hana to approach her corner. Trying not to be rude, she nervously walked towards Jin's mother, looking over a shoulder to catch Jin's look from afar. He had a stormy glower for her, but she figured he might be worried that secrets would come out about their broken friendship. She sent a slight nod and smile his way, letting him feel at ease.

"Mrs Takami, how are you feeling?" Hana bowed at the pretty woman.

"I'm fine, thank you." Sayomi grinned while setting out lunch on the spread blanket. "How are you, Suhana? You seem rather thinner now."

"Oh, I haven't been feeling well," she said with a casual shrug. "My parents send their regards to Mrs Takami, wishing you good health."

"Please do the same for me. Also, you haven't been visiting us." Sayomi tilted her head curiously.

"My mom feels I should be concentrating for the upcoming tests," she said with an endearing smile.

"Ma, I would like you to meet someone." Jin came out of nowhere, and tagging along behind him was Shouko, with a demure demeanour. "She's the girlfriend I've been telling you about."

Hana was shocked when Jin on purpose banged his tall frame against her to block her from Sayomi's vision. His mother gasped in pure delight at the newcomer; instantly, she patted the empty space beside her in invitation. Hana felt her pulse rise but continued to breathe evenly through her nostrils while awkwardly standing to one side while Jin's mother focused her easy smile on Shouko, waiting for her to sit down with them as well. Hana's face crumpled under an onslaught of emotions, and she moved back one step at a time, waving both hands, before turning to walk away, hugging herself.

She could not dispel the sickening image of the three of them, relaxed with each other, whereas Hana could only stare as an outsider. With her stomach tightening, she rested under the shade of the tent, ignoring the cheery atmosphere and struggling to avert a panic attack. Even though Jin hurting her over and over, she could not push him away from the depths of her mind.

Soon, Jin was standing on the track while the rest of them, except Hana, yelled for him to do his best. Everyone heard the other competitors bantering him, despite their awareness of how strong Jin was in sports. Shouko came to stand beside Hana, along with some of her friends; their playful voices grated on Hana's nerves.

Just then, the runners started off. The crowd cheered, roaring multiple names to urge on the athletes. Cut up in the atmosphere of excitement, even Hana continuously cheered for him. "Run!" she cried, jumping up and down, eyes fixed on Jin. "Hurry!"

On cue, everyone around her raised their voices and their fists, proudly looking on as their friends gave a supreme effort. Hana covered her mouth, amazed at Jin and his competitor running neck and neck. Abruptly, Jin passed off the baton, stumbling a few steps before tumbling onto the track. Hana's ears rang from the crowd's shrill cries and whistles; in the meantime, Jin was flat on his back, humorously panting to regain his lost energy.

"We won!" Ino clapped ecstatically. "Everyone, we won!"

"Yes!" they all joined in.

Hana clapped too. For the first time, she was starting to enjoy the event. Suddenly Jin, with the rest of his relay team, joined them, and because in an excess of joy he grabbed Hana's shoulder, a gleeful expression on his sweaty face, and shook her frame.

"Did you see that, Hana?" he yelled, his eyes gleaming with excitement. "I literally flew with wings attached on my ankles!"

"Yes, I saw you!" she eagerly replied, looking into his face.

"Jin!" Shouko came over with stunned features.

As if roused from a dream, Jin released his grip from Hana's shoulder, shock transforming his expression before he turned to focus on the other girl. Hana allowed the rest of the classmates to swallow her up as they reached out to congratulate them, and she drifted off like a fish jostled by a dangerous wave.

During the rest of Sports Day, she withdrew. She remained reclusive when the eve ushered in the traditional bonfire, with students gathered to relax and chat with each other.

"Hey." Ino walked over to sit beside her. "I'm so tired."

"Hm," she murmured, never glancing away from the crackling fire.

He peeked at Hana's dull face. "You okay?"

"No," she replied quietly.

"I'm sorry for asking that stupid question." He shook his head but sighed aloud. "Hana, how long will you keep this up?"

"What do you mean?" she whispered, watching Jin and Shouko holding hands at the far end of the field.

He searched her face. "Stop hurting yourself. Look at me. Suzumi rejected me, but I move along because that's the sad truth. At the same time, I got to see her true nature, saving me from a messy break-up."

"Ino, do you know how long Jin and I have been friends?" Hana felt the stab of pain in her heart when the loving couple strolled out of sight. "We were inseparable, but right now, my brain cannot take the hint that our friendship is no more."

"I may look like a bumbling idiot, but I do see what goes on around me." He sat cross-legged, taking in the scenery. "You have lost weight."

"Glad someone notices me dying one day at a time," she whispered brokenly. "My days have become a living shadow—crying, writhing in agony, crying, and taking medicines."

"You are suffering, not him." Ino shrugged. "Jin is floating on could nine with his girlfriend, whereas you're lapsing into illness."

"How do you know I'm sick?" she asked, finally peeking at him.

"I don't share much about myself, but I'm a regular patient visiting my family doctor." His face contorted into a sheepish, frustrated expression. "I've been sick since middle school."

"Oh." Hana blinked once in realisation. "My mother is beginning to notice my transformation, although my lies are getting drier."

"I know earlier I've said that I give out bad advice. But watching Suhana in this state pains me; move on—leave Jin behind."

The words instantly pierced Hana's heart, bursting the bubble of tears choking her throat. As they began to flow, she stared blindly at her hands in between her crossed legs, watching the droplets falling on her olive skin. Then she stared up into the darkening sky with a heavy sigh. Her lips were trembling, but she nodded unsteadily when Ino gingerly patted her shoulder. The kind action seemed to free her to weep silently. The two friends sat quietly side by side until Ino lent his shoulder to cry on.

"I will try my best," she said, choking on the sentence. "I promise."

"Good. In the meantime, concentrate on your health," he said, trying to cheer her up before frowning at her weird expression. "What's the matter?"

"Nothing," Hana whispered the words while placing a hand over her belly. "I will survive this outcome."

"That's the spirit," Ino said with a warm smile. "I admire your inner strength, Suhana. I don't see you as a meek person but as someone who can bear up without crumbling."

"You see too much in this, Ino." She shrugged and then stood up. "I'll be heading home."

"Take care," he said with a wave.

Hana bit her lower lip recalling Jin and Shouko, wondering where they might be. But for the time being she decided to walk forward one step at a time, feeling baffled by the absurd idea that she could forget somebody like him. And not just anyone—Jin, her best friend and a person she had relied on for years, never imagining that the two of them would one day suffer together.

Back at home, she had trouble focusing on the printing in the textbook; her mind was elsewhere—above all on the fear of pregnancy. In the dining room she also had to keep a close watch on the adults; even though they were chattering as normal, in her heart Hana sensed something amiss. Or was it that her mother was busy with some current project and seemed preoccupied, even while braving a carefree outlook? Hana pushed these family matters aside.

Just then, her tired brain conjured up Miko. She gasped to realise that their friendship might not have survived the debacle. She wondered whether the girl would bother to reply to a text. A little jittery, she picked up the cell phone to send a short message. Seconds passed by, then minutes, and soon an hour, as her eyes kept straying to the device on the table. With a heavy heart, she decided to accept that she'd lost another trustworthy companion.

Out of the blue, a notification ring caught her in the midst of scratching her head. She grabbed the phone to read the screen.

How are you? - Miko
Hello, I'm truly sorry for disappearing off - Hana
It's all right - Miko
Can we meet up please? It's urgent - Hana
Sure - Miko

Without a doubt, Hana guessed the girl was not in the mood to rekindle their friendship but shoved the unwanted thought aside because of her rising desperation and typed a location where they could have lunch. She chose a school day so that her mother wouldn't tag along as before. Anxiety ate at her from within as she waited impatiently for the day.

Chapter 23

"Put down your pen. Test is over," their homeroom teacher droned. "Pass the slip of paper forward for collection."

Hana laid down her pencil. She had a terrible notion about her test answers but dutifully passed it forwards and fidgeted her thumbs nervously, watching the slow ticking of the clock above the whiteboard. Class was about to be over. Today she was off to meet Miko. She had told a white lie to her mother about a school activity as usual. In the meantime, the tension between Jin and herself was diminishing because she had made a mental note not to stare at him, figuring people were always watching. She still foolishly yearned for Jin but forced the pain away by looking some other way whenever she stumbled upon the couple. She had given in once or twice and caught Jin staring at her, only to roll his eyes away.

Jolted by the school bell, she slowly arranged the stationery inside her bag. When the boys were asked to stay back to help clean the bathroom, she could hear their voices jumping from one topic to another.

Her fingers brushed the top of the lunch box; it was untouched. She stood up, feeling a little lightheaded. She made a mental note to at least grab some biscuits to sustain her energy, since heavy meals weighed like lead in the pit of her belly. She turned and spotted Ino amongst the others around his place and called his name. Off to one side she could see Jin pause, losing his smile.

"How did you do on the test?" she asked with a smile when Ino got close.

"I think I did well," Ino replied looking serious. "What about you?"

She stretched one corner of her mouth. "I'm ready to accept my failing grades."

Soon she stepped out of the classroom but slowed when she overheard someone mentioning her name. She leaned against the wall, hugging her bag, but the sentences were laden with mirth, and she couldn't make out many words. She was about to leave when Jin's low tone stopped her. Nervously she stepped a little closer.

"She was the one tagging behind you all along," Hiroto said.

"Hey, can we drop the subject?" Ino dared to say. "Jin, your friend is suffering—"

"Ino, do you know the story behind it?" Jin retorted.

"No …," he replied hesitantly.

"Be careful. Hana will latch onto you before confessing her undying love for Ino." Jin's joke drew chortles and gasps from the group.

"Even if Hana admits her love, it must be out of honesty," Ino whispered.

"Ino, what do you know of love, huh?" someone piped in. "I remember Suzumi rejecting you."

"It's good that Suzumi chose that wise decision," Ino said more confidently. "The two of us would never have lasted long."

"So Suhana declared her confession to you?" Clearly they had turned back to Jin.

"Before or after you got together with Shouko?" came another question.

Hana fled down the corridor, fear gripping her heart because of what the rest of the boys might think of her. Already dreading it, on cue she experienced her first anxiety attack, flooded with memories of past bullying and harsh words directed at her. In the process, she forgot about her meeting until Miko gave her a call.

Her impatience quickly gave way when she heard Hana sobbing. "Hey, you okay?"

"No—" Hana had trouble speaking coherently. "Not okay …."

"Where are you right now?"

"I don't know." She sobbed brokenly. "I'm walking away from the school."

"Suhana, please wait for a second to take a good look at the area," the other girl emphasised. "Stop crying for now."

"O-okay." Hana choked on a sob, wiping at her tears. Once she saw where she was, she gave Miko the address, and her friend urged her to stay there until she arrived. Thankfully, it was not far from where they had arranged to meet for lunch.

Thirty minutes had gone by before Hana saw Miko strolling along the busy sidewalk. Not waiting for her, she raced over and collided against her with a hug. Before either of them knew it, she was pouring her heart out.

"Hey! What's the matter?" Miko was gawking at her. "Suhana!"

"Miko!" Hana wailed, feeling hopeless. "Everything's gone wrong for me!"

"Okay, okay." Miko forced her to pull away and dragged her along by the wrist. "Just stop crying, please. Everyone is looking at us."

The moment they were seated in the quaint café, Hana laid out her situation. Because of the burden weighing on her heart, she kept crying, started to feel feverish, but never gave up. Once she had explained the entire situation, she blew her nose in a tissue and then rested her chin on one hand, looking lost. The silence lingered until Miko let out an audible sigh. Hana looked all around, miserably rubbing her face.

"I am stupid to think the two of us will even be seen as a couple," she said, her voice trembling.

"Hana, we have a dire situation at hand instead of that crap," Miko snapped at her. "The first question is, are you pregnant?"

"I don't want to know," she whispered.

"You look so different compared to before. Suhana, first of all, you must take care of yourself."

"It's a pain taking care of myself." Hana sniffled through her clogged nose. "Even if I was rotting away, Jin wouldn't care about me."

"Is that why you're torturing yourself?" Miko looked shocked. "At least think about the baby."

"Miko, I am not pregnant; my belly isn't showing," she shot back, fighting down panic.

"What if you are, Suhana?" Miko asked, clearly concerned. "You know, it's highly possible when that idiot did not have protection."

"He pulled out." Hana blushed, embarrassed at her stupidity.

"Oh, Suhana, what have you done to yourself?" Miko's voice was full of sympathy.

"I fell in love," Hana answered quietly.

"But you handled everything wrong." Miko sighed once more. "What's important for now is to get you healthy again."

"I don't want that." Hopeless tears sprang to her eyes. "I just want Jin beside me like before."

"I'm really sorry, Suhana." Miko leaned forward with a sad expression. "Although it won't be far from the truth if you're carrying his child."

"My mother will kill me," she whispered in a strained voice. "In fact, the thought of seeing Jin's angry face scares me more."

"We have to go for a check-up," her friend insisted. "Just to make sure. If the two of us are alone, you can make a decision to abort—"

"No." Hana fixed her with a stare. "I won't even think about abortion."

"But you just said …." Miko quirked a brow. "I'm really lost right now."

"I know what I said before, but that will not make me choose that path."

"Fine." Miko slumped back with a sullen look and began scrolling through her cell phone.

Hana looked down, feeling the silence growing between them. It seemed they had drifted apart, but just then Miko perked up with a determined look and narrowed her eyes at Hana. She waved her phone towards Hana's befuddled face and scooted forward once again, grinning and wiggling her brows. "Hey, I know of a way to get back at him."

"What do you mean?" Hana whispered still confused by the sudden change.

"There is a group date coming up; follow us." Miko was excited.

"Huh?" Hana blinked once.

"You heard me," Miko said impatiently and rolled her eyes. "It's time you got yourself a real boyfriend."

Hana shook her head. "I'm sorry, but it's too early for me."

"Suhana, you need a good distraction." Miko grabbed Hana's cold hand. "Trust me, when Jin sees you smiling again with another guy, he'll start to remember the times you had together."

"I'm supposed to stay away, knowing he has a girlfriend right now." Her soft words had no force behind them.

"Come with us; we'll enjoy our time together." Miko was grinning. "Suhana, you cannot stay like this forever; it poses a danger to your health."

"But I'm not very good at communicating with new people."

"It's okay, they'll understand. And don't forget, I'll be attending as well," she said with a casual shrug.

Hana suddenly recalled Miko's crush on the young baker. "What happened to Yoshi and you?"

"Never worked out." Miko toyed with her straw. "Yoshi still cares about his ex-girlfriend."

"I'm sorry to hear that." Hana frowned, feeling heartbroken for the other girl.

"That's why I'm going to this group date." Miko looked away. "I want to let go of this emotion that is still slightly attached to him."

"I feel bad for pouring all of my problems onto you, Miko." Hana bowed her head in apology.

Miko shook her head slowly. "You've got a much bigger problem than mine, Suhana. So, what do you think about the check-up?"

"I'll let you know." Hana bit the bottom of her lip. "I'm scared of the result."

"Whatever the result is, I'm sure you will think of a proper solution." Miko suddenly straightened. "All right, I have to get going."

"Are you working at the same place?" Hana slid out of the seating area.

"No, after Yoshi and I broke up, it's better to keep a good distance between us." The girls walked out side by side.

"You're the stronger one between us," Hana pointed out.

"I am far from being a capable woman. In fact, I cried and suffered from multiple hangovers before taking that wise decision."

"Maybe I will do that date." Hana shrugged. "It might help me feel better."

"You will!" Miko hopped once. "Meeting new people excites me."

"What if the people involved don't like me?" Hanna whispered, a little unsure.

"Suhana, you have to work on your self-consciousness," Miko commented before pausing at the traffic light.

"See you." Hana smiled slightly. "Just let me know the details about the date."

"Sure." The girls waved a farewell.

Numb, Hana headed to the nearest train station as the fastest means of transportation. Once aboard, she closed her eyes with a sigh. She couldn't wait for the year to end quickly so the new semester would start, because high school life was giving her a case of depression.

Chapter 24

The school summer holidays were coming quickly. Most of the students hummed with palpable excitement, their energy noticeably elevated, while Jin rested his head on the desk, tuning out noises with a pair of earphones and eyes shut. Their exam results had been posted; gratefully, he had passed, if barely. A small smile twitched the corner of his mouth as he thought about the hard work he'd put behind alongside Shouko, who religiously guided him on certain topics.

Jin had also received financial aid from the school, easing up on the burden of college preparation. The teacher told him about a softball scholarship, to which Jin agreed without any hesitation. The hospital was another matter altogether, and he heaved a pent-up sigh. *I'll just get a part-time job during summer holidays,* he mused—even though the bills wouldn't be settled by half. The fans were on full blast, but he felt caught in a heatwave.

He felt a twinge of returning tension, and his eyelids drifted open. He saw Hana seated on the other side of the classroom. He had been aware of her weight loss for a while. She was drifting away, but his stubbornness kept him from asking after her even while he watched the changes taking place.

But Jin wanted to avoid giving her any more wrong signals; she might take his concern as something else entirely, causing more friction between them. He continued to watch from above his crossed arms, hidden from anyone's view, as she nervously glanced around like a frightened doe. A guilty conscience crept up because of the outburst inside the classroom about the reason why Hana and Jin had split up as friends. She had become a centre of mockery, so of course Jin still felt a twinge in his heart due to his sympathetic nature. Just then, sunlight broke through the clouds to shine directly into their classroom.

At one point, Jin was confused by his own emotions when Hana talked with Ino, who often stood up for her against bullying and abuse. Ino himself was also the subject of speculation amongst the classmates. Only a few seemed to target them, but Jin would not intervene to stop the gossip and abuse.

Before Jin could shut his eyes once again, Hana teetered dangerously to one side. Startled, he jolted upright, his heartbeat skyrocketing. Realising nobody was paying attention, he cleared his throat loudly while resuming his former position. He stared intently at Hana, who began taking notes although nothing was written on the board. A trickle of fear for her health left him feeling unsettled.

"Jin, are you okay?" Shouko's voice caught his attention.

"Huh?" He blinked. "Yeah, I'm fine."

"You seem out of focus today," she said with a smile.

"Don't mean to," he replied softly.

"I won't be long," she promised him while browsing along the section of books.

They were in a huge bookstore at Akihabara. Shouko adored romance comics, just like Hana, who had dropped in countless times before. He used to whine about the hours she took to look at one book. Of course, he got recommended to one or two action genre comics, but just standing in the building brought the memories drifting back.

Jin clung to his anger even now, close to three months after their falling-out. Recently it had abated somewhat when he caught a strange sight from the distance. Hana's stepfather was coming out of a restaurant shoulder to shoulder with a woman. Although it was normal to see different sexes together, this intimate closeness shocked him. The man's face lit up with a huge grin as they vanished from sight. Quickly Jin fished out his cell phone to contact Hana but then stopped himself; he had lost the right to talk with her ever since he decided to let anger get the best of him. Still, he wondered if either Hana or her mother was conscious of the cheating.

"Hello?"

Jin jumped, dropping his device to bounce on the floor. Shouko emitted a cry in reaction to his fright. He bent low to check on the budget phone; thankfully, he could still switch it off and on. He looked up at Shouko, leaning apologetically over him. Several customers looked at them, some of them giggling at his embarrassment.

"I'm sorry!" She bowed a couple of times. "I did not mean to startle you."

"It's okay," he said with a smile.

Jin trailed after Shouko, but he kept on thinking of Hana and the travails she must be facing herself. Jin was aware how much she adored her stepfather; they had a close-knit relationship. While Shouko was again distracted by a lately arrived comic, he decided to wait outside. At one point, he pulled out his cell phone and toyed with it, only to realise that he was skimming through old messages between him and Hana, and his mood turned forlorn.

He sighed aloud. *I shouldn't harbour thoughts like this.*

He was doing his best to move forward after the turbulent end of their friendship, but he had trouble erasing his overwhelming feelings during their lovemaking. Once again, he could not bring himself to acknowledge it and resorted to denying it as deeply as before. He chose to gratify his ugly impulse by behaving coldly towards Hana. Perhaps at first she deserved his harsh treatment, but after two months he began to feel the distance between them. He leaned his head against the building.

Suddenly his body moved forward of its own accord, the heart winning over logical thinking. Nervously glancing behind in case

Shouko had appeared and might stop him in the nick of time, he saw only random people walking in and out of the huge store. He gritted his teeth, rebuking himself but continuing to plough ahead. He entered the train station and boarded just as the door slid shut. He caught his frightened reflection in the glass. He breathed a little unevenly while being pushed by the crowd in the cabin. Then the phone buzzed in his front pocket.

"Hello?" he answered once he was able to loosen the invisible knot.

"Jin! Where are you?" Shouko's voice hinted of panic.

"I ...." Jin's mouth opened and closed, but no sound came out.

"What?" she asked. Then she must have heard the rattling background. "Are you going home?"

"Y-yeah." He gulped, suddenly feeling the unbearable heat. "I'm not feeling well, sorry."

"Is it my fault, Jin?" Her voice wavered. "I made you stay out so late; in fact, you must be bored out of your mind."

"No," Jin said with a mirthless laugh. "I'm used to it."

"Used to being dragged around by me?" Her tone altered a little. "I'm really sorry."

"Please, don't apologise," he said, sighing aloud.

He decided not to mention that the person who would drag him everywhere was Hana, since she had no other friends to share her excitement with. When the phone cut off, Jin got out of the train to settle on a bench. He sat in a daze, staring at nothing, waiting for his heart to calm down. Then a tear rolled down, startling him. With a shaky finger, he swiped at the lone droplet in disbelief before inhaling and exhaling shakily. Finally, he was feeling his emotions breaking down as they had before he allowed anger to take over. Jin guessed the flame had mellowed.

He was afraid to actually spy on Hana when his feelings were aroused, knowing it wouldn't turn out well for him. He glanced down at his hands, reliving the moment when he had caressed her body and felt the smoothness of her skin. His inner fire awakened at the suppressed memory.

I'm in love with Hana, a inner voice said, ringing with truth.

The train wheels clattered on the track before it came to a slow halt. Jin's hair ruffled in the strong gust from the transport, while he went on staring at his hands spread open. The clarity of his emotions frightened him senseless. Suddenly short of breath, Jin blindly looked up through the sheen of tears to see passers-by watching him out of curiosity. By now, the sun had dipped low at the horizon. Jin waited for the next train, feeling the ground rumbling as it zoomed to a stop. When the door opened, he climbed in.

For the next several days, Jin kept on ignoring Hana, impatient for the holiday to arrive. Although they were wearing the school uniform for the summer season, it never stopped either of them from sweating underneath the shirt. Jin had a moment of déjà vu as he sat in the same place, surreptitiously gazing at Hana who dozed on the desk surface, when he recalled that she had barely passed her test as well, a first time for the studious student. Jin saw, that as evidence of her tumultuous mind. They had been friends far too long for him to ignore the uneasy signs within him about her. Then his body froze when he was caught red-handed; Hana was looking right back at him. He shifted his nervous gaze elsewhere, but after a moment's hesitation, he looked back at her.

What am I doing? he asked himself, nearly panicking.

Just as Jin had pointed out earlier, the two of them had gone through thick and thin to become close friends. They were too young to be subjecting themselves to this turbulent experience. At this moment their eyes never wavered from each other; Hana was peeking from above her folded arms while Jin sat slouching, openly watching her from across the classroom. For the entire day, he had shied away from direct contact; Hana had bravely put up with his rejection and his cold demeanour, observing the romance between Shouko and himself. All the while, Jin had hurt her time and time again, disregarding her feelings, all because the idea of being in an actual relationship with his best friend revolted him.

The teacher droned, "Those who have failed your mock test: please attend the extra classes during the holidays." Then he read their names aloud, each one prompting a disappointed groan.

When Hana walked past the front of Jin's the table, he got up from his desk. But as his hands pressed against the table once more, his legs also became too heavy to move. He battled inwardly with a riot of emotions, confusing thoughts, and a sense of uselessness. Then he thought about the hurtful comments he had spread in the classroom and the boys taunting Hana about that confession.

He collapsed into his chair. *I cannot do this,* he silently lamented.

"Jin?" Shouko popped over, smiling. "I have class duties today."

"I'll be going home then." He returned her smile but dropped it quickly.

"See you soon." Then she peered closely at him. "Jin, you look really exhausted."

"I am." He slung the backpack over his shoulders. "Bye."

Without another word, he strode away from her. Suddenly, he bumped into someone. He glanced up to spy Chiyo looking at him in a stunned manner. They were descending on the same staircase. It had been months since they had seen each other. Unsure how to react, he nodded at his former partner; she reciprocated before leaving his side, but they continued in the same direction until he reached the locker section.

He conjured the scene when he and Hana were able to see eye to eye, and a hollow feeling crept into his heart. The word *love* had pounced on Jin out of nowhere. He rested his forehead against the cool metal before changing his shoes and walking out of the school building alongside a sea of students.

"Hey, Jin, do you have some time to spare?"

He glanced behind and saw Chiyo coming closer. She looked in another direction before focusing on him with an unreadable expression. He raised a brow; if she meant to screw like before, he would decline the offer while allowing her to regain her composure, but irritation got the best of him.

"What do you want?" he snapped, regretting instantly.

"Wow, you've become rude." She frowned. "Forget it."

"Look, I apologise for my sharp tone, but I'm not in the right mindset for now," he said, sighing heavily.

"I want us to grab some lunch outside." She crossed her arms. "Well, I am curious about what is happening between Suhana and you."

"Why?" He squinted, confused.

"Just come with me, please," she said. She sounded impatient.

"Fine." He shook his head, and they set off.

Chapter 25

Jin found himself sitting in Chiyo's apartment living room, suddenly nostalgic. In earlier days, by this point the two of them would be at each other, tearing off clothes, yet now they were subdued. Chiyo had changed into a baggy shirt with shorts and as busy rummaging in the kitchen. Jin rested his head on the sofa with both legs stretched out in front of him on the floor, hands hanging useless on either side, and glazed eyes staring at the chipped ceiling. He ignored the lewd noises from the apartment next door. Chiyo had decided to reside by herself, so because of cheap rent, the walls were thin.

Suddenly she burst from the kitchen, yelling at the top of her lungs. "Cut it out already!"

"What happened to the elderly couple living there?" Jin murmured, eyes still closed.

"They moved out two weeks ago, but these college lovebirds are driving me crazy!" she fumed while searching for a broom.

Jin finally glanced up. "What are you doing?"

"What else?" she snapped, banging the wall with the end of the broom handle. "All I am asking for is basic courtesy."

At once the lewd sounds came to a halt, and Chiyo returned the broom to a corner. Moments later she walked in and set at tray with their lunch on the low table, but Jin was not feeling in the mood to eat. Still, the fragrance drew him, and he leaned sideways with a faint sigh and shut both eyes, awakening his other senses. He could hear small noises as Chiyo ate; the television murmured at a low volume.

"What was it you wanted to talk about?" he muttered, moving onto the floor beside the low table.

"You've become a regular subject for gossips in our school," she said with a smirk.

"Just spit it out," he grumbled, now irritated.

"I have no right to dabble in your problem, but after seeing Suhana beside Jin as well as hearing stories from your end, I feel as if I know her." She shrugged and laughed drily.

"So?" Jin remained cold although he saw her react to his indifference.

"You are hurting her," Chiyo said firmly. "I tried my best to ignore your situation; after all, our relationship was purely non-committed, but it seems that I'm destined to catch Suhana at awkward moments."

Jin looked away, his fingers digging into the carpet, recalling Hana in her weak form countless times. His eyebrows dragged downward to match the sad frown on his lips. A mental voice repeated that he had no right to approach her. Meanwhile, Chiyo sat across the small table from him, watching him lost in thought.

"What do you want me to say?" Jin began to inhale and exhale rather harshly.

"I don't really know, but is the circumstances really bad?" she asked, poking her fork at the cooling vegetables.

"Tell me, why should I share my trouble with you?" He felt a burning sensation inside his chest.

"Truth be told, I couldn't be bothered, since we aren't friends, although it got on my nerves to see that girl crying."

"I can't blame Hana for constantly being in tears after how I mistreated her." He was in the midst of defending his best friend when it hit him. The sad reality that Jin found the initiative to speak on behalf of Hana spoke volumes about the situation they were both in.

For a minute or so, he allowed his old frustration and anger to take over his emotions; it felt much better than this new mixture: lost, hurting, and confused at the newborn feeling of love. But now the truth was out in the open.

He watched a fly buzzing over the bowl, and Chiyo swatted it away. Sunlight still filtered in from the blinds, and there was an occasional thump from above.

"Are you okay?" Chiyo asked in a quiet voice.

"I have to go now." He got awkwardly to his feet. "The next time you come across Hana crying by herself, just do me a favour and hug her."

Chiyo remained on the floor looking up at him. "Why won't you?"

"I don't have the right anymore," he said without looking at her. He casually pushed each foot into his worn shoes. He heard her soft footfalls approaching, yet he pretended not to acknowledge her presence. Finally, he adjusted the bag on his shoulder while looking directly into Chiyo's worried gaze. He bestowed a tight smile before opening the door to head out. He was halfway down the rickety staircase when he realised she was chasing him barefoot.

"Wait!" she huffed. "Jin, I'm sure this case isn't as bad as you are making it out to be."

"As much as I still adore Hana, I don't wish to communicate with her," he said, half-turning to look at her.

"Why are you acting so out of character?" she inquired, clearly confused.

"I am not, Chiyo." He tiredly rubbed the back of his neck. "Both Hana and I went out of line, the friendship cannot be salvaged at this point, and I have to think of Shouko as well. Of all people, she does not deserve this."

"So?" Chiyo took a few steps closer. "Suhana has been with you much longer than Shouko."

"I'm sure all of this will die down in a couple of months." He shrugged. "We're still teenagers chasing after love. Come to think of it, the entire drama is rather childish."

She folded her arms. "Who are you relating this to?"

"Nobody," he said, starting down again. *Especially not myself,* an inner voice chided. Jin forced himself to walk at a moderate pace, leaving her standing alone at the edge of the staircase to watch his retreating back. Once out of sight, he burst into an all-out run, arms pumping on either side and his hair flying in the strong breeze, his tears streaking backwards down his cheeks.

Just then, he bumped head-on into a stranger and was knocked flat on his back. He looked up to see a man and his companions. They glared at him furiously. "Oi! Are you fucking stupid, running down the street without looking?" The speaker grabbed him and pulled him up by the collar.

"Let him go; he's just a boy," said another of the men, cautioning his pissed-off friend. "We don't have to waste our time with him."

"Sorry," Jin said, weeping pathetically. "I am so sorry."

"Forget it." The man clutching Jin's collar shoved him once again.

Realising that people all around were watching, Jin quickly snatched his backpack, sniffling unpleasantly. He used his uniform sleeve to wipe his nose while on wobbly feet he walked away. Rushing passers-by either collided with him or gave him a wide berth. When he finally looked around, still hiccupping, he was surprised to find himself in Hana's neighbourhood. Panic settled deep; he twisted one hand in his shirt, fighting the sentimental urge to abandon everything and rush headlong to meet her.

But the memories surfaced of their blow-up in her living room, all his harsh words about her, giving in to his negativity and casting a bad light on Hana in front of everyone. Suddenly he found it hard to breathe. Bending low from the waist to gasp for air, he became aware of hatred directed at himself. He'd been brought up by a single mother who taught him from his youth to be a better person, yet he had disappointed the one person who was more important than anyone else.

"C-calm ... down," he said, straining for air.

Birds chirped in the trees nearby, and the rustle of leaves soothed Jin's ear, reminding him that summer was close. In the background he overheard vehicles zooming by, as daily life went on for everyone else. Once he had regained his composure, he pressed on, allowing his limbs to move on their own. This time, he walked as if his body were made out of a leaf. Numbness had overtaken his entire system by the time he came to a stop and glanced upward to the apartment.

"Hana, look out the window because if you do …," he whispered, lips trembling with his strong emotion, "I'll come to you, so come on—hear me out."

The shut curtains never moved. Instead, Jin sat on the edge of the brick wall opposite the building, where greenery lined the entire section. A car drove into the lot; nothing out of the ordinary occurred. His eyes were still fixed on the same window when evening lowered and night came. He pushed himself upright to shuffle slowly away, once in a while glancing over his shoulder.

Suddenly he felt drained. Fatigue made his body drag, and he figured it was high time he returned home. The walk back helped clear his troubled mind. Once and for all he forced himself to push away any thoughts or feelings associated with his former best friend. Out of nowhere he wheezed a dry chuckle, which turned into belly laugh. He realised that he had stopped and was staggering back and forth during this episode and collected his wits to continue the journey. "I'm still too young for all of this relationship crap," he murmured.

Home at last, Jin reverted to his old self by cleaning up the house. Silence was his companion. Soon the clothes were neatly folded and the fragrant rice was heating in the cooker. He stripped down and went into the bathroom. Cold water sluiced across his lean body while he sat on a small wooden stool to scrub all over with a foam infused with soap. Then he relaxed with both eyes closed, feeling the icy liquid pouring over his face. Clad in a towel and bare chest, he sat alone under the dim kitchen light to eat a bowl of plain rice with soy sauce and yesterday's leftovers from the fridge.

Occasionally his cell phone beeped. Shouko was texting him online about her day and sharing funny stories from her house. Jin dredged up a small smile; he had already pictured her family background as perfect. She was the second oldest with two siblings; the oldest was married with their first child on the way, and her younger brother was a first-year in an all-boys faculty.

He went up the stairs to his bedroom, put on his shorts, and dropped on the mattress. Then his eyes strayed to the game station pushed into the corner. He easily fell into a deep slumber from exhaustion. Even when the alarm clock went off, Jin was snoring aloud, unaware that his mother quietly closed the slightly open door to let him rest.

Jin marshalled all his energy to pedal the bicycle like a madman. The wind swept his hair behind while he grunted for more speed. At one point he called his sweet mother on the phone, and miraculously their line connected. "Ma! Why didn't you wake me up?" he asked.

"You were sleeping so peacefully, I couldn't bring myself to wake Jin." She sounded affronted.

"Peacefully?" he choked. "I'm late for school!"

"They won't fail Jin for skipping one day of school," she explained patronisingly.

"Ma, are you teaching your son a bad habit?" He paused to smile.

"Go to school, be a good boy, and have a safe trip," she chortled before disconnecting the call.

By the time Jin arrived, the gate was closed. Even though he would have been wise to turn back, his persistence got him into trouble. Soon he had to sheepishly explain to the headmaster why he was caught climbing over the gate after flinging his bike into the yard.

In the classroom at second period Jin's cluster of male friends were guffawing at his stupidity. "I can't believe this!" Hiroto said, wiping his eyes.

"If I were you, I'd take a hike—probably go to the arcade," another chimed in, shaking his head.

"School break is one week away," Jin said with a shrug.

"Right, our boy is a hard-working pupil." This came with a slap on the back.

From the corner of his eye, Jin spied Hana staring into space. He uneasily noted that she looked a little thinner and weaker to him. Someone blocked his vision, and he blinked to focus back on his group of buddies. He reminded himself that it was better not to meddle with her, since the poor girl deserved better than his friendship.

Chapter 26

During the middle of clean-up Hana received a message from Miko, who reminded her she would be arriving to pick her up. Hana was a little unnerved by the upcoming event, although it was a normal occasion for extroverted beings.

Two days ago, Miko had mentioned the group date, and Hana had eventually declined the offer. But Miko was persistent, since they needed another girl to make up the entourage. Tomorrow was the start of the summer holiday, and everyone else was set to enjoy adolescent life. Hana, however, had a lot going on. After building up the courage, she had stumbled into a pharmacy to purchase a pregnancy kit. Then she went to a public toilet where she received the positive result.

Raw fear had overcome her. She remained seated in the stall, sobbing behind her hand clamped over her mouth. It was frightening to picture Neena learning of the dire situation, especially when her belly grew as the months passed, and Jin's shame at being told off by everyone else. She felt as though she was coming apart. She already had trouble eating due to stress, even though it was not a grand idea, since she carried a baby inside her belly; still, Hana could not bring herself to consume solid food.

"Suhana?" A voice brought her back from her reflections.

"Yes?" Hana looked up to see a kind face gazing back.

"Are you done washing that part of the window?" Aika looked at it curiously.

"Yes," she said with a nod.

"Finally! It's summer holiday!" Maichiro danced comically.

"My job is starting the day after tomorrow at a crêpe café," Aika explained to the group.

"Whoa, it must be nice to work in a dessert shop," Ikumi sighed, plopping on the floor.

"I just need the cash to support myself," Aika said with a sad look.

"What about you, Suhana?" Maichiro met Hana's stunned eyes with her own.

"W-well, I'm leaving for Yokohama to visit the hot spring resort," she stammered, feeling guilty.

"I've been there countless times. It's a beautiful place with an endless ocean view." Ikumi sat unladylike with legs spread, showing off black running shorts.

"Of course," Hana whispered, a little daunted.

"Are you okay, Suhana?" Aika frowned, a concerned look on her face.

"Yeah, I am," Hana said, forcing a bright smile.

"If neither of you are too busy, maybe you girls can drop by the place I'm working at to eat crêpes," she said, resuming the earlier subject.

"Really?" Maichiro spoke in a gleeful voice.

"You too, Suhana; plan a day together." Ikumi grinned, baring her teeth.

"Me too?" Hana blinked, unable to comprehend.

"Of course! I want to make it up for being rude to you," the other girl mumbled, looking flustered.

"But we cannot say the same for Suzumi," Maichiro hissed in distaste.

"Ignore her," Aika said, shaking her head. "I'm also shocked at Jin treating you so badly."

"It's not his fault," Hana protested mildly.

"Doesn't matter who is at fault! The courage it must have taken for Suhana to confess your feelings to him," Ikumi spoke vehemently.

"I crossed a line." Hana walked toward the bucket filled with grimy water to toss the towel in. "In fact, I am not mad at him. Jin is someone who has a difficult time controlling his runaway emotions."

"Are we done for today?" Maichiro swiped an arm over her forehead.

"My fingers are pruned," Aika lamented while staring down at her hands.

"Let's return to the classroom. I'm eager to get out and breathe in the fresh air!" Ikumi stood up and dusted the back of her skirt.

In the meantime, Hana once in a while giggle at the group's interplay, but her heart grew heavy the moment she stepped out of the school gate to spy Miko engrossed with her cell phone. The girl drew the attention of nearby boys since she wore a different school garb. Miko glanced up to double-take just as Hana reached her. They smiled at each other before Miko caught her in an embrace. An overpowering perfume caused Hana to grimace.

"I've been waiting for you!" Miko gasped in delight. "Your school looks incredible!"

"Thank you," Hana said dismissively.

"Is that all?" She rolled her eyes. "Come on, I don't want you to clam up again."

"I'm not, because there is another problem I'm facing by myself," Hana whispered.

"What do you mean?" Miko frowned.

"I'll tell you when I'm ready." Hana glanced at the floor. "Let's go, shall we?"

"Okay," Miko replied in an unconvincing voice. "Maybe, you don't want—?"

Hana cut her off in mid-sentence. "It's all right, I'll just accompany Miko. Perhaps a new environment will help me."

"Does your mother know about this?" Miko asked, pulling out a cigarette pack.

"About what?" she frowned slightly.

"This group date. Is your mother open-minded?" She held a cigarette between her teeth as the lighter flared.

"I am not sure, but it's better to keep it under wraps. My mother is strict, while my stepfather is more lenient."

"Oh yeah, you told me before. It's amazing to see a relationship so rare between that stepfather and you." She chortled. "We usually hear crap stories, but yours is different."

"I love him." Hana smiled, checking out her shoes as they strolled side by side, but then she started thinking about the tension that had arisen within the household. Although the adults put up a good front around her, yet she had once caught her mother weeping alone in the living room. Hana had silently backed away, but it only spurred her growing suspicions. She had no clue whether those tears were about the marriage or about job stress. But the idea of her parents divorcing frightened Hana because of the adoration she had for her stepfather. there was nobody else in her life as a father figure except him.

"All right, we'll meet you there." Miko's words brought her back to the present.

"Your friends?" Hana asked.

"Yeah." Miko replaced the device inside her skirt pocket. "The guys they've invited are college students."

"College guys?" Hana's eyes widened in alarm. "Wait, they are practically adults."

"Yoshi is an adult too, but you seem fine with him."

"But Yoshi was my co-worker and a nice person too." Hana bit her lower lip.

"What if Yoshi is one of the boys?" Miko squealed behind her hands.

"You said he is still pining for his ex-girlfriend, right?" Hana crossed her arms.

"True." Miko hung her head dramatically.

"It's all right, you'll meet someone better." Hana playfully bumped shoulders with her.

"Hey, Hana, what about you?" Miko slanted her head to watch Hana's face.

"Don't you think we are too absorbed in getting into a relationship?" she asked randomly. "We should be spending our youth by rejoicing because adulthood is not far off."

"You have a point," Miko replied after a moment of silence.

"But we want to celebrate our adolescent life by experiencing the ups and downs of having a relationship," Hana continued in a whimsical tone.

"Where does this mature talk come from, huh?" Miko beamed sheepishly.

"It's called 'growing up'." Hana giggled at Miko's deadpan expression.

"Anyway, let's hurry up." Miko grabbed Hana's hand to rush forward.

The two of them arrived at Shinjuku, where they navigated amidst the crowds. Hana passed a crêpe store, whose familiar name brought a beaming smile to her face; Miko kept on leading the way. Finally, the pair came to a stop in front of a ramen stall before entering together. A raucous laugh reached their ears, and they found a big group of people at one of the tables. All of them sat on the floor, legs crossed. The men entertained the high school girls, one of whom waved a greeting to Miko. She loudly acknowledged her friends, "Yo! I'm so sorry for my late arrival!"

"It's all right," said one of the young males, signalling them to sit down.

"By the way, her name is Suhana, she is my ex-colleague, but we became friends while working together." Miko moved to the side to let them see Hana.

Hana's body stiffened. She caught their eyes looking her up and down and studying her face. She had to push aside the overwhelming urge to check herself for body odour; she wondered if her hair was a mess. This first impression was a disaster. Of course, Miko's friends welcomed Hana as usual; the rest looked on with undisguised interest.

After a round of introduction when one of the boys whispered to his partner, Hana overheard him. "Yes, I can understand Japanese," she announced, startling everyone.

"F-forgive us for the rudeness," the handsome lad replied, placing his palms together and bowing. "It's so fascinating to hear from another culture speaking our Language fluently."

"Thank you." Hana cringed, a little flustered at the attention.

By now, all of them were settling into a casual ambience. They ordered food while the underage girls sipped fizzy drinks. Hana eyed the liquor bottles, but most of the time, she remained silent. Her thoughts dwelt on Jin as well as the baby growing inside her belly, while she forced herself to eat a little out of basic courtesy. All of a sudden, a sharp pain startled her deep in her abdomen. She sloshed her glass of iced tea over the table surface, and those nearby noticed.

"You okay?" Haru seated next to her asked, inching closer.

"Yeah, thank you," she said with a tense nod. "I need to get my medicine."

Hana did not wish to admit it, but she was a little addicted to a pain medication, since it helped ease the agonising pain she more often than not suffered from. Hands shaking unsteadily, she managed to drop a pill on her open palm just as the person beside her waved down a waiter to ask for a glass of water.

"Suhana, what's the matter?" Miko regarded her with a sharp gaze.

"Nothing." Hana forced out a laugh.

"Any of you girls willing to head out for some karaoke?" Asami asked, who was quite a looker.

"Of course!" one of the girls said, jumping at the offer.

"Our treat," the guy chortled.

As everyone was getting to their feet, Miko came over, looking concerned, and took Hana's arm to stop her from moving forward. Hana turned to peek at her; she regretted ruining her friend's fun outing, but at the same time, even though it was difficult, she was forcing herself to enjoy the occasion. She reassured Miko she was having a good time, but her friend nodded wearily; she was not buying the excuse.

"Come on, let's enjoy," Hana said, interlinking their fingers.

"Suhana …," Miko said, dragging out the name.

As they looked at each other, at that moment Hana decided to share the news, but someone interrupted them. One of Miko's friends came up to them only to tilt her head in confusion when she noticed they were holding hands. Finally, the three of them exited the ramen stall to walk towards the entertainment section. Hana listened to their conversations attentively so as to keep up with everyone else.

The gastric pain is getting worse day by day, she mused, mentally feeling the pinch.

Someone pointed out the building. "This should be a good place for us."

"Let's go in," a girl said, brimming with excitement.

They booked a room complete with snacks, but Hana felt uneasy. This was the first time she'd been out with someone other than Jin. Then a message notification startled Hana, and she fished out her mobile. Neena was texting to ask about her location, and panic threatened to overcome her.

A figure loomed over her, and a boy paused by her side. "You okay, Suhana?"

She looked up and nodded. "Yeah."

"Do you want to join us?" he gestured towards the others, already moving forward.

She typed a short text and said, "Of course; just a moment."

She lied to Neena about her whereabouts, saying that her female classmates were celebrating their summer holiday at the school. Neena was not pleased by her staying late but relented when Hana pleaded with her.

"That's the spirit!" Sai yelled a little too loudly.

Hana jumped at his loud voice, and when she stood, he draped an arm across her shoulders. Reflexively she shoved him aside with a disgusted look; she couldn't bear the thought of another man touching her besides Jin, who respected her. The college guy looked at her in confusion, his face ruddy from too much alcohol, when Hana walked away from him in a hurry to reach the others.

Chapter 27

The third time Hana had to take a bathroom break to answer her concerned mother, she was having to elaborate her white lie, using the "summer break" as an excuse to stay behind at school alongside a small group of girls from the same classroom. She had to make sure Neena did not take it upon herself to drive all the way to school to pick up Hana.

Even so, she was desperate to break loose from the current crowd she was part of. No sooner had the rest of them settled cosily in the dimly lighted room than a colourful spotlight flickered across the surroundings. Someone knocked on the door and brought in a tray of snacks along with booze cans, a bucket of ice, and empty glasses. Hana was taken aback to realise that the group of men had ordered the drinks for everyone else including her. She flopped down on the couch, feeling a world of regret as she took in the uncomfortable sight of everyone flinging caution to the wind.

The moment Sai, one of the young men, sauntered over, she promptly declined his invitation, earning sniggers and several offhand remarks, but she had grown up with strict teaching from her parents about accepting anything from strangers. Eventually, she was put to the task of heading to the front counter to order finger food and refills on drinks. During this detour, she realised the karaoke bar had an adult theme and not so family-friendly ambience.

Just as she was returning to the room, one of the doors opened for a group of adults walking out. They merrily ignored her passing by in school attire as she stood aside, peeking at their faces. She had considered multiple ideas in hopes of escaping from the despairing group date because of her inability to enjoy it with the rest of them. At the same time, she was preoccupied with the fact that she was pregnant in the worst situation.

Suddenly she received a phone call. In a fit of frustration, she snatched the device from her front pocket. She was annoyed by her mother's interference, the one time she was willing to stay out late. She didn't need the stress.

"I told you I won't be coming home right now!"

"Huh?" said a male voice from the other end. "Wait, whose number …?"

Hana stiffened at the familiar voice, and chills covered her as she began to hyperventilate. In the middle of the corridor, her legs gave way, and she collapsed to the floor. It was covered by a mat that had seen better days. One fist anchored her on the floor as the other gripped the cell phone so hard that she feared it might crumble.

"Jin," Hana whispered, hearing him curse under his breath at his mistake, but then silence came in between them.

"Um, I dialled the wrong number," he finally replied in a deadpan voice.

"You still have my number?" she asked quietly, despite her trembling with emotion.

"I forgot to erase it from my contacts," Jin responded with a huff.

"I'm happy." Hana squeezed her eyes shut feeling tears rolling down. "It's good to hear your voice so close to my ear."

"I have to put down the phone now," he said in a cold voice.

But she listened to his breathing over the line, neither of them uttering a word while she wept in a wavering voice. She stayed where she was, slumped on the floor, heedless of the litter caught in the mat. Her elation combined with a stabbing pain in her heart. She finally moved the other hand to carefully cradle the mobile in her hand as if she were caressing his cheek. "I ... miss you," she declared in a choked voice.

"You should be moving on now," Jin answered in a low tone.

"Didn't you know? I cannot move forward without Jin walking by my side," she admitted helplessly.

"Why are you doing this to me?" he whispered brokenly. "I'm not strong, Hana."

"Jin, I promise you, I'll be standing behind to lift you up," she whispered.

"What is happening?" His voice broke on the words as if in disbelief.

"Just give me a chance to prove my love for you," she pleaded, holding the thought of a baby growing within her.

"I'm scared, Hana," he finally admitted in a low tone.

"Don't be," she smiled through the tears. "I am here."

"You're crazy," he responded in the same hushed voice.

"I'm only in love with you," she declared straightforward. "Do you think I can keep up this charade for months?"

"No," he mumbled after a moment of silence.

"I love you, Jin," Hana vowed as someone passed her with a inquisitive look.

"Can you meet me at the park tonight?" he inquired in a hushed voice.

"I'll be there at once." She shot to her feet, but dizziness blurred her vision. After several seconds, she managed to take steps forward.

"Wait—before we meet, are you sure, Hana?" He sounded uncertain.

"Yes," she responded as the strong emotions energised her system and began walking back to the karaoke room. "I want to talk to you, Jin."

The moment they disconnected, she was seized with impatience. She figured that tonight there would be a lot of tears, fresh wounds, and—she dared to hope—Jin pulling her into his arms once again. A small sob escaped her at the idea that she would be reliving sentimental emotions and the comfort of familiarity.

Hana knocked on the door once and let herself inside. The room was strangely quiet, although in the background music was playing. "Um, I have to head back home," she explained a little nervously.

"Oh, sure!" Sai nodded his head a couple of times.

But Hana did a double take. At the couch section Miko and the rest of her friends were settled in a lump against one another, unmoving. She was confused by the unusual sight. Just then, someone blocked her view, and she glanced up at Haru's smiling expression. Whenever she tried to look at the girls again, he moved into her line of sight.

She assumed all of them were joking around and gave up on the situation. "What happened to them?" she asked, pointing in their direction.

"They got a little tipsy from drinking too much." Haru chuckled, but his demeanour was changed drastically. "Girls these days are really difficult to look after."

"Oh." She blinked once and picked up her bag, unsure about leaving them behind.

Sai shook his head. "Well, at least you're the sober one amongst them, which is a good idea right now."

"Thank you for joining our group date. I hope you had fun," Asami said, bowing to her. "Although it seems Suhana was drifting off most of the time."

"I'm sorry, but this is my first time in a group date." She shrugged, in a hurry to leave.

When the door closed behind her, she paused for a moment, debating whether she should inform Miko, but the girl was literally snoozing on the sofa. Glancing over her shoulder, still unsure, she stepped away from the room, reassuring herself about Miko's carefree behaviour, but deep in her heart, Hana felt uneasy. Annoyed by her nagging mindset, she sighed and retraced her footsteps towards the booked room. The idea of leaving the girls in the hands of strangers made her rethink about putting herself in their shoes, which spurred her forward.

"I'm coming in," she announced herself before opening the door.

A flurry of movement caught her by surprise, and she was physically dragged inside by a strong individual, muffling her startled cry with one hand clamped over her mouth. Her widened eyes flickering in every direction before they came to rest on the girls situated on the couch. Their unbuttoned shirts revealed their perky bosoms clad in bras. Two of the college boys held a device over their slumped figures.

"Let me go!" Hana shrieked, but her body was flung forward to land on her side on the floor. She caught her breath, shivering and shaking.

"Why the fuck did you return?" Sai crouched beside her, and she flinched away from him.

"What are you doing to them?" she inquired in a loud voice.

"This is none of your concern. In fact, you should be far from here right now." He rubbed a hand over his face.

"What should we do now?" Asami asked, standing behind her.

"I don't know," Sai grumbled, clicking on his camera as if to check the contents. "These pictures won't be enough to upload on the website."

"What website?" she muttered in a stupor.

"Porn website," he chortled dryly.

"What?" She gasped in horror.

Haru spoke up, clearly frustrated. "Sai, stop leaking our information—"

"Shut up," Sai snapped. His face was beet red from their early drinking session, but he was still holding his liquor.

Suddenly fingers dug into her arms. Startled, she found herself on her feet, the person behind never loosening his hold on her. Helpless, she watched in disgust as the drugged teenage girls became the highlight of their amusement. The sound of cameras clicking and male cries of disbelief accompanied their filming, as they now and again copped a feel of the soft mounds for the sake of the video.

Hana's body trembled in fright, both regretting her choice to return here while knowing that if she were in these girls' predicament, the hope of someone intervening would be her sole deliverance. She was seized by panic and helplessness.

"Stop it!" Hana yelled before she was shoved onto another sofa on the opposite side of the coffee table.

"Put something inside her mouth to shut that girl up," Haru lamented when the choice of words causes the others to cackle in mirth.

"If you don't cooperate, I'll tear you apart," Asami joked while Hana glares at him.

A sudden vibration from her pocket alarmed her. Surreptitiously, she fished out the device until a hand reached out to snatch it away. She caught her mother's name on the screen, and her heart lodged in her throat. Tears prickling, Hana started to stand up only to be pushed back onto the seat. Her jaw hung open when those who were videotaping began to focus on her thighs. It was a no-brainer what might happen next.

"Cut it out!" Hana shrieked, pushing herself upright, ignoring the pain in her lower abdomen. "I'll report to the police about this!"

"I actually chose you to be my willing partner," Sai sneered at her.

"Stay back," Hana warned him.

"Or else?" The drunken male motioned towards her. "Oi, Haru, I'll be showing you a great performance, enough to give us a high rating vote on the site."

"There's a camera here!" Hana glances up at the walls.

Asami chuckled, standing in front of her. "Stupid girl, this place is our hunting ground. You should have kept walking without looking back; you'd safe and sound right now."

Jin, her mind whispered that name.

All of a sudden, his hand shot out to grab her arm, and her school bag dropped to the floor. Hana began to struggle, but weakness from lack of nutrition sapped her energy; she could only keep screaming for dear life. She noticed that one of the girls was aware of the dire situation; her terrified eyes locked on Hana's, although the other girl remained immobile, either from the drugs or from consternation at her state of undress.

"Get away from me!" Hana screamed with all her might.

"I had to control the lust, watching your body," he grunted while locking both arms around her.

"I'm begging you, please let me go," she pleaded while kicking at the air.

"Don't record now." Sai waved a hand.

"Are you stupid?" Haru sneered at them. "I won't be recording the rape we'll be caught sooner or later."

"Jin!" Hana wailed aloud when she was shoved to the floor, instantly followed by her attacker.

She tried to scratch at his neck even though his strength was overpowering. Finally, glanced back towards the stiffened girl, who was crying quietly while she watched the ugly incident. Then she squeezed her eyes closed, cutting off Hana from her view.

"Don't move," he grunted while taking hold of her wrists in his huge hands. "I want to experience with a foreign girl."

Another hand found its way lower, since Hana's legs were forcefully spread wide by her attacker's legs. Meantime, the girl's body became rigid in hopes to fight him off. From the corner of her eye she caught uneasy stares from the other men. Hana attempted to slap her adversary a couple of times while someone's hand covered her mouth to keep her from screaming aloud.

"Jin! Jin!" she keened, repeating the name when she could twist her face away from the clumsy hand, tears now streaming.

This is not happening to me, please!

It was over in minutes, but Hana suffered damage that would last a lifetime. She throbbed between her legs; sobbing brokenly, she stayed on the floor, unable to move a muscle. Both mind and body had shut down from the horrific event, and she was barely aware of the sounds around her.

"I think this is enough." Haru frowned, and his disturbed look settled on the girl curled on the floor. "You asshole, why the fucking rape?"

"Shut up," Sai mumbled, rearranging his jeans. "That body off hers got me hot and bothered."

"Oi, listen here!" Asami grabbed Hana's tousled hair. "If you fucking go to the police to report this, we'll spread these pictures, hear me?"

They packed up their stuff, and then their shuffling footsteps grew distant as they left everyone there to regain consciousness. Meanwhile, Hana was still inert on the ground until she felt soft hands lifting her body to envelop her in an embrace. The same girl who had looked away now comforted Hana, who collapsed in her arms.

Chapter 28

*J*in arrived at the promised destination. There he dismounted from the bicycle, gingerly glancing in every direction. His eyes settled on the empty bench beneath the flowerless tree, and he approached it, rubbing his hands in a display of nervousness. He quietly sat down on the cold plank and exhaled foggy breath. Then he pulled out his cell phone to check the time and realised he had dropped by earlier than the appointed timing. He groaned in embarrassment.

But he was mildly surprised by the fact that Hana was not there first and rushing over to him. Jin shut his eyes and tilted his head backward, feeling the caress of the chilly breeze. When his eyelids opened, he saw the moonlight outlining a cloud as it ducked behind, and for the hundredth time he was bewildered by his own actions.

Casually, he fiddled with the cold device before pressing on several icons to open up Hana's message. He went on typing out a string of words only to delete them and slump back on the bench. He propped his long legs out straight, and frowned. He crossed his arms and tucked his hands under them on either side to create more warmth. Even though he was clad in a thick sweater and jeans, the cold air managed to curl invisible fingers around him.

"Where is she?" he murmured to himself.

In retrospect, he had no idea whether Hana was socialising with anyone or keeping everything to herself. When guilt resurfaced to twist his heart painfully, he reviewed his mistakes, acknowledging how impetuous he had been in an act of pettiness, confusion, and fear. He gave himself a pep talk about mistakes, their young adolescent age, and learning to uncover hidden feelings.

With growing agitation, Jin climbed to his feet to throw a glance where Hana would normally appear. Suddenly, his brain conjured an image of her, and his heart accelerated a little because, knowing Hana, she would rush over. After making sure he was by himself, he put out his arms as if to embrace a person; instead, emptiness and silence enveloped him.

"I'm an idiot." He snorted at his stupidity. "Where are you, Hana?"

He was aware of his heartbeat as the time approached. He was unable to comprehend that something might occur between the two of them and not sure if he could shut off his inner voice or the actions of his body. In fact, he wanted to apologise profusely and if possible plead for Hana's forgiveness; he was ready to clear up for her at school.

As the time stretched out, Jin began to speculate whether Hana would appear as she had agreed over the phone. Instead, he was warming the bench and leaned forward to hang both hands between his spread knees. He expelled a foggy breath before looking up for the hundredth time to stare at the spot with a sceptical expression. He peeked at the phone screen to read the number, realising it was too late for either of them to meet up. Reluctantly, he rose to his feet, unsure whether he should beat a retreat or remain in the same area.

His fingers hovered over the buttons before he decided to dial Hana's number. When the line connected and began ringing, his heartbeat was erratic, yet nobody picked up the call. Instead a robotic voice informed him that the party could not be reached. He tried several times, receiving the same answer. Then he raised his eyes toward the sky and sighed aloud, clutching the cold metal, feet as if rooted in the ground, as he internally manoeuvred through his mixed emotions.

"I wonder why you never came, Hana," he whispered in ragged voice. "This was your only chance to make me yours."

Perhaps, another chance? an inner voice enticed him.

But Jin shook his head dejectedly. This was a risky move from the beginning, with so many lives involved. Acting out of selfishness would hurt the innocent. With slow, shuffling steps, he walked away, abandoning his post. His heart was heavy as if beckoning him to wait for her until morning just to make sure. But that could not be the case. She must have had second thoughts about the two of them— or not—but Jin had to be the wiser one and finally move on, even though he was making the least progress.

"Fuck it," he cursed harshly, kicking a rock away.

He decided to walk back and forth, torn by conflicting emotions, but then chose to ride the path leading back out of the garden. His bicycle would let the chilly air calm his heat body. He adjusted himself on the seat and took off on a leisurely ride, the handle weaving from left to right. While his hair fluttered in a gentle breeze, his eyes were bleak. He felt an inward bleakness and a constriction of his heart. He took the familiar route to his neighbourhood and then, devastated, he dismounted the bike to walk into the front yard. He took a moment to pull out his cell phone; he chewed on his bottom lip before his fingers did the work of deleting Hana's number.

After dealing with the bicycle at the lawn, he managed to stumble towards the entrance. Inside, he dragged each foot out of its sandal and padded into the formal living room. He saw his father's small shrine, although it never occurred to him that the kitchen light was turned on.

Just then a slender figure appeared from the kitchen. "Jin! Where have you been?" Sayomi called out, surprising him as he began climbing the staircase.

"Eh? Mom?" his dubious voice felt far away. "What are you doing back here? I mean, it's good to see you home though."

"My new manager told me to return home because Mr Mayushi wished to work double shift." She shrugged, her eyes on Jin as he came down and stood at the bottom of the stairs. "Of course, I feel a little sad that my shift was given to someone else …."

"Oh," Jin murmured. Her sheepish smile told him she was preoccupied about work instead of feeling glad that the two of them could have a little time, no matter the late hour.

"Jin, forgive me." She walked closer right, her smile slowly giving way to a concerned frown. "What's the matter? Where have you been off to?"

"Nowhere." He glanced down at his sock-clad feet. "I'm going to bed—"

"Hold on." Her tone stopped him. "Jin, do you stroll out this late at night when I'm not around?"

Instead of replying, Jin decided to turn around, showing his back as he ascended the stairs, because he was in no mood to answer her badgering questions. He was caught red-handed by his mother about his nightly activity. But he took only a few steps upward when he felt a tug on the sleeve of his sweatshirt. She was adamant, and he sighed; this night could only get worse.

"What?" he asked in a sour tone. "I want to go to sleep—"

"You will not until I get my answer, Jin," she said, glaring at him.

Any normal teenager would be peeved by their parent's interference, but for Jin this little scenarios felt normal. In his chaotic life, reality had its own distinct flavour when it came to his ailing mother, high school moments, or the thrill of being in a relationship and surrounded by friends. The pain in his heart intensified.

"I … went out to meet someone." He looked above her head at the darkened hallway. "We've done this a lot in the past."

"Your girlfriend?" She raised a brow. "Jin, did you—?"

"No." He clicked his tongue in frustration. "Somebody else."

"Who is it?" Sayomi crossed her arms, taking authority. "Are you saying that while I've been at work thinking my son is safe at home either studying or playing one of his games, he's been outside traipsing till all hours?"

"Kind of," he mumbled, a little unnerved by Sayomi's raised voice. "But it won't happen anymore, I promise."

"How can I put my trust in you, Jin?" She stared daggers into his wavering eyes.

The word *trust* hit him harder than it should have. He blinked a couple of times, letting out a pent-up breath. His bottom lip quivered, to his astonishment, because Hana had put so much faith in him; yet Jin had disappointed her. Their angry voices echoed in his memory, the images burning like a glowing ember. He felt the heavy regret of not acknowledging her pure feelings.

"I'm sorry," he whispered in a strained voice while moving backward to hastily climb the stairs, but his mother once again latched on to the back of his sweatshirt.

"Jin, how can I let you go when you're crying?" she said, with a surprised gasp.

His eyes widened when her words sank in, and he jerked one hand upward to touch his wet cheek. He stood in disbelief. In the background, he heard her repeatedly asking for an answer but in a gentler tone, which began to crack his armour. Then he sensed a movement from behind, and in a moment Sayomi was cradling his tear-stained face to gaze directly into his eyes.

"I ... don't know," he replied in a blubbery voice.

"At least tell me," Sayomi's eyes reflected his pain. "Who hurt you?"

"Nobody," he said, squeezing his eyes shut. "Nobody hurt me ...."

"Then?" She tilted her head lower. "I have failed terribly as a mother."

"No," he objected in a harsh voice.

"So please, tell me," she insisted once again.

"Hana." Jin's words came out in a pleading tone. "Hana and I meet up secretly late at night."

"Are you two dating?" Sayomi quirked a brow.

Jin shook his head. "No."

"Oh." She stepped back but linked their fingers to pull him gently to the kitchen.

The tearful boy sat down on a chair. He heard the clatter of cutlery before a water tap was turned on, and soon his mother plopped down opposite him and set a mug in front of him. He took a sip of the proffered drink to gain another moment to collect himself. He was embarrassed to be crying; the last time Sayomi had seen him in such a state, he'd been only a young kid. She waited patiently for him to continue, but when he remained silent, she slid an encouraging hand over his.

"We ... fought, Mom," he began haltingly.

"Hana and you?"

"Yeah." He pressed the heel of his palm against one eye. "I don't know what to do right now. Because of me, everything is messed up."

"Maybe I can help you in some way." Her thumb caressed his hand.

"We made l—" He bit the tip of his tongue, afraid to let a confession slip out.

The living room clock ticked loudly as Jin furtively glanced up to observe his mother's kind expression and swallowed the rest of his words. He was afraid to witness her crestfallen face if he made the mistake of revealing their secret, knowing deep inside his heart that he had shamed his mother by his action.

"What is it?" she whispered. "It's all right, Jin; you can tell me."

"No." He broke down, exhausted by the tumultuous emotions. "Please, don't ask me any more questions."

"Then how will I be able to help you?" She searched his face with her confused eyes.

"I don't wish to know the answer," he said, his voice cracking. "I'm really scared to know."

"Jin." His mother was taken aback by his wailing. "It—it's all right, my son. I'm here."

Her chair scraped as she got up to come around and give him a warm embrace around his shoulders, pulling him against her chest. The sweet sensation of Sayomi's warmth caused him to feel even more vulnerable when he recalled the frightening moment of losing her at the hospital.

"Hana fell in love with me," he sobbed into her chest. "She confessed to me."

"Hana?" Sayomi's voice was filled with surprise.

"But I pushed her away." His shoulders shook with his sobs.

"Did you meet just now?" she whispered.

He shook his head awkwardly. "No."

"How do you feel about your friend?" She rocked on her feet.

"It's too late." He drew a shuddering breath. "We're not on speaking terms."

"But what prompted this meeting?" Sayomi heaved a quiet sigh.

"I—I accidentally dialled her number instead of Shouko's." He gulped audibly. "But I've started to feel something for her."

"For who?"

"For Suhana." He whispered her name after a prolonged silence, his eyes leaking fresh tears while he stared in a daze at the small, dimly lit kitchen from within his mother's embrace.

Chapter 29

Mother and son sat still in the compact kitchen, relishing the comforting silence. She gave Jin some space to collect his composure, his words still ringing clearly in their ears. In the distance, nightlife was lively and loud. The backyard kitchen light flickered once, indicating that it was time for a new bulb.

Finally Jin sighed wearily and scrubbed his puffy face with one hand; his empty cup had left a ring on the table. His mother stared into her phone screen with a blank expression. The silence was often interrupted by her quiet coughs.

"Forgive me," he muttered, breaking the serene ambience. "I feel stupid for sobbing like a little kid in front of you as if this matters. It's just teenage nonsense."

"Even adults can have relationship issues, not just teenagers." Sayomi carefully laid down her phone and faced her son. "You just got yourself cornered by so many things: my health situation, Suhana's feelings growing into something more for you, and then also having to deal with your relationship with Shouko. But of course, I won't put in my opinion because you wish not to see where you're standing right now."

"I'm a coward." Jin's head banged down on the table, relieving his numbness with a measure of pain. "But if you see Hana outdoors, please refrain from hating on her; just pretend that everything is fine between us."

"I came across Neena last week at early in the morning." She rested her chin on a palm. "The woman seemed quite haggard. It may be that Suhana never mentioned the trouble between you two. Instead, I learned something alarming."

"What is it?" he whispered as if fearing the response.

"Her parents are going through a divorce." Sayomi's gentle face twisted. "Either she hasn't told you, or she has no clue of the current situation. Anyway, Neena mentioned that her daughter has developed health issues."

Those words set off internal agony when Jin heard them because of his part in causing her distress. Clenching both hands, he worked to calm his breathing so as not to suffer from another bout of hyperventilating and forced himself to focus on the topic at hand.

"Neena's husband is seeing another woman." Sayomi tilted her head to lean backwards.

"I may have seen him with the same woman mentioned the other day at Akihabara." Mixed emotions tugged at his heart.

"But Neena knows of the relationship, and she encouraged him to proceed." Sayomi's voice betrayed her shock. "When I asked for her reason, she waved a hand casually, but I can tell Neena loves him very much."

Jin frowned in confusion. "Then why did she give her blessing?"

"I don't know." Now she was yawning. "Neena never shared the rest; instead, the poor woman had to head back home. She is dealing with a lot currently—work, family, and her main concern: Suhana."

"D-did she ask about me?" Jin flickered his gaze to stare elsewhere.

"Yes, but she must be in the dark. Perhaps Hana has kept it a secret." Sayomi reached over to take his hand. "Jin, I know this is overwhelming for you—"

He cut her sentence off. "I don't know what to do. I love Shouko, but I'm developing feelings for my best friend."

"Take it easy. Sort out your feelings before delving deeper."

"I hurt Hana too." He gulped audibly, sensing sweat breaking out.

"You're hurting as well," Sayomi countered. "Are you relishing the idea of hurting your friend?"

"No," he whispered, with a slow shake of his head. "I took out my frustration on her."

"Honestly speaking, I find it a little too adorable how Hana clings onto you." She smiled in memory.

"I can't help thinking, what if our relationship doesn't work out and our friendship takes a hit?" He shoved fingers through his messy hair.

"You never know," his mom said as she got up from the chair to rummage inside the refrigerator. "Even if it doesn't work out, if your friendship is strong enough to withstand the break-up, then there's nothing to lose, right? Oops! I voiced my opinion!"

"Never mind." He smiled adoringly at his adorable mother.

"Jin, sometimes, you have to take a risk," Sayomi stated whilst popping a chocolate inside her mouth.

"But I don't want to lose Hana," he said in a strained voice. "I'll be weirded out if we are exes, not sure how to behave around her."

"Is this your first relationship with Shouko?" She brought several chilled chocolates to the table, and Jin eyed them speculatively.

"No," he groaned, feeling heat suffusing his face. "But Shouko is my first love."

"Hm. Well, I'm glad that Jin opened up about your problem to me."

"It's not easy," he whined.

"Do what you feel is right." Sayomi pecked him on the forehead. "I'm off to bed now."

"Good night," he mumbled, watching her retreating figure.

"Don't stay up too late," she called from the hallway.

In the meantime, Jin huffed an exhausted sigh while snatching a chocolate and pop it into his mouth. When sleepiness came over him, he finally trudged upward to the quiet bedroom to take off his shirt. He flung it into the darkness before settling onto the mattress to stare at the ceiling.

After months of evading the taboo memory, Jin shut his eyes to relish the scene that happened in Hana's apartment: her soft body against his hard one, the little sighs escaping from between her lips, innocent fingers tracing over his body, and the light glimmering in her almond-shaped eyes.

At once his body reacted. Instead of relieving himself, he slowly opened his eyes and turned onto one side. His mind clashed with his heart, further confusing him, but the images of "what if" began to come into focus, allowing him to view a whole new world with the two of them together. He was eaten up with urgency to rush to her side, yet he battled to remain in a prone position.

I'm exhausted, mentally and physically, he told himself with a sigh.

The next morning he was back at school to attend extra lessons. He gathered with his classmates as well as students from other classes to take seats in the same classroom before their mentor began the morning by droning on particular topics for the day. Even as the teacher was going through important chapters, the boy could not concentrate; he was lost in another dimension.

He casually gazed out the window to enjoy the bright sky since summer was all about taking a break from the heat; a gentle smile played on his face. He and Hana used to sit at the veranda facing his backyard to munch on watermelon freshly cut by his mother, their bare feet dangling in a basin filled with cold water, and chat. They were oblivious to their stickiness in the humidity and hair tied in a messy topknot. Their childish voices filled the air until late evening, when Hana's parents would drive over to pick her up.

"Aah, I'm hopeless," one of his friends lamented. "I hope my grades will change for the better this time."

"I don't think so," another chimed in, earning an earful from the first.

Outside, their footsteps crunched amongst the pebbles, random bicyclists ringing their bells. Then Jin caught sight of Shouko by the gate. Her face lit up when their eyes connected, and she waved at him. Jin focused on the words he and his mother had shared last night, and he took a deep breath to keep panic from settling deep in the pit of his belly.

Shouko entwined her hands around his arm. "How was the supplementary class?"

"It was okay." He nodded once while waving farewell to his friends, who headed in the opposite direction.

"You must be exhausted, but it's all right." She beamed up at his face. "Lunch is my treat."

"Uh, Shouko, you don't have to—" He paused for a second, only to stumble as she pulled him forwards.

"I want to treat you, Jin." She giggled and then unlatched herself from his side to stand in front of him, spreading her arms wide.

"Yes?" Jin raised a brow in confusion. "We can hug later."

"No, stupid." She barked a laugh. "Do you notice this new dress?"

"Oh." He blinked once. The baby-blue cotton dress twirling around her dainty ankles made him recall their trip into a shop when Shouko was transfixed by seeing it on display.

"Oh?" She canted her head slightly to observe his face.

"I meant, you look adorable in the dress." He tried to give her a bright smile.

"Well, you seem rather uninterested." She continued to move forward without looking to see whether he was following.

"I'm sorry," he said, slinking an arm around her slender waist.

"No worries," she replied at once, but he was sure she was pouting inwardly.

"I promise to make it up to you," he said, lightly squeezing her waist.

"Hm," she said, with an adorable expression.

The couple ventured off to a sushi restaurant to feed their hungry stomachs. Although Jin was able to cajole her as the day progressed, he realised it was difficult to actually act out, and the words began to weigh heavily on his tongue. At the same time, he wondered if it was necessary to change this relationship for one that might or might not work out. All over again, he found himself running in the same circle he had constructed mentally.

Soon they left the restaurant and were walking to Shouko's house; this would be Jin's first opportunity to drop by her place, since her parents were strict about boys coming over. Jin was her first boyfriend, and her family were aware of the bond between them. But today, she had decided to bring him to an empty apartment.

"Make yourself at home," she said, visibly delighted, and Jin took off his shoes.

"Sure. Thank you for inviting me," he nodded once, eyes raking in the view knowing without a doubt she had the same status as himself.

"I'm sorry if the place isn't to your expectation." She shrugged apprehensively.

"You have a beautiful house." He playfully nudged her chin with his knuckles.

"Really?" Shouko blushed prettily and dropped her gaze to the floor.

"I'm saying the truth," he admitted meanwhile following her in a pair of house slippers to relief plastic bag filled with desserts.

"You're so sweet, Jin." She turned to look at him, her eyes shining with admiration and love, before stepping forward to plant a kiss on his lips.

They had shared multiple kisses in the past. Jin had taught her some aspects of intimacy, though at by Shouko's request, they stopped short of consummation. She was shy and often showed signs of nervousness whenever Jin decided to venture a step further, so he put an end to that so she would feel neither uncomfortable nor unsafe around him. He quietly watched his girlfriend move around the bedroom to make the area look more pleasing to the eyes, and she directed him to park on a sofa.

"Are you sure it's safe for me to be here with you?" Jin inquired warily.

"Of course; my parents are working overtime today," was her casual reply. Soon they were sitting on the floor facing the television set on the chest of drawers.

Jin's eyes covertly surveyed the compact surroundings. Unlike Hana's or Chiyo's bedroom pattern, his girlfriend's was ultra girly in rose pastel tones. An air conditioner whirring in the background muffled the sounds from the TV set. As the minutes ticked by, he sensed Shouko encroaching on his space little by little, until her head rested on his shoulder, her eyes still fixed on the screen. He let his eyelids close and leaned against the side of the bed frame. As the pair cuddled on the carpeted floor, his mind drifted off, and Hana's features were crystal clear as he recalled his daydream, evoking a faint smile.

A whisper of a caress jolted Jin back to the present, and he saw her fingers moving above his own. Then his wide eyes looked into her darker ones, and suddenly he grasped the situation that was transpiring. Shouko was little by little opening up to him in the realm of intimacy, and a thrill of excitement shot through him, and a sense of love warmed his heart.

Slowly, he raised a hand to cup the back of her neck and leaned downward to breathe against her trembling lips. Shouko closed the gap between them to fuse their mouths in a long kiss.

She rested one hand on the front of his chest with the other anchored on the floor. Meanwhile, their heads were moving as the kiss lingered, and she was gasping and moaning softly.

"Jin, I want to be with you," she whispered whilst gazing deeply into his half-closed eyes.

Chapter 30

The sentence echoed within Jin's shaken soul. He gazed down into Shouko's molten eyes, unable to comprehend when her gentle hand rested on his right chest where his heart ricocheted in an uneven beat. Nervously, she leaned closer, and Jin saw her look around before pressing their lips together again. Finally Shouko pulled away to catch her breath. Before he could inhale, she kissed him again. Soon their heavy breathing seemed to be the only sound he could hear. They were in semi-darkness because of the curtains, which obscured them from the outside world.

Then Shouko decided to timidly straddle Jin's lap. He adjusted her position, dimly aware of the television still droning in the background. They gazed deeply into each other's eyes, still enjoying the kissing foreplay. She was accustomed to it since Jin had taught her the erotic art.

"Jin," she moaned, shifting on his lap and causing him to gasp in response, "I'm feeling shy …."

"This is natural between two people when they are in love," he assured her in a deep voice. "Relax."

"Okay," she whispered, transfixed by the tanned hand fondling her perky bosom.

The room soon heated up with their arousal, and he heard only the little pleasure noises they made. His pants had become uncomfortable, and he had trouble sitting until Shouko moved sideways, vacating the space. She gave him wet kisses on his flushed neck, and his eyes were closed to ride on the erotic wave when out of nowhere, a familiar face popped up in his mind's eye. Just like that, everything else shattered, and he was brought back to the harsh reality. Hana's features had eclipsed his current feelings.

Shouko's breathless voice tickled his ear. "T-touch me. Please, Jin."

"Shouko …." He breathed out her name, although it came out as a plea.

She glanced up, her eyes gleaming with adoration. "I love you."

"I …" the sentence caught in his throat, and he could say nothing. Once again, he was caught up in the same dilemma. Anxiety was building inside him; he exhaled through his flared nostrils, his tension and his inner voice taunting him. *Coward,* the voice mocked him.

Jin decided to take control of his wrecked mindset and confront the oblivious girl who was unbuttoning his shirt. He firmly clutched Shouko's hand to make her stand still. When her eyes jerked up to look at Jin in befuddlement, he chose to steel himself for the upcoming conflict, knowing the force of nature that would be set loose. He moved his thumb in a little circle on the back of her hand, and when she tried to pull away, he gripped it harder.

"Jin, is everything okay?" Shouko tilted her head, and a light tremor in her voice signalled her insecurity.

"Nothing …," he whispered—meanwhile his other hand curled into a fist on the soft carpet—"is fine …."

"What do you mean?" she implored, with a worried frown. "Jin, is your mother fine?"

"Yes." He nodded once. "But this has nothing to do with her."

"Then?" she inquired, pushing a lock of her hair behind an ear. "Is–is it about me? Do you find my behaviour bothersome?"

"No," Jin denied forcefully. "You are the best girlfriend I've had, Shouko. Thank you for being here for me."

"Oh." She blinked once as her cheeks turned beet red from embarrassment. "You're the only one that is for me, Jin."

"I'm sorry," he apologised in advance. "I'm really sorry, Shouko."

"Tell me, what's the matter?" She cupped his cheeks in both hands. "I'll do my best to kiss your pain away."

"Really?" he whispered, in agony.

"Yes, really." She placed a loving kiss on Jin's forehead. "What is bother—?"

"Tell me, why does my heart feel like an empty vessel without her by my side?" He laid down the question in a tormented voice.

At first, Shouko remained silent, only watching his contorted expression as if to read his mind or somehow stare into his battered soul. A lone tear trickled down her cheek. Her mouth opened, yet what came out was not words but a keening cry. Shouko's painful wailing reminded Jin of someone else, and he quietly stood to walk out of the bedroom, leaving behind the weeping Shouko.

"How can you do this to me?" She raced out of the room to face him in the living room. "What about your promises?"

"I hate myself," he told her bluntly. "I'm feeling a change inside of me."

"I hate you even more!" she yelled in a blood-curdling cry.

Jin couldn't change what was happening; it was too late. But then fear overwhelmed him once again, if possible increasing his confusion, and the pain in his chest returned tenfold. Taking a huge gulp of air, Jin shoved the front door open, subconsciously hearing it bang against the wall, and ran out of the apartment. Raking both hands through his messy hair, the frustrated boy let loose a heart-wrenching shout as he aimlessly ran. By the time he had cooled down, he was staring from a bridge at the train tracks below. In the distance, the sun was setting.

I must be broken inside, he mused.

His phone rang, and after a short talk with his mother, he opted to head back home. He walked slowly, hands tucked into his front pockets, looking around at his surroundings. He felt as if his heart was mending after that last outburst and decided to place a reckless call to Hana; but her cell line was unreachable. By the time he had arrived at his front gate, it was evening and fatigue was taking over his lean frame. Solemnly he entered the silent household.

Close to midnight, he had settled flat on his bare mattress to reflect on the afternoon's debacle. Shouko had not called, and he wondered if he'd made the right choice. Could he have found a better way to broach the sensitive subject? No matter how Jin looked at it, there was no other option for him. He reached for his phone in the darkness to send another message to Hana, who was strangely unavailable.

"Oh wait, she must be on the summer vacation trip," Jin murmured to himself. Eventually, he was dozing off with a loud snore.

The next morning, Jin was busy prepping for his summer job as a convenience store clerk. A faint doubt crept up about Hana—why was she out of reach with her cell phone not working? He had no clue what she had been up to last night; perhaps he would visit her apartment in a day or two. For now, he focused having a clear mind to concentrate on the task at hand.

His work location was closer to his neighbourhood, so he pedalled in a leisurely pace for once, his sweat cooling in the gentle draft. He saw familiar faces on the streets all the way to his destination. A question was gnawing deep in the recesses of his heart regarding both Shouko and him. True, he felt love for her; at the same time, he had to wonder whether the bond they shared was strong enough for him to remain by her side and not think of another person with similar emotions.

I love Shouko, but this feeling has attached onto Hana as well.

Finally, he saw the store and turned to enter the parking area. He walked into the cold interior, nervously clutching the strap of his bag over the chest. A young lady walked out of the back room carrying a heavy cardboard box. Jin quickly rushed to her side, startling her, until he explained why he was here.

She answered with a wide smile. "You're the new kid?" she asked enthusiastically.

"Yeah," he said, nodding as he took the load from her.

"Do you have a uniform?" the perky girl asked over her shoulder after pointing out where he should stack the box of bottles.

"No, the person who took my interview informed me that the shirt would be waiting for me," he replied. Then he put down the box and offered a bow. "My name is Jin Takami."

"Oh, I forgot to introduce myself." She reciprocated his movement. "I'm Ayumi Takegawa, this store's manager."

By late evening, Jin had learned some of the shelf layout as well as starting to operate the cash register. Ayumi seemed impressed by his ability to adapt to the work requirements. He was light on his feet, helping with the heavier loads. When his new co-workers walked in, after introductions were out of the way, for the first time in a long while, he could laugh.

He sent out a fervent prayer: *Hana, please, call me.*

Chapter 31

Yokohama, onsen hot springs resort

The public restroom was vacant except for a lone female sprawled on the floor of a stall, leaning against the seat. She was drenched in her mucus and blood, her face pale and bathed in sweat. The acrid tang of waste lingered in the air. Tendrils of hair partially covered her blank face, and her dark whiskey-coloured eyes stared into space.

Hana was having difficulty processing what had happened and felt frozen motionless. Then her frail shoulders began to tremble before her face contorted, releasing a sob. She lifted both hands to press the heels of her palms against her eyelids. She inhaled shakily before releasing the agony tearing her apart mentally and physically. Her body was weakened after losing blood freely from her nether region; the mind-numbing throb sent black spots swirling in her vision.

She was on a two-day and three-night visit with her parents to their favourite onsen spa, although the vacation was more of a burden for Hana because of the tension between Neena and herself, after that cursed night. She had returned home late to encounter both adults, waiting anxiously in the living room. Hana was petrified to see that the time was half past two in the morning. Her mother stormed up to slap her across the face, making sure she had a satisfactory chance to yell.

They had barely been on speaking terms ever since. During the aftermath, Hana had been assaulted by mixed emotions at the realisation that she'd been raped in front of the drugged girls and had rushed out like a bat from a cave. Everything had gone to hell for Hana. She had lost that one opportunity to return to Jin. On top of everything, her cell phone was missing.

"Pain," she moaned to herself.

That excruciating pain continued to burden Hana's body; she had shrunk into a hollow of herself. She had abandoned the idea of eating and was constantly in tears, which upset her parents. She kept quiet whenever her stepfather approached her, and he could only sit beside her and embrace the broken girl in his warmth.

Now each short breath was escaping spasmodically. She tilted towards the toilet bowl, and one shaky hand reached out to clutch the side before helping her stand upright, Her bleary gaze drifted downward to numbly observe her messy state.

I just had a miscarriage! a panicked voice rang inside her head.

She stretched a trembling hand to push on the flush and watched the nauseating sight as it twirled before clean water displaced the bloody fiasco. Her rears were flowing, and she had trouble standing upright because of the pain in her lower belly. She went to the sink, where she tried to clean up her soaked attire as best she could, fearing that either someone might walk in or, worse, her mother would accidentally find her messy clothes.

Fear seized her heart and she let loose a startled scream at the sudden ringing of her new cell phone courtesy of her stepfather. She took it out of her pocket so slowly that the call ended and rang once again. "Hello?" she whispered in a breathy voice.

It was her stepfather. "Suhana, do you want to come along to visit the town?"

"Go ahead." She closed her eyes while sliding down the wall to sprawl again on the tiled floor. She overheard her mother's concerned voice in the background, but she hit the end call icon and let her hand fall to her side. She was heartbroken that they were not on speaking terms, and her parents were at a loss because of Hana's torrential outbursts, so they decided to visit the onsen earlier, hoping for Hana to feel better. Even then, they couldn't fix her shattered shell, unaware of the reason. The rape nightmare fed her anxiety; she was disgusted with herself for not having escaped before that disastrous incident.

Because of that night, Hana had begun to feel her body crumbling. As her agony intensified before the miscarriage, she saw splotches of blood staining her underwear but never thought much of it. Instead, she was ecstatic to see menstruation, although it was just bits of liquid.

"I was pregnant," she said, breaking into tears again. "How can this be?"

The process of cleaning up was arduous. By the end, Hana had to slink around in her wet clothes just to make sure nobody spotted her, especially at the front desk. Meanwhile her heart was accelerating, and gasped sobs escaped from between her puffy lips. Her whole body hurt at the effort to move in any direction; even a single step caused her to breathe in short puffs. Her footsteps left wet marks but thankfully no traces of blood. When she reached the door to their traditional room, she surreptitiously glanced all around, seeing no one.

What if they are here? The thought instilled fear.

Nonetheless, she moved her limbs forward until one hand nervously reached for the door and slid it open, holding her breath, eyes wide open. She spied an empty room before collapsing to the floor and crawling inside. She shut the door, enclosing herself within the silent room.

By the time she had changed into fresh clothing, her face resembled a spirit, with a pale complexion and blurry eyes and drained of energy. Perspiration bathed her body as she found a bag for the soiled items and gathered her resolve to leave the bedroom to venture outdoors. The bright sunlight momentarily blinded her, and she shielded her eyes with one hand whilst dragging her feet along the tarmac in search of a rubbish bin a little way from the hotel.

The random idea occurred to her that she might be caught up by the law for murdering a foetus; she could just see her mother's horrified expression. At the thought of their embarrassment as well as Jin's combination of disgust and disappointment with her, she realised that her mind just now was disturbed. Her eyes were swollen from the barrage of tears, and her throat was raw from sobbing at the endlessly repeating vivid memories. She hadn't had the chance to speak to Miko, but at the same time, she didn't want to. "It's all her fault," she said vehemently.

After discarding the evidence, Hana wobbled dizzily on her feet but forced herself to make a move. She had to choke back a sordid laugh because all of this had resulted from her poor choices. Her body, fouled by someone else's groping, shivered and shuddered, even though the weather was hot.

Later that evening, Hana rested in her futon, listening to the sounds of chirping crickets. A breeze cooled the wetness on her cheeks, and she well knew she had nobody with whom to share this piece of news. The thought caused an ache in her chest. Finally, Hana was all alone.

As if on cue, she felt a gentle hand stroking the top of her head. Without looking, she knew that it was her mother. Fresh tears dripped onto the pillow, and she sighed shakily.

"Hana?" her mom whispered quietly. "What's wrong, baby?"

With her lips clamped against a spoken response, Hana shook her head awkwardly on the pillow and sniffled loudly. Blindly she reached out to grasp her mother's hand, seeking comfort. After some time, she fell asleep.

Hana woke with the dawn to the deep rumble of her stepfather's voice. Feeling slightly feverish, she took her time gathering up her strength to dress and get ready for the day.

When she joined her parents in the dining nook, Neena came forth to rest a hand on her forehead. "Are you sick, Hana?"

"No," she answered quietly.

"Let's get you some medicine," her mom said, tugging on her arm. "Love, if you weren't feeling well, at least inform us."

"She must be exhausted from the trip," Abe announced with a smile. "Don't worry, we're going home today."

Eventually, after breakfast was served, they drove off from the resort. Hana had been given an antibiotic to curb her fever and dozed off heavily. After the ride back to Tokyo, she woke up feeling slightly better. But when she thought of reaching home, the trauma of Jin's hateful speech, Miko's disappearance, and the rape rose up and seemed to consume her.

Chapter 32

The summer holiday was hellish for Hana. She sank into her eating disorder, acknowledging that her weight numbers were unstable but living in constant panic at the prospect of Neena deciding to drag her to their family doctor for a thorough check-up. The subject had been broached on numerous occasions after her fever. Bedridden, she spent her days in tears.

Meanwhile, her stepfather was acting oddly around her, but she couldn't decipher his behaviour. She had forced out a smile in thanks for his sweet gesture. Once she was alone in her bedroom, with windows draped and a towel over the mirror, she typed in Jin's number and email address but never communicated with him.

"Hana, may I come in?" She heard her mother's voice from outside the door.

She pushed herself upright for her mother's sake, even though the simple task put a strain on her body. She had given up on herself to the point of no longer caring. All of a sudden, she felt a rush of tears but blinked them back and took a long, shaky breath.

She embraced a soft, furry toy animal and called out in a muffled voice, "What is it?" dragging her gaze away from the individual who stepped into the entranceway.

"I want to talk to you." Neena stayed where she was for a moment before stepping forward. "It is something very important, and there is no way for me to break this news to you."

"Huh?" Hana's eyes grew wider, and her breath caught. *Did she find out about me?*

Her mother sat at the edge of the bed, adopting a concerned look after scrutinising Hana's dishevelled state. Then she said, "Your stepfather and I are divorced."

"Divorced?" Hana repeated the word. "You two have filed for divorce?"

"We ... finalised it before the summer holiday," Neena whispered.

Hana gawked at her, unable to utter a single syllable, before rage overtook her, and she flung the soft toy at her mother. The startled woman caught it in mid-air. Before she could stop herself, she shrieked in an ear-splitting cry, releasing a flood of emotions. She had an out-of-body moment, as if looking at her disruptive self from one side, but she could not stop her outburst. Then long, slender arms encircled her and drew her forward to collapse against a warm body.

"I'm so sorry." Neena was crying alongside her. "I'm truly sorry."

"*Why?*" Hana screamed out the word.

"Because I love Abe too much, so I have chosen to leave him," she replied, but what she said confused Hana even further.

"What are you yapping about?" she wailed in her mother's embrace. "That's stupid!"

"It is a mutual break-up—"

"I don't care! Why didn't either of you tell me?" She peeked up to glare at her mother.

"We wanted to wait a little longer, but at the same time, we both felt uneasy to mention this matter." Neena assumed a guilty expression. "Our couple 'love' soon dissolved into friendship ...."

"And you both decided a divorce is the best solution?" Hana gasped in disgust.

"Hana, you will not understand our adult situation for now, but I have another topic to discuss, namely your health—"

"No!" Hana cut her off. "Where is he right now?"

"I told him to leave so we wouldn't have this confrontation ...." Neena's voice trailed off.

"Where is he now?" Hana repeated.

"Hana—"

"Tell me." She tore herself from the hug to stare at her mother's tear-streaked face. "Has he found somebody else?"

"He has my blessing." Her voice was stern, but Hana saw her eyes wavering. "I still love him, but our relationship couldn't last long."

"He chose *her* over us?" Hana hissed in pain while glancing away. "So he abandoned us."

"Abe never abandoned us. He will call often to check on Hana." Neena rested a hand on her daughter's sticky cheek. "He still loves you."

"But not enough to stay here with me," she said in a numb voice. Out of nowhere, Hana began to clarify the messed-up problem. Her mother gave up the one person she adored because of their crumbling relationship so as not to hurt either party, perhaps enduring the thought of her partner seeing someone with whom he might have a better connection. Soon Hana was sobbing once again, back in her mother's embrace, to share the burden. Their crying was soon the only sound in the empty apartment.

"Love," Hana wailed piteously. "I love him …."

"I know, love, I know," Neena rocked their bodies gently.

"Why did this happen to me?" Hana shook her head against her mother's neck.

"It's my fault," Neena patted her head, unaware that the subject had changed.

"No." The girl had no choice but to delve into the pain lacerating her system, although making sure not to share too much. "I fell in love with Jin. I love him so much."

"I had a rough idea of what might be happening between the two of you." With both hands Neena clasped Hana's cheeks to search her watery eyes. "What happened, Hana?"

"I fell in love, but Jin wants us to be friends." She hiccupped several times. "B-but …."

"But what?" Neena frowned in concern. "Hana, please tell me."

"I … the two of us—" She shook her head, feeling a rising blush.

Neena's eyes widened when it finally clicked in her brain. "Jin forced himself on you?"

"No! I s-seduced him …." Hana quickly shook her head, about to rephrase her sentence, but squeaked in panic when a hand almost slapped her face but stopped short.

"I don't know if I should remain angry or let it go." Neena fumed but decided to remain calm. "I'm not a good role model myself, but I am confused by your explanation."

"Just hear me out, and don't ask any questions!" She drew a few shaky breaths and continued until the two of them became quiet.

They shed tears because of men, for their own separate reasons, until Hana felt the pull of dizziness. She slid back down flat on the mattress, exhausted, and rolled over to close her eyes. In moments, she was asleep. For her part, Neena quietly left to swallow the bitter pill of bearing her failed marriage and listening to her daughter's plight.

It took some time, but before the holidays ended, Hana managed to eat a little, and then a little more, because of sympathy for her mother, knowing the older woman had a lot on her plate. Still, more often than not, she vomited up whatever she ate. Both of them had trouble sharing laughter; mostly the walls witnessed their tears and splintered souls. Life took on a different path for either one of them, although Hana was not looking forward to the school reopening.

"Hana, dinner is ready!" Neena called from the kitchen.

"Yes," she responded immediately. But after one step forward, she wobbled on her feet, watching black spots swimming in her vision, before dropping on all fours to intake big gulps of oxygen. Her weakness was growing, but she could not afford to visit the clinic without her mother's knowledge. All hell would break loose in that case; still, she had been toying with the idea of heading to another facility by herself.

"Hana?" The door creaked open to reveal her mother's face. "Honey, what is the matter?"

"N-nothing." The word weighed heavily on her tongue.

"But why are you on the floor in that position?" Neena rushed to crouch on the floor beside her and draw her thick hair over one shoulder.

"I'm fine." Hana struggled to control her uneven breathing.

"Hana—"

"Please," she moaned, sure that she knew what her mother was about to mention.

"Your health is getting worse." Neena's voice conveyed her frustration. "I'm taking you—"

"Stop harassing me!" Hana barked at her mother, who blinked once.

"I am not harassing you! Do you think I can overlook the fact that my child is suffering?" Her voice rose even higher when she stood up. "Fine then! Just stay there!"

The booming sound of the door slamming closed jolted Hana. Her mouth trembled, but she bit her lower lip. As she slowly curled her hands into fists, her breathing at last returned to normal.

Suddenly the door opened again to reveal her mother, carrying a tray of food. With a sour expression she carefully sat cross-legged beside a wary Hana who studied her every movement. After mixing the rice with curry condiment and assorted vegetables with cooked fish, Neena jerked her chin towards a handful of rice.

Hana abruptly realised that her mother was patiently waiting to feed her. "I love you," she said, her voice thick with rising tears.

Neena tilted her smiling face. "I love you too."

Chapter 33

The summer holidays had ended. Jin was riding school early in the morning by himself, looking forward to a fresh start for everyone else. The streets were full of students in different school uniforms; he zigzagged carefully on the walkway so as not to hit passers-by. The breeze ruffled his hair curling on the perched collar and fluttered the tail of his shirt; the bike's chain squeaked steadily.

He had resigned from the summer job just before school was to resume. He was proud to receive his salary and give it to his mother; she refused the offer, but Jin was persistent. A smile lit his face as he took half of the cash for personal matters.

Now he pedalled towards the parking space where he locked his vehicle before sauntering towards the locker hall. On the way he spied Shouko alongside her friends. He felt a twinge of hurt as she ignored him and followed the other girls out of the area.

Jin had called her countless times to apologise, but she was so furious that she had blocked him from all social media. Feeling the weight within his chest, he exchanged shoes, riding high above any trouble and pretending to be fine in the eyes of his friends. They chattered as usual, sharing their summer stories; meanwhile he kept mum as they passed through the halls.

At the classroom he paused to study the seating arrangement scribbled on the board. "Jin, you're sitting beside me." Genji roughly thumped his back. "Girls, back off; he's mine now."

"You're making this weird," one of the girls lamented while her companions erupted in laughter.

Minutes before lessons began, Hana walked slowly into the classroom, head down. Strangely, her body at first glance was slender as if she had lost weight. He wasn't able to believe it might be due to exercise. Upon closer inspection, the girl wasn't nearly the same Hana he'd known all his life.

"Wait, Suhana! You're no longer sitting by the window!" someone yelled when she was about to take a seat.

Jin pretended not to notice her presence. She had not bothered to return any of his messages or missed calls. His leg jerked continuously, and his fingers were mindlessly worrying a pencil. He heard a table hitting the wall and her soft voice pleading at the person involved. The familiar scent of her body somehow reached him as she passed by, and memories of better days resurfaced. Jin squeezed both eyes shut to erase the bittersweet moments because those keepsakes now caused him more hurt than happiness. Soon he felt at ease to look up again.

"Hey, hey, she's here." Jin's same friend snorted while tapping on his forearm.

"Just ignore her," Jin muttered, slouching deeper in his chair.

The bell rang, in answer to Jin's inner prayers. Their homeroom mentor walked in, and everyone stood to greet him in a droning voice. When the class had settled down, he erased the seating arrangement from the whiteboard. The students nonchalantly arranged their papers and books on their desks.

"Oi, Jin." Someone lightly kicked his chair from behind.

"What?" Jin leaned back without glancing over.

"Here." A paper became visible beside him. "Hurry up, take this."

"Huh?" He frowned slightly but took the proffered note and carefully unfolded it to stare in amazement at the handwriting.

"Jin, what do you have in your hand?" The teacher stepped forward with a sceptical look.

"N-nothing." He quickly crumpled it without a glance in Hana's direction it was an apology letter.

I'm sorry.

His heartbeat raced at the sight of those brief words, and emotions rose from deep within his heart. He was shocked to realise he was smiling and hid his expression so as not to showcase it to anyone else. He pretended to act distant, but inside he was blooming. Finally he peered over his shoulder for a look at Hana.

He raised a brow. She was the most studious person in the classroom, yet now she was dozing off in the middle of the lesson.

"Hana!" the teacher called. "No sleeping in my class!"

"Sorry," she mumbled.

Their gazes met, and in reflex Jin looked away. Even though he was the one who had created agony in Hana's life, he had the petty urge to retaliate somehow for her ditching him at the park. Of course, he planned to walk up to her and ask why she had disappeared.

"Stand up right now, Hana!" The teacher barked the order. "Are you still affected by the summer holiday?"

"Your lesson is boring; I don't blame her for falling asleep," one cheeky boy commented, earning a blistering glare.

"Both of you, stand outside now," the teacher responded. Jin ignored the boy's sputtering complaint while a few chuckled at his stupidity.

"OI!"

The shout, alarming the entire classroom, was followed by noises from the screeching table and chair. Voices rose, and Jin snapped his neck around in time to see Hana collapsing on the cold floor and hitting her head. A chill came over him at the sight of the unconscious girl.

The teacher raced over to check on her pulse. Girls were shrieking in confusion.

"Jin! Go check on her!" Ino's voice brought him back to reality.

"Hana!" The name was torn from Jin's throat as he surged to his feet, almost tripping because of the chair leg, and rushed to crouch beside her.

The teacher looked up at him. "Jin, move aside—"

"Hana!" Jin's cry drowned out their teacher's terse voice. "Oi!"

He lifted her frail body in his arms, feeling her erratic pulse. Blinding panic seized him, and his face blanched in horror. A bead of sweat trickled along his forehead, and another descended his spine. He cradled the soft figure closer with one hand pressing Hana's dark head towards his chest. The voices around him sounded far away since his focus was on the immobile individual.

"Jin! Leave this to the teacher." Their homeroom mentor squeezed his shoulder in warning.

"S-she's not breathing!" Jin cried out in protest.

"We have to bring her to the nurse," Ino calmly said to him.

Jin got to his feet, carrying Hana in his arms, and stumbled from the spot, ignoring his teacher's angry expression, and proceeded to the hallway, where he finally broke into a run. Guilt drove him, and both feet literally flew off the ground at each step. He knew his face must be contorted because of the tumultuous emotions he felt. *Don't you dare die, Hana!* He screamed mentally.

He burst into the nurse's office and shouted, "Call the ambulance right now!"

Startled, the nurse approached them. "What's the matter?" She looked serious.

"Hurry!" He yelled the word into her stunned face.

"Jin!" Ino Hayamoto walked up sternly. "Calm—"

"I cannot calm down!" he said in a frantic voice. "How do I stay calm when Hana is dying?" He gently laid Hana on the mattress, sobbing brokenly, often swiping at his salty tears. Trembling, he carefully linked his fingers together with Hana's. Unbothered by the others, he leaned over to plant a soft kiss on her cool forehead. Jin never budged but replaces the lips with his forehead to gaze down at the closed eyes.

"I have made a call to the student's mother," the nurse said; "she is on her way right now."

"Please, wake up," he whispered in a strained voice.

"Jin, go back to the classroom—"

"No!" He cut their mentor's sentence short. "I'm not leaving her alone!"

Ino's face reddened with frustration. "Stop being stubb—"

"I've left her alone for far too long! I'm not abandoning her again!" Jin was breathing hard but stood firm beside the bed. Tears dripped from his trembling chin onto their clasped hands. He squeezed her fingers before lifting her hand to rest it on his wet cheek. For a few moments the others left them alone.

Then he heard Ino's, their classmate, voice again; apparently he had decided to visit them. "Jin," Ino murmured.

"I've hurt her," Jin whispered harshly. "This is all my fault."

"Don't blame yourself." Ino placed a comforting hand on his shoulder. "Come on, she needs some rest."

"I'm not going anywhere," Jin said in a firm voice.

"Listen to him, Jin," their homeroom teacher replied, stepping into view with a stern expression. "Students are not supposed to linger in this nurse room."

"I don't care," Jin said, a little louder. "I want to stay by her side-"

"Whatever problems you have with Hana can be settled later. For now, go back." The man walked closer to grab for his arm.

"Let go!" Jin shrugged him off. "Stay away from me!"

"You will face detention if Jin continues with this absurd attitude!" the teacher shouted, with a glance at the girl lying on the mattress.

"It's all right, he can help me look after Suhana if she wakes up," the nurse finally said. "I'll make sure he returns to the classroom."

"Fine." The teacher nodded once. "Let's go, Ino."

"Okay." The other boy once again squeezed Jin's drooping shoulder and left.

"Is she your girlfriend?" the nurse asked with an endearing smile.

"No," he whispered after a moment. "She's my best friend."

"Oh." She blinked while heading over with a fever patch to place on top of her forehead. "She is lucky to have a good friend like you."

"She doesn't deserve me," he murmured after the nurse moved away.

❧

"Where is she?" A new voice broke into Jin's drowsy state.

Jin was seated beside Hana, holding her hand and resting his head on his other arm. He blinked and stood up. He saw Neena on the other side of the bed looking down at her daughter and crying quietly.

"Mrs Neena?" he said, a little nervous.

"Jin." She wiped a tear and looked at him. "My poor baby is really sick," she said, sobbing the words. "I'm a terrible mother."

The nurse walked closer. "Suhana woke up a while ago—"

"She did?" Jin cut her off in a state of shock.

"Yes, but you were sleeping," the nurse said apologetically.

"I've watched over her health, thinking she was fine, but the signs were there." Neena covered her face with one hand.

"Mrs Neena, please accept my apologies." Jin spoke in a rush while he bowed low, feeling sweat springing to his brow. "It's my fault for hurting Hana terribly."

"Jin," Neena said, watching him closely, "please, stand up to your full height."

"I can't." He continued clenching his fists, forcing himself not to burst into tears. "I shouldn't be asking you for anything, but please, forgive me—"

"I don't know what passed between Jin and my daughter, but she shared some with me." Her voice hinted of simmering anger. "As a mother, I am outraged by the action, but Suhana has said not to hate you."

He closed his eyes tightly. "You have every right to lash out at me."

"Both Suhana and I will be leaving Tokyo," Neena said, startling him. "But I have to get her health back on track."

"Just the two of you?" he whispered quietly.

"Yes, the two of us need a fresh start in life." Her gaze drifted away, and she looked forlorn.

"But what about her studies?" Jin grasped for a topic but realised he was far from changing her mind.

Neena turned to look at him. "Suhana can continue with her studies elsewhere. She often received bullying treatment here."

"Jin, you may now return to your classroom." The nurse smiled gently, guiding him towards the entranceway.

He saw Neena leaning over to kiss a rousing Hana on the forehead as the door slid closed. He leaned his head against the block wall separating him from Hana, hearing the murmur of voices from the other side. Then his heart flinched in pain at her familiar voice. He rested one hand flat on the door, grateful that Hana was awake; she must be hurting from the fall, but she was secure in her mother's care.

He began to conclude that he and Hana would never meet again. His chin trembled from the force of his emotions. After a moment of reflection, he decided to back several steps away from the area, keeping his gaze fixed on the closed entrance. He couldn't escape the feeling that a part of his heart was behind that curtain with the person lying on the mattress. It took a lot of courage for him to walk back to class.

At one point, Hana's mother dropped by their classroom to gather up Hana's things. Jin had difficulty looking in her direction, hearing the sound of her heels clicking within the quietness of the classroom. Eventually, without a word, she walked out of the room, and he released a pent-up breath and glanced at the empty desk.

I am sorry, Hana.

Chapter 34

Eight years later
Osaka

Japan had a reputation for strict laws involving working hours as well as stress-inducing labour environments. High rates of depression and suicide had influenced these regulations, yet some offices imposed less restrictive rules, hoping to allow their workers to have breathers; for instance, dogs were hired to calm the ambience. A compact office of fourteen people might be full of the sounds of keyboards tapping whilst the air conditioner worked to cool the room. At any time co-workers might be found ambling toward the minuscule kitchen to brew coffee or chatting with their colleagues, as the laid-back atmosphere allowed them to set their own pace unless meeting a certain deadline.

Yet a certain company was far from the norm as the male boss was kind to his teams, breaking the stereotype of a bloodsucking leader. Instead he trusted the people working for him. To them he felt like an "uncle" due to his bachelor status. He was hiring those who were qualified instead of checking for a diplomatic background.

The insurance company staff was housed in the second level of an established building. Suhana stood out amongst the mainly Japanese staff with her light caramel skin and thick, lustrous hair reaching just above her curvaceous waist and petite body, far different from the slender figures of other women in the office. Instead of being shunned for her race, Hana was embraced by the group, who readily offered advice and tips.

It had been three years since the shy young woman's first job, in an office setting that did not require her to rush around with papers or repeatedly bow to her angry boss because of late projects or "forgotten" tasks. Still, from that experience, she knew that certain colleagues could be vindictive; once, in a situation of sexual harassment, she had not wanted to draw in gossip and had instead resigned.

Now Hana was sometimes asked to recruit newcomers because of her natural instincts to guide them in a friendly pace, having a keen understanding for those who suffered from nervousness and anxiety in a new element.

Today, they were celebrating the retirement of a colleague whose tenure was impressive. She had been with the team ever since the company first opened ten years ago; slices of matcha cheesecake were passed around; gifts were stacked on the honouree's desk, and songs were sung.

Of course tears were shed as well, and being a sentimental girl, Hana carried a tissue box to wipe her wet cheeks. Jokes surrounded her, but she took it all in stride, knowing they meant no harm. She even joined in to return snarky retorts.

"All right, listen up."

The room grew quiet, and everyone stared at the pudgy man who both encouraged and respected his staff.

"Today is Mrs Yuchiko's last day with us." His voice cracked at the end. "She has been a motherly figure to us all and the best colleague anyone has ever had."

"Thank you, Mr Sukihara. Your words will forever be cherished." Mrs Yuchiko was weeping as she laughed aloud. Hana, temporarily dubbed the "Tissue Girl," busily handed over several sheets. "I hope all of you will have a joyous time in this office and meet a good co-worker too."

"About that," Kaito Sukihara said with a chuckle. "Next week, we will have a new person joining us, so please be friendly, and take him under your wing."

"Awesome," Hikari Namani, who was known to be the drinker of the tight knit group. "Well, that seat was taken fast."

"Don't jinx Kaito and the company," another piped in with a sneer. "Even though we are laid back, many wouldn't take a position here due to the salary; also, they might think this job isn't worth it."

The mention of salary stung Kaito, although he kept his composure intact. Yet a few others choked back their laughter at this blunt observation by one of their tech geek.

The room finally erupted into cheers, and traditional sake was raised in toast. Hana wasn't a drinker, but to respect their culture she took a sip in honour of her colleague before placing the small cup on the table. Quietly, the Indian girl exited the office, heading for the vending machines on the ground floor and a small garden with benches for anyone to sit and enjoy their meal.

She watched the colourful vending machine waiting for her ramen to appear. She was carelessly playing with the name tag hanging around her neck. Tendrils of hair below her neat chignon played about her face, and she wore a simple red blouse that complemented white jeans and ladylike sandals.

The machine beeped to indicate that the ramen was finished, and she gingerly removed it through the opened transparent door. Then she turned to stroll out to the familiar spot under a cherry tree, sighing in relief that nobody else was there. She sat happily to begin her lunch—only to realise she had forgotten her drink.

"Hey." A male's voice behind her stopped her in the act of getting up. "The drink's on me."

She spied her colleague sauntering over with a grin, holding two packets of drink that must have come from the vending machine. "Ayato?"

She blinked at the man as he parked beside her and set the packet down close to her. Then he slouched comfortably on the bench, slurping noisily. Hana felt a blush crawling up her skin, because Ayato Kaname was not only her co-worker but also her ex-boyfriend. They had lasted only three months as a couple, but the break-up was partly Hana's fault.

The embarrassing scene replayed momentarily in her head, dispelling her appetite, but a snort made her look up at the handsome male. His warm gaze took in her body language before he rested elbows on his knees with the drink dangling in one hand. His short wavy hair matched his baby boy good looks. He had a medium build and wasn't too tall—just the right height for her to kiss his cheeks without falling over.

He had a reputation as a ladies' man, yet she had learned a lot about him when they were an item. He was in fact a gentleman, knowing how to treat a lady and indeed known to pamper his girlfriends, including herself. It was difficult for Hana to accept his little gifts, and she found it awkward to explain time after time that there was no reason for him to display his "love" by wasting resources on such actions.

"Look, Hana, don't beat yourself up for that night, okay?" He smiled in her direction.

"Hm?" She tensed at the mention of that screwed-up event.

"You weren't ready, and you had told me many times," he said in a soft tone. "We can take this at your own pace."

"I am not the girl for you, Ayato," she managed to croak like a toad. "You deserve someone who is confident and independent."

"But I want you." His dark gaze scalded Hana's damaged soul. "I love you, Suhana."

"No, you don't." Her brown eyes shifted downward to stare at the lukewarm noodles. "I'm broken, and I don't think I'll ever be able to heal properly."

"But I'll be here," he answered before raising a hand to caress her cheek. "Do you think I've never seen that sad face when Hana thinks nobody is looking at you? I don't know what happened in the past, but it must have caused you pain."

The woman's throat filled with a knot, and tears blurred her vision. Once again she relived the moments back when that person still lived stubbornly in both her heart and mind. But she knew that he was also linked to the horrifying incident; the nightmare sometimes replayed, causing Hana to shed tears as she despaired that she might never see him without harking back to the same circumstances.

The scar was too deep for Hana to have a normal relationship, putting her off from making love to anyone. With Ayato, she had tried to be intimate, only to inflict on him a meltdown in the nude as she grabbed onto a blanket. The poor man lay by her side the entire night to calm her down.

The next morning, Hana had asked for a break-up because she couldn't look him straight in the eyes, even though they both worked in the same office. But what happened later surprised her: instead of avoiding her, he was keen on rekindling the relationship. She saw that he was serious with her, unlike his ways with other women.

"Come here," he whispered. "I'm sorry to make you cry."

Startled by his words and by realising that tears were rolling down her heated cheeks, she tried to move away. Yet Ayato was persistent, and soon he was cradling Hana's head against his warm chest. He nestled little kisses on her forehead, making her cry even harder at his understanding and affectionate behaviour. She wished in her heart that she could love him, yet she knew it would never happen.

She hated herself for letting go such a good man who accepted her for who she was, loving her unconditionally. The times she had spent in his apartment were both sweet and exciting until they finally took the chance of making love—only to keep her sleepless for yet another reason. Guilt consumed her for having roped Ayato into her dilemma, when he should be looking for a better life partner.

"Please," Hana whispered before pushing away from his chest. "Go away, Ayato—"

"I won't. Stop telling me to." He gazed intently into her tear-stained face. "Even if it takes a year, I'll wait for you, because I've found the one I want to spend my life with."

"But—"

He placed a finger on her lips before offering a smile, which only frustrated her. His blind devotion was exhausting.

"I'll wait, but for now, we have to head back, or else the rest might think we have eloped due to the measly salary."

He stood up and waiting for Hana to take his outstretched hand. Instead, she rose without his aid, carrying her ramen. She hoped to eat it later, after warming it in the microwave. Still, he tucked her hand in his own, making sure she couldn't shake him off as they returned inside.

Chapter 35

Hana stood in the kitchen placidly cutting up vegetables whilst the television droned on; old habits were hard to shrug off. She lived alone in a compact apartment with affordable rent and a kind old landlady. The whistling of the kettle caught Hana's attention; she took it from the heat and set a pot for the noodles.

After she'd refreshed herself in the shower, it was time for dinner. The place was sparsely adorned except for little oddments hanging on the wall. Although she yearned to decorate, it was always pushed back since she had moved in with Ayato during their relationship but now had returned to her own venue.

She had joined the company as an administrative associate, handling everyone's salary and the database. Now it was the same, except she was the one to provide orientation for newcomers. Some had left after a month of working with them due to the pay, although she understood their reasons. Prices were rising, and having a family to care for was expensive.

She hummed tunelessly under her breath while waiting for the bubbling noodles and vegetables to steam when the first credits rolled on the television screen for a horror movie. With a shrill cry, she skidded out of the kitchen like an Olympic qualifier, only to tumble over an old couch and rolling off the seat to end up flat on her back on the floor. Excruciating pain was centred on her spine, but she groped for the remote control only to mewl pathetically as the images started to play before she could switch the channel.

Just then, her cell phone announced a caller, startling her already frazzled nerves. Gingerly she took the device to stare at the blinking screen. She drew her legs against her chest before answering; it was the one who never let her forget his presence in her life. A glance at the clock told her that Ayato was now perhaps reclining on his bed to call her before turning in for the night.

"Hey," Hana answered breathlessly.

"Suhana." His baritone voice tickled her ear. "Have you taken dinner?"

At the mention of dinner, Hana's eyes widened in horror, and she finally picked up the scent of burning noodles. With a scream she dropped the phone and scrambled for the kitchen, only to bend low, hugging herself with a pathetic groan. The noodles that had not burned were overcooked, and the vegetables were soggy beyond repair. Dinner was ruined.

She was scraping at the pot in a fit of fury, banging it in the sink to ease her tension, when someone rang the doorbell. Frowning with no clue of who this might be, she slowly crossed to the entrance and stood on tiptoe to peer into the peephole. She gasped at the sight of Ayato cradling mysterious plastic bags.

She opened the door to face the smiling man, who patiently waited for her to invite him inside.

"Good evening," he said with a bow. "I brought dinner for us two."

"What?" She blinked in response. "Why has Ayato bought dinner for me?"

"Because … I wanted to?" he raised a brow before shifting on one hip. "May I come in?"

"Oh, sure." She shuffled backward with a casual welcoming gesture. "Forgive my rudeness."

"It's all right," he said with a chuckle as he used his feet to shed his shoes.

Nervous and wary at Ayato's sudden appearance, she watched him saunter over to the tiny living room, which only further narrowed his passage due to the lone two-seater sofa. Suddenly she gasped, glancing down at her attire—she was wearing an emoji bloomer with peach tone spaghetti straps, padded on the front for her abundant bosom, topping off knee-length wool socks, each with two black beady eyes and a red nose.

She hurried into her room and slid the door closed before searching for a robe to cover her body. Then she peered past the door and saw Ayato ready with the assorted plates on the small coffee table. But she did see his red tinted face and realised he must have seen her outfit. She frowned, hoping she wouldn't have to slam the remote on his head in case he made some awkward advance.

She stepped into the living room and caught him smiling at her. She managed only a faint smile, the only emotion she could muster in reply. "What brought Ayato over here?"

Instead of walking over to sit on the springy sofa, she stood near the entrance of the room to study his body language. His body straightened into rigidity when he stood up from the floor and walked the short distance to where she stood. He must have felt her flinch when he cupped her cheek and smiled warmly, never shifting his gaze from her own. "I just wanted to check up on Hana," he said softly. "When you left me hanging on the phone, I had to drop by in case something was wrong."

"But you had the time to stop to buy dinner?" She raised a questioning brow. "What if I'm being attacked and Ayato is still waiting for the food order?"

He barked a laugh, bringing a sincere smile to her face—until his thumb caressed her cheek, making her step back to halt whatever ideas he was getting.

"I'm sorry." He too stepped backward to awkwardly wave at the dinner.

"What?"

"Look, even if Hana had eaten your dinner, then I could pack this back home and give it away to the stray cats."

He seemed confused and perhaps unsettled, so she shrugged and explained the reason she had dropped the phone. A look of understanding came over him, and he nodded slowly. Of course, Hana avoided the real reason she had burned the noodles in the first place.

She peered up at him. "Shall we eat together?"

"Yes." He followed her toward the table, where they sat opposite one another to bow and start to dig in.

The next morning Hana was sitting in her office cubicle typing furiously whilst sucking on a Chupa Chups and ignoring the hubbub. Everyone was working hard to meet the deadline, hoping to satisfy their customers. One was hurrying so fast that he fell flat on his face, sending papers flying in all directions. Everyone paused in their work to either aid him or inquire if he was all right.

On days like this, their boss would periodically demand if any of them had completed the task. Everyone would answer in unison the hated word *No*, after which some of the men would crack crude jokes about the salary. Of course many of them would swallow their laughter, since Kaito would reply silently with his infamous death glare.

Last night, after the dinner Ayato had gone home—much to Hana's relief. Once again, he was blindly chasing her, hoping for any remaining affection. No matter how many times she had explained to him, Ayato would turn down the volume of his hearing to only listen to the good parts of the conversation.

Hana spied an email from her mother; she was touring the globe, even though it was mainly a business vacation. Years earlier Neena had sold their former house to move to another part of the city. There Hana was pushed into an International school where, thankfully, she never ran into bullying and could concentrate on doing well academically.

After sending a short email in reply, Hana looked at the calendar and stared at the notice of when the newcomer would arrive. That meant Hana had to finish tying up loose ends and make herself available to guide him or her for the job; hopefully, that person would decide to remain longer.

Her table was neat, devoid of any pictures or personal memorabilia, keeping the space open for any paperwork. Only a fake plant sat on the desk, scented with perfume to calm her hectic brain.

"Yo, Suhana?"

Her gaze shifted to a colleague, he had been born to be the life of the party and a supportive person. Whenever the boss would take the staff out for dinner on payday, they would gear up for Hikari's antics when alcohol stimulated him to flirt with anyone he encountered.

Of course that meant, they would die of laughing from his singing when Kaito dragged them to the busy district for cheap fun.

"Yes, Hikari?" Hana smiled at the man who wore a casual style, with bright splashes of colour on a loose shirt and harem pants above loafers. "Anything you need help with?"

"I know that you are busy, but can Hana help me with this paper markings?" he begged desperately, looking troubled. "My next pay, I'll buy you a drink, please?"

"As long as it's not an alcohol beverage, then I'm fine." She held out a hand for the papers. "Give it to me."

"*Thank you, Suhana!*" he said with an extravagant bow.

She threw herself into the task, loving the fact that work left no room for dismal musings.

Chapter 36

The plane finally touched down on the tarmac, as passengers sat in their comfy seats awaiting the signal to prepare to exit. The pretty flight attendant bowed in greeting before directing them to walk without pushing in the centre of the aisle. Jin stared at the crowd's glacial pace and checked his wristwatch before glancing at the small window. The view was cluttered with other airplanes either parked or in the midst of taxiing for take-off.

Soon he was able to stand without being bumped. He retrieved his duffle bag from above and joined the slow march with his dark head low.

He arrived at the sidewalk with a trolley carrying his other bags. He paused to look around for a person assigned to greet him. Spying a young man with a signboard written with his name, he headed towards him. There he stopped to bow, sporting a smile. Then he stood to introduce himself to the person, who beamed at him in return.

"I'm Jin Takami, and thank you for meeting me."

"Welcome to Hokkaido, Mr Takami, and it is a pleasure to meet our company's newest member," the man remarked earnestly. "My name is Daisuke Ichinose, and I will drive Mr Takami to your residential area and help with any boxes that may have arrived at your doorstep."

"Thank you kindly, Mr Ichinose, but you really don't have to." Jin followed him, feeling grateful for the hospitality. The young man wore a pale blue shirt that was neatly buttoned and ironed slacks with matching dress shoes. Large-framed glasses perched on his nose, and his cropped hair was stylishly gelled. His height only reached Jin's chin. His friendly smile calmed Jin's mind about being in a new environment.

The ride was silent but comfortable as Jin took in the sights of his surroundings. He had been to Osaka several times during previous jobs. The reason he had quit his last job, as a negotiator for a finance firm, was that it was hectic although the salary was top-notch. Still, he chose to resign and accept an offer in a small office for an insurance corporation.

Soon rows of houses with high fences came into view. This felt more like spying a shrine instead of choosing an apartment. The car rocked to a stop in front of a low building similar to the rest sporting, a high plank fence. A gate led into the front yard; a stone footpath gave it a warm and quite authentic ambience.

"Wow." Daisuke chuckled at the amazing sight.

The owner trots over perhaps to hand over the key. "Jin Takami?" The man bowed when Jin nodded in acknowledgement. "I hope that you will like the accommodation and allow me to show you around the house."

Thankfully, the jovial owner had already seen to the moving of the boxes; they were now neatly stacked in the living room. Each sliding door revealed spacious rooms and a bamboo mat spread on the floor. The bathroom contained a blue basin alongside a wooden chair.

"I'm sorry we don't have a tub," the owner said, bowing in apology.

"It's all right." Jin waved one hand and watched Daisuke peering into every single room and looking impressed.

When the short tour ended inside a kitchen—miraculously it had a single stove instead of using wood to light a fire—the three of them chattered amicably.

Jin was basically in love with his surroundings because he had always preferred traditional ways of living. With the help of his new colleague, he had soon unpacked several cartons. He paused to stare at a picture frame, and his smile faded as he stared at the black-and-white image of the young woman side by side with his father.

He caressed the picture fondly over the cold glass; then he stood upright to set this first item on a small table before bowing in respect. When Daisuke realised that Jin was sending a silent prayer, he quickly stepped near to do the same. He was studying the image before seeing Jin walk away to resume his task in brooding silence.

"You really shouldn't have, Mr Takami." Daisuke chuckled whilst sipping on his beer. "It was my pleasure to help."

"Don't worry." Jin raised his beer can. "We toast our first day of becoming friends and hopefully good colleagues."

"Banzai!"

"Please take good care of me, Mr Ichinose."

They were taking a rest right after rearranging the home. The hours had passed, and now the streetlights outside were lit.

After Daisuke departed Jin's new residence, Jin went back inside to take a "shower" with lukewarm water. He filled the basin from its tap and scrubbed off languidly. He thought he might take a stroll through the neighbourhood to get acquainted with the street.

He put on a pair of jeans and a T-shirt before wrapping a scarf around his neck to go out. He locked the sliding door before donning his boots and walking the short path to step out on the sidewalk. He shut the gate and set out to meet new faces and see the attractive neighbourhood.

Within minutes, Jin had met several residents, even making some friends. As a person from Tokyo, he struck many of them as a curiosity. He drew to a stop in front of the steps leading up to a shrine, but it was closed due to the late hour. He made a mental note to return tomorrow, when he thought of something else.

Tomorrow would be his first day on the new job, but he was confident after chatting with Daisuke. The younger man assured him that the place was hyped and their boss was known to be someone understanding and lenient. He went a bit further to joke about some of his colleagues.

Back home, Jin pulled out two small cups he had purchased for this use. He poured water and placed incense burners and stalks of flowers. Now he sat back on his knees to view the small shrine for his late parents before standing to pace toward the laptop and switch it on. It was nicely ensconced in the dark living room where a breeze from outside cooled the space.

He scrolled numbly through the emails whilst deleting junk. Soon he yawned, figuring it was time to hit the sack.

He unfurled the futon after sliding the glass door shut and plugged in a compact fan. Then he snuggled under the blanket wearing only his boxers. Fatigue from travelling and tidying up the place sent him to sleep easily. When he woke, he was startled to see that morning had quickly arrived—too soon, he felt.

He was still drowsy when he took a bath, but the cold water on his face helped him perk up. He searched his future master bedroom for a suitable ensemble to wear for his first day at work. He chose camouflage harem pants, a tight-fitted black shirt, and a jacket to ward off the chill. Autumn had arrived; soon the weather would turn colder, but Jin enjoyed the changes of season for bringing new hope and memories.

Outside a horn blared. Daisuke was here to pick him up. After praying to his parent's frame, Jin quickly hopped around, making sure nothing important was forgotten. Then he went out and waved at the young man standing near the driver's door.

"Good morning, Mr Takami," Daisuke said with a bow. "Are you ready to leave?"

"Morning, Mr Ichinose." Jin bowed in return before sliding into the passenger seat but not before greeting one of the seniors on a morning walk to the market. "By the way, you may call me by the first name."

"Seems you have already made new friends," the driver chortled. "Which means you have a likeable personality."

"You think so?" Jin raised a brow at the words before relaxing to lean his mussed head back and shut both eyes.

The ride lulled him to sleep as the car zipped along the streets, but Daisuke stopped at one point to wake him up for breakfast. Both enjoyed a hearty morning meal in a busy restaurant.

Finally, the office building came into view. Jin held tightly to his bag strap but felt confident that this new undertaking was a wise choice. Some soul searching following many surprising events through the years had landed him right here. Mostly, the death of his mother had shaken Jin to the core because he had no other living relative and was finally alone in the world.

"Let's do this," he muttered, eliciting a laugh from Daisuke. "Hopefully this will be my last pit stop."

Chapter 37

Jin paused to slip off both shoes and place them in the designated rack and entered the office wearing comfortable house slippers. He followed Daisuke, who addressed everyone gathered in the well-ordered room, people murmured as they spotted Jin, who glanced at each face, hoping for a friendly smile, and bowed several times.

A stout-looking man appeared, introducing himself as Kaito Sukihara, the boss, and welcomed Jin. The rest joined in a straight receiving line to greet Jin more formally. Still, the ambience struck a chord with him; he heard boisterous voices and saw unique characters. Greetings were flowing as they introduced themselves.

"I hope you will enjoy working with us, Takami," Kaito beamed.

Jin's eyes scanned everyone's face only to do a double take when he saw a familiar figure. A pale woman was staring right into his widening eyes with a stricken expression, and the sudden sensation of being deprived of oxygen felt like burning in his lungs. She had not change since the last time saw her—except that the woman now before him was even more beautiful than the Indian girl who often strayed into his recollection.

Jin's mouth slackened. As he kept on staring without shame, she timidly slipped behind one of her female colleagues.

Suhana.

His hands formed fists at his sides; warmth flowed into his countenance, and the tips of his ears grew hot. Finally, the past caught to him as he relived much of it as if it had occurred only yesterday. At the same time, he was hearing Suhana's laughter and seeing her shuddering gaze before her collapse back in the classroom.

"Suhana?" Kaito's voice broke Jin's transfixed gaze. "Where are you?"

"She is right here." Another man chuckled as he drew her by the hand into view. Then he looked at her. "Are you all right? Hana looks as if you saw a ghost."

The group burst into humorous noises, but Suhana only shook her head meekly without glancing up. But Jin waited patiently, holding his breath, until she pointedly lifted those mesmerising light brown orbs toward his own.

"Nice to meet you, Suhana," Jin said, bowing formally. "I hope you will take charge of me from now onward."

"Takami," Kaito said, looking away from the mute girl, "she will be guiding you for two weeks on our daily routine. Please be kind to her. Apart from that, you have a qualified background. How did you come to choose this firm?"

"I couldn't handle the stressful environment where I was," he said, slowing his breath. Then, refocusing on the flustered Hana, he sauntered forward, watching those alluring eyes widen until they looked like saucers. He stood back respectfully but offered a smile. Even as he wondered why she was behaving this way, he figured that he knew very well. Again he was torn by his guilt for the times leading up to her finally quitting the school and moving away.

She looked on the verge of fainting, but Jin pulled her out of her reverie with an apologetic grin. Her answering expression bordered on a grimace as another man beside her leaned close, saying something Jin could not hear. She nodded several times, still apparently unable to speak up.

"Ayato, introduce yourself," Kaito called out to the man as he stood upright.

"My apologies. My name is Ayato Kaname. It's a pleasure to meet you, Mr Takami," he said, with a nod of acknowledgement.

"Thank you," Jin replied, feeling dazed.

"Suhana, you seem pale," said Hiro Kushina, a senior of the team.

"I'm fine, just feeling a little weak at the moment." She offered a laugh, although Kaito looked concerned.

As Suhana's former best friend, Jin knew when she was being less than truthful. A soft grin formed on his face, and he saw that she realised he had caught on easily. She turned to bow at Ayato before returning gaze to Jin.

"For the learning period"—her feminine voice flooded Jin's system with sudden melancholy—"Mr Takami will be sitting beside me to learn the process. I hope you are a fast learner so we can shorten the teaching phase."

"Just call me by my first name," Jin said, but she seemed to ignore him. He studied her, silently appraising the long-haired woman's swaying hips, her petite form still packing those curves. He could see that some places had grown firmer and others seemed softer. His fingers all but itched for her touch. Instead of appreciating their rekindling friendship, Jin realised he was looking at her as a male whose interest ignited from deep within.

They proceeded to a cubicle, where he was presented a chair from a man dressed in cheery colours. Jin bowed, showing gratitude for the thoughtful gesture. Nervously, he stood aside while she cleared the table; finally, he sat down right after her.

Uncomfortable silence reigned between them. Jin couldn't look away from her blushing features. The small cubicle forced them to sit close together, and his heart slammed against his ribs. He jerked to attention when she began speaking in a low tone about job-related matters and introducing him to the work that he would be assigned.

Setting his shock aside, he listened attentively, even jotting reminders in his notepad, never realising that it was lunchtime until someone paused at their table. The scent of food caused Jin to salivate. Again he was grateful for someone's good deeds; this time it was from Ayato.

"Are you coping well, Mr Takami?" Ayato said with a chuckle, setting two coffee mugs on the table where they were dealing with business by phone.

"I'm coping well, thank you," Jin answered truthfully. "Her teaching is easy to understand."

Jin listened tentatively as Hana chatted with her client, although he had his own reasons to study her, watching every little play of muscles. Meanwhile, the return of his old self caught him slightly off guard, but Jin was not really surprised. "She is the perfect candidate for newcomers." Ayato languidly leaned against the entrance of the cubicle. "Our Suhana is skilled at making them feel ease in their new surroundings."

"It's nothing, really," she finally murmured in a deadpan fashion as she set down the phone.

Suddenly, Ayato moved to stand behind Hana. He reached around to rest a palm on her forehead. The action seemed very familiar between them, but Jin saw her lean a little away from the man's touch. He flashed back to times when he had done the same to her and sighed, feeling restless because he yearned to bombard her with questions—but also because their parting might have caused a rift in their friendship.

Ayato's face grew serious. "Should I tell Kaito—?"

"Really, I'm fine, Ayato." She sounded slightly annoyed.

"All right, as you say." Ayato just shook his head before backing away. "I'll head back to my place, but, Jin, please come by if you need any help."

"Yeah." Jin got up to bow before sitting again. "Suhana, you … don't seem happy to see me."

She whispered, "Because I really am not happy to see you."

Jin blinked several times at the girl's frank reply, taken aback and giving himself time to regain composure. But then again, had he expected Suhana to jump right into his arms and cry tears of joy?

"I—I see," he replied quietly. "I'm sorry if I have hurt you in the past."

"The time for forgiveness has passed, Jin."

Hearing her say his first name filled his heart with another emotion. Now he was musing over times wasted and what might have been otherwise.

"I prefer not to talk about that topic ever again," she continued in a dull tone. "They are bad memories to me."

"Even our friendship?" He peered at her sullen face. "Hana, you cannot deny—"

"Yes"—her gaze shimmered with threatening tears—"even our friendship. I don't want to think about those times, so please, let us communicate only about work."

"But what if I want to rekindle our friendship, Suhana?" His voice was insistent. "I think this is fate that we met once again, because I've thought about you throughout the time we've been apart."

"Not now, Jin," she cautioned him. "I don't want any of my colleagues to be aware of our past. because that is all you are to me now—a former friend."

Soon talk time was over and their tasks resumed, but the conversation lingered in Jin's thoughts.

When everyone was clocking out, Jin tried to stay close to Hana's side, but due to the others he became separated as the women headed home in a bunch. Trying not to be irked, he accepted Daisuke's offer of a ride home.

When they stopped for their dinner, though, he only half-heartedly listened to the guy's chatter. Hana was clouding his thoughts. He recalled the very day of their parting from one another. At the beginning, Jin was at flustered, eventually losing sleep and feeling depressed by the abrupt turn of events.

He had confided in his mother when she had asked about Hana's moving away. She was also taken by surprise but only nodded in understanding, since Suhana had gone through bouts of bullying. Yet Jin got an earful after hearing how he had treated his best friend; Sayomi even rapped her knuckles atop his head, only halting when she saw how much he was suffering without her.

As months passed by, everything returned to normal whilst his relationship with Shouko had gone on as strong as ever. As they graduated from high school, she dropped the bombshell that she intended to study overseas; they had promised to enter a distinguished university together in the same capital.

He supported his girlfriend's choice, but distance took a measurable toll, and eventually a break-up ended their romance. Many had been rooting for them to be married, perhaps even before finishing the semester. Word spread, to his annoyance, and people offered condolences while others encouraged him never to give up on the lost bond.

Shouko was still in contact occasionally, sending emails every few months. In truth, Jin had missed her. He regretted their break-up, but he had enjoyed a few casual relationships along the way to a career-driven adulthood carved out for him, when he indulged less playtime and focused more on creating a path for the future.

"Mr Takami? Are you listening to me, Mr Takami?"

"Wh-what?" Jin jumped slightly, feeling guilty for spacing out on Daisuke. "Please forgive me; I am feeling rather exhausted."

"You should have told me sooner." He chortled and stood up, ready to leave. "Come on, I'll drop you off before heading home myself."

"Thank you, Mr Ichinose." Jin bowed with a sincere smile. "Everyone has been so kind to me."

"That's how we are, drop the "Mister"," he said with a nonchalant shrug. "We are more than just colleagues there."

They stepped from the crowded restaurant into the evening breeze. The sky had turned dark when Jin waved at the retreating car. He stood at the front of his rented home before entering the front yard. Inside he hurried to the bathroom for a shower, with images of Hana still assailing his brain.

Chapter 38

*T*he smell of cooked rice filled the kitchen along with the noise of a knife rapidly cutting vegetables. Yet Hana's mind was elsewhere. The sight of Jin standing amidst the small crowd at the office had caused her emotions to explode in all directions. Past memories had resurfaced like demons when she realised that the new colleague she had been anxiously awaiting all week was none other than him.

Back in the office, Hana had struggled for patience, wishing not to break down emotionally and embarrass herself. Having Jin nearby was her weakness. The years apart were nothing to her, except that what between them was the hurtful past and her feeling of abandonment by the one person that she loved deeply.

A sudden sting on her finger reeled her back to the present, and she sucked air through her teeth when droplets of blood fell on the chopping board. She crossed to the sink and cleansed the wound before dressing it, his mature features floating before her mind's eye. He seemed to have changed within the past few years, growing handsomer. Yet she was not a foolish teenaged high schooler; she had changed as well.

The distance was enough to finally allow her feelings to be somewhat detached—but not to the point where her love for Jin had vanished. Still, trepidation kept her on her toes.

No man could take Jin's place in her heart, although had also caused plenty of damage. The one memory that would haunt her to her grave was suffering a miscarriage—sitting on cold bathroom tiles to lean back against the wall, fluttering her eyelids shut, groaning, and sighing aloud.

But now he was back, once again in her life.

She recalled his shocked face when he spied her, followed by a smile that literally took her breath away. She felt her forehead, sensing a sharp headache due to her wayward brain. She figured it was hopeless when it involved her weakened heart; she needed to let her brain take over—if she could maintain her good sense.

Now she was an adult, not the girl who used to follow her heart, only to end up in a disaster that almost cost her life. She would be wise to keep her distance from Jin, who hadn't gone through both the emotions and agony of losing an unborn child as well as being a rape victim.

She recalled and dismissed the fact that in her single bedroom sat a lone bear, because once upon a happier time, a certain boy had given her the plush toy from their visit to the arcade store.

Leaning casually against the cubicle divider that separate the middle walkway next morning, Jin took his time waiting for Hana's arrival to begin their day. Now that autumn had arrived, with a light, steady drizzle, he left early for work using public transport, allowing some quiet moments with himself.

Upon arrival, he had changed his shoes for office slippers before entering the chilly room and greeting the few already deskbound. Thanks to one of the kind female colleagues, Jin was able to navigate the tiny kitchen, where he spotted Hana's mug and filled hers and his own with steaming coffee.

Last night, he hadn't been able to sleep, reliving the past as if it was just yesterday, sometimes chuckling at random moments; other times, gazing into empty space. Meeting her yesterday had evoked long-forgotten days and long-dormant feelings for the young Indian woman. Yet now, Jin was a grown man with a different perspective.

He knew that his former self had been unkind and rather egotistical—enough to lose the one person who had been a constant in his life.

Hoping to rectify for his past mistake, he desperately yearned to make amends with Hana and rekindle whatever bond they still had. Usually, if old friends were to suddenly bump into one another, a celebration followed in an endless night of drinking and sharing the crazy times. But only anger and regret cloaked by uncomfortable silence reigned between them.

Finally, the entrance door flung inward, and Hana strode in. Her long hair was in a neat braid, and she was clad in rainbow tights and a wool coat covering her shapely figure. When she doffed the coat, Jin saw that she had on a burgundy long-sleeved velvet jacket, and slippers covered her dainty feet.

When her wide eyes locked onto his own, Jin bowed in a morning greeting right in the middle of the pathway; she bowed in return before mumbling a greeting. As she passed by, he caught the sweet lingering scent of fresh lime. He was following her when she paused with a raised brow and seemed to stare in a stupor at the mug on her desk.

"Your morning coffee," Jin remarked softly with a ghost of smile.

She turned slightly to regard him with a closed expression but nodded in gratitude. Then, before she could settle on her office chair, Jin slid it into place in a gentlemanly fashion, again startling his former best friend. This time despite her quizzical look, she did not reject the kind offer.

Jin was praying that the day would unfold with both of them becoming closer, but he slouched in disappointment as she began the day in another spirit. "I want Mr Takami to go through these leaflets," she explained, using his surname in an aloof tone. "And here is the stamp that needs to be on each one."

She had definitely changed over the years. Instead of the shy girl he used to know, this woman was oozing quiet confidence, which meant she had no reason to hide behind him. Even her clutter-free desk seemed rather detached; there were no holiday pictures or little trinkets to reflect her personality.

They worked quietly in her cubicle until nearly lunchtime. Then, as Jin was looking around, his eyes shifted downward, and he grinned. Tucked neatly away from easy view was a comic. Perhaps the old self of Hana was still there, hidden behind that façade. He reached forward and pulled out the comic book, only to turn rigid at the image splashed on the front cover.

Maybe her taste in genres had broadened. Heat flushed Jin's face at the sight of two male characters locked in some sort of bondage game. Then the compact sized comic was snatched away, further startling Jin, but he was now facing a red-faced seething Hana while she jerkily hid the volume inside the file cabinet.

"Who gave you the right to snoop in my belongings?"

A hush fell over the entire room, and typing ceased as Hana stood yelling down at him.

Kaito came out of his small office. "Suhana, what's the matter?" He sounded shocked.

Instead of answering, Jin watched her anger draining away before she shook her head slowly without looking at anyone. He felt guilty for putting her in the spotlight and hoped the boss wouldn't scold her over Jin's blunder.

Just as he was about to speak, Kaito once again questioned her. "Maybe you need a day off, Suhana?" he continued. "You seem a little—"

"My apologies," she said, bowing. "I didn't mean to yell aloud."

"All right, the person you need to apologise to is Jin, for whatever reason," he remarked before ambling away. "Lunchtime, everyone."

"Hana"—Jin got up as well hoping to stall her—"I'm sorry, but it wasn't my intention to snoop."

"You are forgiven," she replied without glancing at him. "In fact it is my fault."

"No—"

But Jin never had the time to finish the sentence as Suhana strode away towards the entrance. He didn't plan to lose the moment but took the initiative to be the one making the first move to heal their bond.

He followed her out of the office and saw her gazing up at the elevator number descending to their level. Quickly, Jin changed into his shoes before trotting after her just as she stepped into the elevator car. Then he was bumped from behind by someone, which made him stumble, muttering expletives.

"I'm sorry!" said the interloper. It was Ayato, who rushed to the closing elevator and managed to fling himself between the doors and in. Jin could only watch the two of them side by side before the door slid shut. He turned and ran down the staircase, but on the ground level he immediately became lost. Several minutes later he was able to track down the vending machine; emitting an exasperated sigh, he once again cursed Ayato for his pushiness.

Chapter 39

The pair looked crestfallen as Jin approached them, but Ayato spotted him and perked up slightly. Jin paused in front of them carrying his own lunch, purchased from the same vending machine. He made a mental note to look for possible shops nearby where he could buy lunch.

"Takami," Ayato greeted him before standing up. The man seemed lost for words. "About just now, please forgive me—"

"It's all right," Jin said, waving him off with a smile, but quickly turned towards Hana, who stood as well.

"I'll take my leave now," she murmured but glanced up at him. "I didn't mean to yell earlier, but please, don't touch my belongings ever again."

Jin took the hint that he and she should not act familiar with each other, which made him frown. Yet he shrugged off the irritation because Hana hadn't forgiven him for the past, which hung heavy between them, and Jin figured that it might be better for them to steer clear.

"I understand, Hana," He purposely used the familiar name, and she looked at him for a second before moving off. "Please accept my sincerest apology."

By now, he was staring at her retreating back, but he paused to examine the unreadable features of Ayato, who had sat down and was also gazing after her. Still, Jin was caught up in his own situation due to her cold attitude. He wondered how he might approach her without being pushed aside yet again.

Jin cleared his throat. "May I?"

Ayato blinked a few times as if just realising where he was and that he wasn't alone. He managed a warm smile and nodded his dark head once in permission, scooting a little to make space. Jin sat down on the vacated space and ate slowly and pensively; silence reigned between them, but soon it became apparent they were thinking of the same person.

Ayato chuckled warily. "You seem rather informal with Hana after the second meeting."

Jin paused, wiping his mouth with a handkerchief to glance toward Ayato, who stared blithely ahead, but he detected no malice from him. Instead Ayato had an odd expression, resembling a smile but also something else. He slowly put away the soft material in his pocket, preparing a measured answer.

Then Jin wondered whether Hana would be comfortable if the rest of their staff knew about her history with him and decided not to say anything. Certainly he respected her privacy, but he had another reason, more personal to him, as well: Jin preferred to keep them under wraps and not allow outsiders to peek inside.

"It's just a slip of my tongue," he lied with a slight huff. "I don't mean any disrespect toward Suhana."

"Don't need to apologise to me." Ayato chuckled warily, looking a bit deflated whilst rubbing one hand behind his neck. "Anyway, please don't take her words to heart."

"Of course not." Jin blinked at the irony, recalling their younger days when harsher words had been flung back and forth. "She had the right to yell at my face."

"Women—they're quite sensitive, aren't they?" With this Ayato chortled drily, finally peeking at him. "Don't mind my asking, but is Takami single?"

"Eh?" Jin blinked at the sudden question about his private life. He studied the man sitting beside him, but Ayato's face wore a carefree grin, making Jin brush away any doubts. He tucked his empty bowl between them before reclining back on the bench to enjoy the cold chill, figuring it might drizzle yet again.

"Well, are you single, or is your girlfriend coming along currently to live in with you?" His eyes twinkled with curiosity.

"I don't have a girlfriend." Jin smiled lazily. "What about yourself?"

"Single. I hope to change that status soon." Ayato sucked in his lower lip with a forlorn look and stood to his full height.

"Is break time over?" Jin stood up as well before wrapping the spoons he had brought from home in a paper towel and throwing his empty carton into a recyclable bin.

"Shall we leave, Mr Takami?" Ayato smiled at him.

"Yes," he replied with a nod.

Back in his seat once again, he was close to Hana, who avoided any contact; the only subject permitted between them was training him. For the first time in his work life, Jin found himself consumed with boredom and pettiness because the girl who'd once doted on him was now pretending they were complete strangers.

Soon it was time to head home. From one side Jin saw Hana packing her valuables in a tote bag.

"So uh, where do you stay?" Jin spoke hurriedly when she stood upright.

"Why?" She frowned suspiciously as she stepped out of the cubicle. "Have a safe trip home, Takami."

"Suhana—"

Hikari popped up out of nowhere to intervene. He stood before them beaming, excitement palpable in his gaze. "Takami, come on," he said, beckoning with one hand. "We boys are going for dinner before venturing our separate ways."

Hopelessly Jin gazed at the empty entrance door, knowing Hana was probably scampering to escape his presence. With no other choice he agreed, feeling miffed by the lost chance. Jin was desperate to move on after tearing down whatever obstacle stood between him and Hana.

Ayato, Daisuke, and surprisingly their leader joined them as well. Everyone exited the office to fit into their tech's car and drove off. Jin sat thankfully against the door, since his mood was deflated.

Their destination was a small udon stall in the middle of a quieter street, and they were grateful that seating was available for their number. Curtains flapped whilst gas lamp flickered, and an older man was staffing the constricted area by himself. After taking orders from each one, he expertly worked on their dinner.

"So why did our Suhana shout at Takami?" Kaito inquired from the other side of Hikari. "I've never seen her out of line. In fact I have to speak to her about her disorderly behaviour."

Sake was poured amongst them whilst everyone chattered amicably. Still, Jin was questioned repeatedly about the incident between Hana and himself.

"Please do not reprimand her; it's my mistake, after all," Jin began to explain.

"Don't worry," Ayato inserted while patting on Jin's back reassuringly. "He has a good sense to not allow this small issue to make him quit."

"I never thought of quitting this firm." Jin raised a brow whilst sipping his sake.

"Suhana hasn't lost her cool until now," Hikari chortled, working on his second round. "Takami must have truly irked her."

"They already apologised to one another," Ayato said in his defence. "It's all settled now, and Kaito has no reason to punish anyone."

"Are you going to punish her?" Jin swivelled in his chair to stare at Kaito, aghast.

"It's bold of Ayato to assume that I won't let Suhana off the hook for this." Kaito chuckled warily but then let out a shrugging sigh.

"My apologies for causing any necessary trouble." Jin felt guilt tripping him again.

Their hot bowl of udon arrived, and after politely addressing one another all of them dug into the hearty dinner. By turns they praised the cook for the delicious meal and ordered more of the alcohol before each one set down his chopsticks, feeling satisfied.

Beside him, Ayato was busy checking his cell phone, his expression forlorn, and sat rigidly.

"Daisuke, please let me off in front of my house?" Ayato's feature was flushed.

"Sure," Daisuke readily agreed.

The close-knit bond amongst them made the atmosphere relaxing and certainly laid back. Then Ayato rose after sending a text. "I have to leave." He sneezed all of a sudden, glancing towards Kaito. "Excuse me, *uncle*, but can you make another udon meal for a takeaway?"

"Hey, you'd better pay for that one," Kaito snapped. Jin chuckled because of the man's expression. Then he settled comfortably with both elbows on the scratched table, watching the old man at front whipping up the dish.

"Where are you going?" Hikari frowned slightly, already in a festive mood. "It's the weekend tomorrow. Why not just hang out with us?"

"He has places to go," Daisuke grumbled from the other end. "Leave him be."

"New girlfriend?" Hikari was persistent.

"No," Ayato chuckled, collecting the takeaway after paying the sum for both dinners. "All right, see you guys on Monday."

The ambience grew quiet as everyone stared at the man leaving except Jin, who was at loss for whatever reason. He scanned their faces with a confused countenance. "What's the matter?" he casually asked.

"Nothing." Daisuke laughed with a wave of his hand.

"That girl needs to give Ayato a chance." Hikari shook his head but earned a blistering glare from the tech geek.

"Whatever their problem, it's not ours to delve into," Kaito finally remarked, heaving a sigh. "So don't be a busybody, Hikari."

The topic quickly changed, but Jin was too busy thinking about Hana. Instead of listening, he wondered where she was right now and yearned to have a chat with her.

Chapter 40

Early evening, Jin was jogging along the pathway clad in a hoodie over a long-sleeved jumper, grey sweatpants, and running shoes. Perspiration dotted his face and body, yet his mind was elsewhere whilst he listened to rock songs through Bluetooth headphones.

He was analysing Hana's words from their earlier meeting, dodging his intention to be closer. How could Jin approach her when she'd pegged him as a Lothario? Their week was almost up, and he would soon have his own desk. But giving up was not an option.

As colleagues, they had to share phone numbers, so he had been texting Hana, yet no reply had come. Every time he spotted a perfect chance to have their little chat, someone would intrude. Although Jin was glad that she had finally found close friends, yet it irked him no end.

The road was wet from the light rain; passers-by were either snug in raincoats or carrying umbrellas. Jin turned a corner off the busy street to enter a café as a break from the exercise and stood behind the short queue to order a cup of strong coffee with sandwiches before settling down. He pulled out his cell phone to switch on the Wi-Fi.

Drinking the bitter brew gave his inner system a jolt, but he paused on Facebook when he read Shouko's status and "liked" it.

He shouldn't have lashed out at Hana. Instead of going a step further and breaking off their friendship, Jin could have stepped back and calmed down. He had let both pride and ego rile him up, and he now wished to turn back time and change the course of events but something else niggled at the back of his mind.

Soon, he was out of the café and jogging back to his house, knowing it was time for Hana to acknowledge him.

The desk was untouched whilst Jin anxiously awaited Hana's arrival. He felt let down when Kaito informed him that she had an appointment with another staff which meant she would be returning later. He used the computer gingerly, afraid for another meltdown from her. He recalled the week's lesson and began working.

By mid-afternoon, he was stretching languidly and yawning as the hum of the air conditioning and the sounds of rapid typing and low murmurs lulled his senses. Someone would occasionally pass by to head for the tiny kitchen to make a hot drink due to the chilly atmosphere, Eventually he stood and walked to the boss's office to bring a USB on which he had saved some document.

"Thank you, Takami." The man grinned looking distracted. "Have you taken a break?"

"No, Mr Sukihara," he said with a bow. "I've been busy with the document. May I ask a question?"

"Yes?" Kaito was already in the midst of plugging the USB into his computer.

Jin had second thoughts about his question. "Never mind, it's not important," he said before excusing himself, only to be halted in mid-step when Kaito addressed him.

"Takami, do you mind getting a cup of green tea for me?" He looked apologetic and held out a stained white mug. "You may go and take your lunch."

"Thank you." Jin bowed a second time before exiting the room and heading toward the lone kitchen.

Ayato was standing there and nodded at him. "Afternoon, Takami. Got the documents done?"

"Thankfully, yeah," he said with a chuckle before starting the process to make the drink. Silence fell between them.

"I'll take my leave," Ayato eventually said with a nod and a tight-lipped smile. Jin noticed something in his hand but shrugged nonchalantly.

After delivering the boss's tea, Jin went back to his desk and sat down, only to pause at the sight of cookies. A neat red bow sealed the cellophane packet, and a note attached. Frowning, he leaned forward curiously, lifted the gift, and started to read the words set out in masculine strokes.

Please give me a—

"Is this why Takami was on the receiving end of our Hana?"

A female voice behind Jin made him flinch. He pivoted on the chair to gawk at the narrow-eyed woman, Kim, but a smile played on her lips. Warmth crawled up his neck as he hastily set the item down. She chuckled as she walked around to the side of the desk and snatched the gift card.

As she read it aloud, his eyes widened in alarm: *"Please give me a chance—Ayato."*

He looked towards Ayato, who was leaning back lazily in his seat, slowly twirling back and forth and chatting with someone on the other end of line. He seemed to sense Jin staring because his bored gaze now collided with Jin's. He rolled his eyes expressively, but Jin was too shocked by the note to guess what he meant by that.

Ayato likes Hana?

Suddenly, as if their link was still strong as ever, the girl of his past entered the office, and their gazes connected momentarily. An old memory came to him of them riding the bike, Hana seated on the front basket screaming and cackling, and his heart hammered faster in his chest.

Hana, perhaps wary, must have seen something on his face because a deep flush coloured her own. She slowly walked to the desk they shared for the last time, and her eyes widened at the sight of the cookies. She surreptitiously glanced over at Ayato.

Like a wooden doll, Jin arose from his chair, staring intently at Hana. Before he knew what was happening, Jin was tugging her forward out of the cubicle as she sputtered behind him, trying to dislodge his hand gripping hers.

"Jin! What are you doing?"

The familiar name washed over him, yet he stubbornly marched out of the office door with her, leaving everyone inside gawking in stunned silence.

When the elevator slid open thankfully, it was empty. Just then he heard Ayato's stern voice calling them. Jin slammed one fist on the highest floor button, and the door shut at the very moment his frustrated colleague glowered at him whilst tripping over his feet.

"Jin! Have you gone—ick!"

He quietly put both hands beside her head before leaning closer whilst breathing through his nose. His dark gaze trailed over her features as she stared wide-eyed at this sudden turn of events. Her eyes filled with tears before she looked away when the elevator shuddered to a halt.

Once again he dragged her outside, and they walked toward the rooftop, where they were met by a strong breeze. Even after hearing Hana's cry, Jin did not stop. His heart was pounding, and an array of emotions surged through him. When he brought them to a halt, his tapered fingers tightened around her slender wrist.

"Let me go!"

Without pausing he pulled her closer until their bodies touched before backing her gently against the wall. Her frightened eyes collided with his furious ones. This was a perfect location so nobody could stumble upon their encounter—although Jin was beyond caring right now. The only thought bothering him was that Ayato and Hana had a past together.

"Why aren't you talking to me?" Jin fumed, leaning against the wall and trapping Hana between his arms.

"I already said—" An edge on her voice hinted at annoyance.

"I'm sorry, Hana." He apologised, realising how the tables had turned.

"It's not that easy, Jin!" she screamed as well.

Finally, tears rolled down her ashen cheeks before Jin wiped one salty track with his thumb, yearning to make amends with her. Realising that someone else was chasing Hana had made him suddenly desperate.

Desperately jealous.

"I know as a teenager," he started yet again, forcing himself to calm down, "I fucked up a lot."

"You hurt me," she sobbed with abandon. "Jin, we cannot go back like before."

"Yes we can," he whispered endearingly. "I know we can, Hana."

She pushed at his chest, but Jin wouldn't budge. In fact he leaned lower to breathe against her ear. Her petite frame grew rigid at the action sensation. He fluttered both eyes closed and smiled softly.

"Because we were meant to happen, Hana." His voice held a promise because he wanted to fight to have back what the two of them had shared long ago.

Chapter 41

*W*e were meant to happen ….

The words seem to bounce within Hana's brain. She was still trapped between the cold wall and Jin's warm body. Her breath came in tiny puffs, yet fear constricted her heart. Flashes of the past that she kept locked away finally appeared in kaleidoscope shades, and she recoiled.

"No," she whispered in a strangled tone. "You are wrong—"

"I'm not," he retorted. "Even if that night hadn't happened, still somewhere in the future both Hana and I would have made love."

Tears choked her as she shook her head, trying to deny every word before squeezing her eyes shut, sending salty tracks down her cheeks again. She gasped for breath as she gripped a handful of his coat trying to force him away, but he wouldn't budge. Yes, that night had been important to her, but for Jin, it was a wall that grew up between them.

"You shouted at me, Jin!" She glared daggers at him. "I 'took advantage' of you—those were *your* words!"

"I was scared, Hana." He curled one hand at the back of her neck and grasped firmly so they were looking eye to eye. "Can you understand the feelings I was experiencing back then? My mind was running in every direction because I was adamant that both of us could never connect on that level I was wrong—"

"Stop it, Jin, please." She covered her wet face with shaking hands.

"—because that night I fell in love with you." His voice broke at the end, his lips wavering from suppressed emotion. "My blindness and stubbornness caused us so much pain and misery. I did not want to lose you, Hana; you mean so much more to me. Those feelings hit me slowly, but when they did, guilt erupted in my soul."

By now, Hana's sobs were heavy, and for a moment she leaned her forehead against his chest, feeling that familiar heartbeat. It was too late to salvage their relationship. Ever since that horrible night, a deadly cocktail of pain, suffering, and jealousy had led her to loneliness, eventually breaking her apart.

"You have Shouko." Hana bit the words out. "She has your heart, not me."

"I waited for you at the park!" Jin couldn't contain his riotous feelings any longer. "Where were you, Hana?"

"Suhana! Takami!"

Hana lifted her head at Ayato's voice before staring into Jin's dark hazel gaze, seeing the desperation and guilt surging there. Suddenly she recalled that tumultuous night when she had accidentally dialled Jin, hearing his voice from the other end of the line as the two of them promised to meet up. If only she hadn't turned back towards her friends and revisited that room of wickedness, perhaps they could have achieved what she had been longing for.

"It's too late, Jin," Hana shook her head pitifully. "I don't think we can go back to how we were."

"Why?" Jin was adamant because he had seen a flash of emotion in her readable eyes. "When you called me, you begged me, I gave in as well because at that point both my heart and body missed your presence."

"I can't tell you," Hana whispered in a strained voice but this once let herself touch his cheek.

"Suhana, are you here?"

The voice was louder than before. Any moment Ayato might catch them in this position. But Jin was not moving an inch, his features grimly locked while resting his cheek in her palm. Her brows furrowed in concern, though; she wished for more.

Weakness almost overcame her, but then she leaned backwards. *"Ayato! We are here!"* she called out, glancing away.

"Why did you call him?" Jin scowled when they heard someone approaching. "Because we are not done—"

"Just listen to me: we are done." Hana looked him deep in the eyes. "The wounds I cling to are deeper than they seem on the outside."

"What do you mean?" Jin inquired in a baffled tone. "What happen—?"

"Hana?"

Both of them turned their heads to stare back at a confused Ayato, who looked intently at the two of them standing very close. But then his face flushed, and his brow furrowed as he glowered at Jin, who—to her surprise—looked defiant.

"Let her go, Takami," Ayato warned in a low voice.

"Kaname, we are having a serious discussion," Jin replied, not budging an inch.

"What sort of conversation requires the two of you to stand so close?" Ayato's jaw twitched while he glared at Jin.

"Hana and I go back—"

"Stop it," Hana interrupted whilst pushing at his chest with both hands.

""Why?" Jin snapped. "I'm not saying anything out of the line, Hana. We were once childhood friends."

"Childhood friends?" Ayato blinked a couple of times.

"Jin, stop it," she said, this time in a louder tone. "That is all in the past!"

"So you're the guy ...," Ayato mumbled in a state of shock. "Why didn't the name click for me sooner?"

"What do you mean?" Jin turned to watch him.

"Leave me alone!" Hana screamed in a state of panic when she saw recognition blazing in Ayato's eyes.

"Hana!" Jin yelled, but she deftly escaped reach to race for the door.

She was almost to the elevator when she heard another noise from behind. Ayato had caught up just the door slid open for them to walk in. The faint background music contrasted with the current tension, and Hana pressed a hand against her chest to control her breathing. She couldn't look at Ayato, whose burning gaze she could almost feel.

"That's him," Ayato whispered incredulously.

"Don't tell him anything." She finally glanced up at his face. "Please."

"As you wish." Ayato hung his head. "But by the looks of it, he wants to be with you." He peered at her sideways. "The one person you've prayed for is pining for you right now."

"You don't understand." She shook her head. "Leave it be."

When the elevators halted at their level, they entered to head back towards the office. Before venturing inside, Hana tried to rearrange her hair, although it was a failure. She knew her co-workers must be wondering what had happened for Hana and Jin to behave in such an unprofessional manner. At the thought, Hana's mind ventured towards Kaito, and she shuddered. He must be livid.

A hand clamped onto her shoulder, startling her. She turned to look up at Ayato's reassuring smile as they walked in together. As they did, a few heads popped over the cubicle walls, and Kaito strode out of his office to observe from under arched brows.

"Suhana—"

"I'll explain," Ayato walked in front of her blocking the view.

"Mr Sukihara." A new voice approached from behind them. "This is my fault. I allowed my feelings to rule my mind."

Hana peered over her shoulder and saw Jin walking up to them. A nagging voice forced her to back away from Ayato to face Kaito, who was beet red with anger. Although Ayato was doing his best to help with the problem, Hana wanted to take responsibility; with her head held high, she gauged Ayato's reaction.

Kaito sighed and turned back to re-enter his doorway. "Both of you in my office, please."

"Oi, what happened?" Hikari whispered, but Ayato squeezed her hand reassuringly as she stepped into the boss's office.

The man sat in his big chair behind the desk glaring at them. "Well?"

"I am to blame for the misconduct," Jin began before Hana could utter a word; he had a serious expression. "I promise it won't happen again."

"Don't break your word to me. And you, Suhana?" He gave her a questioning look.

"I will not misbehave." She bowed deeply to stare at her work slippers. "I'll make sure to punish Takami for acting out of line." She peeked at Jin from the corner of her eye and saw him purse his lips while adopting a deadpan expression.

When Kaito began to lecture them, she tuned the voice out to ponder the earlier episode. She had forgotten that evening when she and Jin were supposed to meet; because of the rape, she had shut off all other memory of the night. After Jin's confession, Hana picked up pieces of their conversation, but her palms began to feel sweaty, and she was breathless and light-headed. She swayed on her feet until a strong grip on her shoulders made her look up into the same eyes that still sometimes haunted her dreams.

Black orbs with chestnut flecks, they glimmered in concern. Hana realised she had almost blacked out, and Kaito was directing Jin to bring her to a meeting room at the other end of the hall. Without relinquishing his firm grasp, Jin gently guided her towards their location. When the two of them got out of Kaito's office, more apprehensive stares tracked them.

"I'm sorry," Jin whispered close to her ear.

"You don't have to," she replied in a quiet voice.

They walked inside the spacious office where chairs were pushed neatly along the single long desk. Jin carefully got Hana seated before moving off to bring her a paper cup of cold water. She watched his back amazed by the fact that they were breathing in one room.

"I was raped ... that night after we ended the call." Hana was surprised at herself when the words spilled out effortlessly.

She never dared to look up, but she caught sight of Jin pausing as he carried in two paper cups. A long moment of silence passed before the cups fell on the floor, and water seeped into the carpet. She forced herself to peer at Jin, only to widen her eyes when she saw tears trickling onto his cheek.

"Hana, tell me you're lying." His voice was harsh, his face pale.

"I can only remember bits of our conversation, but I know that my heart felt happiness after a long time. The love I had carried was finally reaching out to you, but ...." Hana had an out-of-body sensation. Her fisted hands began to tremble, and her breathing became difficult as she opened up about the sordid encounter for the first time with anyone. "I—" A sob escaped from her, muffling her words. She squeezed her eyes shut, unable to block out the images and sounds from that night.

Then familiar arms gathered her closer. She caught the same scent he had worn in years past. He was bent from the waist to awkwardly embrace her. He laid one hand along the side of her face as his other arm encircled her shoulders in an effort to share his strength.

"Tell me who did it." His voice was suspiciously low. "Hana, tell me the name, and I'll search high and low for that bastard."

"I was invited to a group date by Miko." She hiccupped and gripped his forearm. "They were college boys. I'm to blame for my misfortune—"

"No! Hana, you are not at fault for the—the incident."

"Then why didn't I agree to my inner voice and leave at my first chance?" She wept quietly. "I lied to my mother. I actually cared more about what those people might think of me for leaving halfway through their stupid 'date'."

"I'm so sorry, Hana," he whispered in a cajoling tone that broke her. "I was really a fucked-up person to hurt you so much back then."

"After the call we had, I ran back to the gathering to pick up my belongings, but the girls were suspiciously slouched together on the couch." Hana tripped over the words that were coming out in a hurry. "The men explained light-heartedly that the girls were drunk, which I understood because Miko and her friends consumed alcohol.

But even when I was leaving the scenario, my brain kept bugging me to return."

"You have a gentle soul," Jin commented, massaging the side of her head. "A brave girl."

"I ran back." Her voice rose and took on a keening sound. "I blocked it out of my head, but sometimes the nightmare frightens me as if I'm back again reliving it."

Before she knew it, she was on her feet and caught in the iron embrace. His arms were like steel bands on her back as he pushed her head against his neck. She was a heaping mess as the tears poured. The words that had been locked so deeply away, now that they spilled out, had left her bereft.

"Did you make a police report?" Jin's muffled voice tickled her ear\lobe.

"No," she said, leaning against his chest, feeling his heartbeat. "I was too scared to tell anyone."

"Miko actually visited the school grounds several months after your departure," he said, scoffing in disbelief. "I knew she was waiting for you, but I ignored her until she approached me one day. When I told Miko you had quit, she was stunned. It was my bad judgement not to ask her, but I was dealing with the fact that all this … *drama* could have been avoided if my cowardice hadn't clouded my brain. You left me. I was hurting inside."

"How can you say that when you love Shouko?" Hana felt the familiar jealousy gripping her heart just as she shoved at him and stepped back. "You've deluded yourself."

"I know, but—"

Hana palmed away her tears. "Promise not to tell this to anyone."

"Who would I tell—?"

"Just promise me. Not even my own mother!" she beseeched him.

"I promise." He started towards her, only to halt when she raised a restraining hand.

"Jin, this will never happen between us. You told me that up front, and I was too stupid to actually see the truth in it," She gave him no chance to talk. "We may be friends, but the feeling won't be the same."

Before Jin could brainwash her again, she hastily left the stuffy office, leaving him behind. She knew she was acting like a coward, but she felt the old anger. She had lost to Shouko; perhaps those two were in a relationship.

Then she paused in mid-step and looked back at the closed door, wondering whether he had foolishly decided to cheat on her. But then she shook her head. Jin couldn't handle one girl; thus two would cause him to move out of the country.

What had happened?

Chapter 42

*H*ana sat at the entrance of her home watching the light rain. She wore several layers of clothes to ward off the cold. A mug of steaming coffee tickled her taste buds as she stared into space, reminiscing about the past. She thought of how her stepfather and mother were frequently invited to some corporate event, leaving her alone in a quiet house.

If only she'd had a pet for company back in those days, perhaps missing Jin wouldn't have been such a huge matter.

She felt the irony of gently sipping her coffee while memories of hurtful events battered her thoughts, especially all the hurtful taunts and how her different skin tone affected her life. In those young years, the sting of such matters lingered. Although she was ignored by everyone, Jin took her side quickly. She brushed away the thought with a loud sigh and a shake of her head.

"The past is in the past," she muttered to herself. "Nothing can be fixed."

A chilly breeze stirred loose tendrils of her hair, and she closed both eyes, enjoying the moment. Earlier today she had made a weekend visit to town to purchase ingredients to stock up the kitchen and stimulate ideas for tonight's menu. She had settled on a simple Indian dish consisting of flatbread and spicy flavoured potatoes.

At times her mother would whip up traditional meals, that her stepfather often complimented. He enjoyed the taste of foreign delicacies gracing the dining table. She suddenly flashed back to a time when Jin had dropped by and was adventurous enough to take a bite of curry chicken and basmati rice infused with spices and cashews.

At first, he had an odd expression, chewing experimentally before taking another spoonful of rice covered in thick curry. His handsome face lit with pleasure as he quickly adapted to the taste and asked for a second plate.

She heaved a sigh and stood up. "I should distract myself." She stepped inside and closed the door. She washed the dishes lying in the basin, enjoying the rush of cold water. She adjusted her cell phone to silent mode, but the buzz of any notifications would alert her as to who might be contacting her.

Both Jin and Ayato kept on clogging her notifications although she knew that her behaviour was petty toward Ayato, but Jin was adamant to "chat" for old times' sake. She wasn't fooled about his true motive because he had been vocal enough to say that he hadn't given up.

Cursing under his breath, Jin glowered at his text messages that had gone unanswered, running a hand through his hair in frustration. He now had his own desk at the office, yet at times, he would peek at Hana sitting opposite him, wondering what pain she must have endured, thanks to his selfish behaviour.

Fear of falling in love had made him turn away, even though he knew she had only him as a confidant. Still, he remained hopeful. When Hana had told him about her rape, cold rage had taken over, blanking all other thoughts for seconds; yet he needed to focus on the woman in his arms.

If Hana had given him the opportunity back then by telling him about the night's events, without a word he would stormed out of the classroom in search of the bastard who had hurt his best friend. She knew how he would fly into a rage whenever he learned of anyone bullying her.

Jin was consumed by the urge to search for those responsible; his agitation sent both hands trembling and all but blinded him with bloodlust. He could at least have asked Hana's location so as to pick her up; perhaps that would have saved her and even the others from the assaults they suffered. The whole picture finally clicked inside his brain; Miko had a ghostly pale expression, with dark circles under her eyes, and incredible weight loss.

"Why?" he mumbled in his pain. "Why didn't you just tell me?"

He recalled the last incident in the classroom, after he had forgiven her and indeed yearned to embrace her petite figure once again. He slid down on the wall to sit with knees bent, holding his heavy head. She had gone through so much.

Once again Ayato couldn't make any progress with Hana. He stared down at the device gripped in his hand, waiting vainly for her to respond to his texts. Finally he had fallen in love with someone whom he planned to spend his life with, but he found himself in a rivalry with Jin Takami for her favours.

Now Jin wished to reunite with Hana, but Ayato wasn't about to let him step between them just because they'd had an earlier connection. He had seen Hana break down sometimes, wondering who she wept for. Judging now, Ayato could put his finger on the person behind those tears. A sense of urgency and desperation tore at him, but he was a wise man, not allowing emotions to guide his mindset.

He paused for a second wondering if it was wise for him to visit Hana; in the end he rejected the idea. He grabbed an umbrella and headed out for dinner. He had seldom cooked during their relationship; Hana would concoct delicious dishes here in his place, although even then, she often showed signs of wariness around him.

Soon the weekend was over, and Ayato was rushing to work. He was suffering a slight flu and was sneezing, for once hating the cold weather. He entered the office wearing a pair of home slippers and walked between the short cubicles to greet his co-workers. But he caught sight of Hana reading a comic before starting her day and eating fruit salad.

"Don't come closer, or you might catch my cold," he cautioned her when she approached his cubicle with a concerned frown.

"Why must Ayato come to work if you're feeling under the weather?" she chided him before leaving for the kitchen. She returned with a mug of hot water. "Drink this to help with your congested lungs."

"You know how much I hate hot drinks," Ayato whined, even though he was elated at her attention.

"Someone needs pampering." Hikari, the office clown, leaned over the cubicle wall with a grin. "Drink up, Ayato."

"Mind your own business," he growled. "Hana, you can set the mug over here—"

"I know you won't drink it," she interrupted. "You overwork sometimes—"

"I didn't catch the cold by working," he grumbled, but inwardly Ayato felt warm spreading within his system. "Fine, if Hana prefers, I'll drink this poison …."

He swallowed his mirth at her irritated countenance and off to one side saw Jin staring at them intensely. Ayato smiled at Hana after emptying the mug, yet she too paused in the middle of turning away when she saw her ex-classmate, who looked inscrutable.

"Takami." Ayato greeted him with a nod and a sudden sneeze.

"Are you all right?" Jin inquired with a half-smile. "Kaname isn't looking so well."

"I'm fine, thank you," Ayato answered, waving everyone away from crowding his space, especially the few women, because they would take on the task on getting him fit again by urging all sorts of herbs and other cures on him.

"Ayato." Kaito, carrying a stack of papers, stopped in passing. "Go on home before you contaminate us all."

"But—"

"I really appreciate your attendance," the head of the office said in a firm tone, softening it with a smile. "Take a few days off for a good rest."

"Don't worry," Daisuke said. "I'll visit Ayato later on and even bring some dinner."

"I'll grab the beer!" Hikari cheered aloud.

"You and alcohol cannot part," Daisuke complained Then he glanced at Jin, who was ignoring everyone. "Even Jin will come along."

"Eh?" Jin blinked at the sudden invitation. "Thank you, but I'll pass up the offer."

"Don't be a party pooper," Daisuke said with a smirk. "We'll have male bonding over a round of beer and delicious dinner!"

Ayato saw Jin grudgingly nod before locking eyes with him for several moments.

Ayato packed up his belongings to leave the office, waving at the men, who were already hyped for the visit, but he figured it would be a tense gathering for at least two of them because they yearned for the same woman.

Chapter 43

*W*hen the doorbell rang, Ayato took his time rolling out of his messy pillows and blankets, feeling feverish. He wore long cotton pants and two long-sleeved shirts with a mask covering the lower portion of his face. He sniffed as he shuffled toward the door and unlocked it to greet his boisterous companions, all of them carrying stashes of supermart plastic bags.

"You look like roadkill," Hikari commented, ignoring his host's severe glare. "Anyway, we came by to make you feel better."

"Thanks," Ayato croaked. "Come in."

"Kim sent her condolences," Daisuke commented, lugging a bag of hot soup.

"Man, I want a girl caring after me too," Hikari whined as he collapsed on the couch.

The last one to enter was Jin, looking uncomfortable as he mostly had done ever since his heated argument with Hana. Everyone now knew about their past relationship, of course, but only superficially—their lost friendship and this delayed reunion.

But Ayato had a better idea, right now they seem at odd with one another but being a good host he welcomed the trio to sit. He lived in a studio apartment, which meant the area was spacious; the room had bare whitewashed walls, and a single coffee table was surrounded with colourful beanbags serving as chairs—and a punching bag.

Hana lived with him only after he had convinced her they would sleep separately. He understood the reason, now instead of merely thinking she was shy. But Ayato still kept the futon where he lounged, allowing her to make full use of the single mattress; the apartment would be clean, unlike now.

A sudden thumping broke Ayato's train of thought, and he blinked at Hikari, who was goofing around near the punching bag. Daisuke walked out of the kitchen minus the shopping bags. Last but not least, Jin was gazing silently into the distance near the window; by the looks of him, Ayato wouldn't be surprised if he was mulling about her.

Hikari made himself at home to slouch on a beanbag, finally bored of the swinging bag. "Daisuke, where's the beer? Bring it over."

"Yeah, yeah." Daisuke sighed but got up to bring the carton. "Jin, here."

"Oh." Jin jerked slightly at the mention of his name. "Thank you."

"Any work sent home to me?" Ayato ended with a sneeze, eliciting a shiver. "Fucking cold, I hate this."

"As always, Ayato being a hardworking stiff," Hikari joked, sipping his brew. "Kaito prefers you healthy again, so lay off the work for now."

"Nice place you got here."

Finally Jin joined in the conversation, but Ayato caught on his halting speech and only nodded in reply. He was at a loss for words, wondering what he could add. The other two exchanged glances, clearly noticing the tense atmosphere between them.

"Hikari." Daisuke got up with a huff. "Help make the porridge and our dinner so we can all eat sooner."

"Sure, why not?"

Silence reigned once again; the only sounds floated, muffled, from the kitchen. Jin's expression caught Ayato's attention. He had a faraway smile bordering on sadness; he must be reliving an old memory. Ayato was curious if it had to do with Hana, and he let loose his tongue. "How long have you two known one another?"

"Huh?" Jin jerked his eyes towards him. "Who are you talking about?"

"Don't feign ignorance, Takami." Ayato he lowered his voice, not wanting others to listen. "Please tell me, I'm only intrigued with the both of you."

"Hana and I were childhood friends; we shared our ups and down," Jin began tentatively. "Whenever she was bullied, I would stand up for her, Hana was introverted, timid, and easily flustered, but she had me by her side to teach her to adjust to her surroundings. More often than not, others mistook her silence for arrogance, even though it was the opposite: she yearned to make friends and experience a carefree life just like the rest of us."

"What about her parents?" Ayato listened to the story with interest.

"She has a good background; Neena, her mother, worked in a museum, while her former stepfather was a businessman. They had a spacious apartment; sometimes you feel overwhelmed standing inside." Jin shrugged, looking reflective. "Unlike me, I had a rough childhood watching my mother killing herself by working double shifts for the two of us, and I abhorred myself for not being able to help share the burden."

"I'm sorry." Ayato had no idea how else to reply.

"Hana started to develop feelings for me," Jin sighed aloud. "I read that as some nonsensical notion of a naïve female acting out of desperation because she once begged me to … to be with her for the first time. Of course, I declined her stupid offer. In between the mix-up, Hana must have ignited that love, but by then I was in love with someone else."

"What?" Ayato gasped; this was more complicated than he'd predicted.

"My friend never gave up her love. While fighting to win my affection, if only she could fathom how afraid I was of losing her. Hana was the only person that I could show my true self; I didn't have to pretend to be somebody else. We would sneak out in the middle of the night to meet if either of us felt bad."

"I'm beginning to envy the friendship you two have." Ayato had a sinking feeling that there was no way he could win against Jin. He looked away.

"Everything happened all at once, and we bonded one night, but in my panicked state, I was drowning in fear and guilt for cheating on my girlfriend. It all muddled my mind, and we had a huge row. I distanced myself from Hana and ignored the signs that she was suffering. It felt good to be vindictive, but at the same time, she was someone else I had conjured out of my brain. By the time I figured out that I'd been in love with her ever since that one night, it was too late. I've hurt her to the point of hating myself."

"Dammit, where's a drink?" Ayato muttered as a headache started pounding behind his temple. "Continue while I crack a cold one for us."

"Eventually, the pull was strong, and I gave in after listening to her soft voice." Jin's vocal became hoarse. "We promised to meet up at our location, and I waited for her until the next morning. She ...."

"Hey, Jin, it's all right now." Ayato clamped a hand over Jin's shoulder when he saw the anxiety twisting his face. "You have another chance to make amends."

"You love her," Jin said, after taking his time to settle down. "Do you think a person like me deserves her?"

"I do love her," Ayato said without hesitation. "I'd be glad to whisk Hana away from you, but she still loves you, Jin."

Jin looked up to stare at Ayato, a mixture of confusion and elation on his face. Then he gulped down the pint from his chilled can in a visible effort to call up his mature self and face reality. "She hates me, Kaname," he said, with a laugh of disbelief.

"Stop being formal with me." Ayato shrugged without looking at Jin. "I'll support your quest, but if you hurt Hana once again, there's—"

"I won't," Jin cut in with a tone of finality. "At this point, you may ask about me," he said, sarcasm dripped from his voice. "Do you live alone?" Then he smiled as they heard the stove clicking shut.

"I have a mother and younger sister living together, but I chose to move out—nothing drastic, just for the sake of privacy." He snorted. "I had to make excuses to my exes for not being able to bring them home. Actually my parents are divorced, and while they went through that messy process, I stepped into the role of taking care of my sibling."

"You're a great guy." Jin saluted him by raising his can before taking a sip. "Your little sister is blessed to have a brother like yourself."

"I guess so, although I had my own issues to deal with—you know, the typical teenage angst. If it weren't for that brat, I might have spiralled out of control." Ayato chortled at the memories. "She's closer to me more than our mother. When I announced that I wished to move out, she didn't talk to me for a week."

"Do you still talk to her?" Jin seemed intrigued.

"Yeah, she calls me every day to relate stories about her high school. As a big brother I have to make sure no boys take advantage of her." Ayato watched as Hikari and Daisuke arrived with a bowl of porridge.

Jin turned to look at him. "Is it okay with Ayato if I take my leave now?"

"Where are you going?" Hikari had overheard his question.

"Sure, I'll send you off." Ayato got up to join Jin, and they ambled towards the door. In silence, Jin put on his shoes. Meanwhile, Ayato shivered when a soft breeze blew his way, and he heard someone's shuffling feet. He turned to regard Jin in a new light.

"By the way, Hana and I lasted for three months." He hope this might put Jin at ease. "We never got to second base."

"Oh." Jin uttered the word beneath his breath.

Ayato had seen hidden depths in Jin, having spent only hours with him. He was hurting just as badly as Hana; both were holding on to old scars with no way of letting go.

The chilly breeze slapped Jin's tear-stained features, turning them pink. He was blindly heading home but halted at the walkway, surrounded by abundant cherry blossoms, to view the road below on the other—a pretty sight if only he was standing here to enjoy the scenic spot instead of sobbing for his lost mother.

He glanced up at the sky, and the first flake of snow kissed his upturned nose before another followed soon, and white crystals soon blanketed the ground. A vision of white.

Hope?

A turn of fate?

Or a kiss from heaven?

"Ma ... show me the way."

Just as he was about to close his eyes, something buzzed in his front pocket, and he fished out the device. Strangely, the number wasn't local; in fact, it was an overseas numeric code. He stood staring at it as the call rang off—only to ring once again.

"Hello?"

Chapter 44

Heavy snow blanketed Osaka Street, lending an ethereal atmosphere. People were bundled up to ward off the freezing draft. Cars crawled along the icy road. Schools and offices had closed for the week due to the lowest temperatures of the year, although some still had to brave such weather.

The live news blared on the living room TV as Hana shivered underneath several heavy blankets. She sneezed and sniffled from between a snow cap and a mask; her teeth were chattering. She wondered whether the storm would worsen; it had been three days since she had gone to the office.

She was worried about the remaining work she had to quickly submit, her laptop was a waste of electronic device, yet the weather kept her from venturing out. It would be a miracle for her to step across the threshold without contracting pneumonia, since her body still wasn't accustomed to winter, even though she had lived in Japan her entire life.

"Achoo!"

She had been holed up at home for four days when her anxiety for the task finally drove her to decide to visit the office. As if getting ready for a battle, her figure grew thick with heavy clothes; she could have rolled down a hill without injury. Around the office at least the streets nearby would have been cleared.

The slap of chilly wind made her stagger backwards, but she stubbornly plodded on, leaving deep footprints behind.

Her nose was covered by her woollen scarf because of her bad sinuses. She carried a bag capacious enough for a ration of food supplies, although it contained paperwork. She frowned at the suddenly darkening clouds rolling in, realising that the weather was about to turn still uglier; still she summoned the strength to waddle forward.

She recalled the first time her colleagues had seen her literally stumbling into the office, resembling a dumpling due to her many layers of garments. They were amazed at how many jackets and scarves she had on. Of course, inwardly her feathers were ruffled; she was a little sensitive to their joking at her expense. Only Ayato had seen her hurt expression and called for a stop to the good-natured ribbing.

Seeing no taxis, she was rethinking this reckless outing, wondering if she still had time to return home before the storm began. By the time she did stop a cab, the stinging breeze had freshened, and those who had dared to venture out were also rushing carefully.

She plunged into the backseat of the cab and huffed out the address. "The weather is unpredictable," the driver said good-naturedly. "Why are you going out in these conditions, Miss?"

"I have work that needs my attention," she replied, peering out the window. "Hopefully the storm will pass soon."

"I'm not sure about that." The driver frowned, leaning forward to hear the radio.

The weather forecaster warned everyone to stay indoors; those caught outside should quickly search for a shelter as the storm approached. Hana felt a trickle of doubt and fear as this was the first time Osaka had ever undergone such a terrible event.

Soon they reached the office building, with visibility dropping. She paid the cabbie and advised him not to drive under these conditions. The old man's features brightened at her thoughtfulness, and he promised that he would head for the nearest mall to wait out the storm.

Hana raced for the entrance—slipping and sliding. She felt she must look like a rag doll and she flailed and squealed.

"Suhana?" The security guard looked shocked. "What are you doing here?"

"Afternoon, Mr Yumei," she said, bowing at the middle-aged man. "But I have something to do back in the office."

"Oh." He pointed upward. "One of your colleagues is upstairs, so the door is not locked."

"Thank you." She bowed again and proceeded to the elevator, muttering, "What a crazy climate."

She worked her fingers to warm them up and stuffed her gloves into her tote. She wondered who had also braved the storm, what project had to be finished to satisfy what client. The corridor was eerily quiet, so that the whistling of the blizzard was all she could hear. The dimly lit area sped her heartbeat.

She twisted the doorknob and timidly entered the shadowy office. The tiny kitchen light was on, and she felt a little better to hear someone making drink.

"I'm coming in," she announced so as not to startle anyone else in the room.

Her heart seemed to stop and then to pound faster when she saw the surprised countenance of Jin staring right back at her. He was holding a steaming mug. His wavy locks were mussed, possibly from running his fingers through them multiple times. He wore a light mustard-shade long-sleeved turtleneck and a pair of tight jeans with rips in the right knee.

"Hana?"

The sound of his soft voice hit her gently at first; her initial instinct was to run out, but she remained rooted where she stood. She fortified her heart as she pretended to busy herself near the coat rack.

Finally she turned, releasing a held breath because he hadn't dared to sneak up behind her. Instead he ventured toward his side of the desk to carefully set his mug down on the surface, which was littered with papers.

"Why are you here?" Without meaning to, she sounded accusatory.

"Working," he said with a casual shrug, smartly ignoring her tone. "Why are you here in this crazy blizzard?"

"I have work as well." She brought her voice under control. It was stupid to blame him for being in the same space when he was the first to arrive.

She sank onto her chair to begin switching on the monitors and took the necessary papers from her bag. The light overhead flickered, alerting the pair of them, but nothing was said. She nervously peered at Jin, only to look away since he was watching her intently.

To her relief, Jin never bothered her further; perhaps he was keen on enjoying the weekend without worrying about the past. When he let out a cough, her body jerked, causing her fingers to blindly type gibberish; exasperated, she tapped on the Backspace key.

"Here." A mug settled on the side of her neat desk.

She looked at it for a moment of stupor before glancing up at his gentle grin. "Thank you," she whispered, hoping to act busy so he won't drag in any subject.

Light footfalls receded from her side. She gingerly peeked at Jin's back as he peered outside through the drapery on the window. One hand rested in his back pocket as the other held the white folds aside. Then he stepped away with a sigh. "We may need to stay indoors for a longer—"

"I'm sure it will end soon. We don't have to be here for long."

"By the looks of it, I'm not so sure." He shrugged. "But I don't mind heading home early if possible."

Overcome by curiosity, she rose and headed for the window, where she gasped in shock. Billowing clouds of white enshrouded everything in icy cold snowfall. She prayed inwardly that everyone might survive when she recalled the cheery cab driver's face.

"Don't worry." Jin voice's seemed closer than before. "We are safe here."

She looked over one shoulder, but he seemed oblivious to the intimate distance between them as he, too, frowned at the sight outside. His masculine scent enveloped her senses; he seemed to be leaning gently against her back. She struggled to compose herself because he was the person from her nightmare—no longer the Jin she had known before he destroyed her completely.

It even seemed he was leaning in to take a whiff of my hair when a knock came from the entrance. She yelped in fright before shoving Jin aside like a rag doll, jerking away from his innocent touch.

As he walked toward the door, she saw his stony features and figured he must have sensed her resistance to his closeness. She cursed her stupidity but heard the guard's voice when the door opened wide. She had guessed correctly as the guard's smiling countenance came into view.

Jin turned and said, "He is informing us that if we are hungry, he wouldn't mind going to the vending machine to get something for us."

"You don't have to, Mr Yumei," she said, moving toward the two men. "We will be leaving later, so please don't bother yourself."

"Eh?" he blinked. "But the storm—"

"Won't last for long," she declared confidently.

"Oh?"

"Never mind," Jin said, taking over the conversation. "The kitchen is thankfully stocked with provisions enough to feed us for some time."

"If you encounter any problem, please don't hesitate to call me," he said kindly.

"Yes," they answered in unison.

They returned to their stations to resume work. Occasionally Jin either coughed or cleared his throat; somehow in the course of minutes or hours, it became a source of comfort to know she was not alone.

At length her demeanour relaxed as the cursor hovered over the Save icon; her work had been completed. It was time-consuming, but she could finally rest at ease, knowing she was ready for whatever work arrived later. Suddenly the entire room was plunged into darkness. Gawking at the blank screen, her body stiffened for a second as she thought for a moment that she had gone blind.

"*What?*" Jin's roar made her jump in fright.

"Jin!" The blinding darkness along with the howling from outside fed her fear. "*Jin!*"

Soon she became aware of a single emergency light. It shone weakly, but it was enough to halt her rising panic. Jin walked toward her and grasped one arm tightly to pull her into his arms. She wrapped her arms around his lean waist, entwining her fingers and squeezing her eyes shut to calm her racing heart.

"Shh, I'm here," he cajoled her quietly. "In case Hana hasn't noticed, I'll always be here for you."

Chapter 45

The warmth of Jin's embrace paralysed Hana's decision to step away from his once familiar arms. She listened to the beat of his heart inside his stolidly breathing chest. Her icy fingers were numbed as held his waist, but her tears welled at his words.

She sensed his lean fingers on her back as he pulled her closer, and a lone tear slipped down my cheek.

Her mind warred with her battered heart, which wept for Jin in a small corner constantly missing him. Just this one time, she let him hug her as if they would never have another moment together or accurately or any future contact.

"Why do you keep on fighting me, Hana?" he whispered.

Her lips trembled before a choking sob escaped in answer. She shut her eyes, but finally the tears rolled down as if they would never stop. If only their separation had been due to a simple situation that did not include the rape and the miscarriage. She then could at least hand him a second chance, even if he had been selfish with Shouko back in high school.

The sudden recollection of Jin's teenage girlfriend burst her bubble. She pushed Jin away, but as she pulled back her hands he quickly covered them with his own. Instead of hearing his heartbeat now, she felt it letting her know that he was truly here standing in front of her.

In fact, a tiny part of her was still fighting tooth and nail to get them back together—happy that he finally saw her not as the "girl best friend" but as a grown woman who had dearly loved him all those years.

Who was I kidding? an inner voice mocked her.

She still loved Jin because he had been her only weakness; for him she could lay bare her sins, but he didn't deserve her. So she fortified the walls again, because in a moment of weakness she might say something that he shouldn't hear. This was her secret, just like the heinous incident at the karaoke room, but her emotions might loosen her tongue.

"Shh …."

His fingertip was rough on her cheek. She realised that she was wailing, and his hand cupped the back of her head as he leaned forward to press a kiss to her forehead.

"I promise Hana that I won't ever leave you." He whispered the words intimately. "Every day that we're together, I'll make up the loss of our time by showering you with love."

"No, you can't, Jin." Her voice was shaky from restrained emotion that filled her to bursting. "When I tell you that we cannot be together … what will happen to Shouko? Will you hurt her the same way you hurt me in the past?"

"No." His voice seemed strained. "We broke up a long time ago."

"Is that why you are chasing after me, Jin?"

"No."

"Then why?" She frowned at the shadowy figure looming over her. It seemed from the silence outside that the storm might have abated. She had longed to hear his answer even while dreading to ask for it, because, truth be told, if Shouko was still by his side, Jin wouldn't bother to glance in her direction.

Silence fell between them, and without actual words exchanged, that was her answer. She took a step back, shaken by the scene that had somehow unfolded between them.

Then warm fingers wrapped around her wrist. "Why? Because I fell in love with you, Hana." His tone never wavered. "Now, why do you seem to push away time after time?"

"How many times must I repeat this?" She twisted her wrist to free herself from his strong grasp. "I'm tired of explaining to you every single time we stray to this useless topic."

"Have you pushed Ayato away as well?"

The mention of his name flipped a switch with her, since she was face to face with the truth. Inwardly, she had blamed herself for not being close to any boys back then besides Jin and couldn't say why that was. She had used hurtful memories as a weapon to keep the hatred flowing through her system, but as Jin's words hit her full force, it seemed she could no longer avoid seeing the truth.

"Hana?" he gently urged. "Am I right? The man is serious about his feelings for you, but I won't lose you to him."

"How can you lose to him when I'm not willing to reciprocate his feelings?" Her voice rose slightly due to her agitation.

"If you don't want me, at least think about his feelings," Jin retorted harshly. "Since Hana harbours the same pain from years ago, then where does that leave him? Have you thought about that?"

"You have no right to lecture me!"

"I have." His tone continued at the same volume. "Because Hana isn't accepting my suit and because I see Ayato going through the same right now—and you are hurting him this time around."

"Shut up!"

"I won't!" He released the hold on her wrist. "Why are you being so stubborn? Talk to him, and give that man a chance!"

"I thought you didn't plan to give up on me!"

"I'm not stupid enough to let that happen, but I have seen the look in his eyes, and you seem to be oblivious!" He raised his voice a decibel higher. "I was a bastard before, but I'm not the same person anymore!"

"You don't know anything, Jin!"

"If you tell me, then I'll know, Suhana!"

"Because you're irreplaceable to me, Jin!" She shrieked out the words. *"No man can take your place in my heart! Not now or ever!"*

Her voice echoed through their surroundings as if underscoring her sentiment. Her breathing was ragged, but it tore at her physically to actually reveal the truth when she had purposely silenced her inner voice. Her fists were shaking as she recoiled in shock at the conviction behind her own statement.

"Hana …."

"Leave me alone," she whispered in ragged voice. "Please."

"But you just said—"

"Saying it is different than living with it physically."

"You love me, yet you don't want me."

"Yes …."

"I'm confused," he responded in a defeated voice. "How can I prove to Hana that my feelings are stronger than ever?"

"Don't prove it to me," she replied in despair. "Because my feelings are more tangled, Jin—you don't need to be with someone like me."

"What makes you say so, Hana?" He took a step forward, but she responded by moving backward.

Her panic was rising because he seemed to be breaking through her walls, yet also she was not surprised at that. "Don't do this to me, Jin." She sobbed once again, feeling the noose tightening around her neck. "Please …."

"Fine." He surrendered, or so she thought when he stepped toward her and lifted her up bridal style. "Rest easy. I pushed you too hard; forgive me."

"Put me down, Jin," she said, clutching his masculine shoulder.

"Don't fight me, just for tonight, Hana," he pleaded gently. "I promise not to touch you or do anything that you deem uncomfortable."

He backed against the wall before sliding down, holding her tenderly onto his chest above his spread legs. One hand cradled her head, and she heard a soft sigh escape him. He must be pretending to fall asleep so he wouldn't break his promise and do something unthinkable, like kissing her.

She let her body turn soft and controlled the rhythm of her breathing; just for tonight she would give up searching for new ways to cast Jin aside. She replayed their earlier exchange, filled with wonder as always, and borrowing his warmth. On cue, his arms tightened further, and she rested her cupped hands on his chest under her head.

When his first snore reached her ears, she timidly peered upward to study his soft features in the dark. She could still make out certain changes; he had a more mature face than the rebel Jin she had known most of her life. The earring stud twinkled. She made sure he was asleep rather than pretending to be before allowing herself a sad smile.

Jin was the only person who knew when she was lying or hiding truth from him. Suddenly beyond caring whether he might be playing a cruel trick on her, she carefully laid a hand against his cheek to caress it, giving herself the permission to touch him, because there shouldn't be any such occasion in the future. Just this once would suffice her.

She connected this to when they had first made love, their young hearts unaccustomed to such strong emotions, treading on unfamiliar ground.

A lone tear trickled down her cheek, surprising her that she had any left to shed. She moved her hand to slide her fingers into his thick locks. He murmured incoherently and went on snoring softly. Shouko had been stupid for not trying to salvage their strong bond; if Hana had been in her shoes, she'd have tried anything to make their relationship work and never let the bond break loose.

She replaced her head on his chest, finally closing her eyes, at peace.

Chapter 46

Jin Takami paused to stare down at Hana's unoccupied desk. He reached one hand to place a strawberry-flavoured Chupa Chup on it. Sucking one himself, he felt a sense of melancholy, but whatever doubt he'd had was gone. He slumped in his chair as it sagged backward under his weight.

A week had passed since the blizzard debacle. They were able to return home only hours after someone had shovelled the thick snow from the entrance. But Jin was finally able to follow a reluctant Hana to her home in a brick double-storey neighbourhood set a short distance from a temple and shops.

Of course he wasn't invited inside as he stood near the gates watching the nervous girl entering into her quarters before beating a hasty retreat for his own. Thankfully, nobody from the office had seen them locked in a tight embrace; yet again, it wouldn't have bothered him. He'd prefer that Ayato had witnessed their "passionate" sleepover, although for entirely different reasons—as well as her waking up with a jolt. Jin figured she would lie about being close to him when, in the dark, as he pretended to be asleep, she was caressing his face.

He pressed the button for his computer to whir to life, waiting patiently as he casually swivelled back and forth using one foot. He checked his email only to do a double take at Shouko's name seeming to sizzle and smoke on the screen. He recalled the call he'd received as the first snowflake drifted down on the streets of Osaka.

At that moment, the door was flung open to reveal a his co-workers, but one stood out in her adorable attire. She wore a fluffy pastel pink sweater over tight leggings and boots; it was still snowing, although not as badly as before. She walked to her area without glancing at him, only to halt in mid-step to gaze, dumbfounded, at the little token.

Instead of glancing back at Ayato, she directed wide eyes over to Jin, who saluted her using his half-eaten sweet. At first, she stared with an unreadable look but broke into a small smile, though it never reached her haunted eyes. The urge to stand and walk toward her had him tightly gripping the edge of his desk.

He leaned back to contemplate replying to the email and finally saved it. He'd been a little ticked off when she had wanted to break up, although they were in a long-distance relationship. He had done everything he could to salvage their strong tie, but he realised that she might want to explore her new surroundings as she was studying law in America.

He had planned on flying over to surprise his girlfriend, but the sad reality hit them both, Now Jin somehow had a strange feeling that she wanted to patch things up with him.

"Listen up, everyone." Kaito walked out of his office. "We shall be having yet another of our monthly vacations; set the date as we will be heading to Hakodate for a bonding trip."

"Now you're talking!" Hikari whooped since his life revolved around alcohol and food. "I'm sick of this cold! I want to visit a hot spring and drink sake while eating raw seafood."

"I'm drooling now," Daisuke said. "It'll be a perfect opportunity to hide away from all this white powder."

"Oi, Daisuke." Hikari turned in his chair with a deadpan expression. "I never pegged you as a drug dealer."

"Shut up!" Daisuke shot back indignantly. "Idiot."

But everyone laughed at the banter until work soon distracted their attention. Once in a while Jin stretched his back or sauntered into the tiny kitchen to make tea for himself. Once Hana came in, making him jerk upright; he had been leaning against the counter munching on leftover biscuits.

"Thank you for the lollipop," she announced without glancing in his direction. "You remember my favourite flavour."

"How can I not remember?" Jin answered breathless. "Just because we were separated doesn't mean you haven't been on my mind, Hana."

For the first time, she was taking the initiative to speak to him. He decided to tread lightly, breaking down the walls surrounding her one brick at a time.

She finally peered at him cautiously. "How is your mother? I'm sorry for not asking about her health; it is rude of me."

"Never mind," he said, waving one hand. "She is doing fine. I hope to bring you over to see her someday."

"Oh." She blinked. "Is she here as well?"

"No," he replied in a quiet tone. "She is resting back in Chiyoda."

"Resting? I remember Mrs Sayomi's health was declining," Hana commented, missing the point, although Jin never blamed her for thinking his mother was still alive.

Just then, Yoko, one of their co-workers, entered the kitchen in a spritely manner, waving at them both. She was the perkiest person perhaps in the entire world. She greeted them in her adorable squeaky voice before rushing out with a bag of melted cheese potato sticks to energise her whilst typing mundane emails to several companies.

Somehow, at the mention of a vacation, the office had brightened up. Even Jin was looking forward to spending free time with Hana, hoping to get even closer to her.

"I must head back," Hana said with a shrug and a half-smile. "Give your mother my regards."

As he stared at her heading back to her desk, his gaze strayed downward to her swaying hips, and a smile formed albeit slightly twisted. He casually took a sip only to hiss in pain at the burning sensation. He had completely forgotten that the liquid was piping hot.

They did not see that Ayato had been watching them from afar.

A TV game show was on in the living room as Jin took a break from exercising; his jogging had been cut short due to the weather. He heaved a fatigued sigh before flipping through the channels, pausing on a thriller movie whilst wandering to his cell phone to make a call to the one person who had no way of slipping through his fingers.

"Yo," he greeted her with a smile, conjuring an image of Hana's frustrated expression. "Taken your dinner?"

"Yes, Ayato came by earlier to take me out for dinner," she said. "Is that why you called?"

"No," he whispered in a low tone. "I just wanted to hear your voice."

"What?" She sighed in exasperation. "Jin, you hear me every day in the office; it's the same boring voice."

"Not for me." He lifted his can of beer to chug before running a hand through his rumpled dark locks. "Hey, mind if I drop by?"

"No, thank you."

"Stubborn woman," he grumbled but didn't miss a beat. "Can't I enjoy reminiscing about our high school days with you?"

"No, you can't, considering my high school life sucked, unlike Mr Popular," she snapped, yet Jin couldn't keep from laughing.

"I was quite the lady's man, eh?" He bit the corner of his lip.

"Shut up, Jin," she retorted, although without heat. "More like servicing for the girls."

"Hey, call it whatever you prefer," he joked before waggling his brows. "But you couldn't hide the fact that even our senior, Chiyo, wanted me."

"You gave out your virginity to her, right?" Hana spoke in a fake gagging voice.

"I may have given her my first, but you have my heart," he blurted only to wince at the error.

"Funny, because I do not remember being kissed at the school festival or shown off to your friends as your girlfriend." Her voice rose. "Instead, you detested the sight of me and made sure everyone saw that!"

"I'm sorry, I'm sorry," he apologised fervently. "I was an idiot—"

"Still are; now get lost," Hana said dismissively.

"Wait!" Jin hung his head backward to stare dumbly at the ceiling listening to the beeping tone and cursing himself inwardly.

Time stood still for him as he pushed away from the counter to finish the beer, since he had to head out for takeaway dinner and also stock up the kitchen, preferably from a convenience store.

He stood behind a short queue carrying an overflowing handheld basket and fished out his wallet when his turn finally arrived. He greeted the teenager working behind the counter and waved one hand as he left the air-conditioned store. Puffs of steam wafted from his mouth as he took the journey back home.

He returned along the pathway to the familiar neighbourhood, with a queer expression as he thought about the two women in his life.

"I'm home," he said upon entering the front entrance to slide his shoes sideways and made a beeline for the kitchen.

He lit the stove under the cooking pot for the rice grains to cook. He had brought home salted mackerel and egg soup. In the meantime, he undressed on autopilot to take a warm shower, dousing himself in steaming water and enjoying the slight sting of the heat.

He shut his eyes, imagining Hana's dainty fingers covered in soap caressing his nude body. But he quickly erased the thought when his loins stirred at the idea of them behaving as a couple and got out of the bathroom. He put on a comfortable outfit as the fragrance of cooked rice brought a rumble to his belly.

But dinner was quiet and cold, the only sound that of the chopsticks clicking on the platter.

Chapter 47

Hakodate

The entourage finally arrived at their destination after a long flight and time spent in local buses. The town was mesmerizing as ever, with modern architecture blending in with old charm, and crowds of locals and tourists clogged the bricked streets. Gingerbread buildings added picturesque sights for everyone.

Kaito was able to book rooms for everyone; the women slept in one room whilst the males shared the space in another.

At first the group felt sluggish, due to exhaustion from the trip, yet their energy was revitalized the moment they saw their surroundings. Naturally, they chose to either part company in small groups or huddle together for a memorable journey alongside their colleagues and friends.

"Hana," Jin called, "why don't you come with me?"

"Why should I?" She frowned, ignoring the giggling women around her. "I'll follow them—"

"But I need your advice for gifts," he persisted. "And you're my friend, so your help matters to me."

"But—"

"Suhana," Daisuke chuckled softly, "Jin is literally begging you, so why don't you go along with him?"

Of course, Ayato became dissatisfied and butted in asking to tag along, finally ruining Jin's plan to woo his childhood girl. He aimed disgusted looks at Ayato, who avoided his stare. But Hana agreed quickly, clamping down his annoyance that she would only travel by his side if someone came along.

Jealousy bloomed within Jin's chest when she beamed at Ayato. He read her grateful expression as if Ayato had saved her from some terrible experience.

As everyone scattered in groups large and small, silence hung amidst the trio but only temporary.

"So what gift do you have in mind?" she inquired in a thoughtful manner.

"I lied," he answered carelessly. "Since you are being adamant on not enjoying this trip with me."

"Jin!" She gawked, halting in mid-step. "Are you serious?"

"Yeah." He rubbed his jaw sheepishly. "Come on, it'll be fun for us two."

"You forgot me," Ayato murmured darkly.

"And you," Jin shrugged nonchalantly. "Too late for you to back off, Hana."

Surprisingly, Hana caved in. Jin was expecting for her to throw a hissy fit as they stood undecided. Still, she mumbled underneath her breath heatedly and stomped away, leaving the pair behind. Jin rushed up to her, alongside the persistent Ayato. They walked either side of her, touring the local streets. Her anger soon melted, and she enjoyed the scenery.

"Oi, Jin." Ayato nudged his arm with his elbow. "She wouldn't have joined you if I never stepped in."

"Thank you, but I never asked for your help." Jin spoke without glancing at the other man, but he caught himself grinning. "Hana may act as though she doesn't want to be by my side, but I can see her slowly succumbing to me."

"Go for it." Ayato smacked him on the back, perhaps a little too hard.

Jin smiled. "I can read her like an open book." He moved away to stand closer to her.

"Ayato," she said, unaware of who was standing beside her, "do you think this will be a nice souvenir?"

"You want this keychain?" Jin murmured whilst inspecting the object, fully aware of Hana flinching from his voice. "I'll buy that for you."

"You don't have to. I can buy it myself."

"Stubborn woman," Jin muttered but took the item.

"What did you say?" This time her voice rose a decibel higher.

"Nothing, nothing." He waved both hands in the air as if surrendering. "You have sharp ears, Hana."

He watched her sharp gaze rolling in exasperation as she moved on to another part of the shelf in a souvenir store. The building was vintage with wooden walls and a lazy fan whirling overhead; Japanese tunes from a bygone era sounded over a radio. An old man in a white singlet and straw hat sat on the opposite counter.

Even Ayato began to search for a souvenir to take back home, perhaps for his family, so Jin browsed the area casually. He paused at a section to look at a paperweight. There were several designs of pretty geisha and even sea creatures for him to choose from; in the end he chose from the latter. Since the price was affordable, he brought several of the items toward the toothless owner, who grinned merrily.

A good sale for today.

"Why are you buying so many?"

He turned to confront a curious Hana, staring at the newly purchased paperweights, and winked at her. "I bought for everyone," he simply answered. "Don't worry, yours is in this bag as well."

"Like I'm worried about that," she snorted before stepping ahead for her own small selections. "I plan to take a ride on the cable car."

"Shall we head there?" Ayato suddenly perked up. "It's on my to-do list here in Hakodate, but are either of you feeling hungry?"

At the mention of food, Jin's belly knotted in hunger, and they left the cramped store in search of a restaurant.

Their first day was spent in joyful companionship, although their initial plan of riding the cable car had to be cancelled. Weariness had kicked in right after they'd indulged in a hearty meal, and the trio retraced their steps to the hotel. Afternoon was winding down, and with night approaching, they spotted familiar faces as well in the hotel's lobby.

"Oi, Ayato!" Hikari parroted, sauntering over. "Shall we go for a round of karaoke?"

"Eh? Where and how did you manage to find one?"

"Leave it to Hikari," Yoko giggled, although she was eager for a night spent singing and being jolly. "He'll be that one person you can trust to locate a karaoke bar."

"Aren't you at all tired, Hikari?" Kaito grumbled since he was tuckered out.

"Too bad our vacation is cut short," Hikari complained, drawing more chortles.

"I'm heading up to the room." Hana waved at them and started towards the elevator.

"Wait up." Jin broke away from the rest to accompany her. "As much as I would love to have a cold beer right now, I'm dead beat."

"You can drink at the hotel's bar," she remarked as the door slid open for them to enter. "Except you're tired."

"But I don't have anyone to join in." He sighed, since he already had one person in mind. "Care to accompany this man?"

"I don't drink," she snorted, looking up at him. "I'll be a boring partner."

"But I want you to sit with me." He playfully nudged her. "At least we won't spend the evening alone."

"I'll need a bath, and that will take a long time." She mildly evaded his request.

"Don't worry, I want to freshen up as well." Jin quirked a brow and cajoled her with a gentle tone. "Meet up at the lobby eight o'clock sharp?"

A chime sounded, and the door opened to reveal their level. They stepped out in unison and walked alongside Hana to her room. He leaned against the wall in silence, still having no reply from her. He figured she had dismissed him the moment she'd unlocked the door with a card, and he took off. "I'll see you later … Jin," she said softly, but never glanced up from the floor.

Warmth enveloped his heart, and he couldn't hold back a wide grin as she finally looked up at him. Her wary eyes studied his features, and he backed away slowly, still holding onto her gaze. When he reached his door, Hana broke off their stare to disappear into the room. Jin let himself into the men's neat closure.

Rows of futons were arranged opposite each other in the middle of the room, although no toilet was located in here. A sliding door led onto a small balcony overlooking the district. He crouched next to his bag to dig out his attire. Figuring the bathhouse must have clean towels for guests, he exited the room.

Before leaving Jin wondered if he should wait for Hana but dismissed the idea; that would put her on edge. Finally she was willing to spend some time with him, and he acknowledged that he was walking on eggshells for fear she might reject their time together. He sauntered off for a much-needed R & R, glad that the bathhouse wasn't full of other guests.

The lobby was buzzing with newly arrived guests. Jin stood wearing a navy yukata and a maroon obi around the waist; on his feet were house slippers supplied by the hotel for all guests. Just then, Hana appeared, and for a few seconds he had a flashback of the past Hana bounding towards him, still clad in her school uniform.

Right now, she looked nervous, but he was taken in by the sight of her thick mane hanging at mid-length, framing her oval countenance, and her hazel eyes glowed at him from across the room as she approached. His eyes lingered on her small mouth; her lips looked to him like the softest he'd ever seen, and he yearned to feel them moving over his fevered skin when making love.

Hana also wore a yukata, neutral in both design and colour, but that could not stop him from fantasizing about peeling away the layers to reveal her bronze skin, a feast for his eyes and his mouth.

"Stop looking at me like that," she whispered as she stopped beside him and turned her face away.

"Like what?" he whispered in return, stepping closer and catching a floral scent.

She glanced up at him, showing vulnerability, which tugged at his heartstrings. "Is this why Jin wanted me to come here—to torment me further?"

"I'm sorry," he apologised hastily. He clasped her cold hand and ushered them along toward the restaurant, where a kind hostess announced herself. "Come, I'll treat you to a dinner."

Chapter 48

They shared dinner and conversation; then Hana found herself accompanying Jin outdoors amongst the locals under a bed of scattered stars. Despite his chortle after two pints of alcohol as well as the delicious seafood, melancholy settled over her as she studied Jin's handsome face with his cheeks tinted pink.

But he wasn't drunk. She was amazed that this grown up Jin was able to hold his alcohol, reminding her that times had changed.

Someone bumped into her, causing her to knock against Jin's side. His hand naturally crept around her waist. She jerked wide eyes upward to meet his hypnotizing dark ones. Her heart skipped a beat for the first time since she had come to terms with her feelings involving Jin back when she was a teenager.

Panic settled in, and she pushed him backward. She couldn't allow herself to fall for this trap yet again.

"Beautiful night, eh?"

She jumped at his voice and glanced at him, but he was busy staring up at the sky with a small smile softening his features.

Her eyes traced his profile against the sky. His lean face was more mature, his piercing eyes from the past still twinkling at her. She felt the strong urge to once again caress that cheek, to kiss his lips, to know if they tasted the same or not, now that they were adults.

"Yes, a beautiful night," she replied, trying to shrug off this growing feeling. "Hakodate is a beautiful place."

Something lodged within her throat at those words. No matter how she struggled to appear aloof towards Jin, as the months went by and they worked under the same roof, her barrier was slowly crumbling.

"Hana." His voice, a mere whisper, was suddenly close to her ear.

"J-Jin!" She gasped aloud. "We are out in public."

"What?" He chuckled and drew even closer. "I'm not doing anything indecent except walking and talking with you."

"Idiot," she groused, but a smile tugged at her lips when the slip of tongue revealed that she'd been regarding him from afar. "You're still acting the same as before."

"Huh?" He pulled a startled face. "What do you mean?"

No turning back now; instead, she indulged in a bit of play. "When Jin is angry, you tend to pout or give out the silent treatment."

His flushed countenance grew even ruddier as he turned away to gaze at the other bank of the river. They were now strolling on a cobbled street, and a couple of rickshaws rattled past to lend their touristy charisma. A picturesque bridge crossed the river nearby to meet a matching path at the far end.

Streetlamps were coming on and glowing brightly, as the stores beckoned more people. School kids, perhaps on tour with their teachers, were squealing in groups.

Just then, fingertips grazed against hers, and oxygen seemed to fly from her lungs. She felt tears gathering but blinked them away, moving slightly away from him. Noises surrounding them, yet her feeling being alone was surreal. She abhorred how their teenage years had twisted them. Perhaps if nothing had happened, maybe now, the two of them would be welcoming these newfound emotions.

"Hana?"

"Yes?" she whispered warily avoiding his gaze.

"I want to hold your hand; may I?"

She finally looked up to him, gauging for any hint of irony, even as she chided herself for overreacting.

Should she?

She paused in the middle of the street to really look at Jin. As if of its own accord, her hand rose in mid-air to clasp the warmth of his. Their fingers slid together, and a sense of familiarity lulled her senses. She let him gently lead her and resume their stroll. She couldn't look away from his joyful face.

Does he truly feel that excited to hold my hand?

Aimlessly, they enjoyed the night scenery in comfortable silence until they headed back. She caught herself unconsciously leaning her head against his shoulder. Instead of plaguing her with a taste of gall, she found they lifted a small weight from her shoulders.

Perhaps Jin's behaviour could be the answer for her not to feel suspicious; or maybe her past prayers had been answered? But something else nagged her; he needed to know about the miscarriage.

Jin leaned down to look at her. "Why are you so quiet?"

"I don't know," she replied in a delicate whisper.

"Hana, are you all right?" He stopped and turned to look at her with a worried look.

"There's a secret that I've been holding on to for the longest time." She drew in a deep breath, aware of her sweaty palms and irregular heartbeat.

"What is it? Wait—let's go back. You seem pale all of a sudden." Jin had a serious tone as they returned to the hotel, but Hana had no idea of where she should tell him this story. The idea of him coming inside her room felt weird after their many years apart.

"Is there any place you wish to sit down?" He took her cold hand and squeezed it.

"My room," she announced when he had no luck seeing a place that offered privacy. She would rather delicately break the news to him in a private place rather than out in public. Jin simply nodded. She kept forgetting he was not a teenager any longer; instead of sly remarks, he gently guided her towards the elevator lobby. They waited patiently to reach her bedroom, shared with two other female working in the same vicinity, Yoko and Kim.

"Is everything okay?" he asked once again.

Hana nodded and gestured for him to sit in the chair next to the small table for meals. Then she kneeled in front of him to take both his hands. "Jin, I know you're doing your best to win me over, but that won't happen."

"Is this a joke?" Jin frowned before snatching his hands away. "I'm leaving—"

"I had a miscarriage."

"What—?" Jin looked baffled. "What did you just say?"

"I had a miscarriage with our baby," she whispered, feeling a blockage in her throat.

"Your jokes have gone too far," he retorted. Then Hana saw his gaze turning dull.

"I wish that I were lying to you, Jin." Her voice was steady, startling her, as well as her absence of tears. "I had a miscarriage alone in a bathroom stall. I was frightened. Even though the signs were there that I was pregnant, I was too afraid to accept it as reality."

Jin bent over to cover his face with his hands. The atmosphere in the room changed, and Hana rocked back on the balls of her feet, now crying softly and swiping at the tears. Out of nowhere, she hear choking noises coming from Jin and saw him sobbing fitfully.

"Jin—" She gaped as he shot from the chair, his face contorted with tears and pain.

"Excuse me," he said in a harsh voice. "I have to leave right now."

"Jin, wait," she called to him. Only to gasp when he pivoted to glower at her.

"Why didn't you tell me about your pregnancy?" he shouted.

"I was not sure," she replied, distraught, her body rigid in denial. "Jin, I was scared, lost, in agony!"

He gave her a long, hard look. "You never went for a check-up?"

"I didn't. The thought that my mother might get wind of it terrified me." Suddenly overcome with that old loneliness, she burst into tears. "I was only a foolish child."

She felt her knees weakening and toppled onto the floor to bend low, wailing her heart out behind both hands, cursing herself for her stupidity. Then Jin was sitting beside her and pulled her body onto his lap. The two of them suffered together, each lost in their own misery.

Finally Hana sensed Jin's unbridled emotion growing from quiet sobs into a howl of unspeakable pain. Instantly she embraced his head under her chin, feeling him shake with every breath.

"I hate myself!" Jin said over and over. "I am nothing but a bastard to you!"

"Jin, please …," she said in a choked voice. "You're not."

"Don't lie to me," he wailed, pressing his head against her.

"We have a lot of sorrow between us," she said, caressing the back of his head. "Now you know the reason why I'm always pushing us away? I know you have changed, but we have strayed so much. We can never go back to how we were in the past. There's too much baggage to carry, too many bitter memories."

They remained where they were until Jin had calmed down, although he never bothered to shift from within her calming embrace. They were silent, and Hana suspected he had come to his senses, learning that there could never be another chance for them.

"I have to go," he whispered but didn't move from the spot.

"Yes." She rested her chin on his head.

Before the rest of the group arrived, Jin left the room without a backward glance. Hana stayed on the floor. She turned her head to look at the wall and broke down because Jin walked away, taking the warmth she once yearned to feel surrounding her. But now she had gotten her wish by pushing him away.

Chapter 49

*E*ver since their return from Hakodate, guilt had been gnawing at Hana from within. Now she stood staring dumbly at Jin's shut gate. The front yard was quiet; she gingerly peered in every direction, unsure how to approach the one who now had begun to bug her internally. She unlatched the front gate and stepped onto the compact lawn that led to the entrance. Since today was Jin's day off, she wondered if he would be inside; she forced herself to move forward instead of fleeing.

"Jin?" she called out as she knocked. "It's me, Hana. Are you in there?"

She gingerly glanced around the surroundings, subconsciously admiring the garden when the front door slid open to reveal a dishevelled person. Despite his bloodshot eyes with dark circles underneath and pallid brow, he still looked handsome in her eyes. She pushed away that hopeless remark and offered instead a smile.

"Hana?" he murmured in a stupor. "What are you doing here?"

"I have dinner for us both." She shrugged. "May I come in?"

"Sure." He stepped aside, allowing her to enter the neat room. At once a small shrine caught her eye. At first, she couldn't make out the person behind the frame, but then a chill seeped into her heart as it beat ever so slowly, and a gasp escaped her. Jin's mother had passed away.

"Jin?" she whispered, incredulous. "You told me—"

"I lied," he murmured in a monotone. "She passed away a long time ago."

Stubbornly avoiding her gaze, there and then Jin was showing her his true behaviour, someone from the past that she could relate to. His jaws were locked, and his arms were folded across his lean chest. Her heart shattered into tiny shards, and she returned her gaze toward the shrine.

Without looking away from the frame, she placed the packed dinner on the floor and then tiptoed over and knelt down. She took a single incense stick to light it and set it on a bowl of ash. Then she rang the bell and clapped twice; choking on a sob, she prayed for Sayomi's soul to rest and asked for forgiveness.

"I am sorry," she whispered quietly.

She turned back only to see the room was empty. She stood and was about to look for Jin when she heard someone snivelling outside. She found him standing outside just a few paces from the entrance. Without a word, she wrapped her arms around him from behind and held him against her.

"I'm here …."

He pivoted in her arms and enfolded her tightly in his embrace. Tears moistened her neck as he sobbed quietly, hiccupping once in a while. She was rubbing his back when he slid to his knees, and she followed, caressing the dark head now resting on her chest.

"Why did … this … have to happen?" he rasped. "Nothing good came out of this …."

Instead of replying, she pulled him even closer as tears leaked from her eyes. He had just spoken the actual truth. They had suffered too much and still were suffering. What made them think that anything good would follow if they began a new relationship?

Yet Jin's words had opened a crack in her heart, and she wanted to hear more.

"Were you … alone?" he whispered.

"Yes." Her voice was thick from emotion; she knew what he meant. "I was all alone when the miscarriage happened."

His arms tightened in answer, and she felt a butterfly kiss on her neck. A shiver ran down her spine. Soon her fingers began to sift through Jin's soft strands. They became aware of sounds from outside. Laughter and screams rows skyward from neighbourhood children, yet darkness shrouded their small corner.

"You must have suffered a lot," he remarked in a dull voice. "Where did this ... miscarriage occur?"

"During summer holiday," she replied. "I started having labour while rushing for the hotel's public bathroom and sat throughout the process. The pain was unbearable. Then it was also rather embarrassing, because I was a mess—"

"I'm sorry." He leaned back to face her. "I'm truly sorry, Hana. I was a real bastard to you."

"Hush now; it's all in the past."

The sentence hit her with an unexpected weight as she said it. She had related her dark secret to the one person she had promised herself not to confide in when it came to her misgivings, let alone her other feelings. Fate had worked in many ways but perhaps couldn't save their relationship. This might be the best chance for them to finally close the chapter and move on.

"That's why I kept telling you we could never work out as a couple." She forced out the words.

"Hana—"

"Nobody knew about my miscarriage. In fact, I feared visiting the hospital because I couldn't dream of causing that hurt to my mother. And you might have come to know also. I was even terrified that the police might decide that I had killed my own flesh and blood."

Jin leaned closer to plant a kiss on her forehead, staying still for seconds before resting his head on her chest once again.

"This is our goodbye then," he said with a wan smile.

Her vision blurred, and she let loose a choked sob. Jin straightened to clasp her against his warm chest as they cried, reliving every moment they had spent together.

Her trembling fingers curled within his stray locks. "I'm sorry," she said through her tears. "I loved you once ...."

And still do, her heart answered.

When night fell, Jin was lying on his back and staring sightlessly at the wall. Hana had gone home a short while ago, but she had carved away some of his heart when she insisted that their romance could never happen and that he was wasting time on her. Still, now that he was facing this dilemma as an adult, how could he walk off and leave her alone?

He sat up and hugged his knees, gazing at the picture of his mother's smiling face.

Hana was adamant, even though Jin knew she still loved him. Saying goodbye was also hurting her. Yet she had decided for both of them.

Would she still accept Jin if he walked up to her and told her that he still wanted her? Or would it cause more chaos in their life?

"What now?" he spoke in a rough tone.

On cue, his cell phone vibrated from an incoming call. His heart skipped a beat as he wondered whether this was Hana, wanting to admit that it was a mistake to announce their farewell. But the number was from overseas. Realising who the caller might be, he held his finger over the screen as if to end the call but then slid to the answer button.

"Shouko?"

"Jin! How are you?" Her voice was ecstatic. "I miss you!"

"Why did you call me, Shouko?" he asked in an exhausted tone.

"I called you because I want you back in my life, Jin, and this time it will be for the long haul."

He frowned. "What do you mean?"

"I love you, Jin." She breathed the words. "I know it was my fault for letting you slip out of my life, and I've regretted it ever since."

"I'm not sure about—"

"Please, don't deny us this opportunity," she said in a rush. "I want you to consider, but please, don't push me away."

"I'll … I'll think about it." He sighed wearily. "Look, I'm busy right now."

"Oh, okay—I'm sorry." Clearly she was not pushing. "I'll call you soon to know the answer. Also, I wanted to inform Jin that you could fly here, to where I'm staying until my studies are over. Then maybe the two of us could return to Chiyoda together."

Jin ended the call, feeling as if he had been dragged underwater by a tsunami and slammed against the rocks.

Ayato sat and studied Hana's solemn expression. She and Jin had become more distant, but underneath, he could see that they were hurting tremendously yet could not approach each other to resolve the matter.

"Hey, Ayato." Hikari paused near his desk to borrow a stapler before moving away to his own desk.

The blur of a body passing caught Ayato's attention. He saw Jin heading for the kitchen whilst talking to someone on the cell phone. He leaned back to resume typing, but his gaze strayed toward Hana. As he stared raptly at her, a strong suspicion arose that she had once again developed feelings for him.

What a mess, He exhaled. *Where do I stand now?*

Chapter 50

Hana glanced at her watch whilst rearranging her cluttered desk. It was time to clock out. She reminded herself that she had to stock up her pantry and planned to visit the market.

A sudden craving for fast food made her mouth water. She grabbed her comic to continue reading it at home. Her back made audible pops when she stretched it, and she sighed wearily. She thought again about quitting this job, aware that her body was complaining from endless hours of sitting and staring at the screen.

She mused about inviting her mother for a trip around the world but dismissed the idea at once. It would be better to use that money to set up her own business.

Maybe I should get married and become a housewife.

At the thought of marriage, her betraying gaze moved to Jin's empty seat. He had packed up fifteen minutes ago. As usual, he would stop by and say farewell before leaving.

Somehow she sensed a shift between them, because her hatred for him had subsided, both confusing and terrifying her. She had held on to that feeling like a mantra, yet her emotions were at war with her brain, which was being practical rather than impulsive.

"Hikari," she called over to him as he typed on miserably, "I'm heading back home now."

"Oh." He blinked in a dazed manner. "Take care, Hana!"

"Don't work too hard." She smiled at him as she changed into her shoes. "See you."

She pushed aside the thoughts whirling in her head to inhale before exhaling quietly when she heard murmuring. It came from the elevator section, and the voice was a familiar song in my heart.

"I have to decline your offer, Shouko."

Shouko? her inner voice screamed.

She backed away a step to lean against the wall and eavesdrop; that was the only option, as the area was occupied for the moment. As she listened to Jin's baritone voice, she stared numbly at the opposite wall. *They're still in touch even after their break-up.*

That should say a lot about their relationship.

"I met a girl," he was saying in a calm voice. "Yeah, we both work in the same office, and I have feelings for her."

Why doesn't he just mention me to her?

She balled her hands into fists to smother the jealousy growing within as the call continued. It seemed Shouko was asking all sorts of questions, and he was answering patiently.

He didn't show me this kindness when I was hurting in school, her inner voice reminded her.

She squeezed her eyes shut whilst denying the ugly emotion oozing into her erratic heart. Jin had been more than kind to her; in fact, he had said that the person he had "strong feelings" for was Hana.

Silence now met her ears, and she peered around the corner and saw Jin gazing at his cell phone. *He still loves her,* her heart wept.

That thoughtful expression finally sealed the deal as she watched Jin step into the elevator and the door closed. She strode reflectively to the now empty spot, contemplating her next move. A grin crept onto her face, although her reflection was double-edged.

During lunch break the next day, Hana left her office desk to take a seat on a bench. It had been a long while since she could enjoy this luxury; finally the weather was getting better, though the wind still carried a slight bite. She was unpacking her bento box when someone cleared his throat.

Her heart jumped at the thought that Jin had followed her. Her sudden mood change exemplified the confusion he had stirred up for her. In fact, Ayato was standing before her holding two vending machine coffees. At his handsome smile, her guilt was back. She had been too preoccupied with Jin, spending even less time with the person now sitting down at her side.

"Here is your coffee." He set the cups down between them. "Doesn't it feel great to be eating outdoors?"

"True," she said with a smile. "Have you taken lunch?"

"Yeah, but I thought I'd find Hana here." His wink was playful.

"Thank you for the drink. I'd love your company."

"That's why I'm here," he replied simply.

A comforting silence settled between them whilst she ate her fried rice. Soon she became full and neatly packed the box. She wiped her mouth with a napkin and sighed with a warm smile. For a minute, she could enjoy the scenery and pretend that her life was not a complicated mess.

Ayato's next words stopped her heart from beating. Out of the blue, he said, "Suhana, will you marry me?"

"Ayato!" She gasped in horror. "What are you saying?!"

"Sorry," he said, chuckling light-heartedly. "I was only joking."

Her heart was still slamming in her ribcage, but then the atmosphere grew dreary, and she sat there in a stupor. "I'm sorry," she murmured.

Ayato skipped to another subject while her head was reeling. "What are you going to do about Jin?"

"Why are you asking me?" Her voice was a little harsher.

"Because I can read your expression like an open book," he replied. "When you think nobody is watching, Hana's eyes will stray toward him and hurriedly glance away."

At first, she wanted to deny it, but it had all turned exhausting. She knew she could no longer put up a front. She turned from his unflinching stare and gazed blindly at her surroundings, coming to terms with her decision, even though she was taking it without the other party's own choice.

"Nothing."

"What?" He blinked. "What do you mean by nothing?"

"I mean I'm doing nothing." Her bleak eyes turned back to his. "Another person from his past is calling for him."

"Who is that?"

"His ex-girlfriend." She quirked her mouth sideways. "She wants to be with him."

"How has Hana come to this decision?" His tone was sceptical. "Did Takami tell you this?"

"No." She leaned back on the bench, sipping at her lukewarm coffee. "I overheard the conversation. They are still in touch with one another."

He shrugged. "Some exes do keep in touch. I still do with one or two only because our bond is stronger as good friends than when we were in intimate relationships."

"But this is different, Ayato." Her voice crackled with frustration. "Shouko is calling him back to her, and I heard him declining."

"So now you have the chance." He inched closer. "Why are you still pushing him away?"

"Because", she said, staring into his eyes, "they deserve to be together."

"Jin loves you, Hana." He scoffed. "Wait, what did he say to her?"

This time she looked away, fidgeting with her cup as she recalled the words.

"Why are you throwing away this opportunity?" he continued. "Are you harbouring negative emotions from the old times?"

"It's not like that anymore."

"Then what?"

"Jin should be with someone more carefree and not carry a burden."

"You don't love as much as you think." His words were biting. "If I were you, instead of mulling this to death, I'd be grabbing the chance to declare my feelings."

A little hurt by his words, she lashed out, "Then why didn't you?"

"How can I when the other person doesn't reciprocate my feelings because she is in love with someone else?" he snapped. "But that's not the case here. Jin pledges his heart to you, and Hana disrespects his feelings."

"I'm not disrespecting him." Her voice rose a notch. "You don't understand—"

"I do understand." He cut off her reply, making her react to this new Ayato sitting beside her. "Hana is being stubborn; you prefer to play out this sacrificing being when the man is clearly waiting for you."

"Ayato," she said with a tremor in her voice, "you're acting rather mean."

"I am." He took a deep breath. "Right now, I'm feeling sorry for Jin because he fell in love with someone who couldn't see the answer in front of her. But you are using Shouko as a tool so that Hana has a reason to reject him."

"Go away," She whispered.

"Fate is giving Hana another chance for you to be with that one person you claim to love deeply."

"I don't think so."

He sighed wearily. "I hope you don't regret this decision."

She got up to throw her half-empty cup into the nearest bin without a backward glance. She walked toward the building in wooden steps. What Ayato didn't understand was that she was doing this for their own good. He hadn't seen Jin's face after his call ended.

Chapter 51

"Jin, do you want to have dinner with me?"

Jin glanced up at the speaker while rearranging his desk to put an end to an exhausting week of non-stop work. Moments ago, he had been casting impatient looks at the slow-ticking clock, but now he would rather head home later.

Hana stood at the entrance of his cubicle, inviting him with a warm smile, which brightened his fatigued soul. A spark of hope lit in his heart, but he schooled his features in case she should see something unintended on his stunned face.

He returned her smile. "Sure, why not? I'm done over here."

They walked together towards the front door while glancing toward a stone-faced Ayato, whose dark eyes were fixed on his computer screen. Jin changed his shoes quickly to follow Hana, reminding himself that they were behaving as friends rather than proving their love for one another. He inwardly repeated that thought as a wake-up call while standing beside Hana, who seemed unusually perky.

"So where are we planning to have dinner?" he asked as they left the elevator to venture out of the building.

"Somewhere nearby?" She gazed up at him. "We will have more time to spend together."

The evening sky was painted in a riot of burnished colours, with diamonds twinkling between puffy clouds drifting before a light breeze.

Jin tried to gather his thoughts but failed after peering down at Hana, who was chattering about work-related stories. Truth be told, he couldn't restrain the feelings deep in his heart for this woman. Unfortunately, he couldn't speak for her.

Somehow her demeanour—as if nothing had transpired between them—confused him as he struggled to decide whether or not she truly loved him, and that muddled his thinking.

Throngs of people surged along the sidewalk, either workers set free or students still mingling, not ready to depart from their friends. Families were out together since it was Friday evening, having chosen to dine outside.

"I used to come here." She pointed to a long queue of hungry people; Jin only nodded, keeping a hand on the small of her back.

He was thankful he'd worn a coat, since the evening had brought on bone-chilling cold. Whenever he exhaled, a cloud of fog hung before him.

"Who has been with you to dine here?" He leaned closer to breathe in her ear.

"Ayato, when we used to date," she replied softly.

The mention of the other man's name damped Jin's mood. He knew that the pair had once been close to being announced as a couple.

"I'm sorry about your relationship not working out." He offered sympathy, although his feelings were another matter.

"It's all right," she replied nonchalantly. "I have trouble getting into relationships."

He was dying to argue with her one-track logic, but he prayed for control and throttled the urge. Instead, he was about to change the subject in favour of a mundane conversation.

She interrupted his thoughts. "Let's go some other place. The queue is not moving at all, and I'm hungry."

"Well, you should have told me earlier," he grumbled—rather adorably, he thought.

"I'm sorry." She rolled those expressive eyes while stifling a laugh. "This is your punishment."

"Why?" He scowled almost on the verge of pitching a fit.

Instead, she grasped his hand and led him away. They ditched the queue, but Jin pretended not to notice their hands in close contact. He was afraid to twitch his fingers, fearing that she might pull her hand away. His mind was in turmoil, whispering what-ifs as if purposely taunting him. Right now, he felt as if they were like any normal pair hopelessly in love.

They sat side by side at a busy front counter in a loud establishment. The head chef, a skilled old hunchbacked woman, delivered bowl after bowl of udon that packed a punch.

"So tell me, Jin."

Hana's lilting tone distracted him from the cold brew in his hand. "Tell you what?" He raised an inquisitive brow and took a sip. Then he looked at her with a hint of a grin. "If you're asking me something private, then you're out of luck."

"Is there someone you wish was your girlfriend?"

Her question caught him by surprise. Finally, the puzzle pieces were coming together, and Jin was certain as he stared at her grinning expression. Somehow her eyes conveyed desperation, and her laughter seemed forced. Evidently her "calmness" was meant to say that they might now hope for a new beginning.

"You tell me," he said, playing coy for the moment. "Who do you think?"

She blinked at his evasive response. "Well, I'm sure you have someone that you want to be with."

"You're right," he said in a strained voice, slamming both palms on the counter.

Several customers craned their necks to stare at the sudden commotion, but Jin's unwavering glower was fixed on Hana. As he watched her fingers fidgeting, all but hearing the thoughts turning and sifting in her mind, his anger slowly grew. He felt used, thinking Hana preferred his company as a trade-off.

She turned to him pasting on a smile. "Well?"

"She is here with me," he answered quietly. He retrieved his wallet and dug out a few notes to pay for both their dinners, ignoring Hana's reaction, if any. Instead, he grasped her wrist and physically dragged her out of the place. Their hurried steps clattered along the pavement, allowing his rage to calm down, and soon they were walking aimlessly. Hana must have sensed his mood and was keeping quiet.

Calm down, he mentally scolded himself.

He looked over one shoulder. Hana looked crestfallen. When his heartstrings tensed at the sight of her moist eyes. Soon he caught sight of a park, still clutching her hand. He led them into the park; he figured they wouldn't be the only ones visiting.

By now, the surrounding area was lit by streetlamps. Cyclists passed by with their red lights blinking behind them.

Again Jin glanced over his shoulder and saw Hana rubbing that button nose with the sleeve of her faux fur coat. She must have sensed him watching because she caught his eye. He held his chin high with an animated look, swallowing his mirth and hoping to make her feel even more guilty.

As they turned a corner in heavy silence, moonlight revealed a vacated playground, and an idea struck him. Without warning he abandoned the asphalt walkway and jogged towards the swings, whilst behind him Hana struggled to match his fast pace and surely questioned his motives.

"Sit," he ordered in mock anger as they paused near a lonely swing.

"What?" She gasped but then studied his face. "Jin, are you all right?"

"Just listen to me." he gently urged her.

WIth a puzzled look, she sat down warily on the seat. He waited for her to grasp the chain links carefully before he pushed her from the back. Her startled gasp was followed by girlish giggles, and soon she asked him to push her even higher; he chuckled every time she let out a squeal.

"Higher!" she exclaimed, her peals of laughter seeming to fill the night sky. "Jin, don't stop!"

"I won't," he whispered like a promise.

Stop loving you, Hana, he finished silently.

He stepped a few feet away and watched her swaying back and forth, basking in her carefree laughter. Without hesitation he stepped forward again and wrapped both arms around her from behind— startling her, as she was now stranded in mid-flight. Since she couldn't let go of the chain, he took this moment to embrace her tightly.

"Jin?" Her voice was incredulous. "What are you doing?"

"Since no feelings are involved, why do you worry about one hug?" he whispered close to her ear.

Silence greeted him, and he buried his nose in her tresses, squeezing her body, and feeling the weight of her breasts resting on his forearm.

"Right."

Jin might not have detected her whisper if he had been listening to the wind or the other people in the park. He let out a shaky breath as he sensed another feathery light weight on his shoulder. He knew without looking that she had leaned back to rest her head there.

"I cannot forget you," he said. "I heard you say that we aren't able to become a couple, but my heart says otherwise."

Her shifting weight caused him to take a peek, and he saw her leaning backward awkwardly. Their eyes met under the night sky, and he felt himself being drawn into those wide pupils where he read so many emotions swirling subconsciously. He moved his head inch by inch, letting her figure out that he was reeling in for a kiss.

"Hana …."

"Mm," she hummed.

The only sound in his ears was his pounding heart. He was stunned that she hadn't shot him down for admitting his feelings. The flecks of hazel in her orbs came into view now, since he was close enough for them to share their breath and for the tips of their noses to graze. At last he pressed a kiss to her waiting lips—a kiss that had been in his mind ever since their first meeting.

Chapter 52

The shrill ring announcing a caller exploded the delicate mood. Without looking, he guessed the caller was Shouko; they had been carefully cementing the bridge between them. She often asked about the mysterious other person in his life, but Jin hadn't told her about Hana. Somehow that seemed rather personal.

"Jin?"

Hana's soft voice reeled him back to the present, where she was still caught in his arms. Slowly he lowered her back onto the swing, as she stared back at him oddly. Finally the ringtone halted; heavy silence hung over them until it rang again. He pulled out the device to study the overseas number, with her name flashing like a neon sign.

"Who is it, Jin?" Hana tilted her head. "Won't you answer the call?"

"Umm … no." He glanced at her before looking away to regard the dark playground.

She studied him for a moment. "What's the matter, Jin?"

"Nothing," he huffed out, plopping down on another swing.

"Then why are you so stressed out?" she pressed.

"I am?" He emitted a strained laugh. "I mean, do I look stressed out?"

"Yes," she replied in a frank tone. "It's Shouko calling you, right?"

Astounded by her statement, Jin could only gawk at her features, shrouded in the surrounding gloom.

"What makes you think so?" he whispered warily.

"I overheard your conversation with her," she answered quietly. "I'm sorry, Jin."

"Oh." Jin blinked, the cold device between his warm hands. "What else did you overhear?"

"She wants you to visit her," was her matter-of-fact reply.

He let out a tired huff. "What else?"

"You told her about someone catching your attention," she said, prodding him on purpose.

When she said nothing more, Jin glanced down at the clasped hands between his legs but then sensed another presence. Hana's soft fingers glided over his own, and she squatted in front of him with a serene look. "I want Jin to fly over—"

"Hana." He cut her off sternly. "How can you say that?"

"Jin, listen to me." She scooted forward while speaking hurriedly. "You don't know what to expect. You once told me how important Shouko is to you, and your connection is strong."

"There is a saying about walking away from your former times," Jin argued. "That saying goes for me as well."

A dainty hand sidled up to his cheek. He felt it tremble but quickly rested his own hand on it. Goosebumps prickled his skin at the contact.

"You are feeling guilty for me, Jin," she whispered gently. "This 'love' that you feel for me is nothing but regret that you have hurt me long ago."

"Guilt?" He frowned, a little confused.

"Yes," she said with a decisive nod. "But the feelings you have for Shouko are real."

"Are they?" he mumbled.

"I once loved you, Jin." She released a laugh that sounded fake to his ears. "Maybe … I still do."

"Then why are you pushing me away?" His voice hinted of desperation.

"Because I want Jin to know if staying away will diminish this 'love' that you developed for me or if Shouko still has your heart."

"What if I never returned?" Jin narrowed both eyes. "Would you be ready for that answer?"

"Then we have the answer." Her voice cracked. "Give Shouko the benefit of the doubt, Jin."

"Are you able to handle coming to know that I want to be with Shouko?"

"Jin, it was my fault to bring this entire mess upon us."

"Stop blaming yourself," he replied fiercely.

"You warned me time and time again." Her voice rose, urged by suppressed emotions. "But I used Jin, disrespecting your advice, for my own curiosity, because I was blinded by the urge."

They remained in the same position for quite some time. He watched Hana's silent tears, letting her words sink into his system. Soon he felt the start of a pounding headache. Cautiously, he stood upright, never relinquishing Hana's hand; he was afraid he might be actually losing her.

He had a strong notion of what would occur if he paid a visit to Shouko's residence; although they had cut ties, Jin had suffered a little. After all, the pair had gone through a strong relationship until the long distance had taken a toll upon them.

Guilt? Regret?

Monday had been a drag for Jin. When he made the first call to Shouko, she was startled by his gesture.

Of course he had told her about the arrangements regarding his visit—after Shouko's excitement settled down—and continued with further details. Once again he was keeping Hana in the dark.

Right now, he was leaning back on his office chair while staring at Hana over his linked fingers.

"You have to be the saddest man on earth," Ayato said, ribbing him.

Jin rolled his eyes. "What do you want, Ayato?"

"I want you to disappear from Hana's life," he replied, accepting the challenge. "I think it's better to cut the string of connection between you two."

"Why?" Jin glanced at him, hovering against the wall of his cubicle. "I know that you want Hana."

"At least there's no tragic history I'm holding against her." His remark struck a chord in Jin's heart. "The best for you two is to cease breathing in the same atmosphere."

Instead of replying, Jin looked away, only to make eye contact with Hana. She waved a hand and offered him a smile that squeezed his heart.

"Can you make her happy?" Jin asked the question in a hushed voice.

"I love her."

Guilt?

His eyes strayed to the computer's screen, where an email icon blinked continuously, her name pulsing as if for his attention. Jin's mind was muddled from overthinking, but this conversation held a deeper meaning. Ever since his arrival, he and Hana had been at war.

Hurtful words were exchanged, tears were shed as they relived the history and learned about secrets that were beyond irreparable. Maybe it was a wise choice to step back and take a long breath.

"Will you promise me to make Hana forget my existence?" Jin's voice had a rusty edge.

"I promise, but—" Ayato frowned, clearly frustrated. "Why are you so easily giving up Hana to me? I expected a little possessiveness from Jin."

Jin chortled, drawing a few curious looks from their co-workers including Hana, whose neat brows were raised. In reply, Jin leaned forward before shaking his head; Hana nodded slowly, still clueless.

But Jin knew that he preferred Hana smiling again rather than crying all the time, ever since he had arrived.

"I want her to be happy again."

Silence fell between the men. Ayato regarded Jin's crestfallen face while the said person settled back in his chair, moved the cursor, and opened the new email.

"What about yourself?" Ayato sighed from behind.

"I'm leaving," he replied in a terse voice.

"What?" Ayato gawked comically.

This time, his loud voice caught everyone's attention, and everyone looked at them. "Oi, what's going on?" Daisuke's voice echoed from the other end. "What are you two hens gossiping about?"

"N-nothing," Jin quickly interjected before Ayato could make an unnecessary scene. "We were just chatting about the scores for our baseball home team."

Because Hana didn't know about his decision to depart from the company, of course the idea left a deep gash in his heart. At the same time, Ayato's words only confirmed their conversation at the playground.

Their relationship was based on a toxic and charged history.

He felt personally responsible to pursue Hana from the beginning, thinking he could actually heal her soul and make amends without any consequences. Disregarding the depressed girl's own emotions and thoughts, instead Jin forced his opinion on her. Maybe they weren't truly meant to be together in the first place.

Back at the playground, Hana had reminded him of her teenage self—squatting in front of him and imparting wisdom as they talked.

A warm hand on his shoulder told him that Ayato was still standing on his side of the cubicle. Now he leaned over with a serious expression.

"Whatever is Jin's decision," he whispered, disappointment written on his face, "I respect your word."

"Thank you." Jin could only nod.

When office hours had ended, was about to meet with Kaito to hand over the resignation letter—he had typed and printed it in the afternoon—when Hana came over to his side.

"Are you all right, Jin?" Her voice was wary.

He opted for a carefree grin. "I should be the one asking you that."

She offered him a half-hearted smile that faded when she saw the letter on his desk. "May I know to whom that letter is addressed?"

"I'm resigning, Hana." He chuckled drily, not glancing at her. "I'll be leaving soon, perhaps in a week."

"Oh." She blinked as if taken aback. "Th-that was fast."

"True." He paused in the middle of picking up his bag. "I may need to think about us and to know if Shouko might be the one for me."

"I'm happy for you!" she said with a fake enthusiasm.

Hana rushed forward to envelop him in a hug that sent him hurtling back to the moment when he'd told his best friend.

"Hana—"

"I have to leave early," she said, cutting him off, a wide grin on her face. "I'm reading the latest romance novel and totally hooked on the male character."

Jin waved his fingers while watching her walk away in a hurry. Then he shuffled over to the boss's office. When he was invited to enter, he explained his situation to the quiet man, feeling mentally exhausted.

"I know that Hana and you have had some tension, but I never figured it was this much." Kaito sighed aloud. "Of course you may resign, since I do not like to see my workers stressing over any matter that will cause work-related issues."

"Thank you, Mr Sukihara." Jin signalled his gratitude by bowing low.

Soon he was out of the building and into the humid outdoors, ignoring the pain in his heart but steeling himself. If this meant that both of them might have peace of mind, then he must act accordingly. But Jin knew without a doubt that Hana would live in a part of him until his very last breath.

She meant that much to him and more.

Chapter 53

$\mathcal{H}$ana stared dismally at the television, where a Bollywood movie ran in the background. Her mind was elsewhere. As she sat on the couch with her legs tugged against her chest, images of Jin's face blocked everything surrounding her.

Ever since he had turned in his resignation letter, he had retired to his home. He was taking the week to tie up loose ends and working from his place. A group of the men from the office dropped by his location to help with the packing.

Her patience was about gone, due to the silence on her cell phone and wondering if he was talking with Shouko at any given moment. Were they reminiscing about a past that excluded her?

She had finally realised that Jin was part and parcel of her life. Without him close, it was difficult to go through the daily motions. Before he'd come crashing once again into her life, she had almost come to terms to move forward, but now she had grown use to his presence.

Although this realisation had come too late, still no tears had wet her cheeks. All she could do was stare at the empty desk back at the office. Somehow, she yearned to hear his smooth voice whispering bittersweet promises in her ear.

Jin would be departing within days. She had recently overheard Daisuke commenting to Hikari about Jin's odd behaviour. He had withdrawn drastically.

Even as the movie credits rolled, her eyes stayed on the screen as her riotous thoughts surged.

Just then, she heard a knock on the door, and she sprang from her seat to answer it. She strongly sensed that Jin was standing outside to bid a final farewell. Maybe ... just maybe he wanted to inform her that he'd cancelled the flight and wished to stay here with her.

When she opened the door, her heart seemed to sink through the floor. Standing on the other side was Ayato, whose silent expression spoke louder than words. He must have read her crestfallen features and concluded that she'd been hoping to see someone else. She immediately felt guilty for behaving in such a hurtful manner.

"Hana," he greeted her softly. "Good evening, I brought us light dinner in case you haven't had yours."

Suddenly she found herself engulfed in his embrace, clutching the back of his shirt as if she were drowning. Which was partly true; she was drowning in her own misery caused by none other than herself.

Ayato seemed shocked at her reaction but quickly recovered. "I'm here," he whispered in a cajoling voice. "I'm always here for you."

"I know," she answered quietly. "I know you will be here for me."

Finally, she felt the urge to cry but held back, because in recent months that was the only emotion she'd felt. The two of them ambled into the apartment, each with an arm around the other's waist. "Ayato ...," she said in a wavering voice, "I'm so sorry."

"It's all right." He smiled down at her.

"I don't know what to do," she answered shakily. "I should be loving you right now, Ayato; instead, I'm constantly pushing and causing you hurt."

"Then admit that you don't want Jin to leave." His eyes boring a hole into her own.

Their gaze unflinching. "I don't want Jin to disappear from my life again."

"Stop him," he urged. "He's going through the same upheaval as we are."

"But I can't." Hana's heart was beating madly. "Ayato, I'm too late, and I have a strong feeling that Jin still harbours feelings for her."

They stepped back from the hug but kept their eyes trained on each other. After Hana's admission, her heart felt free. Although the timing was far from perfect. The three of them were caught in a web of feelings, yet she took on the blame. If she had only been true to herself from the beginning, Ayato and she wouldn't be standing here still hoping for her.

"Hana, don't do this to yourself again."

"Please tell me what to do." She sobbed aloud, feeling lost. "I need you now."

In silence they stood in the middle of the living room, suffering.

The next day at the office, Hana sat on Jin's chair, stroked his desk with her hands, and laid her head down on it. She closed her eyes to allow past memories to filter into her mind: faint laughter, exchanged banter, and mostly their unwavering connection that had bound them together for the long journey right through high school.

"I was a coward," she whispered.

Thankfully, the office was empty, and she needed this moment to herself as feelings clouded her systems.

"Please don't leave me, Jin," she pleaded, over and over again, choking on the words. "Please don't abandon me again." She rested her forehead on the backs of her fingers clutching the edge of the desk.

She heard distant voices from the corridor, so she hurried back to her desk, where she pretended to focus on the computer. When colleagues spilt in one by one, she nodded a morning greeting and even shared a joke or two. Then Ayato's face came into view, and they stared at each other, recalling the night before. He had stayed overnight. He had shared her grief and pain as an understanding friend.

"Morning, Hana," he said with a mischievous wink. "You're early today."

"Morning, Ayato." She smiled at him. "I have extra work to finish, so …."

"I see." He paused for a second before moving off to his side.

Tomorrow was the day when Jin would fly off to another part of the planet. She wondered if she would even survive the heartache. A sense of urgency began to gnaw at her during the afternoon and again later, when her file was being processed.

"I think you should say something to Jin."

"Ayato?" She pivoted to study his serious expression. His words fanned the urgency within her, but she had to remained composed.

There was nothing to be done at this point in life. In fact, it was a lesson that she would live in regret and what-ifs. She knew that whatever happened in the future, at least it wouldn't be as tragic as what she was going through right now. With Ayato by her side as a pillar of support, she could walk with her head held high.

"I can talk—"

"Goodbye, Ayato." She beamed at him. "Go home, and stop worrying about me."

"But—"

"Please," she said with a pointed look, "I'm fine, truly."

When he exited the office, she sat back to pull the cell phone from her purse toying with the device, adopting a nonchalant pose.

Even as she stepped outside the building, which now housed more recent memories of Jin and herself.

The night was dreadful for her. More forgotten scenes from the past bombarded her whilst she lay awake on her mattress, smiling in the shadows. She felt ensconced in the warmth of those times when the man she had viewed as a father still lived with them, joyous moments spent together as families.

As she turned on her side, the teddy bear caught her gaze, and she tugged it close with a sad smile. She fervently wished she could have taken a different course; perhaps Jin would be here with her.

She felt crushed under the weight of regret.

This only proved that the selfishness in her still existed, because she made everything about herself—pushing away Ayato's kindness, using him for her own gain—but now that she had succeeded in pushing Jin away, her inner self finally came to its senses. Somehow, she'd become a grown adult, but her behaviour hadn't changed.

Morning arrived with pelting rain that matched her own solemn mood. Angry black clouds hung low.

The ticking of the clock reminding her of the hours slowly ticking by as Jin drew further and further away from her. His flight was at midnight.

Hunger was forgotten, the weekend nothing but a blur of passing hours and the unreality of lives obliviously continuing around her.

Chapter 54

*H*er restless emotions led her to the park she and Jin had visited. She sat down on the swing in the murky weather, embracing the chill while the drizzling rain pitter-pattered. She clutched the icy metal of the chain and stared off into space for an hour or so, waiting for the day to end.

Staying at home only made her glance at the clock every minute, watching the numbers pass every hour. Somehow today, it was dragging.

Anxiety suffocated her while that same urgency troubled her fatigued mind; she hadn't slept a wink the night before, replaying the times when Jin begged for her forgiveness, again watching him break down when he learnt of her miscarriage. *How can I move on when I'm still clinging on to the past fervently?*

Her tears mixed with the rain, and she squeezed both eyes shut. Only the beating of her heart signalled that she was still living and breathing. She couldn't turn back the time to change the course of their destiny.

"Jin," she whispered over and over. "Jin, Jin, Jin …."

Come back to me, she pleaded.

Laughter broke out just then, and she peered forlornly at a happy couple getting wet from the drizzle but not caring.

Dear God, what should I do?

Darkness soon settled in. Evening had arrived while she sat contemplating and regretting all her decisions.

Once again, Shouko won.

"Tell me," she said, glancing up at the sky. "Will I suffer forever or grasp my own happiness? If so, will Jin accept me after I gave him a push to his current love?"

Thunder answered her, and she snorted at her goofiness. She knew she might be on the edge; perhaps she really was.

"Excuse me?"

She turned her head toward the voice and saw an old woman holding an umbrella. She looked worried.

"Yes?" She straightened out of her slump. "Do you need my help?"

"No, but I was wondering why you're sitting here." She limped forward and shaded Hana under the umbrella. "I couldn't help but feel a sense of worry."

"Oh." Hana blinked at her thoughtful kindness. "Thank you."

"I'll drop you back to your house—"

"It's all right, Aunty, but I'm in no mood to return home." She was confiding in a complete stranger.

"Oh." The woman frowned before nodding. "Did you argue with your family?"

"No," she whispered, listening to the rain on the umbrella.

"Then what is the matter, dear?" The woman gently placed a wrinkled hand on her arm. "You'll be sick if you don't stay out of the rain."

"I'd rather be sick physically than mentally," she blurted, tears forming to mix with the rain droplets on her face. "Sorry, I'll leave now."

"You'll need this umbrella." The woman smiled kindly, extending the handle to her. "I have three grandchildren, and they are all girls; I've learnt to read their faces."

Hana frowned at the woman, wondering where she was leading the conversation, but she stayed awhile to hear the rest. She stayed seated but didn't take the proffered umbrella. Then, as she looked into the old woman's weathered features, all of a sudden she missed her mother's warm embrace.

"And what did you learn?" she asked, swallowing the rasp in her throat.

"I learnt not to turn my gaze away from those haunting eyes," the woman said, with a glance upward into the rain.

Hana's eyes widened at her sudden remark. Her heart skipped as she studied the wrinkled face smiling back at her. At odds with herself, she took the plunge and asked the stranger a question burning deep in her mind. She had that homely aura surrounding her.

"My best friend left me again." Hana pressed her fists against her eyelids. "We were separated for many years before fate decided that the two of us should meet once again. I pushed him from my side, but right now, I am dealing with agony of separation from him."

"What is it you want?" the woman asked, gazing directly at her.

"I don't know." Hana stifled a sob, peeved at herself for being a weak person. "What can I do right now?"

"Move on from him." The woman's sympathetic expression softened her blunt words. "If he doesn't want to be your friend anymore, then you have no choice but to let your memories suffice."

"But …." Hana's heart protested against this logic. In fact, she faced the opposite situation: Jin had yearned to stay by her side.

"Are you okay, dear?" The older woman clutched the umbrella against a gust of wind.

"Please find shelter." Hana got up from the swing, grasping the woman's arm gently. "I'll take my leave now."

"Are you sure you don't need the umbrella?" the woman called as Hana ran from the spot.

I'm coming for you, she shouted silently.

"Jin!" The name sprang from her mouth as her running feet splashed in the puddles.

She stopped beneath an awning to dial Ayato's number and waited impatiently for him to answer.

"Hello—"

"Ayato!" she screamed into the speaker. "I need your help, please!"

"Hana!" He sounded panicky at once. "What's wrong? What's happened?"

"I need you to drive me to the airport!" she wailed in terror as lightning flashed in the distance. "I want to stop Jin from leaving! I—I love him!"

"Where are you now?" he replied calmly. "Tell me the location."

After telling him where she was, she looked up at the sky. Sudden urgency galvanized her whole being, and it felt as if a huge weight had been lifted off her shoulders. She watched the rain drizzling down like tiny diamonds, and a smile formed on her face. After suffering for many years, Hana could feel the spark of joy inside her. She stood beneath the rain to wash away the sentimental emotions.

That was how Ayato found her: soaking wet. "You'll catch a fever," he yelled from the driver's side while Hana raced towards the passenger door.

"To the airport!" Hana, shivering from head to toe, turned to gaze at him.

He cursed under his breath, reached back and rummaged in the backseat, and retrieved a small towel. "Dry yourself, silly woman," he chided her before driving off towards their desired location.

"I love him." She acknowledged the meaning of the words as she heard herself saying them with so much conviction.

"You two are made for each other," Ayato said as the rain swelled to a downpour.

"What if ...?" Hana shook her head whilst wiping her forearms with the towel.

"It's real this time," he reassured her, pressing on the gas a little but being careful not to skid.

"I want to give the girl inside me that happiness she craves." Hana sucked in a breath, once again in tears. "She deserves to see Jin, she deserves to smile—she deserves a closure from the olden days."

Both Ayato and Hana were on edge as they beat several red lights. Hana studied the bleak scenario; only a few people were rushing beneath the torrent. Then her eyes sparked in reminiscence at the sight of two high school students standing under a shelter as the car stopped to wait for the light to turn green. The boy playfully stuck his hand out to collect rainwater to dump on his companion as she squealed in mock outrage.

"Suhana, you'll make it this time," Ayato said out of the blue as he reached across to cover her hand with his own.

She offered a gentle smile. "I hope you will find love with someone even better."

"I'm nursing a broken heart," he said with a humourless chuckle. "Not so fast."

"I'm sorry," she whispered as she covered his hand with her free one.

"You don't have to be." He turned to wink at her. "Just smile from now on, but then I'll fall hopelessly in love with you again."

"Thank you for not leaving my side, Ayato." She looked straight in his eyes, honesty effortlessly shone on her face.

"Let go of my hand, Hana, before I change my mind," he said quietly. She let him slip his hand away to grip the steering wheel.

Soon, they were heading towards the intersection that led to the airport. Ayato stepped on the gas and switched lanes, easily cutting off several cars. Before the car rocked to a stop, Hana flung the door open, only to feel a rough tug on her arm. She turned to look at Ayato, who was giving her a pleading look. He unbuckled his seat belt to envelop her in an embrace. On cue, she threw her arms around him.

"All the best," he laughed before giving her a shove. "Go and stop that idiot."

She catapulted from the seat and ran, skidding inside the airport because of her slippery shoes, and raced towards the departure hall. She paused to read the huge screen to spot Jin's plane with relief; he was still here. Undeterred by the stares and the bone-chilling air, she zigzagged through the human traffic, her heart beating wildly.

"Excuse me!" Hana called out to the ticket taker at the departure hall. "I am looking for someone; please help me!"

"Oh," the lady said with a surprised blink while Hana, panting, shifted on her feet to survey the crowd. "I'm sorry, but all of the passengers are now queuing up for their flight," she replied while checking her wristwatch.

"Please, I am begging you." Hana clasped her hands in a beseeching gesture.

"There is nothing I can do to help you right now." The young woman had an apologetic expression. "Hey, wait!"

Hana had decided to rush forward, only to be caught quickly by a security guard, who dragged her flailing body backwards, drawing more stares from onlookers, while the attendants directed the man in charge to take her out of the airport. Meanwhile, police officers were jogging towards the commotion.

"Jin!" Hana cried in a shrill voice, ignoring the warning from the security guard, who was having trouble moving her.

"You are disrupting the airport with your behaviour," he said, his arms lifting her by the armpit.

"Jin! Jin Takami!"

"We will have to arrest you, Miss, if you do not heed our warning," a police officer said in a brisk voice.

"Jin! Where are you?" she hollered at the top her lungs. "I'm here for you! Jin Takami!"

"Lady!" The officer grabbed onto her forearm, but because of her rush of adrenaline, she was able to shake him off. Meanwhile, a crowd had formed around them to observe the odd scene.

"Leave me alone!" Hana wailed. Then cold dread seized her as the announcement for Jin's flight rang through the building.

"Miss!" The officer was startled when she collapsed on her knees, blinded by tears.

"I am too late," she said, to nobody in particular.

"Please follow me, young miss." The same attendant crouched beside Hana, frowning at her.

"Please stop the flight from leaving," Hana tried for the last time. "I don't want him to leave me."

"I am sorry, but …." The attendant was talking to Hana, but her gaze drifted beyond the official's shoulder.

The hair on her neck rose, and everything else went into slow motion. A whoosh of breath went out of her; she couldn't believe her eyes. She rose from her tangle of arms and legs and started toward him as their eyes connected across a distance. Meantime, Jin, the one who had captured her heart, dropped his backpack and slowly walked forward. Then he broke into a run just as Hana threw her arms open. They ran together, and Jin twirled them in a circle as Hana hugged his head and utterly relaxed in his arms.

"I love you, Jin."

Chapter 55

$\mathcal{J}$in's heart accelerated in jerks when the familiar voice calling his name had led him to glimpse the one person he least expected to meet.

He saw Hana stretch out both arms enticingly as if waiting for his next move. Suddenly, another emotion overwhelmed his entire system. As he dropped his backpack on the cold tiles, his feet began shuffling one step at a time before taking off in a sprint. "Hana!"

He enfolded the weeping girl in a bone-crushing hug whilst burying his face against her slender neck and beginning to twirl. His warm breath clouded, and locks of her dark chocolate hair flew out behind her.

His fingers dug into her back in an effort to crush her to him. Yet he couldn't hold himself back as he nuzzled even closer. The sensation of her dainty fingers sifting through his hair brought a comical grin to his face.

All this time he had been sinking into utter depression and denial. He had no idea whether this decision was wise and whether he could truly forget a girl he'd once called his best friend. But Hana had come here for him, taking away the last of his doubts. He had made a firm decision to be for her from now on—because he'd been about to commit the same grave mistake as he had before.

"I love you, Jin," she whispered the cherished words through her tears. "I always have, ever since that day."

"I know," he nodded, raining kisses on her face. "I know ...."

"Don't ever leave me," she wailed, cupping his face between her hands.

"I swear on my life that I'll remain by your side till the end," he promised, gazing into her tearful eyes. He let go of Hana so she could stand, leaned forward, and kiss her mouth as he gently took her in his arms again. They were greeted by resounding claps and cheers from hugely grinning strangers, and Hana hid her own smile against his chest.

Jin took her hands in his own. "Hana, this is what you want?"

"Yes," she replied, placing one hand over his heart. "I'm sorry for pushing you—"

"Shh.: He placed a finger against her mouth. "Come on, this isn't the place."

The two of them apologised to the workers involved, and after a stern warning, they were allowed to retrieve Jin's pack and leave the airport. He was feeling surreal. He held on to Hana's hand, afraid this might be a dream. But she was walking beside him, dripping wet. She must have been caught out in the rain.

"Let's start fresh," Jin said, kissing her on the side of her head. "Time to get you dried off quickly before you fall sick. By the way, did you run all the way to the airport?"

"Ayato drove me here," she replied in a nasal voice, already sniffling from a possible flu.

Jin made a mental note to thank Ayato for helping them reach this point. When they emerged from the terminal, the rain had stopped. Jin spied a cab, and they managed to climb. Jin gave her address, since the place he rented had been reclaimed by the owner.

All they could hear was their breathless laughter when Jin carried Hana through her doorway bridal style. Presently he began gently helping her strip off. They went into the bathroom where he turned on the tap to fill the tub. Then he turned to eye Hana, who shyly glanced away. He took off his own clothes and soon stood naked. He closed the short distance between them to kiss her again.

"Jin, I'm feeling embarrassed," she said in low voice but squealed when he scooped her up and carried her to the tub, brimming with hot water. As he carefully lowered her in, water sloshed onto the tiled floor. He stepped in behind her to settle down and bring her body to rest against his front. They remained for some time in a comfortable silence.

"Do you feel warm now?" he whispered into her ear.

"Yes," she replied, watching their linking fingers in awe. "Jin, make love to me."

"Let your body warm up all the way." He bumped his cheek against hers. "Your health is more important to me."

An hour or so later, they saw their fingertips wrinkling and decided they had been there long enough. Jin got out to dry himself before loosely tying the towel around his hips. He asked if she had another towel somewhere. Hana directed him, but he had trouble locating it. She went on enjoying a satisfying bath until at last he found one hidden in a drawer in her bedroom.

"Jin! Did you find the towel yet?" she called from the bathroom.

"Yeah!" he yelled in answer, returning to the toilet and beckoning her to step out of the tub. He opened the towel for her and wrapped it around her warm body. She took a moment to blow-dry her wet hair in front of a mirror. Her giggling was infectious, and the two of them behaved like adolescent teenagers when he suddenly felt shy as well.

By nightfall, the pair were cosied up on her mattress after filling up on what was in Hana's kitchen. Their anticipation grew whenever their eyes met; they knew what would transpire behind the bedroom door. They talked to ease the rising tension until Jin could no longer hold back. He entwined her fingers in his own and led her inside, where he watched her pull off her robe and let his own fall to the floor.

The air was chilly after the rain as the two of them huddled beneath the blanket. Jin started to trail tiny kisses on her shoulders towards her neck and chin while she caressed his back. The lovemaking was intimate, a healing process for them that rekindled the passion they had shared the first time, when his body had reacted quickly to her alluring softness.

Hearts melted as one; their breath warmed each other's skin; quiet sighs and deep grunts of appreciation were their only accompaniment. Sweat shone on their bodies as he enjoyed her soft sounds as she clutched the blanket and arched upward with pleasure.

"Jin," a voice called out from somewhere.

"Hmm …," he moaned, burrowing further into the sheets. "One minute …."

"Jin, it's afternoon. Wake up." Hana shook his aching body, finally pulling him out of his slumber.

"What?" He turned to see the sun filtering from the open window.

"You slept like the dead." She laughed at his stunned face. "I'm cooking us lunch. Also, the bath is ready."

"I love you," he said, watching a deep flush suffuse her face.

"I love you too." Her soft voice showered him with happiness. "Now, hurry up before the water gets cold."

"All right." He yawned and stretched languidly, watching her moving out of the bedroom to give him some space. Soon Jin found himself taking a relaxing bath with low music drifting from the living room.

A loopy grin formed on his face when he ducked under the water to wet his hair, knowing this was the best day of his life. He had finally made a breakthrough with the one person who mattered the most to him. Love bloomed inside his heart.

Chapter 56

Chiyoda, Tokyo
Five Months Later

The warm breeze followed Hana in when she walked into a café. She scanned the faces until she saw a familiar face sitting in one corner. The person had a lost expression as she stared out the window.

It took a lot of courage for Hana, but she had listened to Jin's advice to close each chapter of the old life. In fact, it was inevitable. Shifting from Osaka to their hometown in Chiyoda had been a hectic process; the journey was rough, yet the two of them were impatient to start anew.

She had chosen to live with Jin in his childhood home. It felt more welcoming than the apartment where she'd grown up. When she called her mother from Osaka to tell how she'd reconciled with her best friend as well as embarking on this new journey as a couple. Neena was shocked by the news and anxious about their relationship, but Jin had reassured her, and finally, she gave them her blessing.

"Welcome," a waiter greeted Hana, breaking into her thoughts. She realised she had been standing by the entrance, staring at the corner table. The one sitting there was giving her a wide-eyed expression.

"I'm sorry," Hana said with a wave towards the smiling waiter and resumed her walk towards the table.

Her former colleague, Miko, hastily got up from behind the table. She had changed drastically from a rebel teenager into a beautiful young lady. Her wavy dark brown mane had a fringe of bangs covering her forehead; on her still-slender frame she wore a baggy cream cardigan and torn jeans. The two paused to observe one another. A cry escaped from Miko when her arms curled around Hana, who returned her hug, both of them allowing mixed emotions to pour out.

"Hana"—Miko gasped the name in a thin voice—"you're looking so radiant."

"Thank you." Hana huffed out a laugh, surprised that she'd been expecting anger. Instead, Miko was glad to meet her. She moved backward to look her over. "How are you?"

"Even better, now that I got to see you." Miko was smiling through her tears as they held hands before they took seats opposite one another.

A young waitress approached them. "Would you ladies like to order now?"

"Yes." Miko glanced at the girl before pushing the menu forward to Hana. "It's my treat today."

"What?" Hana shook her head, but Miko was adamant. Hana gave in and ordered a cup of tea; so did Miko.

When the waitress left, they sat in awkward silence, neither one ready to open the Pandora's box, but it had to be done. Hana took a deep breath for courage. She caught a nervous look from Miko just then and realised that she had been living with her own demons as well. In some way, Miko must be weighed down with guilt for dragging Hana along to the group date.

Hana reached one hand across to calm Miko's fidgeting fingers and gave her a gentle smile. "It's all right," she whispered in a calm voice. "You don't have to worry about me being angry today. We need to break all ties with that particular night. When we walk out of this café, it will be with a fresh mindset."

"You should be screaming at me." Miko was not ready to forgive herself and hung her head. "I didn't know you were … abused. Then when my friend who saw it came up to me, it was too late because you were not in that school anymore."

"Neither of us knew what was going to happen behind that karaoke room. We were gullible girls." Hana crossed her ankles under the table. "I want to beg for forgiveness too."

"Why?" Miko asked in a loud voice. "You are not at fault, Hana."

"I was too much of a coward to head to the police station." She lowered her gaze to the table when the waitress returned and set their steaming beverages in front of them.

"We were all afraid back then, but my friend got the courage to report the men involved—and they were caught." Miko fisted both hands. "Those bastards denied it at first, insisting we were the ones to con them for money, but the investigators found numerous pictures of other high school girls as well as porn videos. Thankfully, other victims came forward to testify."

"I wish I'd been here to help." Hana sighed feeling dejected. "I hate myself—"

"Don't say that, Hana. You were dealing with your personal issues. In my heart I felt that I was helping to bring justice for you as well." Miko stared into the distance. "I take sleeping medication."

"Both of us went through a lot during our teen years," Hana explained, stirring her tea and watching it swirl. "I'm amazed that we're still breathing and sitting here facing each other again."

"Truth be told, I started to take my life a couple of times but gave up halfway." She snorted sardonically. "I'm a coward too."

"Miko, promise me that you won't hurt yourself from now on." Hana gave her a stern look. "It's time for you to make amends with your inner self."

"How?" Miko looked desolate, her lips trembling. "It takes a lot of strength for me to wake up and live day by day. My parents saw me lurching out of control and stepped in to help me find the path once again."

"Then, for their sakes, learn to let go," Hana whispered with conviction. "If you have nobody to talk to about the demons that might resurface, I am only one call away."

"Hana—" Miko gave her a grateful look before lowering her head on her folded arms to weep brokenly. Hana gave her space by remaining quiet. "Thank you, thank you very much …."

By late evening, they had settled down to cover the rest of the topic. Finally Miko was able to laugh, her eyes glinting with delight and excitement while Hana shared news of Jin and herself becoming a couple. Of course, Hana also shared her own secret about the miscarriage. The women bonded all over again, as they ventured out to see Jin standing at the side of the building, decked out in a formal suit, as handsome as ever.

He'd been given a branch by Kaito, whose friend had a company in Tokyo. Their former boss was saddened to see them leave yet happy that they had settled whatever issues had stood between them. He handed Jin a name and number, asking him to give that person a call. Thanks to Kaito, Jin had a job offer. Meanwhile, Hana spent her time at home taking care of their household. When to her astonishment she learned of her pregnancy, the two of them began to baby-proof the double-storey house.

Jin walked over to join them. "Do you want more time together?" he asked, kissing Hana on the cheek.

"I have to leave now; my daughter is waiting for me at home." Miko stepped away, waving at them, but Hana stopped her.

"You have a daughter?" she asked with an incredulous look.

"I didn't tell you?" Miko blinked once, letting out a peal of mirth while shoving her hand inside her handbag. "She recently turned five years old. I'm scared of her."

"Why?" Jin's eyes widened in fear as he and Hana leaned in closer to get a glimpse of an adorable, cherubic face. "She is so adorable, but why are you terrified of her?"

"She has the same temper as I did when I was a kid." Miko rolled her eyes.

"What about your husband?" Hana grinned at her as the trio made a move for the Yamanote Line.

"It was an accidental pregnancy with my ex-boyfriend. Our relationship fizzled out, but I told him thank you for the little bundle baking inside my belly." Her dry recitation drew laughter from the duo.

Hana and Jin waved at an ecstatic Miko, as the couple decided to have a leisurely walk. With one hand tugged in the crook of his arm, Hana set a slow and measured pace under the twilight sky. In amicable silence, she leaned her head against his shoulder to sightsee. Finally they reached their former meeting place.

"You must be tired," Hana told him as they sat down on the same bench.

"I want to have some fresh air before heading back home." He sighed with a cheeky smile aimed at her.

"What is it?" She leaned an elbow on the back of the bench to face him and pressed a finger on his cheek.

"Judging by the two of you, I can assume the meeting was worth it," he said softly.

"Thank you, Jin," she replied sincerely. "You have been the light in my life since the beginning."

"You as well." He pecked her on the forehead before quietness reigned once again. Then he surprised Hana by getting up from the seat to bend on one knee in front of her seated position.

"Jin." Hana's eyes widened, and she felt her heart rate accelerating. Their gazes locked together.

"Suhana, you have been my closest friend. We've experienced ups and downs in our lives together." He took her hand as tears shimmered in his eyes. "From the start you could read me like an open book. Your undying devotion always set me smiling again, your presence soothed me, your hands calmed me down, but I was blind not to see that the one dear person standing in front of me was my future wife."

"Jin—" Hana was sobbing, with one hand over her mouth.

"Hana, you have reprised the role of being my best friend, my lover," he said in a wobbly voice. Then he pulled out a ring. "This time, I want you to be my wife. Let's spend the rest of our lives in harmony, through the good times as well as the bad, I promise to you that I will never abandon you as I did before. Will you marry me?"

"Yes!" Hana shouted her answer, knocking him to the ground as she seized him in a hug. They sat like a pair of kids on the leafy ground as she watched Jin putting the engagement band on her ring finger.

"I love you, Hana."

Epilogue

One Year Later

The atmosphere was heavy even though sunlight shone from the bright baby-blue sky; cold water splashed within the small bucket borrowed near the grave entrance while Hana, Neena and Hana's one-year-old daughter stood by two graves side by side. Jin came with the bucket and a ladle, and the trio began cleaning the cold stone engraved with the name of the deceased. Hana gently guided her daughter's hand to help with her older sibling's grave.

They carefully cleared out the growing weeds, silently working together, while Neena cleared off the vase to insert a fresh bouquet for Jin's mother as well as for her grandchild. As always, tears continuously dripped from the faces of the grieving; incense sticks were lit, their aroma floating in the air, and water was poured from the ladle.

Sweet dumplings were served for Sayomi along with a small plush toy for the other. Soon all four of them placed their hands flat in front of them, bowing a little to say something about their everyday situation and to ask for their blessings. They sat to watch the grave until their daughter began to make a fuss. Hana got up hoisting the little one into the crook of her arm, while Jin joined her.

"Mom?" Hana was able to speak after clearing her throat.

"You two can go ahead; I'll stay here for a bit longer," Neena said, smiling at the pair. "Don't worry about me."

361

"Come." Jin gently wrapped one arm around Hana's waist to guide the three of them to the entrance of the cemetery.

"Seika," Hana softly chided her daughter who was tearing up figuring out that the poor child was feeling hot and probably hungry. "Jin, are you all right?"

"Yeah." He nodded once, ruffling one hand over the child's small head. He helped Hana into the passenger side before heading for the driver's door.

In the span of a year, Hana and Jin had got married, inviting their ex-colleagues as well as those from Jin's current office. Miko and Neena bore witness on the auspicious day. It was a small celebration, a traditional Indian and Japanese wedding. She was six months pregnant by then; the two of them shared expenses. Meanwhile, Neena pitched in a little to help with the catering.

During dinner, Ayato and Miko met, and the duo clicked. Hana watched from afar as her former flame was enamoured by the toddler beside her friend, and a smile grew on the blissful bride's face. It was a memorable day for all of them; afterward Hana enjoyed the blurring scene passing by as Jin drove towards their desired location.

Now they chose to spend the day outside Tokyo at their favourite haunt, and they took lunch at a beautiful location overseeing the vast ocean, while Seika was given royal treatment by the staff. The young child had a mixture of her mother's and father's facial features: bright brown eyes, dark curly hair, and a button nose, along with Jin's temperamental character.

By late evening, the three of them had reached home, exhausted from the excursion. Jin carefully took Seika from Hana's arms while she opened the front gate and the entrance door. Toys were piled in the corner; Neena spoilt her granddaughter whenever she dropped by to visit. Jin and his mother-in-law were on good terms, having put the past behind them.

"Were you this much of a handful as a baby?" Hana mocked Jin, who swatted her butt.

"She takes after you," he said over his shoulder while walking upstairs carrying the little one, who dozed peacefully. "I had a difficult time looking after you."

"As if," she chortled, following behind him.

Once they had settled Seika in the baby crib in their bedroom, the couple admired the child, standing close while Hana rested her head on Jin's chest, leaning into his strong arm wrapped around her slender waist. Finally, they moved away to settle down on the veranda overlooking the rear garden; even though it was night-time, the summer heat had not abated.

This was where Hana had first kissed Jin. A smiled tugged at the corner of her mouth; it felt like a dream now, when she thought about that incident. Jin returned with watermelon cut in small cubes, his pants folded to his calf. Meanwhile, Hana had tied her thick mane in a bun and pulled her flowy skirt to her knees.

"I have to help Mr Ito fix the light bulb tomorrow," Jin explained as he popped a cube into his mouth and wiped away the overflow of juice. Hana took one and relished the sweet taste on her tongue. Her legs swung lazily back and forth as she watched the stars above. Jin leaned back on both hands.

At one point, Shouko had called on Jin's cell phone. Unaware, Hana picked it up and was startled to hear the feminine voice. In fact, both women were unprepared.

When Shouko learnt of Jin's marriage to Hana, she was taken aback, but the call was made for the last time. When Hana mentioned it to Jin, he went pale, but Hana reassured him. Of course, he had insisted that he was not fooling around; she hushed him by placing a finger on his lips, explaining that she trusted him.

"Why are you smiling like that?" Jin leaned closer to plant a kiss on her chin.

"Nothing." She pushed him gently with a giggle. "Jin, where do you think we would be right now if the two of us had never met?"

"You mean, if we weren't friends or never crossed paths again?" he asked, tugging one leg against his chest.

"If we never crossed paths again," she whispered the sentence.

"I don't know," Jin replied after a minute of contemplation. "Probably not over you."

"Really?" She bit her lower lip, and a hint of slyness dripped from her voice. "You'd have to be dating someone by now."

"Possible," he mused but glanced at her. "My world wouldn't have been complete without my best friend beside me."

"You are my lifeline, Jin." Hana leaned closer to settle her head on his shoulder. "I wouldn't bother dating anyone."

"I must have been in love with you even before Hana felt such an emotion, but the dumb boy inside me had to be pushed over the edge to confirm that fact." He chortled. "Hana?"

"Yeah?" She peered at his face up close.

"There is no other for me than you." He cupped her face between his wide palms, caressing her. "No matter where you are, I will find you, because you are the most important being in my life. You are irreplaceable to me."

THE END

Lightning Source UK Ltd.
Milton Keynes UK
UKHW010634070820
367857UK00001B/36